By John Jackson Miller

STAR WARS®

A NEW DAWN

STAR WARS®
A NEW DAWN

JOHN JACKSON MILLER

Del Rey | New York

Published in the United States by Del Rey, an imprint of Random House, a division of Random House LLC, a Penguin Random House Company, New York.

DEL REY and the HOUSE colophon are registered trademarks of Random House LLC.

This book contains an excerpt from *Star Wars: Tarkin* by James Luceno. This excerpt has been set for this edition only and may not reflect the final content of the forthcoming edition.

ISBN 978-0-553-39286-9
eBook ISBN 978-0-553-39287-6

Printed in the United States of America on acid-free paper

www.starwars.com
www.delreybooks.com
Facebook.com/starwarsbooks

2 4 6 8 9 7 5 3 1

First Edition

Book design by Elizabeth Eno

To my mother, who taught me to love books and movies

ACKNOWLEDGMENTS

Since first seeing the movie that would later be known as *Star Wars: Episode IV: A New Hope* in the theater as a youngling, I've been interested in what life was like under the Empire. *A New Dawn* gave me the chance to explore that subject in a story set several years before the *Star Wars Rebels* television series. *A New Dawn* depicts the characters Kanan and Hera as developed by that program's executive producers Dave Filoni, Simon Kinberg, and Greg Weisman, and I am appreciative to them for their suggestions and guidance.

Thanks as well as to Rayne Roberts, Leland Chee, and Pablo Hidalgo of the new Lucasfilm Story Group and, as always, to Jennifer Heddle, Lucasfilm's fiction editor. I am further indebted to Random House for giving me the opportunity: lead editor, Shelly Shapiro, and editors Frank Parisi, Keith Clayton, and Erich Schoeneweiss.

I owe all again to wife and proofreader Meredith Miller—and a special thank-you to science-fiction sage and longtime friend Ken Barnes, for helping me think through some of the astronomical details.

Finally, I owe a debt to all the writers who've worked in the *Star Wars* universe to date—and to the millions of readers who've supported their works. The stories we love may not always fit neatly into a single timeline, but they will always matter.

John Jackson Miller

A long time ago in a galaxy far, far away. . . .

FOREWORD

Star Wars is an incredibly creative galaxy, where storytellers have sent Jedi on countless missions, explored numerous planets, and discovered hidden treasures since 1977. I grew up with the original trilogy, and as the years passed by I read the books and comics, I played the games, I saw the re-releases, and I could not believe it when one day I sat in a theater and the screen said EPISODE I. It was a day I had waited for, for a long, long time. I went to all the prequels on opening night, stood in lines like we all did, went to the "Midnight Madness" toy releases. I really enjoyed the community that had grown up around the *Star Wars* universe.

Little did I know that before the final prequel film was released, I would move to Northern California and begin work on *Star Wars: The Clone Wars,* right alongside "the Maker" George Lucas. I felt like I had won some *Star Wars* lottery, but I also felt a tremendous responsibility to all the people I knew who loved *Star Wars*: to make sure that I "got it right." As my own personal Jedi training began, I always had George there to answer the deeper questions, to make certain that we got it right, that we truly made *Star Wars* the way he wanted it. He used to joke with my crew and me, telling us that he had been teaching us the ways of the Force so that one day when he retired *Star Wars* could keep on going without him. I'm not sure we ever believed him, until it happened.

So how do we move forward? And how do we make sure we get it right? Very simply, we trust in the Force, and we trust one another. We came together as a group and found the best talent: people who, like you and me, love *Star Wars* and want to make it great. Who want to capture the feeling that it gave all of us, that inspired all of us. More than at any other time in its existence, new *Star Wars* stories are being told every day. More important, the old concept of what is canon and what isn't is gone, and from this point forward our stories and characters all exist in the same universe; the key creatives who work on the films, television, comic books, video games, and novels are all connected creatively for the first time in the history of the *Star Wars* universe.

A New Dawn is a result of this method of story collaboration here at Lucasfilm. As executive producers of *Star Wars Rebels,* Greg Weisman, Simon Kinberg, and I had input on the story and characters, working with author John Jackson Miller. I even got to make comments on the look of Kanan and Hera for the cover—maybe a small detail to some, but it was exciting to be a part of that process, and to know the characters would remain true to their intended design. I really hope you enjoy this story, and that it enriches your experience and knowledge of the characters in *Star Wars Rebels.* There are still countless worlds to visit, countless aliens to meet, and with the incredible talent we have coming to work at Lucasfilm the way forward looks clear.

Last I must thank you. Whether this is your first *Star Wars* adventure, or one of many over the years: Thank you. Thank you for your dedication to and passion for the *Star Wars* galaxy. Because of fans like you around the world, the Force will be with us, always.

Dave Filoni
Executive Producer and
Supervising Director, *Star Wars Rebels*

STAR WARS®

A NEW DAWN

For a thousand generations, the Jedi Knights brought peace and order to the Galactic Republic, aided by their connection to the mystical energy field known as the Force. But they were betrayed—and the whole galaxy has paid the price. It is the Age of the Empire.

Now Emperor Palpatine, once chancellor of the Republic and secretly a Sith follower of the dark side of the Force, has brought his own peace and order to the galaxy. Peace, through brutal repression—and order, through increasing control of his subjects' lives.

But even as the Emperor tightens his iron grip, others have begun to question his means and motives. And still others, whose lives were destroyed by Palpatine's machinations, lay scattered about the galaxy like unexploded bombs, waiting to go off. . . .

Years earlier . . .

"It's time for you to go home," Obi-Wan Kenobi said.

The Jedi Master looked at the blinking lights on the panel to his right—and then at the students watching him. The aisle between the towering computer banks in the central security station was designed for a few Jedi doing maintenance, not a crowd; but the younglings fit right in, afraid to jostle one another in the presence of their teacher for the morning.

"That's the meaning of this signal," the bearded man said, turning again to the interface. Rows of blue lights twinkled in a sea of green indicators. He toggled a switch. "You can't hear anything now, or see anything. Not here in the Jedi Temple. But away from Coruscant, on planets across the galaxy, those of our Order would get the message: *Return home.*"

Sitting on the floor with his classmates in the central security station, young Caleb Dume listened—but not intently. His mind wandered, as it often did when he tried to imagine being out in the field.

He was lean and wiry now—ruddy skin and blue eyes under a mop of black hair. He was just one of the crowd, not yet apprenticed to a mentor. But one day, he'd be out *there,* traveling to exotic worlds with his Master. They'd provide peace and order for the citizens of the Galactic Republic, defeating evil wherever he found it.

Then he saw himself later as a Jedi Knight, fighting alongside the Republic's clone warriors against the enemy Separatists. Sure, Republic Chancellor Palpatine had promised to resolve the war soon, but no one could be so rude as to end the war before Caleb got his chance.

And then, finally, he dared hope he would become a Jedi Master like Obi-Wan—accepted while still young as one of the wise sages of the Order. Then he'd *really* do some great feats. He'd lead the valiant battle against the Sith, the legendary evil counterpart to the Jedi.

Of course, the Sith hadn't been seen in a thousand years, and he knew of no shadow of their return. But in his ambitions Caleb was no different from the younglings around him, whatever the gender, whatever the species. The adolescent imagination knew no bounds.

The sandy-haired Jedi Master touched the panel again. "It's just in test mode now," Obi-Wan said. "No one will respond. But were there a true emergency, Jedi could receive the message in several ways." He glanced down at his listeners. "There is the basic alert signal. And then there are other components, in which you might find more detailed text and holographic messages. No matter the format, the basic purpose should be clear—"

"Go home!" the collected students shouted.

Obi-Wan nodded. Then he saw a hand being raised. "The student in the back," he said, fishing for a name. "Caleb Dume, right?"

"Yes, Master."

Obi-Wan smiled. "I'm learning, too." The students giggled. "You have a question, Caleb?"

"Yes." The boy took a breath. "Where?"

"Where what?"

The other pupils laughed again, a little louder this time.

"Where's home? Where do we go?"

Obi-Wan smiled. "To Coruscant, of course. Here, to the Jedi Temple. The recall is exactly what it sounds like."

The teacher started to turn back to the beacon when he spotted Caleb Dume jabbing his hand in the air again. Caleb wasn't one to sit in front for every lesson—no one respected a teacher's pet—but shyness had never been one of his afflictions.

"Yes, Caleb?"

"Why—" The boy's voice cracked, to mild chuckles from his companions. He glared at the others and started again. "Why would you need all the Jedi here at once?"

"A very good question. Looking at this place, one would think we had all the Jedi we need!" Obi-Wan grinned at the students' Masters, all standing outside in the more spacious control room, looking in. Out of the corner of his eye, Caleb could see Depa Billaba among them. Tan-skinned and dark-haired, she had shown interest in taking him on as her apprentice—and she studied him now from afar with her usual mostly patient look: *What are you on about now, Caleb?*

Caleb had wanted to shrink into the floor, then—when Obi-Wan addressed him directly. "Why don't *you* tell *me*, Caleb: What reasons would *you* expect would cause us to recall every Jedi in the Order?"

Caleb's heart pounded as he realized everyone was watching him. In his daily life, the boy never worried about being hassled for sounding off; the kids he regularly trained with knew he never backed down. But there were students in the gathering he'd never seen before, including older ones—not to mention the Jedi Masters. And Caleb had just blundered into a chance to impress a member of the High Council in front of everyone.

Or it was a chance to founder on the question, and take their abuse. There were so many possibilities—

Including a trick question.

"I know the reasons you'd call them back," Caleb finally said. "*Unexpected* reasons!"

Riotous laughter erupted from the others, all semblance of respectful order disappearing at Caleb's words. But Obi-Wan raised his hands. "That's as good an answer as I've ever heard," he said.

The group settled down, and Obi-Wan continued: "The truth, my young friends, is I simply don't know. I could tell you of the many times over the course of the history of the Order when Jedi have been called back to Coruscant to deal with one threat or another. Some perilous times, which resulted in great heroics. There are truths, and there are legends touched with truth, and all can teach you something. I am sure

Jocasta, our librarian, would help you explore more." He clasped his hands together. "But no two events were alike—and when the signal is given again, that event will be unique, too. It's my hope it will never be needed, but knowing about it is part of your training. So the important thing is, when you get the signal . . ."

" . . . *go home!*" the children said, Caleb included.

"Very good." Obi-Wan deactivated the signal and walked through the crowd to the exit. The students stood and filed back out into the control room, appreciating the wider space and chatting about their return to their other lessons. The field trip to this level of the Jedi Temple was over.

Caleb stood, too, but did not leave the aisle. The Jedi taught their students to look at all sides of things, and the thought occurred to him there was another side to what they'd just been shown. Brow furrowed, he started again to raise his hand. Then he realized he was the only one left. No one was looking, or listening.

Except Obi-Wan, standing in the doorway. "What is it?" the Master called out over the din. Behind him, the others quieted, freezing in place. "What is it, Caleb?"

Surprised to have been noticed, Caleb swallowed. He saw Master Billaba frowning a little, no doubt wondering what her impulsive prospect was on about now. It was a good time to shut up. But standing alone in the aisle between the banks of lights, he was committed. "This beacon. It can send *any* message, right?"

"Ah," Obi-Wan said. "No, we wouldn't use it for regular administrative matters. As Jedi Knights—which I very much hope you will all become—you will receive such instructions individually, using less dramatic forms of—"

"Can you send people away?"

A gasp came from the group. Interrupted but not visibly irritated, Obi-Wan stared. "I'm sorry?"

"Can you send people away?" Caleb asked, pointing at the beacon controls. "It can recall every Jedi at once. Could it warn all of them away?"

The room behind Obi-Wan buzzed with whispered conversations. Master Billaba stepped into the computer room, apparently wanting to put an end to an awkward moment. "I think that's enough, Caleb. Excuse us, Master Kenobi. We value your time."

Obi-Wan wasn't looking at her. He was staring back at the beacon, too, now, contemplating. "No, no," he finally said, gesturing to the crowd without turning. "Please wait." He scratched the back of his head and turned back to the gathering. "Yes," he said, quietly. "I suppose it could be used to warn Jedi away."

The students fairly rumbled with discussions in reaction.

Warn Jedi away?

Jedi didn't run! Jedi rushed toward danger!

Jedi stood, Jedi fought!

The other Masters stepped in, beckoning to Obi-Wan. "Students," said one elder, "there's no reason to—"

"No *expected* reason," Obi-Wan said, pointing his index finger to the air. He sought Caleb's gaze. "Only what our young friend said: unexpected reasons."

A hush fell over the group. Caleb, reluctant to say anything else, let another student ask what he was thinking. "What then? If you send us all away, what then?"

Obi-Wan thought for a moment before turning toward the students and giving a warm and reassuring smile. "The same as any other time. You will obey the directive—and await the next one." Raising his arms, he dismissed the assembly. "Thank you for your time."

The students filed out of the control room quickly, still talking. Caleb remained, watching Obi-Wan disappear through another doorway. His eyes turned back to the beacon.

He could sense Master Billaba watching him. He looked back to see her, alone, waiting in the doorway. The frown was gone; her eyes were warm and caring. She gestured for him to follow her. He did.

"My young strategist has been thinking again," she said as they stepped into the elevator. "Any other questions?"

"Await orders." Caleb gazed at the floor, and then up at her. "What if orders never come? I won't know what to do."

"Maybe you will."

"Maybe I won't."

She watched him, thoughtful. "All right, maybe you won't. But anything is possible," she said, putting her arm on his shoulder as the door opened. "Perhaps the answer will come to you in another form."

Caleb didn't know what that meant. But then it was Master Billaba's way to speak in riddles, and, as always, he forgot about them as soon as he stepped out onto the floor where the young Jedi trained. On any given day, room after room would see the mightiest warriors in the galaxy teaching the next generation in lightsaber combat, acrobatics, hand-to-hand fighting—even starship piloting, using simulators. Every discipline imaginable where a kinship with the mystical Force, the energy field all Jedi drew upon for strength, could come in handy.

And those he saw were just a tiny fraction of the Jedi Order, which had outposts and operatives throughout the known galaxy. True, the Galactic Republic was at war now with the Separatists, but the Jedi had thwarted threats for a thousand generations. How could anyone or anything challenge them?

Caleb arrived in front of a room where his classmates were already at work, sparring with wooden staffs. One of his regular dueling partners, a red-skinned humanoid boy, met him in the doorway, training weapon in hand. He had also attended the lecture. "Welcome, Young Master Serious," he said, smirking. "What was all that back there with Master Kenobi?"

"Forget it," Caleb said, pushing past him into the room and reaching for his own training weapon. "It's nothing."

"But wait!" The other boy's free hand shot up into the air, mimicking Caleb's questioning. "Ooh! Ooh! Call on me!"

"Yeah, you're going to want to focus, buddy, because I'm going to whip your tail." Caleb smiled and went to work.

THIS IS OBI-WAN KENOBI
REPUBLIC FORCES HAVE BEEN TURNED AGAINST THE JEDI
AVOID CORUSCANT, AVOID DETECTION
STAY STRONG
MAY THE FORCE BE WITH YOU

Phase One:
IGNITION

"Emperor unveils ambitious plan for Imperial fleet expansion"

"Count Vidian contributes star power to new industrial inspection tour"

"Leftover unexploded ordnance from Clone Wars remains a concern"

—*headlines, Imperial HoloNews* (Gorse Edition)

CHAPTER ONE

"Sound collision!"

Only a moment earlier, the Star Destroyer had emerged from hyperspace; now a cargo ship careened straight toward its bridge. Before *Ultimatum*'s shields could be raised or cannons could be brought to bear, the approaching vessel abruptly veered upward.

Rae Sloane watched, incredulous, as the wayward freighter hurtled above her bridge's viewport and out of sight. But not out of hearing: A tiny scraping *ka-thump* signaled it had just clipped the top of the giant ship's hull. The new captain looked back at her first officer. "Damage?"

"None, Captain."

No surprise, she thought. It was surely worse for the other guy. "These yokels act as if they haven't seen a Star Destroyer before!"

"I'm sure they haven't," Commander Chamas said.

"They'd better get used to it." Sloane observed the cloud of transports ahead of *Ultimatum*. Her enormous *Imperial*-class starship had arrived from hyperspace on the edge of the appointed safe-approach lane, bringing it perilously close to what had to be the biggest traffic jam in the Inner Rim. She addressed the dozens of crewmembers at their stations. "Stay alert. *Ultimatum*'s too new to bring back with a scratched finish." Thinking again, she narrowed her eyes. "Send a message on the Mining Guild channel. The next moron that comes within a kilometer of us gets a turbolaser haircut."

"Aye, Captain."

Of course, Sloane had never been to this system, either, having just attained her captaincy in time for *Ultimatum*'s shakedown cruise. Tall, muscular, dark-skinned, and black-haired, Sloane had performed exceptionally from the start and ascended swiftly through the ranks. True, she was only substituting on *Ultimatum*, whose intended captain was serving on assignment to the construction committee—but how many others had helmed capital ships at thirty? She didn't know: The Imperial Navy had been in existence by that name for less than a decade, since Chancellor Palpatine put down the traitorous Jedi and transformed the Republic into the Galactic Empire. Sloane just knew the days ahead would decide whether she got a ship of her own.

This system, she'd been briefed, was home to something rare: a true astronomical odd couple. Gorse, out the forward viewport, lived up to its reputation as perhaps the ugliest planet in the galaxy. Tidally locked to its parent star, the steaming mudball had one side that forever baked. Only the permanently dark side was habitable, home to an enormous industrial city amid a landscape of strip mines. Sloane couldn't imagine living on a world that never saw a sunrise—if you could call sweating through an endless muggy summer night *living*. Looking off to the right, she saw the real jewel: Cynda, Gorse's sole moon. Almost large enough to be counted in Imperial record keeping as a double planet with Gorse, Cynda had a glorious silver shine—as charming as its parent was bleak.

But Sloane wasn't interested in the sights, or the travails of all the losers on Gorse. She started to turn from the window. "Make doubly sure the convoys are respecting our clearance zone. Then inform Count Vidian we have—"

"Forget the old way," snapped a low baritone voice.

The harshly intoned words startled everyone on the bridge, for they had all heard them before—just seldom in this manner. It was their famous passenger's catchphrase, quoted on many a business program during the Republic days and still used to introduce his successful series of management aids now that he had moved on to government service.

Everywhere, the Republic's old ways of doing things were being re-placed. "Forget the old way" really was the slogan of the times.

Sloane wasn't sure why she was hearing it now, however. "Count Vidian," she stated, her eyes searching from doorway to doorway. "We were just setting up our safety perimeter. It's standard procedure."

Denetrius Vidian appeared in the entryway farthest from Sloane. "And I told you to forget the old way," he repeated, although there was no doubting everyone had heard him the first time. "I heard you trans-mit the order for mining traffic to avoid you. It would be more efficient for *you* to back away from *their* transit lanes."

Sloane straightened. "The Imperial Navy does not back away from *commercial traffic.*"

Vidian stamped his metal heel on the deck. "Spare me your silly pride! If it weren't for the thorilide this system produces, you'd only have a shuttle to captain. You are slowing production down. The old way is wrong!"

Sloane scowled, hating to be talked down to on her own bridge. This needed to seem like her decision. "It's the Empire's thorilide. Give them a wide berth. Chamas, back us a kilometer from the convoy lanes—and monitor all traffic."

"Aye, Captain."

"Aye is right," Vidian said. Each syllable was crisply pronounced, mechanically modulated, and amplified so all could hear. But Sloane would never get over the strangest part, which she'd noticed when he boarded: The man's mouth never moved. Vidian's words came from a special vocal prosthetic, a computer attached to a speaker embedded in the silvery plating that ringed his neck.

She'd once heard the voice of Darth Vader, the Emperor's principal emissary; while electronically amplified, the Dark Lord's much deeper voice still retained some natural trace of whatever was inside that black armor. In contrast, Count Vidian had reportedly chosen his artificial voice based on opinion research, in a quest to own the most motiva-tional voice in the business sector.

And since he had boarded her ship with his aides a week earlier, Vidian had shown no qualms about speaking as loudly as he felt necessary. About *Ultimatum,* her crew—and her.

Vidian strode mechanically onto the bridge. It was the only way to describe it. He was as human as she was, but much of his body had been replaced. His arms and legs were armor-plated, rather than synthflesh prosthetics; everyone knew because he made little effort to hide them. His regal burgundy tunic and knee-length black kilt were his only nods to normal attire for a fiftyish lord of industry.

But it was Vidian's face that attracted the most awkward notice. His flesh lost to the same malady that had once consumed his limbs and vocal cords, Vidian covered his features with a synthskin coating. And then there were his eyes: artificial constructs, glowing yellow irises sitting in seas of red. The eyes appeared meant for some other species besides humans; Vidian had chosen them solely for what they could do. She could tell that now as he walked, glancing outside from convoy to convoy, ship to ship, mentally analyzing the whole picture.

"We've already met some of the locals," she said. "You probably heard the bump. The people here are—"

"Disorganized. It's why I'm here." He turned and walked along the line of terminal operators until he arrived at the tactical station depicting all the ships in the area. He pushed past Cauley, the young human ensign, and tapped a command key. Then Vidian stepped back from the console and froze, seeming to stare blankly into space.

"My lord?" Cauley asked, unnerved.

"I have fed the output from your screen to my optical implants," Vidian said. "You may return to your work while I read."

The tactical officer did so—no doubt relieved, Sloane thought, not to have the cyborg hanging over his shoulder. Vidian's ways were strange, to be sure, but effective, and that was why he was on her ship. The onetime industrialist was now the Emperor's favorite efficiency expert.

Gorse's factories produced refined thorilide, a rare strategic substance needed in massive quantities for a variety of Imperial projects. But the raw material these days came from Cynda, its moon: hence the traffic jam of cargo ships crisscrossing the void between the two globes. The Emperor had dispatched Vidian to improve production—a job for which he was uniquely qualified.

Vidian was known for squeezing the very last erg of energy, the very last kilogram of raw material, the very last unit of factory production from one world after another. He was not in the Emperor's closest circle of advisers—not yet. But it was clear to Sloane he soon would be, provided there was no relapse of whatever ailment it was that had brought him low years earlier. Vidian's billions had bought him extra life—and he seemed determined that neither he nor anyone else waste a moment of it.

Since he'd boarded, she hadn't had a conversation with him where he hadn't interrupted at least a dozen times.

"We've alerted the local mining guild to your arrival, Count. The thorilide production totals—"

"—are already coming in," Vidian said, and with that, he marched to another data terminal in the aft section of the bridge.

Commander Chamas joined her far forward, many meters away from the count. In his late forties, Chamas had been leapfrogged in rank by several younger officers. The man loved gossip too much.

"You know," Chamas said quietly, "I heard he bought the title."

"Are you surprised? Everything else about him is artificial," Sloane whispered. "Ship's doctor even thinks some of his parts were voluntarily—"

"You waste time wondering," Vidian said, not looking up from where he was studying.

Sloane's dark eyes widened. "I'm sorry, my lord—"

"Forget the formality—and the apology. There is little point for either. But it's well for your crew to know someone is always listening— and may have better ears than yours."

Even if they had to buy them in a store, Sloane thought. The ragged fleshy lobes that had once been Vidian's ears held special hearing aids. They could obviously hear her words—and more. She approached him.

"This is exactly what I'd expected," Vidian said, staring at whatever unseen thing was before his eyes. "I told the Emperor it would be worth sending me here." A number of underproducing worlds that manufactured items critical to the security of the Empire had been removed from their local governors' jurisdictions and placed under Vidian's authority: Gorse was the latest. "Messy work might have been good enough for the Republic—but the Empire is order from chaos. What we do here—and in thousands of systems just like this one—brings us closer to our ultimate goal."

Sloane thought for a moment. "Perfection?"

"Whatever the Emperor wants."

Sloane nodded.

A tinny squawk came from Vidian's neck-speaker—an unnerving sound she'd learned to interpret as his equivalent of an angry sigh. "There's a laggard holding up the moonward convoy," he said, staring into nothingness. Looking at her tactician's screen, Sloane saw it was the cargo vessel that had bumped them earlier. She ordered *Ultimatum* turned to face it.

A shower of sparks flew from the freighter's underside. Other vessels hung back, fearful it might explode. "Hail the freighter," she said.

A quavering nonhuman voice was piped onto the bridge. "This is *Cynda Dreaming*. Sorry about that scrape earlier. We weren't expecting—"

Sloane cut to the point. "What's your payload?"

"Nothing, yet. We were heading to pick up a load of thorilide on the moon for refining at Calladan Chemworks down on Gorse."

"Can you haul in your condition?"

"We need to get to the repair shop to know. I'm not sure how bad it is. Could be a couple of months—"

Vidian spoke up. "Captain, target that vessel and fire."

It was almost idly stated, to the extent that Vidian's intonations ever conveyed much genuine emotion. The directive nonetheless startled Chamas. Standing before the gunnery crew, he turned to the captain for guidance.

The freighter pilot, having heard the new voice, sounded no less surprised. "I'm sorry—I didn't get that. Did you just—"

Sloane looked for an instant at Vidian, and then at her first officer. "Fire."

The freighter captain sounded stunned. "What? You can't be—"

This time, *Ultimatum*'s turbolasers provided the interruption. Orange energy ripped through space, turning *Cynda Dreaming* into a confusion of fire and flak.

Sloane watched as the other ships of the convoy quickly rerouted. Her gunners had done their jobs, targeting the ship in a way that resulted in minimal hazard for the nearby ships. All the freighters were moving faster.

"You understand," Vidian said, turning toward her. "Replacement time for one freighter and crew in this sector is—"

"—three weeks," Sloane said, "which is less than two months." *See, I've read your reports, too.*

This was the way to handle this assignment, she realized. So what if Vidian was strange? Figuring out what the Emperor—and those who spoke for him—wanted and then providing it was the path to success. Debating his directives only wasted time and made her look bad. It was the secret of advancement in the service: Always be on the side of what is going to happen anyway.

Sloane clasped her arms behind her back. "We'll see that the convoys make double time—and challenge any ship that refuses."

"It isn't just transit," Vidian said. "There are problems on the ground, too—on planet and moon. Surveillance speaks of unruly labor, of safety and environmental protests. And there's always the unexpected."

Sloane clasped her arms behind her back. "*Ultimatum* stands at your service, my lord. This system will do what you—what the Emperor—requires of it."

"So it will," Vidian said, eyes glowing blood-red. "So it will."

Hera Syndulla watched from afar as the scattered remains of the freighter burned silently in space. No recovery vehicles were in sight. As unlikely a prospect as survivors were, no one looked for any. There were only the shipping convoys, quickly rerouting around the wreckage.

Obeying the master's whip.

This was mercy in the time of the Empire, she thought. The Imperials had none; now, to all appearances, their lack of care was infecting the people.

The green-skinned Twi'lek in her stealth-rigged starship didn't believe that was true. People were basically decent . . . and one day, they would rise up against their unjust government. But it wouldn't happen now, and certainly not here. It was too soon, and Gorse was barely awake politically. This wasn't a recruitment trip. No, these days were for seeing what the Empire could do—a project that suited the ever-curious Hera perfectly. And Count Vidian, the Emperor's miracle man, practically begged investigation.

In previous weeks, the Imperial fixer had cut a swath through the sector, "improving efficiency." On three previous worlds, like-minded acquaintances of Hera's on the HoloNet had reported misery levels skyrocketing under Vidian's electronic eyes. Then her associates had simply vanished. That had piqued Hera's interest—and learning of the count's visit to the Gorse system brought her the rest of the way.

She had another contact on Gorse, one who had promised much information on the regime. She wanted that information—but first she wanted to check out Vidian, and the system's notoriously anarchic mining trade offered her a variety of chances to get close. Industrial confusion, the perfect lure for Vidian, would provide excellent cover for her to study his methods.

Emperor Palpatine had too many minions with great power and influence. It was worth finding out whether Count Vidian had real magic before he rose any higher.

It was time to move. She picked out the identifying transponder signal of a ship in the convoy. One button-push later, her ship *was* that vessel, as far as anyone trying to watch traffic was concerned. With practiced ease, she weaved her freighter into the chaotic flood of cargo ships heading to the moon.

None of these guys can fly worth a flip, she thought. It was just as well it wasn't a recruiting trip. She probably wouldn't have found anyone worth her time.

CHAPTER TWO

"Look out, you big idiot!"

Seeing the bulky thorilide hauler coming right at him, Kanan Jarrus forgot about talking and abruptly banked his freighter. He didn't waste time worrying whether the bigger vessel would veer in the same direction: He took his chance while the choice was still his. He was rewarded with survival—and an alarmingly up-close look at the underbelly of the oncoming ship.

"Sorry," crackled a voice over the comm system.

"You sure are," Kanan said, blue eyes glaring from beneath dark eyebrows. *I see that guy in an alley tonight, he'd better watch out.*

It was madness. Cynda's elongated elliptical orbit meant that the distance between the moon and Gorse changed daily. Close-approach days like today made the region between the worlds a congested demolition derby. But the appearance of the Star Destroyer and its destruction of the cargo ship had created a stampede in space. A race with two terrified groups bound in opposite directions, hurtling toward each other in the same transit lanes.

Normally, Kanan would be the one pushing the limits to get where he was going. That was what kept him in drinking money, the main reason he had a job. But he also prided himself on keeping his cool when others were panicking—and that was surely happening now. Kanan *had* seen a Star Destroyer before, but he was pretty sure no one else around here had.

Another freighter moved alongside. He didn't recognize this one. Almost shaped like a gem, with a bubble-like cockpit forward and another for a gunner seated just above. It was a nice ride compared with anything else in the sky. Kanan goosed the throttle, trying to pull alongside and get a glimpse at her driver. The freighter responded by zipping ahead with surprising speed, claiming his vector and causing him to lay off the acceleration. He gawked as the other pilot hit the afterburners, soaring far ahead.

It was the one time he'd touched the brakes all trip, and it was instantly noticed. His comm system chirped, followed by a female voice, sounding none too happy. "You there! What's your identifier?"

"Who's asking?"

"This is Captain Sloane, of the Star Destroyer *Ultimatum*!"

"I'm impressed," Kanan said, smoothing the black hairs on his pointed chin. "What are you wearing?"

"What?"

"Just trying to get a picture. Hard to meet people out here."

"I repeat, what's your—"

"This is *Expedient,* flying for Moonglow Polychemical, out of Gorse City." He rarely bothered to activate his ID transponder; no one ever managed space traffic here anyway.

"Speed up. Or else!"

Kanan sat lazily back in his pilot's seat and rolled his eyes. "You can shoot me if you want," he said in a slow almost-drawl, "but you need to know I'm hauling a load of explosive-grade baradium bisulfate for the mines on Cynda. It's testy stuff. Now, *you* might be safe from the debris in your big ship over there, but I can't speak for the rest of the convoy. And some of these folks are hauling the same thing I am. So I'm not sure how smart that'd be." He chuckled lightly. "Be something to watch, though."

Silence.

Then, after a moment: "Move along."

"Are you sure? I mean, you could probably record it and sell—"

"Don't push it, grubber," came the icy response. "And try to go faster."

He straightened one of his fingerless gloves and smiled. "Nice talking with you, too."

"*Ultimatum* out!"

Kanan switched off the receiver. He knew there wasn't any chance of his being targeted once anyone with a brain understood what he was carrying. For their own protection, miners only used "Baby"—the sardonic nickname for baradium bisulfate—by the gram down in the mines on Cynda. Any Imperial would think twice before targeting a Baby Carrier too close by—and the Star Destroyer captain in particular would be less apt to call on him again about anything after that conversation.

That was also according to plan. He'd rather avoid that meeting, no matter what she might look like.

He mouthed Sloane's words mockingly. *"Go faster!"* He was already flying the freighter at close to top speed. When fully loaded, *Expedient* wasn't going to give him even that much. The sarcastic name was his idea. The freighter was Moonglow's, one of dozens of identical vessels the company operated; the ships met with disastrous ends often enough the firm didn't bother naming them. "Suicide fliers" didn't stay in the game long, either, provided they survived, so Kanan had no idea how many people had flown his ship before him. Giving the Baby Carrier a name was just his attempt to give it even a single amenity.

It'd be nice, he thought, if on one of the planets he visited he could fly something with some class—like that ship that had just raced past him. But then, whoever owned it probably wouldn't let him take the liberties he did with *Expedient*. Like now: Seeing two mining haulers heading right for him, he banked the ship, corkscrewing between them. They slowed down: He kept on going. *Let* them *watch out for* me.

His carefully secured payload didn't react to the sudden motion, but the maneuver did produce a dull thump from back in the cargo area. He turned his head, his short clump of tied-back hair brushing against the headrest. Through the corner of his eye, Kanan saw an old man on the deck, half swimming against the floor as he tried to get his bearings.

"Morning, Okadiah."

The man coughed. Like Kanan, Okadiah had a beard but no mustache—but his hair was completely white. He'd been sleeping back with the baradium bisulfate containers, on the one empty shelf. Okadiah preferred that to the acceleration couch in the main cabin: It was quieter. Figuring out which way was forward, the old man started to crawl. He addressed the air as he reached the copilot's seat. "I have determined I will not pay your fare, and you shall have no tip."

"Best tip I ever got was to pick another line of work," Kanan said.

"Hmph."

Actually, Okadiah Garson had several lines of work, all of which made him the perfect friend to have, in Kanan's eyes. Okadiah was foreman for one of the mining teams on Cynda, a thirty-year veteran who knew his way around. And down on Gorse, he ran The Asteroid Belt, a cantina favored by many of his own mining employees. Kanan had met Okadiah months earlier when he'd broken up a brawl at his bar; it was through Okadiah that Kanan had gotten the freighter-pilot job with Moonglow. Even now, Kanan lived in the flophouse next door to the cantina. A landlord with a liquor supply was a good deal indeed.

Okadiah claimed he only partook of his own ferments when someone got hurt in the mines. That was a handy conviction to have, considering it happened nearly every day. Yesterday's cave-in had been so bad it kept the party going all night long, causing Okadiah to miss his shift's personnel shuttle. Baby Carriers didn't get many passengers who had any other options for getting to work, and Kanan didn't take riders. But for Okadiah, he made an exception.

"I dreamed I heard a woman's voice," the old man said, rubbing his eyes. "Stern, regal, commanding."

"Starship captain."

"I like it," Okadiah said. "She's no good for you, of course, but I'm a man of means. When do I meet this angel?"

Kanan simply jabbed a thumb out the window to his left. There, the old man beheld *Ultimatum,* looming behind the frenetic rush of space traffic. Okadiah's bloodshot eyes widened and then narrowed, as he tried to determine exactly what it was he was looking at.

"Hmm," he finally said. "That wasn't there yesterday."

"It's a Star Destroyer."

"Oh, dear. Are we to be destroyed?"

"I didn't ask," Kanan said, grinning. He didn't know how an old miner on an armpit like Gorse had come by his genteel manner of speech, but it always amused him. "Somebody got on the wrong side of her. Know anyone on *Cynda Dreaming*?"

Okadiah scratched his chin. "Part of the Calladan crew. Tall fellow, skinny Hammerhead. He's run up quite a tab at The Asteroid Belt."

"Well, you can forget about collecting."

"Oh," Okadiah said, looking again out the window. There was still a bit of debris from the unlucky freighter about. "Kanan, lad, you do have a way of sobering a person up."

"Good. We're almost there."

Expedient rolled and angled downward toward the white surface of airless Cynda. An artificial crater had been hollowed out as a landing approach zone; half a dozen red-lit landing bays had been gouged into its sides, connecting with the mining areas farther below. Bringing *Expedient* to hover over the crater, Kanan turned the ship toward his appointed entrance.

Okadiah turned his head forward and squinted. "There's my transport now!"

"Told you we'd catch up."

They *had* caught up, but it wasn't purely from Kanan's efforts. The Empire's unreasonable directive had played a role. The personnel transport Okadiah was supposed to have been on had attempted to enter the bay too quickly and had clipped the side of the doorway. Now it sat blocking the entrance, disabled and partially hanging over the edge. It was in no danger of falling, but the magnetic shield that would seal the cavern against the void could not be activated. Space-suited workers were visible in the bay, staring haplessly at the wreck.

"Move it," Kanan said over the comm.

"Stay put, Moonglow-Seventy-Two," crackled the response from the control tower at the center of the crater. "We'll get you in after we get the workers suited and off-loaded."

"I'm on a schedule," Kanan said, shifting *Expedient* out of hover mode and moving toward the entrance.

Objections came loudly over the communicator, getting Okadiah's attention. He glanced at Kanan. "You are aware we're carrying high explosives?"

"I don't care," Kanan said. "Do you?"

"Not at all. Sorry to disturb. Carry on."

Kanan did, expertly bringing *Expedient*'s stubby nose toward the exposed side of the personnel carrier. He could see the miners inside its windows, clamoring futilely at him as his ship made contact with a clang.

Expedient's engines straining, Kanan gunned the ship forward, dislodging the personnel transport from the edge. The noisy scrape reverberated through both vessels, and Okadiah glimpsed nervously back into the cargo section. But in moments both ships were inside the landing area. The magnetic shield sealed the landing bay, and Kanan deactivated his engines.

Okadiah whistled. He regarded Kanan with mild wonderment for a moment and then placed his hands on the dashboard before him. "Well, that's that." He paused, seemingly confused. "We drink *after* work, is that correct?"

"That's right."

"Entirely the wrong order," the old man said, wobbling slightly as he rose. "Let's get to it, then."

CHAPTER THREE

The horn-headed Devaronian miner charged from the disabled personnel transport across the pressurized cavern's floor.

"You punk kid!" he yelled as Kanan exited *Expedient*. "What were you trying to prove back there?"

Kanan was still in his early twenties, but he hadn't answered to "kid" ever. And certainly not when the name came from a dunderhead like Yelkin, whose job it was to drill holes for explosives. Kanan turned and walked alongside his ship, opening up cargo hatches as he went.

The muscular miner stomped after him and grabbed at his shoulder. "I'm talking to you!"

With quick reflexes, Kanan grabbed Yelkin's hand and spun around, twisting the other man's arm. Yelkin winced in pain and fell to his knees. Kanan didn't let go. He spoke in low, calm tones into his captive's pointed ear. "Your ship was in the way, pal. I have a deadline."

"We all do," Yelkin said, struggling. "You saw them shoot that freighter. The Empire's come to check up—"

"Then go faster. But don't go stupid." Kanan released his hold, and Yelkin fell to the ground, gasping. Kanan brushed off his long-sleeved green tunic and turned back to *Expedient*.

Several miners arrived at Yelkin's side. "Blasted suicide flier!" one said. "They're all cracked!"

"Someone needs to show you some manners," another said to Kanan.

"So I've heard." Unworried, Kanan looked around the landing bay.

The loader droids that normally helped hadn't arrived, evidently unable to make sense out of the impromptu parking situation on the loading floor. It looked like it was going to be another one of those days when he had to do everything.

Kanan unloaded a hovercart and parked it in front of the ship. Then he began the laborious process of hefting down metal crates. Cynda's lesser gravity made the cases somewhat lighter than they had been on Gorse but no less bulky—or hazardous—to carry. Heaving the first crate, he carried it toward the milling miners.

"You're in the way," he said. "For the moment."

Okadiah appeared on the far side of the spacecraft. "Gentlemen, I think a maxim is in order: Do not aggravate the man who carries high explosives."

The miners parted, glowering at Kanan as he passed. Rubbing his arm, Yelkin snarled at Okadiah. "You take in some real pieces of work, boss."

"Like I did all of you, one time or another," the old man said. He pointed toward the south, and a bank of elevators. "Let's get the shift started. If the Empire's inspecting today, Boss Lal will be here, too. At least pretend to work." He smiled toothily. "And let me add—in honor of that poor sap outside who got himself blown to smithereens—it'll be happy hour all night tonight at The Asteroid Belt. We'll even pick you up and drive you home."

Momentarily assuaged, the miners turned and made for the elevators. Okadiah watched Kanan set a case down on the hovercart. "Still winning friends and influence?"

"Don't know why I'd do that," Kanan said.

"Ah, yes. You're not staying. Like you told me: You never stay."

"Clothes on my back," Kanan said as he turned to grab another crate. "Travel light, and death will never find you."

"I said that, didn't I?" Okadiah nodded. "You'll work the bar tonight?"

"If you can afford it."

Okadiah winked and ambled off after his co-workers. Kanan did keep the bar on occasion, but on some nights he was his own best customer. He'd also tried his hand as bouncer, although again, he'd wound up starting as many fights as he'd stopped. Still, this system had been closer to a home than any he'd known in years of wandering. It would be a hard place to leave.

But he would. The day job was wearing on him. Giving up on the loader droids ever arriving to help, Kanan finished filling the first hover-cart and pushed it into the freight elevator.

As the doors closed behind him, he thought on it. He might miss Okadiah's place, yes, and he'd certainly miss Cynda. In all his travels he'd never encountered a place quite like it. The landing bay didn't look like much, but he knew to watch for the big show as soon as the elevator doors opened.

They did, a thousand meters below—and Kanan was bombarded with a coruscating display of lights and colors. He was in one of the countless great caverns beneath the surface. Crystal stalagmites climbed and stalactites hung all around. Each one acted as a prism, refracting the lights of the work crew; to move was to see kaleidoscopic change. Better still, the crystals gave off warmth, making Cynda's many oxygenated caverns as bright and pleasant as parent-planet Gorse was dark and sticky.

Back before the Empire, the place had been a natural preserve. Cynda had been the literal bright spot in the lives of Gorse's residents; tourism had been the moon's—and Gorse's—number one draw. And while Republic scientists had learned early on that Cynda's interior contained massive amounts of thorilide, no one had wanted to mine for it while the workable nightside of Gorse still held any of the substance at all. As far as Kanan knew, no one even bothered looking for thorilide on Gorse's dayside, where the heat was enough to melt any droid in manufacture.

But then, almost exactly on the day that Chancellor Palpatine proclaimed the first Galactic Empire, a report had revealed that Gorse's mines were exhausted. The refineries went idle. The Empire wouldn't stand for it—and didn't need to. Cynda was right there, readily available to exploit.

Kanan saw the results now as he pushed the hovercart from the intact antechamber into the main work area. Pebble-sized crystal fragments littered the floor, and his boots crunched as he walked. Only the big industrial lights illuminated the cavity; the ceiling couldn't be seen at all in the smoky haze above. A sickly burnt stench hung on the air.

The Empire had defiled the place, but it could hardly resist. Useful as thorilide was in its processed form, in nature it had a fragile molecular structure. Efforts to free the substance from comets, already an insanely difficult process, often resulted in the collapse of the compound into its component elements. But Cynda was the mother lode in more ways than one, for its tough crystal columns managed to preserve thorilide inside them, even when blasted from their bases. Given how the prismatic structures reacted to laser torches, blasting was the only way.

The need for explosives had given Kanan a job, but it had also given Gorsians cause to object. Some were more vocal than others. And a few were downright loud about it.

Like that guy, Kanan thought, recognizing a voice coming from the far end of the work zone. *Oh, brother. Skelly.*

"You're not listening," the redheaded man declared, gray dust puffing from his protective vest as he waved his arms. "You're not listening!"

In the perfect echo chamber the cavern provided, no one could help but hear Skelly, and if there were any stalactites left intact, Kanan half expected Skelly's voice to bring them down.

But Kanan saw that the target of Skelly's harassment wasn't paying much mind, and he couldn't blame her. A four-armed, green-skinned member of Gorse's Besalisk subcommunity, Lal Grallik was the enterprising chief of Moonglow Polychemical. Running it kept "Boss Lal" jumping from planet to moon and back. Skelly was just one more nuisance to deal with. "I *am* listening, Skelly," she said. "I could probably hear you down on Gorse."

I'm sure she wishes she were there now, Kanan thought. Short and compactly built, Skelly had one mode: intense. Kanan was vaguely aware of the fortyish man's war record as a tunneler; the scars and pockmarks on his face read like a walk through recent military history. But while Kanan felt for anyone who'd gone through all that, he had little patience for the way Skelly always talked as if he were trying to yell over a barrage. The man could out-shout a jet turbine.

"I'm trying to save people's lives here," Skelly said, busy auburn eyebrows lowered in all seriousness. "Your company, too." Seeing Lal return her attention to the electronic manifest in her four-fingered hands, Skelly turned around and shrugged. "No one listens."

Kanan knew Skelly worked as a demolitions expert for Dalborg, one of the other mining concerns. Okadiah had explained that Skelly had been fired by every major firm in the last five years. The only one Skelly hadn't yet landed with was Kanan's employer. It wasn't too small a firm, Okadiah had said: just lucky. Kanan agreed. Skelly knew what he was doing with a demolition charge, but a variety of neuroses came with the package. And he always looked as if he'd slept on the floor. Even when Kanan did that for real, he made sure he looked presentable.

Skelly turned to face the Moonglow chief. "Look, Lal, all you have to do is suspend blasting past Zone Forty-Two. You and the other firms, just for a while. Long enough for me to test my—"

Lal looked at him in disbelief. "I thought you said you were giving up!"

Skelly's small eyes narrowed. "You'd like that, right? I forgot. All you guild outfits are the same. Out for yourselves . . ."

Kanan tried to tune it out as he pushed his pallet past. "Coming through."

Lal, clearly pleased to have someone other than Skelly to talk to, looked down at the load Kanan was hauling and checked it against her manifest. "Glad you made it, Kanan. I heard there was some trouble out there."

"No concern of mine," Kanan said, parking the hovercart. "Here's your bombs."

"This batch goes to Zone Forty-Two," Lal said, waving some workers over. She nodded to Skelly, who smoldered as he stared at the hovercart. "Someone's favorite place," she whispered.

Skelly leaned on the hovercart handle. "I've told you, we can't keep blasting down there. Not with these—"

"Take them home, then," Kanan said, walking around Skelly. "Blow yourself up." He began to unload crates of explosives one at a time for the workers to carry away.

"Wait," Skelly said, finally noticing the freighter pilot. He stepped beside Kanan and looked back at Lal. "You'll listen to Kanan, right? He's one of your top explosives haulers—and one of my best friends."

"Right on one. Wrong on the other," Kanan said, continuing his job.

"Kanan flies with this stuff," Skelly said. "He knows what it can do. He'll tell you: Using microblasts to cut crystal is one thing, but you shouldn't use it to crack open walls! He knows—"

"I'll tell you what I know," Kanan said, turning and poking a finger in Skelly's sternum, knocking him back a step. "I have a deadline. I've got more to unload. So long." He returned to the empty cart and turned it around.

Lal stepped aside to take a call. "Imperial channel," she said, waving Skelly off. "This is important."

"This is important, too," Skelly muttered to no one. Seeing Kanan pushing the hovercart away, he started marching after him. Catching up, he tried to match the pilot's pace. "Kanan—pal, why didn't you back me up over there?"

"Get lost, will you?"

"Lost is what we'll all be if this keeps up," Skelly said, huffing and puffing. "I know what the baradium family of explosives can do. Better than anyone. I've done the yield estimates. I've even studied the seismology of this moon—"

"You must be fun on holidays," Kanan said, pushing the cart back into the elevator.

"—right down to what they never consider: the core!" Skelly kept talking as he pushed his way into the car with Kanan. "It's sturdy up here, but way down deep? This moon could snap like a protein cracker!"

"Ah."

"*Ah* is right. I knew it! You agree with me!"

"No, food reminded me," Kanan said, drawing a pouch from his jacket. "I skipped breakfast."

"I'm serious," Skelly said, reaching into his own vest. He wore a single glove over a right hand that Kanan had never once seen him use, except as a pincer: There was something gripped in it now, not much larger than a coin. "It's all on this holodisk. I've got my work right here. You know those groundquakes we get on Gorse when the moon passes close by? The only reason it isn't worse on Cynda is because the crystal formations keep the tension in check. But we keep blowing them apart! If I can get just one person to read this—"

"Why does it have to be me? I'm nobody."

"Everybody comes to Okadiah's!" Skelly said. "You're there all the time. You can talk to people."

"Why can't you?" Kanan knew why. "Oh, yeah. He banned you, for aggravating people."

"Just have a look." Skelly waved the disk before Kanan.

"Get it out of my face, Skelly. I'm serious." Kanan threw his food pouch to the deck of the pallet. Pushing back against workers for other firms always caused a hassle; Okadiah had warned him against it. But Skelly was friendless, and for good reason. Kanan was near his limit.

Skelly's face twisted into a disdainful snarl. "Yeah, that's right. I forgot. You're paid by the shipload, right? And now you're all going to be running like eskrats, because the Empire's dropped by." He got in the taller man's face. "Well, the Empire had better watch out, or it's going to have a real disaster on its hands!"

"Last warning!"

Skelly opened his mouth again—but before a syllable emerged, Kanan's fist slammed into Skelly's teeth. Five seconds of violence later, the elevator doors opened to the landing bay—where waiting loader droids saw Kanan pushing the pallet with Skelly's crumpled body atop it.

"Good, you're here," Kanan said. He shoved the cart at them. "Put this somewhere."

As Kanan headed back to *Expedient* for another load, a dazed and flustered Skelly looked up at the puzzled droids. "Nobody listens."

CHAPTER FOUR

"I have a ping on Cynda cam five-six-oh," the operator in the second row said. "Threat to the Empire in spoken Basic. Elevator cam. Thirty-eight decibels, clearly intoned."

Across the crowded data center, Zaluna Myder didn't look up from tending to her plants. "Who was listening?"

"A transport driver."

And us, Zaluna thought to herself as she turned back to business. Her gray hand swept at the air in front of her—and a new half-meter-tall hologram appeared on one of the display platforms surrounding her work dais.

Hundreds of thousands of kilometers above Gorse, a couple of people were having a conversation in one of the lunar mining station's elevators. Or they *had* been having a conversation, until one person had decked the other. And it was all unfolding again, seconds later, in three static-laced dimensions in front of Zaluna's enormous black eyes.

Focusing on the moving image, the Sullustan woman reached for this hour's mug of caf. Now in her fifties, Zaluna spent an hour each day in the corporate gym, but she still knew it was past time to do without the artificial stimulant. On the other hand, her work had only gotten busier—and the caf was the only vice she'd ever had. She knew for certain that fact put her in the distinct minority of Gorse's residents—because in the last thirty-plus years, Zaluna Myder had seen and heard everything.

She had to. It was her job. And in the earpieces plugged into her giant shell-like ears, she heard the words that had caught the system's attention: "*. . . the Empire had better watch out . . .*"

She glanced down at the terminal operator in the second row. "The listener was a transport driver, you say. Anybody we—"

"Migrant, no record," he replied. "Nobody we care about."

Zaluna didn't need to ask whether the *speaker* was someone they cared about. His words alone were enough. The surveillance supercomputers had comprehended the statement, measured it against mysterious metrics, and kicked the incident up to the Mynocks, who'd taken it to her.

Myder's Mynocks. That was what the shift on her floor was named after she rose to supervise it. She had no children or grandchildren; she hadn't needed any other family, ever. Standing here on her platform she was queen, lending her guidance to the surveillance operators and taking the occasional spare moments to tend her potted plants. She'd had the misfortune to be born onto a world where the sun never rose, but at least her office had full-spectrum lighting.

Zaluna had been a fixture since her late teens here in World Window Plaza, the upside-down and truncated cone that was still the newest building on Gorse. Transcept Media Solutions had built the structure— which had no windows at all—as a local repository for marketing data about the planet's residents. There wasn't much commerce on Gorse unattached to the mining industry, but that didn't matter: When people did leave, they took their purchasing preferences with them. And thanks to the monitoring stations it maintained, Transcept would have their profiles when they arrived elsewhere. That information was surely worth something, although who'd want it or why was a subject Zaluna rarely considered.

Few people apart from poor transient laborers left Gorse anymore, but that wasn't a concern. First the Republic and later the Empire had become Transcept clients—and Zaluna had kept her dream job. Watching and listening: That was what she'd been born to do. Not because of her giant Sullustan eyes and ears—though they missed nothing—but because as long as she could remember, she had loved to observe and absorb information.

And neither did Zaluna forget anything.

"Ah, our old friend," she said aloud as her finger movement brought the holographic image to a halt. "Skelly, no surname. Human, born Corellia, forty standard years ago. Demolitions expert, Dalborg Mining, Cyndan operation. Last known address, Crispus Commons on Gorse. Clone Wars veteran. Injured, hand replaced. Two teeth missing—"

The operator in the second row looked back at her, amused. "That's him," Hetto said. "But I haven't even pulled up the file yet."

"You did eight days ago," Zaluna said, sipping from her mug. "No need to tell me twice."

"You're scaring me, boss." Laughter came from along the lines of desks.

"You could use a good scare, Hetto. Back to work, all of you."

The operators hushed immediately—and Hetto smiled and turned back to his terminal. Over two decades she'd watched his youthful brashness turn into jaded irascibility, but he still relished getting a rise out of her.

Zaluna had never expected to command a room of any kind. The diminutive Sullustans—at just over a meter and a half, Zaluna was taller than most—were one of the least threatening peoples on Gorse, a world where folks did a lot of threatening. Long before she had been promoted to her superior position, Hetto had taken to walking her to and from her tough neighborhood. She appreciated the gesture, but in fact she faced danger gamely. Theft on Gorse was a constant, like the ground-quakes that rocked the world. You might get knocked down now and again, but you simply had to get back up.

It had started before the Empire, under the Republic: The Mynocks had been tasked with screening electronic communications and certain monitored public places for "conversations suspected to pose a threat to the lives of Republic citizens." As the Clone Wars had dragged on, "the lives of Republic citizens" had evolved into "Republic security"—and under the Empire, that phrase had morphed into "public order."

No matter, Zaluna had thought. *They're just words.* She'd never had a problem with listening to those of others for a good cause. The mining business attracted a lot of rowdies, yes, but worse things grew in darkness. It was smart for law enforcement authorities to use the latest tools to keep tabs on miscreants.

And there was no shortage of things to listen for. During the Clone Wars, the Separatists had hatched many plots against the Republic; watching out for them was just common sense. Even the Republic's supposed defenders, the Jedi, had turned traitors—if you believed the Emperor's account. She wasn't sure she did, but she was fairly certain that if there *was* a plot, then someone like Zaluna had probably first flagged it.

Privacy? In her younger days, Zaluna had found it a silly concept. Either thoughts were in your head, or you let them out. The only distinction between a whisper and an intergalactic broadcast was technical. A listener with the means to hear had the absolute right to do so. Really, the *obligation* to do so—else the act of communicating was a futile one. Zaluna didn't speak her mind nearly as often as Hetto, but when she had something to say, she definitely wanted people to listen.

But times had changed. Under the Empire, words had become causes with greater effects. People she'd monitored had disappeared, although she'd never found out why. And the job had ceased to be as much fun.

Skelly's frozen image lingered there before her, his mouth stuck open mid-rant. It seemed a perfect pose—and she knew she'd see it again. Because Skelly, she knew, was red-stamped. Records digitally stamped with a red star indicated visits from Gorse's mental health authority.

"He gets any more stars, he can open up his own galaxy," she said. She took a deep breath, relieved. Red-stamped people tended to stay in the medical system, rarely escalating to anything else. They were freer with words than most, rarely intending action. And Skelly had been fun to listen to in the past, at least. She unpaused the feed. "That's that, then. I'll close out the—"

"Incoming message," Hetto said, speaking abruptly. "The official channel."

That doesn't happen every day, she thought. "Put it through!"

A macabre form appeared holographically in the space before the brown-clad supervisor. His mechanical voice spoke precisely and clearly. "This is Count Vidian of the Galactic Empire, speaking to all surveillance stations under my authority. I am launching inspections of mining operations both on Cynda and at the processors on Gorse. All such locations are now under Security Condition One. No exceptions."

Zaluna gawked at the life-sized figure. "Excuse me. *All* the mining operations? Are you aware how many—"

Count Vidian did not wait to hear her finish. The transmission ended.

Hetto spoke first, as always. "What the *hell?*"

"Yeah," Zaluna said, under her breath. Then she let out a whistle. The mining trade employed tens of thousands of people.

"Is he serious? Does he even know what he's asking for?" Hetto threw up his hands. "Maybe we need to get a red stamp for *that* guy's file. I swear, some of these Impies must be out of their minds! That, or—"

"Hetto!" Zaluna snapped.

Except for the low murmur of audio feeds coming from the monitors, the room fell silent. More quietly this time, she said, "We do what we're told."

Zaluna traced her jowls with her fingertips as she tried to remember the last time Sec-Con One had been invoked. It hadn't happened since the Emperor first drafted Transcept into Imperial service to deal with the Jedi crisis. It meant escalating every case under watch to the highest level—and Zaluna had a sense of what that meant.

It was nothing good.

Her eyes had returned to the live feed of Skelly on Cynda, the connection she had been about to close without action. "Bump him up, Hetto."

"But he's a red-stamp."

"Which counts for nothing today." The supervisor straightened. "Whatever his condition, Master Skelly's mouth is going to earn him some time with our friends in white."

And good luck to him then, she thought.

CHAPTER FIVE

"Count Vidian, this is an honor," gushed the tall cape-clad Neimoidian waiting at the bottom of the Imperial shuttle's landing ramp. Despite the short notice, every firm working the moon had sent someone to the party meeting *Cudgel,* and the director's big red eyes practically beamed with pride. "The Cyndan Mining Guild welcomes you," he said, a wide, thick-lipped smile on his noseless green face. "I'm Director Palfa. We've all heard so much about—"

"Spare me," Vidian snapped, and half the listeners on the cavern floor took a step back, unnerved. "I have a schedule—and so do you. When you bother to keep it!"

The director's throat went dry. "O-of course." The others averted their eyes, afraid to stare at the cyborg.

Good, Vidian thought.

In the waning days of the Republic, Vidian's management texts had become pop-culture hits despite—no, *because of*—his reluctance to appear on the business HoloNets. He wasn't shy or ashamed of his appearance; he just didn't like wasting his time. But while the mystique added to his public reputation, in person his physical presence was a large part of his managerial success.

The turnaround expert, he had written, *is a germ invading the body corporate. It will be opposed.* Whenever someone sought to make over an organization, entrenched bureaucrats always tried to intimidate him.

But two could play that game, and Vidian had been winning for fifteen years.

The legend of Denetrius Vidian had started five years before that, on what doctors expected would be his deathbed. But he'd survived, spending his bedridden time turning his meager bank balance into a fortune through electronic trading. In time, he purchased expensive, high-tech prosthetics, crafted to his own specifications. He did not look like other humans, but then humanity had abandoned him first, leaving him to rot in that hospice.

So Vidian had optimized his physical features in keeping with his now-famous trinity of management philosophies: *"Keep moving! Destroy barriers! See everything!"* Simple rules, which he diligently applied at every opportunity.

Including now, as the coterie made for the elevators. "The tour you ordered will cover some distance," the director said. "Would your lordship like to rest first?"

"No," Vidian said, marching so quickly the others had trouble keeping up. He moved faster now than he ever had in his youth; physical age no longer mattered. Some joked that Vidian was half droid, but he knew the comparison was inapt. Droids shut down. Vidian had spent too many years lying around already. So he had compounded his successes by working 90 percent of every day. *"Keep moving: With an able body, the mind can achieve anything!"*

Leading Vidian from the elevator onto a lower floor, the director paused in his blather about Cynda's wonders. "I'm sorry," he said, presenting his comlink. "Would you like to call your vessel to report your arrival?"

"I just did, while you were prattling in the elevator," Vidian said.

Palfa seemed puzzled. He hadn't seen or heard Vidian do anything. The count had installed a variety of comlink receivers into his earpieces; by routing his artificial voice through them, he regularly placed calls without ever appearing to open his mouth. Vidian hated getting information from intermediaries, who often distorted things for their own reasons; his communication capabilities were just one more way of cutting out the middle. *"Destroy barriers: Get information directly, whenever possible!"*

"This chamber leads to one of our mining levels," the director said, gesturing to the workers hurrying around. "What you're seeing is a typical day here—"

"A lie," Vidian said, continuing to walk. "I'm reading the live feed from your reports as I speak. You've doubled your pace, but will return to mediocrity when the Empire turns its eyes away. Be assured: I will see it does not."

A rumble came from the group of mining company representatives around them. But there was no point in their arguing. With a vocal command that made no external sound, Vidian cleared the daily production reports from his visual receptors.

Years earlier, he'd realized how leaders, from floor managers to chief executives, were often blind to the basic circumstances around them. Vidian didn't want to miss a detail. His optical implants not only gave him exceptional eyesight, but also eliminated the need for vid monitors by projecting external data feeds onto his own retinas. *See everything: He who has the data has the upper hand!*

Vidian looked back at the group of worried mining officials. Many were out of breath from trying to keep up with him, including a Besalisk woman. There were several of the multi-armed humanoids working at Calcoraan Depot, his administrative hub: members of a reasonably industrious but otherwise unremarkable species. Before he gave her a second thought, freight elevators opened on either side of the chamber. Stormtroopers rushed from the cars.

Right on time. Vidian pivoted and pointed to five different corridors leading from the chamber. Without a word in response, the squads split up and headed into the tunnels.

Director Palfa was startled. "What's going on?"

"No more than I said." Vidian's tone was as casual as his meaning was ominous. "You are managers. We're helping you manage."

. . .

Hera wasn't about to bring her ship into the Cyndan mining complex for an unauthorized landing. Joining the convoy, however, had gotten her close, and once out of sight of the Star Destroyer, she'd parked in orbit. Her ship's small excursion vessel had taken her the rest of the way to a little maintenance outbuilding on the surface.

She'd studied just enough about the mining trade to know what to pretend to be: a maintenance tech for bulk-loader droids. The rest she'd thought up on the spot.

"This is the wrong entrance," the guy inside the airlock had said.

"Oh, gosh, I'm sorry. It's my first day, and I'm late!"

"And where's your badge?"

"I forgot. Can you believe it? My first day!"

The man had believed it, letting her pass with a smile that said he hoped she'd keep making wrong turns in the future. People of several different species found Hera appealing to look at, and she was happy to put that to use for a good cause.

But as she walked carefully through the mining complex, she increasingly realized how difficult that cause had become. Gorse and Cynda produced a strategic material for the Empire, yes, but they were well away from the galactic center. And yet Hera spied one surveillance cam after another—including several that the workers clearly weren't intended to see. If Coruscant-level security had made it out to the Rim worlds, that would make any action against the Empire all the more difficult.

Another good reason to visit my friend on Gorse after this, she thought, darting lithely beneath the viewing arc of another secret cam. A rendezvous with any mystery informant was dangerous; she'd learned that quickly enough in her short career as an activist. But her contact had proven knowledge of Imperial surveillance capabilities, and she'd need that to get to the important stuff, later on.

Finding out more about Count Vidian's methods, though, she'd have to do through old-fashioned skulking. He was on Cynda now, she knew: She'd seen him once already from afar, passing through the caverns with a tour group. It was tough to get closer. The transparent crystal columns were pretty to look at but lousy cover.

Darting through an isolated side passage, she thought she'd found a shortcut to get ahead of him. Instead, she found something else.

"Halt!" A stormtrooper appeared at the end of the corridor, his blaster raised.

Hera stopped in her tracks. "I'm sorry," she said, putting her hand to her chest and exhaling. "You scared me!"

"Who are you?"

"I work here," she said, approaching as if nothing was wrong. "I may be in the wrong place. It's my first day." She smiled.

"Where's your badge?"

"I forgot." Dark eyes looked down demurely, then back up. "Can you believe it? My first day!"

The stormtrooper studied her for a moment—and then saw the blaster she was wearing. She moved before he did, delivering a high kick that knocked the blaster from the startled stormtrooper's hands. Seeing his weapon clatter away, he lunged for it. She easily sidestepped him—and pivoted, leaping onto the armored man's back. Losing purchase on the crystalline floor, he stumbled, her full weight driving his head into the side wall. His helmet cracked loudly against the surface, and he slumped motionless to the ground.

"Sorry," Hera whispered over the fallen trooper's shoulder. "Charm doesn't work on everyone."

CHAPTER SIX

"Hurry up! Hurry up!"

Skelly looked back in annoyance as Tarlor Choh rushed about the cavern, egging workers on. A tall light-skinned fellow, Tarlor was Dalborg Mining's imbecile for Zone Thirty-Nine—not to be confused with all the *other* imbeciles managing their firm's efforts in this underground pocket. There were official imbeciles in all the other zones, too, Skelly knew—and not one of them had a whit of sense.

All were currently in a tizzy. For hours, arriving workers had reported the Empire spurring them along, even circulating a tale of the Star Destroyer blowing up a freighter captain for slacking. Now word had come through Tarlor that the Emperor's top efficiency expert, Count Vidian, would be inspecting.

Skelly saw it as deliverance. The top government inspector—coming right to him? Well, not to *him*, of course, but this was close enough. And better still, it was Denetrius Vidian. A business mogul under the Republic, true, but perhaps the only one Skelly respected. Vidian fed on blundering corporations, profiting from fixing their mistakes. Vidian's famous treatise, *Forget the Old Way,* was the only business holo Skelly owned.

If Skelly could get his research to Vidian, the Empire would understand—and it surely had the power to stop what the mining companies were doing.

Tarlor loomed over him. "Skelly, get those charges set!"

Skelly simply sighed, then returned his attention to the crystal column he was kneeling beside. Having prepared a suspension of baradium bisulfate in putty, he began caking a ring of the pasty substance all around the stalagmite's base.

It was slow, painstaking work—and hard to do neatly when he was irritated at the universe and everyone in it. Kanan, of course: Skelly's mouth still hurt from the man's punch. Who did he think he was? Tarlor plagued him, too—along with all his managerial kind, especially since Dalborg had recently busted him down from explosives supervisor to lowly demolitions placement tech.

And most of all, he hated his right hand, for being useless and forcing him to do the finely detailed work with his left. He could just bear to look at the fake hand now; it had been curled into a claw most of the time since that terrible day back in the Clone Wars.

The Clone Wars were yet another thing to be upset about. Everything about that conflict had been a lie. The Separatists had been this big enemy, and yet when the Empire was declared they'd melted away as if at the push of a button. The big corporations had staged the whole thing, Skelly was sure. Wars sold more ships, more weapons, and more medical devices. And in the Clone Wars, even the *soldiers* on both sides were manufactured goods.

The Republic and the Confederacy had been partners in the same corrupt game. The Empire was probably just another iteration of all that, to Skelly's thinking; no more or less immoral. To corporate oligarchs, political allegiances were just another change of clothes. This decade, central rule was in fashion. Something else would come along soon. The beast had to be fed, with lives and limbs on the battlefield and with the sweat and blood of the workers.

The problem was that blowing things up was the only thing Skelly had ever been taught to do.

He didn't fault himself for that. He was the product of a system that built only to destroy, as he saw it. He'd learned from the best—and learned well. Everything always came down to that simple list, taught to him during his first day in military demolitions: *Pair your ordnance with your initiator. Ignition leads to reaction leads to detonation.* Whether applied to compounds of baradium or its tremendously more powerful isotope, baradium-357, those steps referred to a series of complex reactions that had the same simple result.

Now forty, Skelly thought that list also applied to life. You started with a festering problem. Someone initiated a change. The system reacted to that pressure. And then, *bang,* you had your solution. It had always been his method. He'd been the one to initiate changes, whenever possible, starting back on the battlefield. It was why he'd volunteered for everything. Whenever battlements were too dangerous to storm, Skelly risked his life to burrow beneath, planting the explosives that made the decisive opening. He did that and more.

But then had come the Battle of Slag's Pit. A foolish charge on behalf of an idiot general, hoping to use demolitions to buy a Separatist fortification cheaply. The ground wasn't firm, the explosives were the wrong kind—and Skelly had raised hell about it.

No one had listened. No one ever listened.

The general had rank. All Skelly could do was enter the breach himself, relying on his innate talent to save the day for his fellow soldiers.

It hadn't been good enough.

The Clone Wars had ended while he was comatose; he'd later learned that none of his companions had been saved. His hand was another crushing blow. The medical droids had assured the platoon they were carrying all the spare parts necessary for proper battlefield surgery. But they'd lied. They only had a Klatooinian prosthetic hand left for Skelly, which had never worked right with his human neurology. Worse, their blundering had damaged his arm to the point where a proper replacement would never work, either. Skelly had just stuck a glove on the stupid thing and tried to go on.

Poverty had followed. He'd had no choice but to return to demolitions work—and there, he'd only found confirmation for all his beliefs about corporate malfeasance. They were just as careless as the military types.

It would have been unbearable had his travels not taken him to Cynda.

As someone who had spent much of his time underground, he'd been astonished by the beauty of the moon's caverns. Thoughts that moved too quickly through his head seemed to slow down here. He'd imagined his role a responsible one, for a time: If the moon was going to be exploited anyway, he'd make sure it was done in a cautious manner, protective of the world and the people working on it. Cynda had countless caverns; it was unimaginable to think the corporations could ruin them all.

But now, Skelly could imagine exactly that. Cynda would become one more ripped-up place, to add to the pile of torn-up lives.

The detonator armed, he replaced the applicator in his toolbox. One more stalagmite, ready to be decapitated. Rote work, and boring—but nicely done. Someone had to care.

"He's over there," Skelly heard the supervisor say. He stood up from his work on the stalagmite and turned around. There, being led by Tarlor, was a group of four Imperial stormtroopers.

Ah, Skelly thought. It seemed soon for the inspector's advance team to be here, but that didn't matter. "Hello!" he shouted. Toolbox still clutched in his good-for-little right hand, he saluted with his left. An impulse act: He wasn't part of any military organization, but their armor looked much like that of the clone troopers he'd once served with, and he was glad to see them, in any event. "I'm Skelly. I've been writing to your oversight offices for months—"

"What?" Tarlor blurted.

"—and I'm glad to see someone's listening." Skelly looked past the stormtroopers, who continued to march toward him. "Er, is Count Vidian here?"

The lead trooper stopped and raised his blaster rifle. His companions did the same. "Skelly, you're under arrest."

Skelly laughed nervously. "You're joking. Why?"

"You're charged with speaking to the detriment of the Empire."

Skelly's eyes widened—and his mind raced. "Wait! Did Kanan report me?"

Tarlor shook his bald head. "He's all yours. Skelly's always been trouble—and Dalborg Mining doesn't want anyone around that'll upset Count Vidian. Please tell him we cooperated fully." He looked over at Skelly and spoke acidly: "Looks like I just won the pool. *You're fired!*"

Skelly sputtered. "W-wait. This is a mistake! And Tarlor, you don't have the authority to—"

Before he could finish, the stormtroopers began to advance toward him. "Put that toolbox down!" the lead trooper said, just steps away.

With a blaster pointed at him and coming his way, Skelly made a decision. His left hand in the air, he crouched. "Okay, fine. I'm doing it. Just give me a second here." He knelt—

—and grabbed for the remote control he'd left on the ground. He tumbled behind the crystal column he'd been working on and rolled up into a ball, covering his toolbox with his body. Before the stormtroopers could follow, Skelly pressed the button.

The baradium bisulfate affixed to the column near Skelly detonated—and the massive diamond-hard cylinder fell forward, exactly the way he'd known it would. Away from him—and toward the stormtroopers. One screamed loudly, crushed immediately by the base of the falling column. On striking the surface, the entire structure shattered into daggerlike fragments.

Skelly didn't see what happened to the other stormtroopers because he was already up and running. He sprinted into an unlit passage leading from Zone Thirty-Nine into a service shaft. He knew from memory that it led to ventilation tunnels and other routes, pathways that could take him all over Cynda's underworld.

Wheezing as he ran in the dark, Skelly tried to comprehend what had just happened. So someone *was* listening to his words, after all. But they hadn't gotten his meaning.

Fine, he thought. He recognized the feeling of the toolbox full of explosives, still clutched in his immobilized right hand, bouncing against his leg as he ran. It gave him comfort, and he smiled.

There's more than one way to send a message.

CHAPTER SEVEN

Vidian had never seen corporate hacks scatter so quickly. Since he'd declared Security Condition One, the surveillance operators on Gorse had provided him with the names of forty-six potential agitators working in the Cyndan mines. Vidian's news that the stormtroopers were making arrests had sent the executives off to alert their employees of the new scrutiny.

Other organic beings, for their supposed sentience, were really no better than droids, Vidian thought. They could be made to act according to program.

With the right encouragement, of course. Flanked by a pair of stormtroopers, the count glared at the guild chief—the only person left on the tour. "Palfa, your members will name a morale officer in each work crew to ensure the Empire is supported in word and deed."

The director cast his eyes to the ground. "My lord, I don't know how such a program will be received. It's the kind of laborers we attract. Rough characters. It's hard to control what they think—"

"When they think at all. Drunks and brawlers don't concern me. But they aren't all harmless! Consider this report I've just heard." Vidian paused to tune his earpiece. "An arrest attempt has been made on your Level Thirty-Nine—and the suspect responded by assaulting the troopers!"

The director shook his large head. "That's terrible. I'm sure our security personnel have caught him."

"They haven't. But my troops will." Vidian switched off his audible communications long enough to give a command. "There," he said, speaking aloud again. "I've sent your office a copy of my remedial political program. Make sure your member firms adopt it immediately."

"Yes, my lord."

"Then we continue."

The dejected director led Vidian into a work zone. Like everywhere else, this space was populated by itinerant laborers, beings only slightly more effective than droids. Some passed through with explosives for other chambers. Others stood hip-deep in mounds of shattered crystal, sweating profusely as they shoveled thorilide-containing chips into bins for shipment. Cynda's interior was naturally dry; the light haze on the air was entirely organic perspiration. Vidian was glad his sense of smell no longer existed.

The rabble with the rubble, Vidian thought. Their kind had been present on countless other production worlds he'd been tasked to straighten out, and they were terrible clay to work with. Even with the troublemakers removed, few could be taught anything new—and their lifestyles outside only served to make them less effective on the job.

But they were boundless in number, and that gave him something he could do. He walked into the workers' midst and slapped his metal hands on the backs of one laborer after another. "You. You. You. And you." Each looked up, startled by the cyborg's touch. Human, nonhuman—their only common trait was their advanced ages. "Too old. Too slow."

Ignoring the mix of angry and insulted looks he was getting from the workers, Vidian called back to the guild chief, "Palfa, another directive for your members. New age caps on laborers, effective immediately."

Palfa spluttered. "But—but they're still productive!"

Vidian turned his soulless eyes toward Palfa. "And you are being unproductive," he said, stalking toward him. "Your guild is a haven for traitors and loafers!"

"My lord, perhaps I can suggest some way to—"

Vidian didn't wait to hear Palfa's suggestion. His arm lanced out and caught the director by the collar. Yanking downward, he pulled the screaming bureaucrat's cape over his head and forced him to the rocky surface. The stormtroopers watched, blasters drawn, as Vidian rained powerful blows on Palfa's body.

The count stepped back, satisfied, as the cloth-covered guildmaster's body stopped moving. Vidian looked admiringly at his hands; they still had their sterling shine.

"My lord!" one of the stormtroopers said.

"Eh?" Vidian looked at the soldier—and then back at the group of workers he'd been standing amid. They were all staring at him. "Industrial accident," he said. "Get to work—unless I told you to get out. Your firms will find more suitable labor for you on Gorse. Unemployment in a strategic resource system is unlawful. The Empire does not tolerate layabouts."

Seeing the wary workers complying, Vidian nodded with satisfaction. *Management, the Imperial way.* It was so much more efficient than under the Republic—and it came to him easily. Firing a manager inspired only the ambitious who wanted to take his or her place. But murder motivated everyone. It belonged in every supervisor's tool kit.

He changed his audio channel. "Captain Sloane, are you listening?"

From *Ultimatum*, the captain's voice filled his ear. "Affirmative."

"Inform Coruscant that there is an opening atop the Cynda Mining Guild. I'm sure the Emperor can send us someone appropriate."

"Done. Sloane out."

Leaving the stormtroopers to mind the workers as they disposed of the body, Vidian continued his tour alone. In the next chamber, he found another work crew—and while he had no intention of personally going through and identifying every slacker, he couldn't resist when he saw a white-haired man kneeling as he cleaned his pick.

"You're definitely too old," Vidian said, grabbing at the man's collar.

"Yeah? Well, you're too ugly," the man responded before he even turned to see who had accosted him. When he did, he cried out in revulsion. "What are *you* supposed to be?"

Vidian didn't react. He read the old man's badge. "Okadiah Garson." Not one of the names on the dissident list, but it didn't matter. He was through here. "Stop gawking at me like a fool."

"Sorry." Okadiah pointed to a spot behind the cyborg's ear, where his synthskin didn't completely cover the scar tissue beneath. "It's just—you missed a spot there."

"It's not for vanity. It's for the benefit of those who lose efficiency when confronted with the extraordinary." He tightened his grip on Okadiah's collar and shook. "I find this galaxy already has enough *ordinary* beings. Maybe you'd like to have your skin removed, as well, to see what it's like!"

"Maybe you should let him go," a voice said from behind.

Vidian looked back to see a dark-haired young man standing with a heavily laden hovercart in the opening to a tunnel. He held a blaster pointed straight at the count.

"Well, well," Vidian said, not in the least concerned for his safety. "We have a gunslinger. Or perhaps we've found our missing saboteur!"

In his travels, Kanan had seen a lot of people with prosthetics. Most were decent individuals, using technology to overcome misfortune. But the cyborg that had Okadiah by the collar had really gone to town with it. He looked like a war droid playing a human at a masquerade party.

"I'm no saboteur," Kanan said, still holding his weapon. "Heard a scream—sounded like trouble. What's this about?"

"I am Count Vidian, here for the Emperor. And I am doing his work." Vidian, seeming totally unconcerned by Kanan's blaster, started to lift the writhing old man by the neck.

Kanan fingered the trigger of his weapon. He had no desire whatsoever to tangle with the Empire, much less the top Imperial in the area. He was thankful when another way occurred to him. "There's something you should know." He lowered his blaster as he trod cautiously onto the work floor. "You're about to mangle the man who knows how to mine thorilide better than anyone."

Vidian paused. "Doubtful. He can't have the strength to dig or haul much."

"He teaches those who do," Kanan said. "Moonglow's the most efficient producer for its size."

Vidian shook Okadiah for a short moment before abruptly dropping him to the cavern floor. "At last—someone who understands what's important," he said. "You're fortunate I've already beaten someone else to death today, gunslinger. I have a schedule to keep." With that, the cyborg abruptly turned and exited with his guards.

Kanan holstered his blaster and turned back to check on Okadiah. Being tended to by his fellow miners, the old man rubbed his neck and looked at Kanan. "You always have to poke the gundark."

"Just following your lead," Kanan said.

Yelkin, the miner he'd tangled with that morning, rolled his eyes at Kanan. "I don't know why you didn't shoot that creep! Someone said he killed the guildmaster!"

"I pick who I party with," Kanan said. He walked back to the hovercart and activated it. "I don't mess with the Empire—and it doesn't mess with me."

"Zone Forty-Two awaits, gentlemen," Okadiah said. "I want to be done with this day."

Far across the wide chamber, Hera lowered her electrobinoculars. She'd had a bit of luck in the last hour, when all the stormtroopers had left her area. From what she'd been able to overhear, they were all after someone who had violently resisted arrest. She was interested to learn that story, but Vidian had to come first—and so she'd kept following along, trying to find safe places in each cavernous chamber from which to watch.

She'd been unable to get within a hundred meters, but she'd seen enough to know he was a vile thing, completely worthy of an important station by the Emperor's side. She'd seen both his attack on the poor guildmaster and how his escort had reacted to it: as if managerial murder was the most normal thing in the galaxy. And she'd seen him harassing the old man, moments earlier. It was good luck that the younger guy had come along. At least someone had a spine.

Watching the dark-haired man leaving with his hovercart, Hera felt a moment's impulse to follow him. People with the will to stand up to the Empire were worth knowing. But then she remembered that this wasn't a recruiting trip. She needed to keep after her objective.

Maybe next lifetime, pal. Hera slipped down from her perch and took off after Vidian.

CHAPTER EIGHT

More stormtroopers ran past as Kanan pushed the hovercart down the last tunnel to Zone Forty-Two. No doubt they were still looking for the idiot who had flipped out and attacked them in Zone Thirty-Nine. Lal Grallik had popped into the work area long enough to confirm the rumor that it was, indeed, Skelly on the loose. Kanan wasn't in the least surprised—or upset. At least Skelly was out of his hair.

It wasn't unusual to see stormtroopers in the Empire. But while he had hopped around some, Kanan's travels through the galaxy had tended toward a spiraling path, moving outward from the galactic center. Core Worlds, Colony worlds, Inner Rim: Each represented a new frontier for him. And each had turned out the same, with Imperial presence starting at nil and gradually growing. Kanan sometimes wondered how the stormtrooper uniform suppliers kept up with the demand. When the Imperials reached the fringe of the galaxy, what would they be wearing?

Not that the sight of stormtroopers alarmed him. No, like the woman who had spoken to him from the Star Destroyer, they were all functionaries. Organic droids, trained to react a certain way and seek out certain targets. Vidian was maybe the most literal expression that he'd seen: all their robotic efficiency and general nastiness bound up in a mass of metal, with a little skin on top. The best way to avoid being hassled by them was simply to fit perfectly into the stereotypes they were expecting to find.

On worlds like Gorse, the Empire expected to find workers of the sort drawn to low-skill, high-risk jobs. Rowdy and rambunctious characters—just not rebellious. Threats to their own sobriety and to one another, but never to the Empire. Not politically active, or even conscious.

It happened that those were the planets Kanan found the most fun. The role of roughneck suited him. He traveled the galaxy, looking at the sights—and sometimes the ceiling, after the odd fight or drunken binge. He'd visited more places than he could remember, and, beyond Okadiah, he'd never learned the names of most of the people around him. Why bother, when you were just going to leave?

Kanan pushed the cart into Zone Forty-Two. Deep beneath Cynda's surface, it was the largest chamber yet opened—and more important, sensors had found large recesses hiding behind its walls: other areas sure to be thick with minable thorilide. For weeks, various teams had triggered controlled blasts—barely audible over Skelly's objections—trying to get at the rich deposits. In a newly hollowed alcove, Moonglow's techs were working on their own attempt.

Kanan parked his cart outside the opening and pounded on the outside wall. "I'm thirsty. Let's get this done!"

Yelkin appeared from inside the hole, now wearing a white safety vest. He frowned when he saw Kanan. "You again."

"You bet."

Aggravated, the Devaronian surveyed the load of explosives. "We're measuring the length of the borehole for the charge. It should be just a—"

"Wait," someone called from inside the carved-out area. "There's a problem."

Kanan sighed as Yelkin hustled back inside. Kanan was about to start off-loading the crates himself when he glanced back into the recess. Beside Yelkin, he saw another technician sticking a long prod into a hole drilled for explosives. Or trying to. "Something's already in there!"

Kanan's eyes widened—and for the first time, he looked down at the ground outside the short tunnel. There was something he'd seen before: small and brown, discarded nearby.

Skelly's toolbox.

Kanan yelled into the opening. *"Get out! Get out!"*

He didn't have to yell a third time. The techs were moving.

"Someone's wired something already," Yelkin said in a panic. "There's a timer! Thirty seconds—"

No disarming that! "Forget it!" Kanan yelled. "Go!"

Moonglow's demolition techs kept a portable siren in the blast area; it was right in Kanan's path. He activated it. All across Zone Forty-Two, workers charged for the exit tunnels to the west.

Ahead of him, Yelkin stumbled across the craggy surface and fell. Kanan, on a headlong run, slowed as he approached the miner—the only other soul left in the enormous crystal atrium. But Yelkin wasn't asking for help. He was pointing, instead, to something Kanan had forgotten about.

"Kanan! Your cart!"

Kanan looked back at the hovercart with its full load of baradium bisulfate—a hundred times more material than Skelly would have been carrying in his kit—and remembered the demolition guys' adage: *It's the secondary that does the damage.* His cart could bring down half the cave network.

Kanan bounded back toward the opening—and its ticking bomb inside—and seized the hovercart. Turning with it, he ran, pushing it as fast as he could across the long clearing.

Yelkin wasn't moving, he saw—he'd twisted his ankle. Kanan pointed the cart toward him as his boots pounded the surface. His voice echoed across the chamber: "Yelkin! Grab for it!"

It wasn't easy to see or hear much after that.

Light from the blast came first. Emanating into the work area from the blasting tunnel, it reflected dazzlingly off the crystal structures above and to either side of Kanan. The sound came next, a muted boom.

Kanan had just reached Yelkin with the crate-topped hovercart when the shock wave hit him in mid-stride. The cart's repulsors were still working; its front bumper caught Yelkin in the gut—and now both they and the hovercart were carried forward, Kanan's hands locked onto the handle for dear life.

Searing cracks resounded across the atrium. Kanan, now a passenger hanging on like Yelkin, knew what was next. Like icicles on a summer day, meter-wide stalactites across the chamber began falling across the ground they'd already covered. First the crystal knives—and then the rock and stone suspended above them, all plummeting into the open space.

Seeing the first shard strike nearby, Kanan hit the ground with his heels for the first time in seconds. Without thinking, he leapt.

Leapt, as he hadn't in nearly a decade, farther than any mortal normally could. Leapt, atop the crates filled with deadly explosives on the careening cart. Leapt, to where he could reach out and grab the shoulder of the unaware Devaronian, clinging for dear life.

The western opening through which the other miners had evacuated was just ahead. Pulling the hapless Yelkin fully onto the hovercart in one motion, Kanan hit the ground off the left side with his next. Guiding the airborne vehicle like a wader moving a raft, he slung the cart toward the exit tunnel. He stumbled, a step shy of safety, as he tried to follow. Twisting faceup as he dropped, Kanan hit the ground. He looked up into the onrushing mass—

—and stopped it, with his mind.

It was an odd feeling, like putting on an old article of clothing. It was like the leap, something he had sworn never to do. Not in front of anyone, to be sure.

But now he had done it. All light was gone, but he could sense the black mass of debris quivering a meter from his head, even as he heard apocalyptic clamor all around. Instinctively, Kanan dug his heels into the tunnel floor and forced himself backward, the tail of his shirt grinding against the surface until he was fully inside the reinforced western tunnel.

And then he let go. Let go with his mind, and listened as a mountain, denied, found the space where he had landed.

Vidian was in an upper chamber addressing the droidmaster and his three terrified aides when the floor fell in.

Everything went dark as Vidian, his audience members, and all their furnishings tumbled downward. The fall was brief, with the remnants of what had been the floor beneath their feet smashing to pieces on the tougher surface below. An immense jolt rocked Vidian.

Up to his hips in stone, he took a moment to regain his bearings. His eyes switched to night-vision mode, and he realized that a sinkhole had opened beneath the droidmaster's office: The walls of the room, as well as the hallway leading from it, were intact, several meters above.

Disregarding the pained cries of the others struggling in the rubble, Vidian used his cybernetic arms to dig himself out. Then he began climbing for the aperture above.

"We're trapped down here," a voice called behind him. "Help us!"

"Someone will arrive before you starve," Vidian said, reaching for the bottom of the doorway.

"But there may be aftershocks—"

"Aftershocks? Impossible. This moon's crystal columns are supposed to prevent tremors," Vidian said. The event couldn't have been natural. Pulling himself up and into the intact hallway, he began to suspect what had happened.

His anger returned anew.

In the darkness, Hera felt the world rumbling around her. She'd seen Vidian fall through the floor and disappear; she'd lingered for a few moments, hoping he was gone for good.

No luck, she thought, hearing his voice from the recess up ahead. The moon had tasted him and spat him out.

She heard voices in the hallways around her, and spied portable lights flashing this way and that. There was too much activity now—someone had kicked the insect nest. She needed to use the darkness while she could.

Recon's over, the Twi'lek thought. She turned from Vidian's chamber and ran back up the hall.

Kanan continued to force himself backward as debris struck the ground behind him. Finally, after what seemed like an eon, stillness came.

And then the work lights.

Okadiah arrived at his side and knelt. "Lad? You all right?"

Kanan coughed up dust and nodded. Blinking particles from his eyes, he vaguely saw his hovercart, its securely fastened crates of explosives still there. Yelkin lay facedown atop it, wheezing.

"What happened?" Okadiah asked.

"I didn't see," Yelkin said. He looked back at the rubble-blocked passage. "I guess we caromed into the tunnel! I thought we were goners, for sure!"

"A million-to-one shot," Okadiah said, scratching his chin. He looked at Kanan. "My boy, you *are* the lucky one."

Kanan knew he was anything but lucky. For Kanan Jarrus was Caleb Dume, the Jedi who never was.

And now, he knew, it was time to go.

CHAPTER NINE

The Force was a mysterious energy field that sprang from life itself; that much, every Jedi student knew. The Force could be used for many purposes: protection, persuasion, wisdom—even the manipulation of matter and the performance of great physical feats. Jedi taught younglings all of those things.

But they never taught how to make the Force go away when it wasn't wanted. That was all Caleb—all *Kanan* had wanted from the Force for years. And the blasted thing had just shown up again on Cynda. It had saved his carcass, true—but if anyone had seen, Kanan's life wouldn't be worth a Confederacy credit.

He had left a moon in chaos. Zone Forty-Two's ceiling had caved in, producing tremors that caused dangerous seams to open in some floors higher up. Thankfully, no chambers had vented to space: They were too far beneath Cynda's surface. It was a miracle no one had been killed.

Kanan didn't know if Count Vidian was still there or not, or if the Empire suspected Skelly of planting the charges that caused the collapse. It was a safe bet they did. It was mining in Zone Forty-Two that Skelly had warned about; perhaps he'd decided to bring the roof down before anybody else did. Cynda was laced with tunnels, but the Imperials had numbers. They'd find Skelly eventually, and he'd get what was coming to him.

Kanan had used one of those back tunnels to slip away, leaving Oka-diah and his crew behind. Taking little-used elevators back to *Expedient,* he'd raised ship before security knew any better. He could hear over the transceiver that departures had been grounded. He doubted it would be a problem. The Moonglow techs below would vouch for his having warned them; no one would suspect Kanan of having planted the bomb, at least. He was just returning his ship safely to home base, on Gorse, like he was scheduled to do.

And that would be it. He'd never set foot on the moon again. And tomorrow, he'd find a way off Gorse. It was time to move on.

He'd been in motion since that dark day, years earlier. The darkest of days. The day when life as he knew it had fallen apart, had been blasted apart, by something he hadn't then understood. He still didn't understand much of it. There he'd been, fourteen years old, having relied for his entire life on the Jedi Order for everything: food, shelter, education, and security. Maybe not love, but at least stability, calm, sense.

And then, all at once, the Republic and its clone soldiers had turned against the Jedi. Depa Billaba fought to protect him—and he fought to protect her. She died. He fled. She died *so* he could flee, but to what end? What did she hope for him?

The young Caleb hadn't known. He'd known only that, in the end, the Force hadn't helped her. Or any of the other Jedi he'd heard about.

It's not your friend, he'd told himself. It was one reason he refused to use it, even to make his life a little easier. He'd also refused to take up his lightsaber. He still had it: Besides the finicky Force, it was his last tie to the past. But what good were lightsabers? What good was the Force, if it allowed its most devoted followers to be cut down by rank betrayal?

"A Jedi uses the Force for guidance," his first teacher had said. *Yeah, guidance right into a freaking wall!*

The problem was that the Force couldn't be turned off like a switch. Many of the benefits it conveyed were subtle. They enhanced traits without his conscious effort. No act of will could make it stop; no lapse of belief could make it fully vanish. Kanan would always be better at some things. And that had been the problem of his life. He was still driven to take jobs that interested him, and to excel at them. That was just his way.

But excelling by too much, or for too long, risked notice. And that was something he had been told to avoid.

Obi-Wan had used the beacon to warn Jedi to avoid detection. It hadn't taken long for Kanan to understand why. For days and weeks after the Jedi generals had been cut down by their own clone troopers, the new Empire continued to hunt and kill Jedi. It wasn't just about hiding physically from the Empire. *Avoid detection* meant hiding from everyone the fact that he had a connection to the Force.

The Force was a death mark.

The early months had been a blur of terror for young Caleb. He'd lived constantly with nightmares of what could happen. The Empire had control of the Jedi headquarters. That surely included the database with whatever information the Jedi had on file for Caleb Dume. They would have learned his name, for sure, and likely had images of him taken by the training center's security cams. What else did they have? He'd racked his brain many times trying to remember what, if any, biometric information the Jedi had taken from him over the years. Did they have a soundprint of his voice? A genetic sample? It bewildered Kanan now to think that the Empire might know more about his family history than he did.

Whatever had happened to the other Jedi Knights and their Padawans, he had to assume the Emperor would have been thorough about it. They'd have found a list, or constructed one. They'd have marked off everyone who fell. And they would've known Caleb Dume did not fall when Depa Billaba did.

So in the beginning, Caleb did everything right. When he took jobs to feed himself, he made sure not to excel too far beyond the expected norm. Personally distributing his own payloads on Cynda was a holdover from that; it kept his number of flights per day to a number that was merely exceptional, and not suspicious. He'd resisted friendships and long-term romantic connections, and he'd mostly restrained his chivalrous impulses. The teenager had done all those things, for fear of a middle-of-the-night visit by stormtroopers.

But weeks turned to months, and months to years, and no one came to his home—or cot, or tent, or patch of spacecraft floor—to wake him and drag him away. And the young man now known as Kanan Jarrus discovered that carousing eliminated those worries entirely.

So he'd done more of the same. He'd drunk to forget. He'd brawled to let off steam. He'd taken the dangerous jobs to fund his lifestyle—and then began it all again. He wasn't some chivalrous nomad, skulking from planet to planet doing good deeds and leaving when things got too hot. No, he left when things got *dull*. When the drinking money ran out, or when the bar-owner's daughter suddenly wanted to marry him. Kanan didn't leave because the Empire moved in: He'd stared down Imperials like Vidian before and lived. They knew he was something to ignore. No, he left because where the Empire went, fun usually died.

And he also left whenever he got too comfortable. That was when the Force, tired of being suppressed, would sneak back like an ignored pet. He didn't want it complicating his world, making him feel like somebody's prey again. And he didn't like being reminded about what had happened in that other life.

Watching *Ultimatum* growing in his cockpit window as he headed for Gorse, Kanan thought for the umpteenth time about the text portion of the message from Obi-Wan. *Republic forces have been turned against the Jedi*. There was something in that wording: *have been turned*. It suggested that maybe the people themselves hadn't turned against the Jedi, despite the Emperor's claims to the contrary.

That might have mattered years earlier, Kanan thought, but it hardly did now.

He had always been aggravated by how little Obi-Wan had shared. It made sense that he'd been short of time. And perhaps he hadn't known much, yet, when he sent the warning. But why hadn't he sent another? If he didn't have access to the beacon on Coruscant any longer, wouldn't he have found another way to get a message out, later on?

Kanan knew the answer. *Because there probably aren't any Jedi left to contact. And because Kenobi's probably dead himself.*

At one time, those had been hard thoughts to have; now they only produced a tired yawn. He couldn't see Obi-Wan willingly hunkering down on some remote world, waiting for things to blow over. He'd have had a mission, if he were alive—an important one. He'd want people to know about it. And all the missions Kanan could imagine would have put Obi-Wan into motion all around the galaxy. No, if Kenobi lived, Kanan would have heard something.

But Kanan knew he wouldn't care even if the Jedi Master popped up in the seat right behind him. Caleb Dume hadn't yet been a Jedi Knight, and Kanan Jarrus wasn't one now. None of it affected him, need *ever* affect him. He'd been dealt his hand, and that was what he would play. Play, for as long he could keep from stupid stunts like the one he'd pulled on Cynda.

He just wouldn't play *here* anymore.

He would return *Expedient* to Moonglow; it would be a dumb star-ship thief indeed that would want it. He'd collect his back pay, gather his few goods before Okadiah got home, and be on his way. The Star De-stroyer was still out there, he saw, but it hadn't yet barred commercial flights from Gorse. He would pick a direction and be on his—

Kanan took a second look at the Star Destroyer, now ahead and to his right. From *Ultimatum*'s underside, two four-vehicle flights of TIE fighters emerged and headed in his direction.

Snapped alert, Kanan leaned forward and grabbed the steering yoke. Which way? They were headed right for *Expedient*. The ship had a little rock-shooter of a cannon, nothing more, and the vessel hadn't been re-fueled since that morning, four lunar flights earlier. Kanan switched the comm system from channel to channel, listening for Captain Sloane's voice. Someone, something to tell him whether he needed to fight or fly.

The voice he did hear came from the backseat—but it wasn't Obi-Wan Kenobi, or even kindly old Okadiah. "They're not after you," it said. "They're looking for me."

Kanan looked back.

Skelly!

CHAPTER TEN

"You!" Kanan grabbed at Skelly's collar, yanking him violently forward and slamming him against the top of *Expedient*'s dashboard. Kanan's first instinct was to deal with the stowaway—but the Imperials were still out there, still heading in his direction.

"Look!" Skelly said, gasping for breath, arms flailing.

Kanan followed the upside-down man's gaze and saw, past the TIE squadrons, a *Lambda*-class shuttle departing *Ultimatum*. As its trapezoidal wings folded into flight position, another one followed. And then another—until five shuttles were heading in Kanan's direction. Two TIEs from each group broke formation and moved to flank the shuttles as the others continued ahead, clearing the space lanes. Kanan watched, disbelieving, as the vessels passed over his head on the way to Cynda.

"I told you, they're all looking for me," Skelly said. "Not you."

"Congratulations," Kanan said drily. He didn't let Skelly up. "There's about to be a hundred more stormtroopers on Cynda, thanks to you. I'm tempted to send you back to them!"

Skelly wrested free—and Kanan gave him a hard smack. Blood spurted from Skelly's nose. "You jerk! What did you do that for?"

"You blew up Zone Forty-Two. You tried to kill us!"

"I didn't!" Skelly said, wresting free.

"You're lying!" Kanan grabbed Skelly's left arm and twisted it behind his back. Turning, he started to shove the unwanted guest toward the airlock. "They're looking for you? I'm giving you back to them!"

"Watch it! Not that arm! Not that arm!" Skelly said. Putting his free hand—his mechanical hand—before him, he grabbed on to a handle near the airlock door. After a few moments' scuffling, Kanan realized the hand was in a death grip, and that Skelly wouldn't be going anywhere.

"Fine," Kanan said. He turned and grabbed his holster, which had been hanging on the back of his pilot's seat.

Skelly looked back and sneered. "What, are you going to shoot me now?"

"Maybe."

"That's gratitude! *I saved you!*"

Kanan had the blaster fully out of the holster when he finally registered what Skelly had said. "Wait. What?"

"I saved you," Skelly said. "You and your whole rotten corporate bunch!"

"Saved—" Kanan was flabbergasted. "You brought a mountain down on my head!"

Skelly went silent.

Aggravated, Kanan stood and turned back to the controls to direct *Expedient* onto a path well away from any other convoys, Imperial or otherwise. He glanced back to see Skelly slumped against the airlock door, massaging a hand that had finally come free from the handle.

Kanan lowered his pistol but didn't put it away. Suddenly exhausted, he dropped onto the acceleration couch facing the airlock. "I need a drink," he said, rubbing his forehead. "Now, tell me this again. You were saving us by *blowing us up?*"

"I wasn't trying to blow you up. I was trying to show the Imperial inspectors we shouldn't use baradium to open new chambers. Cynda can't take it."

"You could've killed people!" Kanan said.

"No, no," Skelly said. "You Moonglow guys weren't supposed to be working Forty-Two until tomorrow. I saw Boss Lal's schedule earlier!"

"That was the schedule before the Empire got here. We were working double time. We weren't on today's schedule anymore."

"Oh," Skelly said in an awkward, small voice. "Er—so, *did* anyone die?"

"Glad you care," Kanan said, reaching for his shoulder holster and putting it on. "No. Not that I know of."

"Good," Skelly said. "I was just trying to prove a point—and it worked." He tugged at his collar. "The joint caved in, just like I said. If they've told Vidian I was right, he's probably looking for me now to thank me." He gestured with his left hand to the cockpit window. "That's what all the ships are about. They think I'm down there still. Search-and-rescue!"

"Uh-huh. Which is why you stowed away, instead of staying there."

"I needed a place to wait while the Empire figured out what happened. I had no idea you'd come back so fast and take off!"

Kanan shook his head and holstered his blaster. He didn't know what to believe. But before he could say anything, Skelly got to his feet and walked forward like a man with a purpose.

Kanan stood. "What do you think you're doing?"

"What do you think I'm doing? I'm hailing the Star Destroyer!"

Kanan did a double take. "What?"

"I told you, they're looking for me." Skelly reached for a button, only to be shoved into the passenger seat by Kanan.

Reaching for the seat's restraint harness, Kanan snapped Skelly in. Then he pulled out his blaster again.

"Hey! Don't shoot!"

Kanan didn't shoot. Instead, he activated the safety and turned the blaster over in his hand. Using the butt of the handle as a hammer, he pounded Skelly's harness buckle until it was bent out of shape.

"You broke it. I can't believe you did that."

"It's not my ship," Kanan said. Or it wouldn't be, after he landed. The harness would keep Skelly in place now. "I'm not letting you hail the blasted Star Destroyer!"

Skelly shook his head. "You still don't get it." With his left hand, he reached inside his vest and pulled out the holodisk he'd shown Kanan earlier. "I just need to take this information to Vidian—"

"Vidian." Kanan sat down in the pilot's seat, his head spinning. "That weird guy the Empire sent?"

"Don't you follow the news? Vidian's a fixer. He's like me—he sees what's wrong and he takes care of it. He's probably suspending all work on Cynda right now for an investigation. All I have to do is get in touch with him, show him my facts. He'll whip those corporate hacks into shape!"

Kanan looked out at *Ultimatum,* shrinking in the starboard window—and then back at Skelly. "You really think that's what'll happen?"

"Sure. Once they see what I have to show them, they might even reward you for bringing me in."

Kanan looked back to the controls—and then up. There, from the darkness of Gorse's permanent nightside, he saw something familiar rising into space.

"There's your response," he said.

"What?" Skelly turned his head. He saw dozens of ships: empty cargo vessels, personnel transports, and explosives haulers like *Expedient.* All were headed to Cynda. "The next shift?"

Kanan laughed. "So much for the Skelly Memorial Holiday."

He turned on the comm system. The Imperial traffic was all scrambled, but Boss Lal was talking on Moonglow's dedicated channel. Work zones affected by the collapse were being cordoned off, but mining operations would continue in the other areas. "Count Vidian's orders," she said, launching into a list of rerouted landing instructions.

Listening, Skelly was dumbfounded—but only for a moment. "They've just seen what blasting in the wrong place can do. And they're keeping on?" Shaking with rage, he spat three words Kanan could tell Skelly hated. *"Business as usual."*

Kanan snapped off the comm system and stretched back in his chair.

Skelly, unable to move, stared at him. "Well?"

"Well, what?"

"Well, now what?"

"I'm going home," Kanan said.

"Home?" Skelly asked. "Where's home?"

"I'm taking *Expedient* to Moonglow's shipyard, like always. I'm going to park the ship, and I'm going to turn you over to that security chief husband of Lal's." Kanan turned his attention to flying the ship.

Skelly shook his head and lowered his voice. "Some friend you are!"

Kanan bolted upright in his seat and turned. "Let's get something straight," he said, jabbing a finger in Skelly's direction. "I'm not your friend. I'm not your accomplice, and I'm certainly not your co-conspirator. I didn't help you in this, and I am not going to help you get out of it. I'm done!"

Skelly looked at Kanan for a few moments—and then turned his head away. "Great," he growled. "It's just like always. Nobody ever—"

In the window, Skelly caught the reflection of Kanan standing up. He turned his head to see Kanan walking into the back. "Wait, where are you going now?"

"Somewhere I can't hear you."

Safely back aboard her starship, Hera sent the encrypted message to her contact on Gorse. She was more certain than ever that a meeting was necessary. That the Empire spied on workplaces in a system that produced a strategic material was no surprise. But it had no qualms about using such technologies everywhere, and her contact could tell her a lot about the latest Imperial surveillance capabilities and how to defeat them. She had to risk the meeting, whether she got another chance to spy on Vidian or not.

Hera studied the scene outside. Listening, she took everything in. The Empire was encrypting its own signals, but the mining companies weren't, and she had gotten a clear picture of the hours that had just passed on Cynda.

A miner tagged as a troublemaker or dissident had been identified by Imperial surveillance. But Skelly the demolitions guy had surprised his employers, the Empire, and everyone else by using explosives in order to escape arrest. And not long after that, the big explosion had occurred in a work area—unscheduled, and evidently far more destructive than anything to be found in normal operations.

The Empire had hustled then, sending more than half the Star Destroyer's complement of troop shuttles to Cynda. Since no medical ships were on the way from Gorse—the moon's clinic was limited—she had to assume there were no casualties. That meant the stormtroopers sure to be on the shuttles weren't part of search-and-rescue. They were there to continue looking for the bomber.

But in between the reports of the blast and the Imperial scramble, she'd noticed something else. An explosives hauler—Moonglow-72, by the call sign—had been the only ship besides hers to depart Cynda before the grounding order came. She'd seen it jerk violently when the TIE formations approached—and while the sight of the Imperial fighters might have that effect on any simple tradesbeing, the ship had flown unusually after that, as if no one was piloting. Finally, it had settled on an approach to Gorse that kept well away from the most traveled lanes.

Skelly, Hera concluded, was on that transport.

It was more than a guess, but it was hardly a scientific deduction. She didn't want to let it deter her from her real goals. Her connection on Gorse, she now saw, had just responded to confirm their meeting for later. That was the important thing.

But as she was now going in Skelly's direction anyway, Hera decided it wouldn't hurt to find out what his story was . . .

CHAPTER ELEVEN

Kanan had lived with secret stress every day for years without showing it. It was out of necessity in his case, but it was also a choice. Gloom attracted gloom, as he saw it. Acting like a victim only made things worse.

Gorse and Cynda were a case study. The gravitational dance between the two worlds put both under constant stress, but Gorse wore it worse. Cynda, with its crystal lattice innards, kept it together, foolish acts of sabotage notwithstanding. Gorse, with mud on the surface and mush beneath, suffered incessant groundquakes as Cynda made her close approach. It didn't help residents' attitudes that everyone was trapped in permanent night.

But even a rattled loser could catch a break, and Gorse got one every full moon. Cynda sat huge and glorious in the sky for standard days on end. Streetlights were doused. Crime decreased, marginally. And living on Gorse didn't seem so bad.

Cynda was a few days from full, Kanan saw as he stepped off *Expedient*'s ramp onto the tarmac. He wouldn't stick around to see it. Looking toward the cluster of low buildings ahead, he spied an approaching burly figure with four arms and multiple holsters slung around his midsection. It was Gord Grallik, Boss Lal's security chief husband. Gord was a decent sort, Kanan thought: capable, if a bit doting on his wife.

"Kanan. Heard about the collapse—glad you're safe."

"I'm staying that way," Kanan said, reaching for his ID badge. "Give my ship to someone else."

"I don't blame you," Gord said. He put two of his hands up, reject-ing the badge. "You should talk to Lal first. She'd hate to see you go."

"Not changing my mind."

"Go across to Cousin Drakka's and get a meal. Lal should be down here by the time you're finished." Gord looked up at the moon and shook his head. "I'm sure she's worn out."

Kanan's mind was still back on the mention of food. He'd have to see Lal to get his final pay, anyway. Remembering something else, he snapped his fingers. "Oh, and I brought you a farewell gift."

Gord followed Kanan up the ramp into the ship. There, in the front passenger seat, sat Skelly, still bound to the seat. He had a rag stuffed in his mouth and hatred in his eyes.

"Mmmph! Mrrppph!"

"What in—" Gord put a hand over his own mouth.

"There's your mad bomber," Kanan said. "No bounty requested."

Gord laughed heartily. Everyone around Moonglow knew about Skelly. The security chief examined the smashed restraint buckle. "I'll have to cut him out of there."

"I suggest taking the seat out and him with it," Kanan said, patting Gord on the shoulder as he turned to leave. "You don't want the rag to fall out of his mouth. He'll just start talking again."

Count Vidian sat alone in the troop compartment of *Cudgel* as it rose from Cynda. The newly arrived shuttles had landed behind him, and there was no more point staying on the moon. The stormtroopers, in-cluding his escort, had remained to investigate.

Whatever had happened down in Zone Forty-Two, it had left several areas unworkable. If it had been a deliberate act of sabotage, Vidian's forces would find out. And if the one responsible had lived, well, he would find that out, too. Either the stormtroopers would find the cul-prit on Cynda, or Transcept's surveillance assets would locate him on Gorse. There was no third possibility. The Empire could not be resisted.

No—it *should* not be resisted. The Empire was the only way.

The Empire, Vidian understood, was the logical result of a thousand years of galactic government. For centuries, the Republic had expanded not through force, but by quietly exerting a powerful magnetic pull on bordering systems. The promise of trade with Core World markets had great value, and the prospect inexorably lured nonmember worlds into ever-tighter cooperation with the body.

But the Republic was often slow to invite new systems in. The addition of territories tended to diminish the political power of existing senators. New members invariably aligned themselves with blocs in their own galactic neighborhood—yet most senators who controlled the invitations represented worlds near the Core. The Republic repelled even as it attracted. And there were other constituencies that had slowed expansion. Republic bureaucrats disliked the expense of extending services and protection to the hinterlands. The result was that many useful star systems were left waiting, some for centuries, on the Republic's political doorstep, even though it came at the cost of the body's overall power.

To Vidian's mind, Emperor Palpatine had brought sanity to the Republic's growth policies. In standing up to the secessionists as chancellor, he'd signaled the Republic was no longer some social club that could be exited at will. That move had attracted Vidian's attention, and his financial support. Now, as Emperor, Palpatine had shown an eagerness—no, a *zeal*—when it came to expansion. The Core Worlds had always been the heart of the Republic, drawing nutrients from the periphery. The Emperor had taken that biological model and refined it, improved it. The Empire was growing robustly, with the fat of bureaucracy no longer clogging its arteries and veins. A single brain was directing it, not an aggregation of minds with conflicting ideas.

The Emperor had done everything right—so far. Selecting the count to represent his interests was his best decision yet. Surely no one could be more effective in advancing the Emperor's goals. Vidian was the perfect Imperial man, seeing without sentiment, reshaping what he found, and moving on.

He had but one ritual he held to—and even it was purely practical.

Seated in the low light, hearing only the normal pings from the cockpit and whirs from the Lambda's guts, Vidian commanded his lungs to let out a deep breath. His prosthetic eyes no longer had lids, nor any need for them, so he set them to display nothing. What Vidian did required as few distractions as possible.

Vidian's mind was his most powerful asset—and yet, he dealt every day with its limitations. His artificial eyeballs recorded the sights of his entire waking life, but their storage capacity was limited: The data had to be purged every sleep cycle. Where Vidian had once dreamed in images, now, when he slept, he lost them.

More invasive cybernetic technologies existed that might have given Vidian near-total recall, allowing him to process all the information he had at his disposal. But he had decided against upgrading, afraid to risk harming whatever brain chemistry gave him his extraordinary genius. An irrational fear, perhaps—but while he'd never believed in the Jedi's mystical Force, he did allow that some things might defy logic where the mind was concerned.

So every evening Vidian sat as he did now, reviewing the day's events and deciding which images to commit to permanent storage. Cargo vessels en route to Cynda, yes. The backs of others' heads in countless corridors, no.

He didn't preserve the images of the death of the guildmaster. He knew no repercussions would come from it, and he didn't take undue joy from violence, apart from the satisfaction he always felt in setting a failing enterprise aright. He saved the image of the old man he'd confronted, to remind him to follow up on the new age restrictions, but he deleted the face of the foolish gunslinger. The old man's rescuer was likely just another roisterer, too brave for sense. There wasn't anything special there, either.

But the word the man had said: *Moonglow.* That gave Vidian pause.

He'd seen the name of Moonglow Polychemical for the first time while doing his advance research on Gorse. He'd paid it little mind. It was a small firm, probably a start-up—or maybe a piece of a broken-up conglomerate, being run now by its old employees. That trick never worked, he thought. Why did people always insist on trying to reanimate the dead?

Calling up the company's files over the HoloNet, however, he was surprised by its numbers. The blaster-toting fool was right about its efficiency. The firm's production targets were lower, relative to the other corporations, but it was the only one coming anywhere close to meeting them. Maybe there was something there, he thought: some ideas to steal for the other manufacturers.

Scraping ideas from the bottom of the bin, Vidian thought. It galled him that the state of things on Gorse was such that he'd have to resort to—

"Message from Coruscant, my lord."

At the sound of the captain's voice, Vidian's eyes flickered and reset themselves, and *Cudgel's* passenger area reappeared around him. "Patch it through."

A figure appeared before him in holographic form. Rugged and sharply dressed, the blond young man placed his hands together and bowed. "Count Vidian! Wonderful to see you."

"What is it, Baron?"

Vidian had pleasantries for few—and none at all for Baron Lero Danthe of Corulag. The wealthy scion of a droid-making dynasty had a sinecure in Imperial administration but was always angling to turn it into something more, usually at Vidian's expense. As now. "The Emperor has embarked on several amazing new initiatives," Danthe said, beaming. "We need more thorilide."

"I already know the quotas—"

"Those are the old quotas. The Emperor desires more." Danthe's eyes widened with happy malice. "Fifty percent more per week."

"Fifty?"

"I told the Emperor you were on the scene, and that if anyone could do it, you could."

"I'm sure." Vidian knew Danthe could never have said such a thing: It didn't involve stabbing the cyborg in the back.

"Of course, if my droid factories can help in any way, you have but to—"

"Vidian out." He cut the transmission.

He was still steaming a minute later when he felt the thump indicating the shuttle had arrived on *Ultimatum*'s landing deck. There weren't any "new initiatives," Vidian knew: It was all Danthe's doing, part of his continued pursuit of the count's position in the Empire. Vidian had thwarted the upstart at every turn in the past, but this was something else. Given what Vidian had seen on Cynda, even 5 percent improvement would be a challenge.

Holding a datapad, Captain Sloane met him at the foot of the landing ramp. "You asked for updates every half hour on the chamber collapse," she said. "We've confirmed it was intentional. A blasting team located a device set by the fugitive Skelly."

Vidian wasn't surprised. "The team survived. How did *they* escape?"

"Somebody played hero," she said. "We're trying to find out how—"

"Forget it," Vidian said, looking through the magnetically screened landing bay entrance into space. After a few long moments, he nodded. "It's time for the next phase."

"Of the inspection, you mean?"

Vidian looked back at her. "Of course. It's what we're here for. The thorilide mines on the moon are only part of the problem. The refineries must be put in order. I must go to Gorse."

Sloane blinked. "I had thought you'd decided it was more efficient to meet with the planetary managers here, by hologram."

"I know what I decided. Don't question me!" A second passed, and he lowered his voice's volume. "My plans have changed. I'll need your assistance on the ground."

"I'm . . . not sure what you mean, my lord. Planetary security should be able to coordinate your efforts."

"Captain, I have many more steps to take that will not be popular with the *masses*," he said, hitting the last word with particular disdain. "As we've just seen, they need to know my moves have the full weight of Imperial might." He studied her and thought for a moment before continuing. "You're helming *Ultimatum* only while Captain Karlsen is detached elsewhere, no?"

Sloane averted her eyes a little. "Yes, my lord. There are more captains than postings."

"Then we must build Star Destroyers faster. Perhaps Karlsen can return to one of those, instead—while you keep *Ultimatum*."

She looked up at him. "But he's more senior."

"I hold some sway in certain quarters. Serve me well, and you may find this a permanent position."

Sloane gulped, before straightening. "Thank you, my lord." She saluted needlessly and departed.

Vidian turned to look into space. Gorse was down there, in darkness as it always was; only the lights occasionally peeking through the clouds gave any indication that the black body wasn't just another part of the void.

Gorse had been a disappointment to him before—in ways nobody knew about. And now, it and its lazy workers threatened to do more than disappoint.

But he would deal with it. Efficiently, as only he could.

CHAPTER TWELVE

It had been, bar none, the worst work shift in Zaluna's memory.

The new security condition had been executed earlier, quadrupling the surveillance workload on Myder's Mynocks. Imperial security officials, an occasional sight in the elevators of World Window Plaza, were crawling all over the place—and more startling to Zaluna was the presence of stormtroopers in the building. All were following leads generated by her office and others, preparing to round up troublemakers in advance of what she'd gathered was Count Vidian's impending visit to Gorse.

There had been visits to Gorse's factories by bigwigs before, but none on this scale. Vidian's role in the Emperor's administration was no secret. He'd been a wealthy entrepreneur before joining the Imperial cabinet. The poor planet and its moon of riches were recent additions to his portfolio: He'd never set foot on Gorse before, so far as she knew. So if the security steps were exceptional, they were at least explainable. Gorse needed to put on a good show for the new boss. That the boss himself had ordered the measures was only added inducement. The Sec-Con One had created a frenzy, true—but an ordered one.

While her Mynocks scanned Cynda's caverns for Skelly, Zaluna had looked for the dark-haired character she'd seen Skelly arguing with earlier in the elevator, in case he might know something. A Transcept file hadn't been started on him—it took a while for migrant workers to get one—but she knew she'd seen him several times via various cams in recent weeks. The Rugged Pilot, she'd called him: always steering his cart and minding his own business—except when he wasn't.

She had just found the pilot's name in the Moonglow personnel records when she caught him on a Cynda cam, saving an old man from abuse by the frightening Count Vidian. Vidian, who had earlier done *something* to the guildmaster: The cams couldn't see what, but Palfa had immediately turned up dead, and Vidian had remotely ordered the records of their meeting purged. It was the sort of thing that happened far too frequently these days.

So for standing up against Vidian, Zaluna had decided to reward Kanan Jarrus by leaving him alone. He'd already been intimidated enough for one day.

Work had proceeded normally for a while. Then came news of the explosion and collapse in Cynda's mines—and everything went berserk.

Now the Imperials were on the work floor, quizzing Zaluna and going over recordings of events on the moon. They'd been at it for hours. While public reports from Cynda held that the collapse had been a natural phenomenon, the officers clearly thought a bomber was responsible and had already taken all the files on Skelly and a dozen other potential suspects known to have been on the moon. Making things worse for the Mynocks was the fact that few in the mining community seemed to believe the cover story—which just resulted in even more borderline seditious statements for her team to evaluate. It seemed as if every miner preparing to leave Cynda for the day had said *something* about it in a monitored place.

And the mere presence of the stormtroopers was rattling everyone. Intellectually, Zaluna knew the white-clad figures were on the side of peace and order, but there was no doubting how intimidating they looked. What must it be like to have them come to your home or workplace? She'd always wondered.

They'd all found out. Hetto, normally a source for tiny treasons in the safety of the office or during the isolation of his walks with Zaluna, was clearly nervous. He'd said nothing since the Imperials entered the room, keeping his dark eyes fixed straight ahead on his work whenever the officers came near.

And once, as she'd walked through his aisle, he'd reached out to tug at her sleeve. "Are they talking about me?" he whispered.

"You? Why would—"

"Never mind."

She thought she knew why he was worried. If Skelly had indeed done harm on the moon, her team would get the blame for not flagging him sooner. But the remedy to that was obvious: vindication. And so she continued running her searches of Cynda's surveillance network, hoping to catch sight of Skelly.

Then Zaluna had a flash of insight. *Gorse!*

She paused her search of the lunar surveillance cam feeds and started a new scan of Gorse, instead. The routine took less than a minute to find a vocal and retinal match.

"Got him," Zaluna announced. Down on the work floor, the visiting Imperials paused in their conversations. "Skelly's on Gorse. Moonglow Polychemical's offices, over in Shaketown." It was one of the covert feeds, coming off the corporate security cams.

"Here on Gorse?" The lead officer sounded alarmed. "How did he get down to the planet?" The burly lieutenant stomped up the steps to Zaluna's dais and unceremoniously pushed past her. "Let me see. Out of my way, creature!"

Zaluna thought to stomp on the rude officer's foot. Instead she listened in on her earpiece. "They've taken Skelly into custody. The factory manager's contacting planetary security now." That was plainly the case, from the images: She and the officer could clearly see Skelly secured to a chair and being watched by a Besalisk guard. She'd seen the guard many times over the years.

The lieutenant turned and barked an order, and three of the storm-troopers left the room. "Inform *Ultimatum*," he said to one of his re-maining aides as he brushed past and exited her platform.

The boss saves the day again, Zaluna thought. She exhaled, hoping against hope that the uncomfortable moments for the staff had passed. It wasn't any easier on the watchers than the watched, and she'd never seen poor Hetto looking so rattled. She turned to face his workstation, hoping to find him relieved.

She didn't find him at all.

Zaluna looked around for a few moments before realizing he was behind her, peering up at her through her shelves of plants. He'd gone around to the opposite side of the platform, out of earshot of the Imperials.

"You startled me," she said with a relieved grin. "Thinking of taking up gardening?" Hetto was trying—and failing—to be nonchalant, she thought, pawing through the soil of her yellow stasias.

"They're not leaving," he said softly.

Zaluna cast a quick glance over her shoulder. The gaggle of agents was still off to the side, talking furtively about something. She looked back at Hetto reassuringly. "Don't worry. We found Skelly again."

"That's not it." He looked up at her. "Act like you dropped something."

Hearing uncharacteristic seriousness in his voice, Zaluna lifted one of the pots from the upper surface and knelt, pretending to change the saucer beneath the plant. That brought her face-to-face with Hetto, who reached through the rails and took her hands. "Zaluna, I've . . . gotten *involved* with something. There's someone I've been chatting with on the HoloNet about—never mind. I'm meeting—*was going* to meet her tonight."

"Wait. What are you—"

He moved her hands onto the pot. "The address is on the note on the outside. Go alone. *Please,* Zal."

Zaluna looked down at the pot. Something was half buried in the soil, she saw. It resembled a data cube, a high-density storage medium. Her eyes narrowed, and she shook her head. *Some woman on the Holo-Net?* "Oh, Hetto, what have you gotten yourself into?"

"Nothing you didn't know was coming." He dipped his head and spoke somberly—more seriously than she'd ever heard him speak before. "If my help's ever meant anything to you, you'll deliver this. And . . . I'm sorry." With that, he released her hands and departed from the railing.

Bewildered by the exchange, Zaluna picked up the pot and stood, looking to see which way Hetto had gone. He wasn't hard to find. The big Imperial was back again, having stopped Hetto in his tracks—and there were stormtroopers with him.

"You're Hetto?"

Hetto glared. "I am."

"You are under arrest."

"On what charge?"

"Sedition. We have a record of your comments—comments intended to disturb order." The lieutenant yanked at Hetto's shoulder. "All made while working here—*here!* You've abused the trust of the Galactic Empire!"

Hetto's upper lip curled in defiance. "Galactic Empire? I think you're confused. Didn't you see the sign on the building? I work for Transcept Media Solutions!"

"Same difference! You work for us—and we won't have traitors in our midst." The lieutenant's eyes narrowed beneath bushy red eyebrows, and he looked about suspiciously. "And what about the rest of you? Perhaps you people didn't overlook the bomber on Cynda. Perhaps you *all* looked the other way!"

A shocked rumble came from the other members of the surveillance team. Zaluna moved forward to defend her people. "Now, wait a minute! This team has done everything the Empire has ever asked of it!"

"You'd better hope so." The lieutenant sneered. "Everything that happened here today will be reviewed. If there's anything to find, we'll find it." He gestured to Hetto. "We caught *him,* didn't we?"

Hetto tried to move, but the stormtroopers grabbed his arms. His smirk disappeared. "Hear that, Mynocks?" he announced. "You're all being watched, too." He glared at the lieutenant. "Watching us, watching everyone! Well, go ahead and review all you want. Nobody here had anything to do with your stupid mine collapse—not like you care!"

"Perhaps," the officer replied. "But you know the things you've said in the past about the Empire, Hetto. And so do we."

Zaluna stepped down from her platform, almost ready to take on the stormtroopers herself if she had to. "Hetto, I swear. I didn't know anything about this!"

Hetto looked at her and nodded. "I know, Zal. This isn't the only floor in this building. These days, everyone is watched. *Everyone*. I'm just an idiot."

With that, the lieutenant pointed toward the door, and the stormtroopers pushed Hetto ahead of them. Sounds of shock and dismay came from other employees.

Hetto looked back from the doorway—but not at Zaluna. His eyes were on the yellow plant on the top shelf. And then captors and prisoner were gone.

A hush fell over the work floor.

Eyes glistening, a young woman looked up at Zaluna. "Hetto's been with us for ten years."

"Twenty."

"What'll happen to him? You must know what . . . what goes on."

Zaluna straightened, too uncomfortable to look at anyone directly. "I try not to ask. All of us here—we're a tool that can stop bad things. Like we did—*could* have done—with that event on Cynda today." She shook her head. "I don't know about the rest."

Imperial agents reentered the room. "Back to work, Mynocks," Zaluna said, sounding resigned.

But she only sounded that way. Because after a moment's thought, she marched back up to her platform—and pretended to water her plants.

It was a data cube, all right. And buried with it was a small note, quickly scrawled in Hetto's hand. It bore the name of a local cantina. And one word:

HERA.

Hera would have to work fast.

It had taken her too long to find a place to park her starship. Gorse was a patchwork world, with one dead industry layered over another. The muddy ground wouldn't permit the towering skytowers of the city-canyon worlds; that left a horizontal urban sprawl that seemed to go forever. She'd finally found a spot between some abandoned buildings. Her route here had taken her from one bad neighborhood to another.

She'd arrived at Moonglow's headquarters only in time to see a Besalisk security guard and his helpers carrying someone bound to a starship acceleration seat out of the explosives hauler she'd tracked. They'd disappeared into the factory building after that; by then, Hera was sure the prisoner was Skelly.

Hera wanted to find out more about the man, but she still didn't know whether it was worth any effort. Skelly had evidently driven the Imperials up the wall, and that was a good thing. He might know something useful. Or he might be a waste of time. Her cause required a disciplined approach—not impulsive acts. Or people prone to them.

A corporate shuttle landed, discharging a female Besalisk—the head of operations here, Hera figured. Time was running out. A choice had to be made, and soon. She could see shadowy figures beginning to gather outside the building behind her: criminals, likely, now watching her. They were talking and pointing. Whatever their idea for her was, it was certainly no good.

But she got an idea for them, first.

CHAPTER THIRTEEN

Never make a life-changing decision on an empty stomach. Good advice from Okadiah. But the food over at The Asteroid Belt was only edible in theory, and while Kanan Jarrus wasn't going to change his mind about leaving Gorse, he wasn't going to have his last meal come from picked-over snack bowls atop a bar. Especially not after the day he'd had.

That meant the diner by Moonglow. Just a few meters across Broken Boulevard—no one used the official name, Bogan—the establishment had survived years of hard times in the Shaketown neighborhood not just on the quality of its food but on the strength of its chef. Drakka's volatile temper had made him notoriously unemployable at his cousin Lal's mining firm, but it—and his four almost comically muscular arms—had made him eminently capable of dispatching any troublemakers.

He also made a mean bowl of stew. "Thanks," Kanan said, taking another steaming serving.

The cook didn't respond, keeping his bony beige headcrest down over his work as four massive hands worked the pots and pans.

"I'll miss these great conversations," Kanan added.

Drakka looked up long enough to growl, a creepy sound made creepier by the way the fleshy sac beneath his mouth fluttered. Then he returned to his cooking.

That was fine with Kanan. He prided himself on making it alone. Certainly, he talked to people every day: the people he had to deal with in order to get his job done. Mostly, though, he talked to no more than he absolutely had to. It wasn't because of the secrets of his past; it just suited him. People could be real pains.

Okadiah was the exception. The old man had been friendly from the start, offering a drifter a place to stay and, later, a job. Thorilide mining had left Gorse for Cynda, but the quarries on the south side of town remained, making for a lot of cheap real estate; Okadiah had opened his cantina there, in the neighborhood known as The Pits. He'd hired Kanan to drive his ancient hoverbus, running miners back and forth between the Moonglow facility and the bar. Later, he'd recommended Kanan for the job of flying explosives for Moonglow. No one on Gorse was as kindly to newcomers.

Even so, Kanan had kept the old man at arm's length. There had been someone like Okadiah on all the planets he'd visited: the one person willing to help a stranger, no questions asked. And Kanan had left all those worlds without saying good-bye to those people.

It might have been ironic, if Kanan bothered to think much about such things. The Jedi had always preached against forming connections, to prevent their acolytes from putting too much value in any one relationship. In so doing, they had unwittingly trained their students to be the perfect fugitives, able to cut and run at any moment. As long as they didn't stop to care, they could go on indefinitely.

Even so, Kanan thought as he ate, Okadiah was a little different. Kanan had never known his father; prospective Padawans tended to get plucked from their families very young. Kanan had only known mentors, like Master Billaba—and while he didn't know from experience, he suspected parents were different. Parents taught, too, but without all the judging. Good parents, anyway. And on that score, Okadiah had probably been more fatherlike than any of the other patrons Kanan had found in his travels. Okadiah didn't mind Kanan's prickly attitude, his drinking, or the hours he kept; the old man was right there with him, some of the time. And with dozens of workers on his mining detail, Okadiah could always point to someone worse on all those scores.

But for some reason, Okadiah hadn't treated him like just another member of the crew. The old man had seen something in him—what, Kanan didn't know—and he'd done everything right. Okadiah had never tried to push his help on the drifter; he'd left it to Kanan to decide what assistance to take.

It had worked—mostly. For while Kanan had never shared any secrets about his origin with the foreman, he had stayed on Gorse longer than he'd intended. The explosives hauler, bad as it was; the home across from the bar; and Okadiah, his host: They'd all made Gorse more livable than some of the other places he'd tried.

But he'd seen all the world had to offer. And there were plenty of things he wouldn't miss. One was in the doorway behind him.

"Suicide flier! You show your face here, after the last time?"

Kanan looked up at the mirror behind the grill, already knowing the speaker's identity. "Hello, Charko," he said. He felt for his shoulder holster but otherwise didn't move.

Charko, two meters of horned Chagrian meanness, wouldn't set foot in Drakka's Diner—the cook kept not one but four big blasters behind the counter. Instead, Charko just yelled like an idiot from the open front door. "We're waiting for you, pilot. Come out and play."

The Besalisk cook swore and moved toward his blasters. Charko didn't wait around. The door slammed shut. Unconcerned, Kanan finished his stew as Drakka rounded the counter, four weapons in four hands. A fully armed Besalisk defending his business was a great equalizer.

Charko never went anywhere without at least half a dozen members of his gang, the Sarlaccs. A sarlacc was a ravenous monster that was little more than a mouth; Kanan thought the name was properly descriptive. Charko's Sarlaccs had an endless appetite for the credits of anyone fool enough to wander the streets of the industrial area. The gang activity had provided Okadiah with a business opportunity: opening his cantina across town and busing miners safely past the trouble spots.

Three times, Charko had tried—and failed—to separate Kanan from his hard-earned credits as he'd walked Broken Boulevard. The third time, Kanan had broken off one of the horns on Charko's head; the Chagrian had sworn revenge.

"They still out there?" Kanan asked without looking up.

"They've moved up the way to talk to someone," Drakka growled. "But yeah, they're still there. Idiots." He shut the door and returned to his cooking.

Well, no sense leaving unfinished business behind, Kanan thought as he wiped his face. He pushed back the bowl with one hand and drew his blaster with the other. Kanan walked cautiously to the entrance, blaster in hand. He nudged the door open with the tip of his boot.

"Hey, ugly!" he yelled. "Where'd you go?"

Outside, he spotted Charko's unmistakable one-horned silhouette as part of a shadowy gathering up the street. There were eight or nine of them, all members of Charko's band, but they were ignoring Kanan, talking to someone else.

Before Kanan could see more, the group quickly dispersed, breaking up into groups of three and heading off into the alleys, while whomever they'd been talking to remained, twenty meters up the street from Kanan.

Wearing a black cloak that gave no indication of the person beneath, the figure stood beneath the glare of the moon, watching not Kanan, but the Moonglow facility across the road. Clearly this wasn't one of the Sarlaccs.

Something told Kanan to holster his weapon. As he did so, the watcher turned toward him—and called out.

"Excuse me!" He couldn't see the speaker's face, but the voice was female, almost melodic. "Where can I find the repulsorlift entrance to Moonglow?"

The restless ground beneath Kanan's feet rumbled as she spoke, but he didn't hear it. He was still trying to process the voice, so warm and polite it was totally out of place on a Shaketown street. It startled him so much that he could only manage: "Huh?"

"Never mind," the figure said primly. "I'll find it myself."

With a whirl of her cloak, she headed off in the opposite direction.

Kanan, who had had no mission in life, now found himself with one: seeing who it was that could be attached to a voice like that. Gorse had one last surprise in store for him after all. It didn't matter that she'd been chatting amiably with a street gang. His feet, developing a will of their own, started to move to follow.

They didn't get far, and neither did the rest of him. Cousin Drakka appeared behind him, slapping two pairs of huge grease-matted hands on Kanan's shoulders.

He'd forgotten to pay his bill.

CHAPTER FOURTEEN

"I understand you've captured the suspect from Cynda," the shimmering holographic form of Count Vidian said. "You will be receiving a squad of stormtroopers to take custody of him shortly."

Skelly glowered. Looking through the back of the image, he could see Vidian, but Vidian could not see him. Or maybe he could. Lal had barely informed the authorities that Skelly was there when the efficiency expert had called. It would make sense, Skelly thought, for the Empire to keep an eye on all the producers of a strategic compound like thorilide.

But he didn't mind their spying. He minded the fat four-armed fools in the room with him, who had yet to release him from the chair—and who had decided to keep the gag on him when Vidian called, despite his urgent muffled cries to be allowed to speak.

"Moonglow. Your firm is a newer one?" Vidian asked.

"Only under that name, my lord," Lal replied. "I have worked in this facility for more than twenty years."

Skelly wondered if a hologram could catch how nervous she was to be speaking to the Emperor's man. *She'd better be worried*, Skelly thought. By the time the Empire learned what he knew, the whole Mining Guild might well be out of work.

Lal continued. "We're a smaller firm, but we've made many advances in efficiency. I assure you we knew nothing about—"

"Never mind the saboteur," Vidian interrupted. "I would see these efficiencies. I will begin my inspection there."

"Here?" Skelly saw Lal's eyes widening. She clasped both sets of hands together, prayerfully. "My lord—we'd like some time to prepare for your arrival. It's the end of a very long workday. I know we don't have mornings around here, but could it possibly—"

Vidian waved his metallic hand dismissively. "Diurnal cycles! So annoying. Fine. In twelve hours, then—regard it the reward for your service. But I'll show no leniency in my review because of your help to me tonight. Is that understood?"

"I would expect none, my lord. Moonglow will be ready."

"See that it is," came the cold response. "An Imperial repulsorlift will arrive in five minutes. Have the prisoner ready." Vidian vanished.

Lal sat, dumbfounded, looking at the space where the image had been. Off to the side, Skelly could see her security chief husband, Gord, scratching his head. "I thought you said you didn't think the Empire would inspect here," Gord said. "We're too small."

"I don't understand, either." Lal cast a glance over at Skelly. "I guess it's because of you?"

"Mmmm-mmmph!" Skelly replied.

"Oh," Lal said, flustered. "Gord, get that out of his mouth!"

Gord grumbled. "All right," he said, looming over the seated Skelly. "But I think it's a bad idea."

The rag finally removed, Skelly coughed before turning his ire on the Besalisks. "That was Vidian! Why didn't you let me talk to him?"

Lal goggled at that. "I'm already terrified of him. I definitely wasn't going to let you talk to him!" Almost in a daze, she plopped down in her office chair. "Twelve hours to get this place looking good enough for an Imperial inspection?"

Gord looked back at her. "It's all right, Lal. You run a good place. I'll get the cousins in with some mops and it'll be fine."

Skelly rolled his eyes. The security chief was moon-eyed over his wife, and their mushiness was the capper to a horrid day. "You'd better worry more about what Vidian will say after he talks to me. You and every firm that's ever used Baby to break open a wall up there."

"Forget this guy," Gord said. He snapped his fingers. "Oh, Lal, I almost forgot. That Kanan fellow said he was quitting."

Lal shook her head, disappointed. "I was afraid of that. It was the worst day ever. He nearly got killed. But I wanted to thank him—he wound up saving some of my people's lives."

"Maybe you can talk him out of it," Gord said. A buzzer sounded. "There's somebody at the repulsorlift gate."

"That'd be the stormtroopers," his wife replied. She looked at Skelly sadly. "I *am* sorry."

"Yeah, sure," Skelly said. "You guys'll be the sorry ones."

Gord whistled. Two of his Besalisk assistants entered and lifted Skelly, chair and all. They carried him into the moonlit stockyard at the side of the complex. Equipment lined the inner perimeter of the tall black fencing, with a path between large enough for a repulsortruck to arrive.

Skelly knew what to expect: He'd seen the Imperial troop transports hovering through Gorse City now and again. He hoped this time, they'd take him straight to Vidian. He watched as Gord, leaving Skelly with the other guards, stepped up to the gate and opened it.

No one entered.

Curious, Gord walked into the street. A second later, the burly Besalisk looked back and shouted to his assistants. "Guys—it's Charko! The Sarlaccs are stealing our hovertruck!"

Moving almost as one, Gord's fellow guards drew their blasters and ran out to join him. Alone, Skelly shook his head. In high-crime Shake-town, no supply delivery was safe—not even when Imperials were on the way. He heard blasterfire from the street. Maybe they'd all shoot one another.

Then it occurred to Skelly that the Sarlaccs must have activated the entry buzzer. *Why would they have done that?* Before he could consider it, he became aware of someone behind him—and something pulling at the strap on his left shoulder.

"Are you Skelly?"

"What?" He looked to his left to see a cloaked figure crouching behind his chair. "Yeah. But who are—"

"Hera," the female voice said. A green hand inserted a vibroblade under one of his restraints. "And you're leaving."

"No, wait," Skelly said. "I can't go. I have a story to get out!"

For a moment, the woman stopped cutting, as if puzzled. But only for a moment. "I can help get your story out. But you have to go!"

"Wait!" Skelly had no idea who she was, or what she was talking about. "Listen—"

"I *will* listen. But you have to go," she said, severing the last bond. She ripped the straps free. "I paid Charko for a distraction. But it won't last."

Skelly looked through the gate at the street. It was empty. But he could hear Gord and his companions running somewhere and firing their blasters, and beyond that, the low whine of a repulsorcraft.

He didn't know what to do. The stormtroopers would take him to Vidian, who had the power to stop what was being done to Cynda. But then again, they might not. And the cloaked woman had said something he wasn't accustomed to hearing.

"I'll listen," she repeated. "Go!"

Skelly looked back, only to see she was no longer at his side. Hearing footfalls heading for the gate, he forced his cramped muscles to stand. Walking painfully, he headed for the gate.

"Where can I find you?" he yelled.

The call came from over the fence, outside: "I'll find you!"

She was already gone.

CHAPTER FIFTEEN

Kanan rushed around the corner of a building—only to be nearly run down by an Imperial troop transport. Seeing the boxy repulsorcraft careening straight at him, Kanan dived to the muddy roadway. The long vehicle passed right over him, its metallic underside mere centimeters from the back of his skull.

Now he lay in the mud at the corner of a Shaketown intersection, and there was still no sign of the woman with the alluring voice.

Picking himself up, Kanan wiped off his tunic and stood as more traffic came down the other street, this time on foot: two of Charko's gang members, barreling in his direction with big metal pry bars in their hands. The sound of blaster shots followed behind them.

Kanan reached for his weapon, only to realize the Sarlaccs weren't coming after him—and that the blaster shots were meant for *them*. The hoodlums ran past without stopping, rushing to stay ahead of their pursuers—who turned out to be Gord and his fellow guards, firing blasters.

"You'd better run, punks!" Gord yelled, firing blasters held in all four hands.

Kanan looked down the street after them and then up the route the Imperials had taken. He shook his head. *I'm too sober,* he thought. *Nothing makes sense!*

He walked around the block. At the far end of one street, he could see the Moonglow service entrance. There was no sign of any caped woman there; just the stormtroopers from before, piling out of their repulsorcraft. Kanan quickly turned away.

This was no place to stay on a fool's errand, stormtroopers or not. This end of Shaketown, he recognized, had fared badly in a recent quake; half of it was under renovation and most of it was closed down. Resigned, Kanan decided to give up and head for Okadiah's. *I'm just being silly,* he thought. *Tomorrow's moving day. Time to get packing.*

Then he heard the voice again.

"Fifty up front, fifty afterward," the woman said. "Like we agreed."

Kanan looked down the alley to see the hooded figure facing off against Charko, flanked by several members of his gang. It was like the scene Kanan had witnessed outside the diner—only not. This place was more enclosed: Construction scaffolds rose against buildings on either side of the passage. There was a new menace to how Charko's friends—a mix of tough-looking humans and other beings—stood. And Charko, clutching a bunch of credits in his hand, wasn't happy at all.

"If you've got a hundred credits, maybe you've got a hundred more," the one-horned gang leader said. He took a step forward. Towering over the short woman, he gestured to her black cloak. "You've got room for a lot more cash under there, I'll bet."

Kanan strode into view at the end of the street. "Hey, Charko! You were looking for me. Did you forget?"

Charko and his companions looked back at Kanan. "Never," the Chagrian said. "There's always time for you!"

Kanan saw blasters being raised. His was already drawn. *Six—no, seven against one. That's about right.*

But before he could fire, Kanan saw the woman suddenly twirl in place. With one swift motion, her cloak came off—and became a weapon she cast into the air like a net. Charko turned back to get a faceful of fabric, dropping his credits in the process.

The gang leader stumbled backward, victim of a high kick from his assailant. His friends turned and gawped at what Kanan now saw: a beautiful, lithe, green-skinned Twi'lek, holding a pistol in one gloved hand.

The Twi'lek shot one human Sarlacc point-blank in a single motion, and then rushed forward in the next. As the burly man fell backward, the Twi'lek used his body as a makeshift staircase, giving her the altitude she needed to leap for a horizontal strut on one of the scaffolds. Catching the bar with her free hand, she used her momentum to help her gain a perch, clinging to one of the vertical supports. Turning, she fired her blaster down into the astonished crowd.

"Get her!" yelled a female gang member. But blasterfire was coming from a second direction as Kanan, done with watching, charged into the alley. The Sarlaccs scattered, uncertain who to target first.

With an angry bellow, Charko leapt from the mud, heedless of the cross fire. Turning toward the Twi'lek's position, he slammed chest-first into one of the scaffold supports. The structure shook, and the Twi'lek woman dropped her blaster. Her weapon hand freed, she scrambled like a sand monkey higher up the scaffold—even as it began to fall.

Kanan knew he had to move. He rushed his nearest attacker and grabbed her blaster arm with his left hand. His motion directed her errant shot into the assailant approaching on his right; he followed with a head-butt beneath her chin that knocked her backward. Now he could see the raging Charko trying to upend the scaffold. He dived forward, even as the Twi'lek woman vaulted in the opposite direction high above, to the scaffold on the other side of the alley.

Seized from behind by Kanan, Charko lost hold of the scaffold support—and the whole thing started to come down, all five stories of it. Kanan saw only one place to go: the large picture window of the building the scaffold was attached to. He launched himself and the Chagrian through the window, creating a shower of shards even as an avalanche of scaffolding came down in the alleyway behind them.

Dazed, his blaster lost in the dive, Kanan struggled to regain his feet inside the vacant building, which he recognized as an abandoned cantina. The Chagrian had taken the brunt of the crash, and yet somehow the thug still stood, ready to fight it out.

"You're on my turf now," Kanan said, raising his fists. "I do all my training in bars!"

Kanan and Charko traded punches across the dark quake-damaged room. Kanan grabbed a chair; Charko did the same with half a broken table. The two carried on a parry-and-thrust battle with their makeshift weapons—it was a kind of fighting the Jedi never taught, and it suited Kanan just fine.

Blow by blow, he maneuvered Charko in front of the only remaining intact window. Winded from his exertions, the Chagrian staggered. Kanan saw his opening. A roundhouse kick sent his opponent smashing through the pane behind him.

"Are we done here?" Kanan asked, stepping up to the windowsill. Charko didn't get back up this time. But the others were still out there, Kanan remembered. He readied himself and carefully climbed out the shattered window.

There wasn't anything to do. All Charko's companions were down. Some, Kanan had taken out earlier; others, the Twi'lek had. The rest had been crushed under the falling scaffold. And the Twi'lek herself was nowhere to be seen.

Rubbing his bruised cheek, Kanan searched the wreckage for his blaster. He was in pain: the kind that would pass, but enough to make it tough to go another round with the Sarlaccs. By the time he found his weapon, however, it was clear to him no danger remained.

But something was missing from the scene. The credits Charko had dropped had been plucked from the ground, and small footprints led away from the place where they had lain.

He saw the Twi'lek's cloak nearby, pinned beneath a heavy girder. *She did leave me a souvenir, after all.* With great effort, he pulled the metal aside. He took the garment into his hands and held it up. It was a good find, he thought, as he turned to stagger out of the alley. Because he was beginning to believe she had never been there.

He stopped thinking that when he stepped out into the street—and found himself looking into her eyes.

"Ah," she said, seeing her cloak.

"Ah," he repeated. Kanan stood frozen, studying her under the bright light of the moon. She was shorter than he was, with deep green skin, full lips, and a chin that came to a pleasing point. She wore a gray pilot's cap that allowed exit for two head-tails that hung at a little more than shoulder-length. She wore a brown vest, gold-colored slacks with utility pockets, and black gloves that matched the cloak in his hands.

"I knew I'd forgotten something," she said, removing the garment from his hands so deftly he barely noticed she'd done it. Then she looked at him with concern. "You okay there?"

Kanan nodded.

"You speak Basic?"

"Words fail me."

She smiled. "So they do."

It wasn't a dig—or if it was, it was delivered so gently that Kanan chose not to notice it. He looked back. "That was something back there."

"Yes," she said, still talking in that wonderful voice as she flicked mud from the cloak. "It's a good thing I was here to save you."

Kanan's brow wrinkled, and he looked back. "Save *me*?" He pointed at the bodies. "You had a whole gang after you!"

The Twi'lek lifted the cloak to put it on. "I'd paid them to do a job for me. There was a minor pricing dispute. I could have handled it." Seeing him look back at her, slack-jawed, she bumped a gloved fist underneath his bruised chin. "You did pretty good though. I'm impressed." She studied him. "So, you just randomly go around sticking your neck out for people?"

"No!" Kanan said. "Er—almost never." He blinked as she pulled her hand back. "Wait a minute," he said, gesturing back to the bodies in the alley. "You needed *them* to do a job? For *you?*"

"*Mm-hmm*. And now it's done." She flipped the cloak back into place around her shoulders, turned, and started walking.

"I do jobs," Kanan said, tromping after her. His whole body hurt from the fight, but he didn't want the conversation to end so soon. "You need something done, I'm there."

"No, thank you," she said, continuing on. "I have stops to make."

"Wait!"

Kanan tried to follow, but his body rebelled. Wincing, he grabbed at his knee. When he looked up, she was gone again—likely down one of the side alleys.

Disgusted with the universe, he yelled into Gorse's endless night. *"What's your name?"*

For a long moment, nothing.

And then that voice again, calling back to him.

"Hera."

CHAPTER SIXTEEN

Starships were settlements in the sky. Some were villages; *Ultimatum* was a great metropolis. And yet even Star Destroyers functioned like small towns. A big sink full of gossip—and as with small towns, the contents all tended to flow toward one person, like water to a drain.

Sloane stood at the window as Nibiru Chamas, *Ultimatum*'s unofficial drain, sat casually in the chair in her office. The mining ships were continuing to shuttle back and forth between Gorse and Cynda—faster than before, of course—but her mind was on the list Chamas was reading.

"Count Vidian has designed and issued new traffic patterns for the cargo ships traveling between the two worlds," Chamas said. "He has ordered several changes to the loader droids' subroutines on Cynda that should make them more productive. He has changed the color of the plates used in the communal mess hall—"

"What?"

Chamas chuckled. "That last one is a joke."

Sloane rolled her eyes. "Continue."

"He also ordered a review of Transcept's personnel—you know, the ones who found the madman on Cynda? There has already been at least one arrest for suspicious activity."

"Thorough," Sloane said.

She was thorough, too—or intended to be. She'd been caught flat-footed by Vidian's actions on her bridge, issuing commands to *her* staff.

Ultimatum had the authority to destroy the freighter *Cynda Dreaming;* Vidian had clearly known that. But, while she agreed with that decision, it behooved her to find out more about her visitor, and how he'd interacted with other crews. She wasn't going to be just one more mechanical arm.

"What else has he done?"

"Laid groundwork for his tour of Gorse. He has a full schedule already. He doesn't head down there for hours yet, and he's already reorganized three guilds, ordered the consolidation of several equipment suppliers into a single firm, and even shut down a medcenter, moving the patients to an institution closer to the factories so they can get back to work more quickly."

"That's it?"

"Isn't that enough? He has met several times with the aides he brought aboard and made several calls back to his main office on Calcoraan Depot. There's only one thing he hasn't done."

"Slept," Sloane said. "He doesn't have the time."

"He doesn't have a *bed*," Chamas corrected. "The attendants changing his room found the place wrecked. The furniture, smashed."

"What? When was this?"

"After he came back from the moon—after we piped a second call to him from Baron Danthe. I think our count has a temper."

Sloane chuckled. She'd heard Vidian had a short fuse—and word back from Cynda was that the Mining Guild chief had found out the hard way. "You got him another room, I hope?"

"We have an ample supply. Don't worry, it'll all be put right before our—er, *regular captain* arrives."

Thanks for reminding me I'm just a temp, Sloane thought, walking around to her desk. But Chamas's comment brought her back to what she wanted to know. This next, she wanted to ask cautiously.

"Interesting man, Vidian—and striking that he would choose government service. You said he bought the title. Do you know where he's from?"

"His biography says Corellia. In the Republic days, he was an engineer for a small design firm that worked for shipbuilders. A cog in a small wheel. His suggested improvements were constantly rejected. Then he was struck with Shilmer's syndrome—and spent the next five years while it was eating him alive conquering the stock exchanges from a bed."

"And the firm?"

"As the *legend* goes"—Chamas said the term derisively—"Vidian's first act on regaining mobility was buying the company and putting everyone on the street. But I don't even know what firm it was. There were confidentiality provisions to the severance packages. He doesn't want anyone he's burned sniping at him, ruining sales of his next management holo."

Sloane knew Vidian didn't need the money, but she didn't have any problem with his rationale. A little revenge did wonders for the healing process. It was also a human thing—and there weren't many human things about Vidian.

"If he's from Corellia," she said, "he's probably connected in the shipbuilding sector—and the Admiralty."

It was halfway between the question she'd intended, and the matter-of-fact observation she'd wanted it to sound like. But Chamas was too sly, catching her drift immediately. "In other words," he said with a smile, "can he make your posting here permanent—perhaps by giving Captain Karlsen a cushy job at one of his subsidiaries? Please, ask him for one for me, while you're at it."

Caught, Sloane simply stared. "What's tomorrow like?"

Chamas passed her his datapad showing the stops on Vidian's planned tour of Gorse. It sounded like an exhausting day.

She was struck curious by the first name on the list. "*Moonglow.* Why start with this little one?"

"They apparently captured—and lost—the fugitive from Cynda a few hours ago."

"That'll go over well for them," Sloane said, passing back the datapad. She swiveled her chair to look again out the window at the ships heading down to Gorse. Her brow furrowed as she tried to take it all in.

"So while he's on his world tour, we play traffic officer," Chamas said, standing. "Keeping the rabble back while Vidian adds to his folktale. We should demand part of the royalties on his next holo."

Sloane smiled inwardly. She only wanted a supporting role. It was her job to help the Empire; helping to find *Ultimatum*'s rightful captain a different ship would be a nice bonus.

Stormtroopers had ransacked his apartment hours earlier. That, Skelly thought without the least amusement, officially represented the first attention the Empire had ever paid to the homes in Crispus Commons.

Crispus was a project for homeless Clone Wars veterans in the sector, an idea hatched in the final days of the Republic. The Empire had kept it going, shipping in new residents from time to time without ever adding to or improving on the complex. Skelly thought it spoke volumes about what the Republic and Empire really thought about those who'd fought against the Separatists. *Let's stick them where the sun doesn't shine.*

Skelly had stayed in the dilapidated apartment partly because it was sandwiched between Gorse City's industrial districts. That way, no matter who fired him, his commute never got any longer. But the other reason he stayed was the rusted grating behind the complex's trash bin at the far end of the rectangular exercise yard—and what lay beneath.

Certain no one outside had seen his approach, he slipped behind the bin and into the hole. He closed the grille above him. Passing through an improvised curtain, he fished for the power switch. A crackle or two later, the darkness around Skelly turned red, lit by computer monitors and a single weak overhead lamp.

It had been intended as a bomb shelter, built by the Republic as part of the Crispus project in the unlikely event Count Dooku or General Grievous took a sudden interest in destroying a retirement colony. Its permacrete walls had been a moldy mess when Skelly found the place. But he liked that it had its own generator, and the presence of a giant garbage bin in front of the grating meant he could enter and depart without anyone seeing.

All Skelly's computers were built from kits, making them safe from slicing by the powers that be, corporate or government. Only one machine was attached to the HoloNet grid, and that through a connection hijacked from an Ithorian lunch wagon that parked daily on the other side of the quad. By selecting an intermediary that was mobile and garaged somewhere else, Skelly had cut down on prying eyes and ears.

Everywhere but at work. Skelly had known some of the corporations working on Cynda had installed surveillance equipment, but he'd assumed that was just to keep an eye on productivity—and to prevent the theft of explosive material, which had once been a problem. Evidently, they were now listening in on individual conversations there, too. It was insane. Deaf to his appeals about safety, but nosing in on everything else!

Skelly quickly ate a meager meal of tinned food paste before collapsing, exhausted, on a mat on the floor. This room had been his world, his *real* world, for years. Boards mounted on one wall were covered with hand-scrawled notes about the military industrial complex, and the intricate network of who owned what. A second wall was home to his studies into the history of galactic conflicts; the sides kept changing, but the stories were always the same. Whenever titans fought, the peons did the dying.

The biggest collection of notes, however, was on the wall facing him now. Apart from the curtained opening that led to a little closet, every square centimeter was festooned with notes about Cynda and its geologic structure. Seeing it all made his gut hurt. Skelly had long feared a day like this would be necessary: a day when he'd have to risk everything to get someone's attention. But he'd been deciding things on the fly, and he worried he'd already blown it.

He'd run here from Moonglow's grounds without thinking, after a spur-of-the-moment promise from someone he'd never met—and had in all likelihood ruined his chance to talk to Count Vidian. He still didn't know why he'd fled. Yes, it was natural to fear being taken anywhere by stormtroopers; the Empire's foot soldiers had a bad habit of damaging prisoners in transit. And everyone had misread his attempt to educate them as sabotage. But Vidian was still his best chance, the only one with the authority to effect change. Would Vidian leave Gorse without talking to him? Would Vidian see him at all, now that he'd run?

Staring at his collected writings from his spot on the floor, Skelly let out a low moan. *"Nobody listens."*

"What do you want to say?"

Skelly looked up, startled, to see the cloaked figure that had rescued him. She removed her cowl. "You're her!"

"Hera," the Twi'lek corrected. "Let's talk."

CHAPTER SEVENTEEN

Skelly sat up, alarmed. "How did you find me?"

Hera patted her own shoulder. "If you'll look in the utility pocket on your left shoulder, you'll find a tracking device that I slipped in when I was cutting you loose." She smiled. "I *did* tell you I would find you."

Skelly reached for his pocket and discovered a small chip. He stared at her angrily. "I don't like people spying on me."

"You're in the wrong system, then." Hera simply opened her gloved hand. "I'll take that. Thanks."

"You said my name," he said, suspicious. "How do you know me?"

"You've gotten a lot of people's attention today. I heard about what you did on Cynda. You know—the blast, while the Emperor's envoy was there." She paused, stopping to take in the many notes about the Empire on the wall to her left. "I'm interested to hear your reasons for doing what you did."

Frowning, Skelly stood up. "And why do you care?"

"I'm just . . . interested," Hera said.

Seeing her reading his notes, the redheaded human interposed himself between her and the wall. "Look, don't read my stuff. I don't know you, lady. I don't know that telling you will help anything!"

Hera looked to her right—and saw the other wall and its writings about Cynda. A glint appeared in her dark eyes. "Would you tell me . . . if I was a reporter for the *Environmental Action Gazette*?"

Skelly goggled. "I thought that had shut down!"

"Just retooling," Hera said. "You can be part of the big relaunch."

Skelly studied her. He'd never been in that HoloNet publication's audience, but it had come up several times in his research. It had put a stop to a number of bad business practices in the past.

"Come on," she said, pulling a datapad from her cloak. "I did let you go."

Skelly took a deep breath—and made a decision. "Okay."

He rushed to his wall and pointed to one diagram after another, laying out his theories. Severing a few crystalline stalactites and stalagmites was fine; those were the mere outgrowths of the physical structures that held Cynda together. It was like giving the moon a haircut. But using explosives to break into new chambers was more akin to breaking bone.

"Every chamber they discover has more thorilide than the one before," Skelly said. "And that makes them use more juice to get into the next one."

"And that causes collapses that harm workers." Hera nodded, making notes on her datapad. "While ruining a beautiful natural setting."

"Now you've got it!" Triumphant, Skelly jabbed his fist to the low ceiling.

"Okay," Hera said mildly.

Skelly's face froze. "Okay?"

She smiled gently at him. "This is not big and shocking news, Skelly," she said kindly, returning the datapad to its place. "The Empire hurts workers and ruins things. It does that all the time, everywhere."

"So?"

"You have a problem, like a billion other people in the galaxy. One day, we'll all do something about it. This is good to know, and I feel for everyone involved. But I'm not sure the time is right to do much about it."

Skelly was alarmed. "You're not going to publish—after all this? What kind of deal is this? I thought you were a journalist!"

The woman took a step back—clearly not fearing him, but simply giving him space to rave. "I'm really more gathering information right now, Skelly. Preparing for . . ." She trailed off, then nodded toward the wall with his notes about Cynda. "What you've described is bad, but it's not exactly world-shattering."

"Oh, yes, it is!" Skelly whipped the holodisk out of his vest pocket and held it between his left thumb and forefinger. "Because I believe that if the Empire keeps up, they could blow the whole moon to bits!"

Hera held up a hand. "Look, forget the hyperbole. How much damage are you talking about?"

"I'm not exaggerating!" Skelly said. Pocketing the holodisk, he turned back to the wall and began riffling through attached notes with his good hand. "The moon's already brittle. The elliptical orbit means Gorse and the sun are yanking at it all the time. Gorse releases the stress through groundquakes. But all the energy stays pent up on Cynda, because the crystal lattices go so deep—"

"The bottom line, please."

"Use enough explosives in the right spots, and Cynda could crumble like a senator's promise."

Hera stared at him for a moment. Skelly stared back.

"That's just . . . beyond belief," she said, finally. "The power to destroy a body that size? It's hard to believe something like that exists."

"It exists. It's possible. And I'm beginning to think they don't care."

Hera walked to the wall and started reading. "These notes are all over the place," she said. "I can't make sense of some of it."

"Trust me," Skelly said. "I'm an expert."

"You're a planetary geologist."

"No, I build bombs."

Hera's lips pursed. *"Oh."* She drew the syllable out.

"I know how it sounds," he said, pulling down notes and wedging them into his frozen right hand. "But it's true. The mining companies know, because I've told them. But they cover it up, because they're all part of the conspiracy."

"The conspiracy?"

"The thorilide triangle," Skelly said, astonished that she hadn't heard about it. He moved across the room to the other side, with his wall of corporate shame. "The mining firms are corrupt. They're tied up—ownership, boards of directors—with the shipwrights that have sold the Empire on one construction project after another. Oh, it's all being done in secret, but you can't keep everything secret. A billion Star Destroyers isn't enough. They're building Super Star Destroyers, and Super Super Star Destroyers, and who knows what else!"

"I see," Hera said, gingerly taking a step backward. "And how do you know all this?"

"The HoloNet!"

"Oh," Hera said. *"The HoloNet."*

"It's all one big web, and it goes on forever," Skelly said, eyes fixing on the far wall. He stepped over to it and began fumbling with notes. "Did you know it was the moneyed interests that started the Clone Wars? There was a battle droid manufacturer that had too much inventory—"

Skelly felt Hera's eyes upon him, and the air went out of his lungs. He stopped talking. The notes, the clippings, all swam before him, not making sense.

He'd done it again.

"I'm sorry to have troubled you," he half heard her say. "Good luck."

Skelly kept facing the wall. "Look, I know what I sound like. I've been through . . . well, I've been through a lot of bad things. I get worked up. I don't always say things right. But what I know—it's still real." He took a breath. *"I'm not crazy."*

When he turned, she was gone. He could hear light footsteps heading up the ladder. He followed—but saw nothing but the trash bin and the darkened quad all around.

Deflated, Skelly climbed back inside and shut the grate after him.

He sat in silence at the bottom of the pit. His head buzzed—and hurt, as it had been hurting for a long time. Skelly's sleep cycles had been wrong ever since moving to Gorse, and time in Cynda's always bright caves confused them further. The confusion in the notes still clutched in his malfunctioning hand were one product. But he could still focus to do some things. The data on the holodisk—that, he knew was right. It was his testament, his last chance.

Skelly remembered Vidian's call to Lal Grallik. The count was coming, yes. And Vidian could still listen, and do the right thing. But he would be bringing the rest of the Empire with him, and they could still do the wrong thing.

Skelly sprang to his feet and reentered his sanctum. Opening the curtain to the closet, he exposed his secret workbench there—and, beneath, in sealed packages, the massive stores of explosive baradium he'd smuggled out over the years. Because of his fears about blasting on Cynda, every time they'd asked him to plant charges to open up a wall, he'd used a little less. He just hadn't given them back what he didn't use.

But if they didn't listen to him now, he'd give it all back. All at once, and so they'd notice.

Yes, he would.

Hera shook her head as she stepped back onto the street.

It had been a calculated risk, freeing Skelly. Her assumption in the detour was that anyone rising up against the Empire, in any way, was worth a look. Some could be helpful. Maybe not yet, but in the movement to come. It was important to know their capabilities.

But Skelly would never be of any use, and so she mentally filed him away with dozens of others she'd met just like him. Political activism drew more than its share of crackpots. Some had been legitimately driven to madness by the forces they were fighting against; some had been damaged by war, as she suspected was the case with Skelly. Some had no excuse. But while such people were always the first to revolt, they almost never led successful revolutions. Action against the Empire would have to be carefully measured—now, especially.

Thus far, Gorse had been a bust. Sunless in more ways than one: Its people wandered robotically between the drudgery of work and the dangers of the streets, sensing neither. Even the human who'd helped her against the street gang—whom she now remembered as the man helping the old-timer on Cynda—might easily fit a ready template: the gadabout, looking for a brawl. That would be disappointing, if so, but not surprising: Like everyone else on Gorse, he was trapped in a role the Empire wanted for him. He'd never be a threat. It was too bad: He seemed to know what he was doing in a fight.

But Hera put him out of her mind. Skelly was the side trip; the real goods lay ahead. And she would find them at the establishment whose unsubtle advertisement appeared on her datapad:

The Asteroid Belt

The Pits, Gorse City • Okadiah Garson, prop.

Open all nite

Come in and get belted

CHAPTER EIGHTEEN

"Hey, lady! I'm talkin' to you!"

The big bruiser *was* talking to Zaluna, for no one else was on the street. But she'd chosen to keep going—until he kept after her. Just steps behind her, he yelled again. "I said, I'm talking to you!"

"No, you aren't," she said, continuing to walk through the mud. "If you were talking to me, you'd use my real name."

Picking up his pace, the drunk laughed. "How'm I supposed to know who you are?"

"Precisely!" Zaluna spun and looked keenly at him from beneath her light hood. "Then you have no reason to talk to me, Ketticus Brayl. Go home to your wife and children."

Face lit by moonlight, the behemoth blanched. "Wait. How do you know who I am?"

"That's not important," she said, right hand disappearing in the long, loose sleeve of her poncho—the lightest garment she owned that would conceal her features. "What's important is that you will leave me alone."

Brayl guffawed. "And if I don't?"

"Then you'll have a talk with this." Her right hand reappeared from within the sleeve, holding a slim blaster. "Are we through?"

The drunk goggled at the weapon's sudden appearance. Then he turned away, staggering off into the steamy night. Resuming her journey, Zaluna put the blaster back in its hiding place, glad no one knew it hadn't been fired in the thirty-three years since her mother had left it to her.

It wasn't true that she knew everyone on Gorse and Cynda by sight, of course—but nearly a third of a century of surveillance had put a lot of troublemakers on her watchlists. And many of them seemed to wind up down here, in The Pits. Some miners acted as if the neighborhood, settled to be close to the old quarries, was a decent place to live now that the strip mining had long since ended. Perhaps for them, it was. But in her experience, roustabouts were trouble waiting to happen. She'd monitored too many bar fights in The Pits, watched dozens of people being shaken down on the streets for money or sport. Whatever the firms paid the miners, it wasn't enough to keep some of them from hassling good folks for cash.

Then again, if they were paid more, they'd just drink more—and that seemed to make them all the worse.

The encounter was just one more headache in a day filled with them. After Hetto's arrest, the remaining surveillance staffers at Transcept had worked their overtime in silence, everyone afraid to say anything. Every operator's background was potentially under review, if the Imperial lieutenant was to be believed. Zaluna had hoped that finding the suspect Skelly again would make up for the Mynocks' not having flagged him for capture earlier—but her hopes fell when she learned that Skelly had escaped from Moonglow's offices before the stormtroopers could arrive.

At least no one suspected the Mynocks of signaling him. The factory supervisor had spent an hour defending her security team from the stormtroopers' insults. Still, Zaluna expected difficult days ahead for everyone at the Transcept office.

And even if nothing happened, a job she'd enjoyed working at would never be fun again.

It was a strange thing. So many people on Gorse lived in fear—especially Sullustans and others of smaller stature. Yet working with the Mynocks, she'd felt somewhat immune. There was safety in isolation, security in having information. Yes, her kind of work did have the potential to create problems for others. But she'd suppressed any consideration of that on the grounds that so many of the people she eavesdropped on were bad characters, likely to hassle a poor workingwoman on a darkened street.

But.

Increasingly, there had been fewer and fewer roughnecks being targeted for snooping, and more and more people like—well, like Hetto. And now Hetto himself, who faced an unknown fate. It hadn't made sense to anyone on the work floor. Sure, Hetto had complained about working conditions and pay, but who didn't? Yes, he'd thought what the Empire had done to the once magnificent caverns of Cynda was an abomination, but that was both old news and a common feeling on Gorse.

But the data cube was another thing—and Zaluna now knew it was the reason he'd been targeted. When the shift ended, she'd fled home to see what it was Hetto had given her. He hadn't given her permission to read what was on the data cube, but it wouldn't be her first time to pry—and she had no intention of passing something along to this "Hera" person without checking it out first.

She'd used a reader she'd first owned as a teenager, safely detached from the HoloNet—and studied the contents of the data cube in her closet for good measure. The contents were encrypted using a commercial program, but Zaluna had worked several years in electronic data collection and soon found her way past the protections.

She was amazed at what she discovered. Somehow, Hetto had managed to download the files Transcept kept on everyone it had ever watched on Gorse and its moon, from way back in the Republic era to the present.

She thought for a moment this "Hera" might be from a rival surveillance firm. Corporate espionage—spying on the spies for profit. Hetto, always broke, could have been hoping for a payoff. She didn't want any part of a transaction like that. But thinking on it, she realized Transcept sold data to its competitors all the time, and sometimes on a massive scale. This act didn't seem necessary.

Looking more closely at it, Zaluna realized that the bounty of personal information on the data cube wasn't the important part. Its existence served as a guide to the state of the art in surveillance means. Every image, every voice recording, every bioscan, every electronic communication tied to names in the files was tagged with information describing how it had been obtained. With it, a reader knew the location of every surveillance point on Transcept's local grid.

Who would need something like that?

Maybe it was another Skelly, some crank or mad bomber looking to know the Empire's capabilities, in order to create more mischief. She wouldn't want to be a part of that.

But Hetto wasn't that kind of person. And that suggested someone else who might want it: someone who cared about what the Empire was doing to the people of Gorse.

Someone who cared as much as Zaluna did.

If there was a chance "Hera" was of that sort, it was worth a conversation, no matter what the danger to Zaluna. One conversation, no more; she had no desire to end up like him. But Hetto deserved that much.

It had to be done in secret, though—and that was why her destination bewildered her. *"The Asteroid Belt?"* She hadn't set foot in a cantina in thirty years, but she'd seen enough video to wonder why anyone would ever consider one a place for a surreptitious meeting. *So many eyes! So many ears!* Not to mention the sensory organs of natures she'd never imagined, belonging to all the other species that frequented cantinas.

Running on adrenaline, she'd unpacked all her devices from the training programs she'd been through years earlier, when she'd learned best practices for placing hidden cams and mikes, and for locating existing ones for repair based on their subspace emissions. Detecting them before they detected her: That would be her edge, she thought.

She saw the sign up ahead. There was no sense waiting outside any longer. "Hetto, you poor reckless soul, this is for you." She drew the cloak tightly around her and stepped toward the building.

CHAPTER NINETEEN

The broken-toothed miner spotted Kanan as soon as the pilot stomped into The Asteroid Belt. "I've been lookin' for you," the burly man snarled. "We still got a fight from last night to finish!"

Bruised and dirtied from the Shaketown episode, Kanan started to walk right by. Then his gloved hands shot out, grabbing the miner by the scruff of his hairy neck. Kanan yanked hard, bringing the man's face down with a smash onto an adjacent table, knocking cards and credits from the sabacc game there astray. The startled card players watched in amazement as Kanan pulled the dazed man off their table—and then climbed on top of it himself.

"Now hear this," he yelled to the dozens of patrons crowding the big cantina. "I have had enough of today. Anyone who hassles me goes to the medcenter."

"The Empire closed the medcenter!" someone yelled.

"Correction: Anyone who hassles me goes to the morgue. That is all." In a single swift motion, he reached down for the mug of ale by his feet—the one that had belonged to the guy on the floor. He drank the contents in one swig and stepped down from the table.

From his regular station behind the bar, old Okadiah eyed him. "You astound, Kanan. You look as though you've been through a bar fight, and yet I could swear you just arrived a minute ago."

"That's because I *was* in a bar fight," Kanan said, rubbing his jaw. "Philo's Fueling Station, over in Shaketown."

"But that's not supposed to reopen for three months."

"It'll be a little longer," Kanan said, reaching over the counter to grab a bottle.

"Hmm." Okadiah shined a glass. "One can only surmise the involvement of a woman."

"Add stupidity and mix well," Kanan said. "But what a woman. She was wearing a hood when I first saw her. But her eyes are *amazing*. And she's got moves. I'm telling you, Oke, if she were to walk in here right now—"

"I think you have your wish!" Okadiah said, pointing.

"Huh?" Kanan looked behind him, expectantly. Peering in through the partially opened door was a Sullustan woman in a rose-colored poncho. Clutching a little blue bag in her hands, she cautiously peeked this way and that.

"Hood, check. Eyes, check," Okadiah said, smirking. "But I'm not sure I'll ever understand your type."

The woman slipped inside. The door slammed noisily behind her, startling her for just an instant. But she quickly made her way to a table in the corner—and then another, and then another, working her way across the room as if she were trying to avoid being seen by someone that only she saw.

Kanan watched, puzzled. "What do you make of that?"

"Perhaps the tax agent's in town," Okadiah said.

Finally arriving near the bar, the Sullustan woman looked in three different directions. Then she bolted across the space, arriving next to the seat at the far end of the counter, near Kanan.

Okadiah bowed. "Welcome to my establishment, young lady. My friend here is a great admirer."

Kanan glared at Okadiah. "It's not her, you imbecile!"

Okadiah smiled. "Can we help you with something?"

Her big eyes looked up at Kanan—and her intense expression softened a little, as if with recognition. "There is something. The bar. Would you mind if I went to the other side of it?"

Kanan goggled. "You want to sit on the barkeep's side of the bar?"

"Kanan does it all the time," Okadiah said. "He sleeps there, too."

"Lady," Kanan said, "there are no stools on that side."

"That's okay," the woman replied, her eyes scanning the ceiling. "I don't want a chair. I want to sit on the floor."

Kanan and Okadiah looked across the bar at each other, puzzled. Then they both shrugged—and the woman darted around the opening and behind the bar. Kanan saw her disappear.

"I hate to miss anything," Okadiah said, "but a host must entertain. Jarrus, lad, hold the fort." He pitched his towel to Kanan and bowed to the huddled woman. "Let's talk again sometime," he said, exiting from behind the counter.

Kanan grabbed Okadiah's shirt as he passed. "This is weird. What am I supposed to say to her?"

"You'll be back there with all the booze. Offer her a drink. Or have one yourself."

Kanan weighed the facts and realized his friend had made an excellent suggestion. Hoisting his body onto the bar, he deposited himself on the other side of the counter. There, he saw the Sullustan woman sitting on the floor, leaning back with her head and shoulders inside the cabinet beneath the sink.

"Hey! What are you doing in there?"

"It'll be just a second," she called out.

Kanan waited. Perhaps she had a lifelong ambition to be a plumber.

She peeked out. "Excuse me. Can you hand me the cutter in my bag?"

Stupefied, Kanan did as he was asked. The little bag was packed to overflowing with electronic gadgets.

"Thank you," she said, taking the tool. A few seconds later, she emerged with a look of satisfaction. "There. Taken care of."

Kanan offered his hand to help her up. "What did you do?"

"Neutralized the surveillance cams in here," she said, getting to her feet. "Thanks for the help."

"There are cams in here?"

"There are cams everywhere," the woman said, brushing herself off. Seeming much more at ease, she removed her poncho, revealing a dark-colored outfit. "That's what I was doing when I came in—moving between the blind spots. I figured Transcept hid the transmitter relay behind the bar. That's a favorite spot for cantinas—no one ever wants to clean under the sink." She put her tool back in her bag. "I cut the power to the whole system."

Kanan looked around the room. He still couldn't see where the cams were.

"Don't worry—I made it look as if a rodent chewed into the works. Happens all the time. Someone pretending to be an ale distributor will be by next week to repair everything."

"If you say so." Kanan took a deep breath, wondering if he'd ever done anything other than get soused in the place. Knowing he hadn't, he shook off the paranoia. "How do you know this, Zaluna?"

She stared at him, suddenly serious again. Big eyes got even wider. "How—how do you know my name?"

"It's on your name badge, there," Kanan said, pointing.

The woman looked at him—and then down at the official badge clipped to her work clothes. "Oh," she said, disgusted, ripping the tag off and putting it in her bag. "I guess I'm not very good at this."

"At what?"

Regaining her composure, Zaluna glanced at Kanan and smiled primly. "I am just another customer visiting a cantina. You should pay me no mind."

"Okay," Kanan said, turning away to the bottles.

"But I could use a little more help."

Kanan looked over his shoulder. "Look, ma'am, I've had a long day. I'm really not in the mood to help anyone."

"But you will." Zaluna leaned against the bar and smiled gently. "I know you. I've seen you working—on Cynda."

"How? I haven't seen you there."

Zaluna didn't explain. "You help people. I've seen you do it before. And I saw you saving your friend from Count Vidian today."

"You saw me?"

Zaluna didn't elaborate. But she smiled, a little ashamed of what she'd revealed. "That's one of the rare pleasures of my world. You spend all your time watching for bad people, and you want to forget what you see. But the good ones, those you remember."

Kanan stared. None of what Zaluna was saying made sense. The woman, he now realized, reminded him of Jocasta Nu, the Jedi librarian. They didn't look anything alike, of course. But Jocasta always seemed to know everything, and acted like knowing everything was nothing. That was definitely in this woman's manner.

"What do you want help with?"

Zaluna looked into the teeming crowd. "I'm supposed to meet someone, but I don't know what they look like."

"You don't know what everyone looks like?"

"Not this time. And I need to keep a low profile. Can you look for me?"

Kanan looked down and put his hands before him. "Zaluna, I don't know who you are or who you think I am—but you do *not* know me. I do not go around randomly helping people!"

"That's not what I've heard about you," came a voice from the far end of the bar. *The voice.*

Kanan decided to play it cool, as he turned. *They always seek you out, brother.* "Hey there, Hera," he said, smiling confidently. "What can I get you?"

CHAPTER TWENTY

The Jedi Order was more than an unpaid police force, more than just an exercise club that was into metaphysics. It was a way of life, based on the Jedi Code—and a lot of rules for living that weren't in the Code, that had been tacked on later. One was that Jedi avoided becoming involved in romantic relationships. Once on the run, Kanan Jarrus had found that rule pretty easy to forget about.

Hera's visit here, now, wasn't any kind of date—but she *was* a lovely woman wanting a private conversation, and from his earlier experiences he knew just the spot. The Asteroid Belt had a nice, secluded table in the back where the light was just right and where you were out of the stumbling line of the drunks and the brawlers.

But never in his past visits to the table had he brought along a short, gray chaperone—and Zaluna was talking more with Hera than he was. After being sent to the bar for something for the third time by Hera, Kanan had started to suspect that the Twi'lek really had come here looking for Zaluna after all, and not him.

The two were chatting closely when Kanan returned to the table with the coasters Hera had requested. It was time to step things up. "You can stop talking about how much you miss me, ladies—I'm back!"

"Great," Hera said, in a tone that, for the first time, wasn't music to Kanan's ears. She seemed annoyed at having been interrupted, but he wasn't going to let that deter him.

Looking down, he saw that the chair he'd been sitting in was pushed well away from the table, out into the aisle. Hera's foot had pushed it there, he realized. *So much for gratitude over being saved.* "Standing room only tonight," he said, grabbing the chair and chuckling. "Good thing nobody else grabbed this."

"Good thing," Hera repeated.

Kanan spun the chair around backward and straddled it as he sat down, putting his chest against the back of the chair and crossing his arms over the top of it—a move intended to bring him fully into the conversation. "So what'd I miss?"

Hera looked at him with impatience—until Zaluna reached out and touched her hand. "I think you can trust him. I've watched him longer than you have. He helps people—though he makes a show of doing otherwise. He stood up to Vidian just today."

"I saw," Hera said.

"You did?" Kanan asked, slack-jawed.

Hera seemed to fret. "It's still not smart. You protect secrets by keeping the circle small."

"And you protect yourself by having a witness," Zaluna said. "I've been a professional witness my whole life. If we're really going to discuss this, I'd like one now." She regarded Kanan. "He'll do."

Kanan slumped in his chair and shrugged. "I'll do." *What's going on here?*

Hera seemed to reach a decision. She leaned across the table, her hands clasped together. "All right. I'd come here to meet this guy I met on the HoloNet—"

"Oh, well, there's your first mistake," Kanan proclaimed. "I could have told you—"

But before he could finish his sentence, Hera flashed Kanan a smile that was only slightly patronizing. "Can it wait?"

Mildly chastened, Kanan shut his mouth.

"I was looking for a man named Hetto. He and Zaluna both work for a company with a surveillance contract for the Empire. Hetto had grown worried about what he saw as abuses of authority—and he had already been in contact with other . . . *concerned parties.*"

Kanan could tell from the way Hera pronounced the words that she didn't want to elaborate too much about that. But she did say that it was Hetto she was supposed to have met until his arrest changed that.

"He was arrested for trying to meet you," Zaluna said, shaking her head.

"It wasn't just that," Hera said, sounding soothing. "You know that. Hetto was aware, Zaluna. Awake to all the things the Empire is doing. This meeting? It was him reaching out, trying to do something. You were brave to take it on yourself, to finish what he started."

"I'm not brave," Zaluna said, her voice a little shaky. "I'm an old fool. I remember too much. I remember how it was—and how it got worse, even before the Empire. I remember when people didn't kill guildmasters on a whim and walk away without a thought." Her black eyes glistened. "And I remember when my people were safe. Those employees of mine are my children, and now one of them's in deep trouble." She focused on Hera. "Will they kill Hetto?"

Hera didn't seem to know what to say. Zaluna closed her huge eyes, mournful. Kanan reached out and patted her hand. "Hey, there, maybe your friend's just in a labor camp."

"Kanan is right," Hera said, a phrase he thought sounded wonderful coming from her, whether she meant it or not. "Hetto is a talented person, and they'll want to keep him around, maybe even doing work like he is now. Just someplace else."

"Yeah, and maybe they even have daylight there," Kanan said. He smiled awkwardly at Hera and shrugged.

Recovering her composure, Zaluna reached into her bag and pulled out a data cube. It was bigger than the storage device Kanan had seen Skelly waving around. "This is what Hetto wanted you to have." She peered up at Hera. "You know what's on it?"

"I think so," Hera said. She reached into a pocket and withdrew a small reading device. "May I?"

Zaluna paused, suddenly reluctant. "This is it, isn't it? This is the moment." Glancing all around the bar, she took a deep breath. "It's exciting, almost, being on this side of the cams. You wonder who else is here."

"There's no Imperial agents here, if that's what you're asking," Kanan said. He looked back across the room. "These are all one hundred percent pure shovel-carrying drunkards. I've tussled with too many of them to think they're plants for the Empire."

Hera looked at him. "And what do *you* think about the Empire?"

"As little as possible," he said. "I could take it or leave it."

"Hmm."

She sounded disappointed, Kanan thought, but only a little. Clearly, Hera was politically aware; he knew the sort, having wooed a university woman or ten on more upscale worlds. But those women had all aggressively tried to get him to care about their causes of the week. Hera was letting him be, at least for the moment. *Good for her.*

"You can look at it," Zaluna finally decided, offering the data cube. "That's what Hetto wanted. But—maybe you'd better give it right back afterward. Okay?"

"Okay," Hera said. Taking it, she plugged it into her device and began reading. Kanan saw her eyes widening as she read, and he realized she was savoring something wonderful.

"Juicy stuff?"

"Mm-hmm." She manipulated the device for several minutes. "This is huge. It's not just the information—it's how it was retrieved. The Empire is everywhere."

"But not omniscient," Zaluna said. "Eyes and ears can fail." She nodded to what Hera was holding. "Study that long enough, and you'd see where they fall short."

"This section here. What are these names?"

Zaluna examined what Hera was looking at and cleared her throat. "That's different. Those are all the requests made on the Imperial channel to the Transcept database. People they're interested in. Background checks, video files being pulled."

Kanan took a peek as Hera paged through lists of names. He still couldn't believe any of this business was real.

"I think Hetto was downloading right up until a few minutes before he was arrested," Zaluna said. "There are some really recent ones in there."

Hera pointed to a name. "What's this very last one—*Lemuel Tharsa?*"

"That's one of the command-level requests from the Star Destroyer. Somebody important wanted to know about him."

"Command level? Like the captain? Or Count Vidian?"

"I suppose."

"And who is Lemuel Tharsa?"

"The name doesn't sound familiar," Zaluna said. She took the cube and reader from Hera and ran a search. "Someone by that name did visit the planet twenty years ago—someone started a file on him, at least. No details, though."

"Why would they be looking for someone like that?" Hera asked.

"No idea. Sorry there's not more—back in the commercial surveillance days, there were more legal limits to tracking." Zaluna passed the cube and reader back to Hera. "Of course, I probably saw the guy back then, if it was even the same person. Maybe something will jog my memory."

Kanan chuckled. "Well, you people spy on millions of people. I wouldn't expect you to—"

"Kanan Jarrus, human male, early twenties," Zaluna said, looking up at him. "Freighter pilot, dangerous cargo. Flight clearance seven. Emigrated to Gorse five months ago from—"

Kanan grabbed her wrist. "Okay, you're spooky. I get it." His mouth went dry, and he reached for his drink.

"This is good," Hera said, detaching the reader and passing the data cube back to the woman. "Very good, very worth Hetto's sacrifice—and yours. May I have it long enough to copy it? I'm busy with the reason I'm here, but for this, I'd make time."

Kanan's eyebrow went up. "I thought meeting *her* was the reason you were here."

Hera looked at him kindly. "Kanan, I appreciate what you did for me back in Shaketown—and also your hosting us here. But I've done all I'm going to do to satisfy your curiosity, so—"

"Oh, no!"

Hera and Kanan looked at Zaluna.

"He's here," the Sullustan woman said, looking into the crowd. "Why would he be here, now?"

Kanan looked around, but could only see the bustling patrons. "What? Who's here?"

"What is it, Zaluna?" Hera asked, worried. "The Empire?"

Having already made a decision, Zaluna stuffed the data cube into her bag and stood. "This is too much. I have to go." She turned from the table and headed for the side door. "Good-bye!"

Kanan and Hera looked at each other, puzzled—until they became aware of a figure in a tan overcoat standing nearby.

"Kanan! Just the guy I'm looking for," Skelly said, peering out from beneath his hood. "And I see you've met my friend!"

CHAPTER TWENTY-ONE

"*You!* I thought I'd gotten rid of you!"

Skelly stretched out his hands and smiled broadly at Kanan. "Hello to you, too," he said, speaking loudly. "Don't get up."

Kanan did get up. He grabbed the startled fugitive by the back of the neck and forcibly shoved him down into the seat Zaluna had been occupying. "This is a room full of miners who think you tried to crush them to death!"

"That's all wrong." Skelly started to rise. "Look, I could tell them—"

"Sit down!" Kanan barked, shoving him downward. He looked around the room to see who had noticed. Thankfully, it was chaos as usual—a term that was quickly coming to describe his entire evening.

"Why did—" Hera started to say. "Our friend, the Sullustan. She ran out of here when she saw you. Why?"

"No idea," Skelly said.

"She probably met him in an elevator once," Kanan said.

Skelly pointed at Hera with his good hand. "You should be careful around this woman, Kanan. I don't think she's who she says she is."

"Thanks for the advice. But she hasn't said anything yet."

Hera stood and glanced at Kanan. "I should see where she ran off to. I'll be back."

"No, wait." He rose and touched her shoulder. "Sit with Skelly. Make sure he doesn't do—well, anything. Anything at all."

Kanan walked quickly back along the bar. Reaching the side door, he saw nothing outside but Okadiah's aged hoverbus, parked in the moon-light.

He saw Skelly and Hera talking furtively when he returned. *Did they really know each other?*

"Couldn't see her," he announced.

Hera frowned. "She'd know Skelly was wanted," she reasoned.

"Maybe she'll come back when he's gone." Sitting down, Kanan faced Skelly. "What are you doing here in the first place? Who let you go?"

Skelly pointed. "She did!"

Kanan looked at Hera and gawked. "What?"

Hera simply nodded—and shrugged.

"When? Where?"

"At Moonglow," she said. "He was being held prisoner. I set him free."

"Why?"

"It seemed like the thing to do."

"What, like activating a thermal detonator?" Kanan couldn't believe it.

She seemed unconcerned. "It seemed safe. There weren't any reports of casualties from the moon—"

"I was nearly one. He's a biological weapon." He clapped his hand on Skelly's sleeve. "Now will you please get out of here?"

"I'll go," Skelly said, pulling his hand back. "But I came to see you because I need a favor."

"This should be good."

"Vidian's coming to inspect Moonglow in a few hours," Skelly said.

Hera's interest was piqued. "That's odd. I thought Moonglow was a small operation."

"I overheard him telling Lal. The stormtroopers have already put up a security cordon around that part of Shaketown. So I'll need your ID to get me onto the grounds, old buddy."

Kanan took a large swallow of his drink, then asked, "My what?"

"You said you were going to quit anyway, right? Just let me borrow your badge. I'll give it back after I've made my case to Vidian."

"I won't get it back, because they're gonna shoot you in the head! And Vidian'll have a ball watching." Kanan shook his head. "That guy's horrible."

"He's brilliant. He doesn't take any guff from corporate types."

"That's for sure," Hera said. "He kills them."

"I know a few who deserve it. From what I hear, he does what needs doing." With his left hand, he gestured to his motionless right hand. "And he's not ashamed of his cybernetics. I think he talks my language. We'll consult, like two professionals. I'll save the moon. And then I'll go."

"This is the dumbest plan I've ever heard." Kanan looked over at Hera in disbelief. "This is what you let loose."

Hera sighed. "I saw someone with a grievance. I wanted to know what it was, before the Empire rubbed him out. I wanted to know if he was worth knowing." She fixed her eyes on Kanan and spoke calmly. "You can't always guess what role someone will play."

"You can't pick your friends, you mean?"

"Oh, I'm very selective."

"I bet."

"I have high standards," Hera said. "Only very special people are going to be able to help me right now."

"Like Skelly? Or her?" Kanan gestured with his thumb to the door Zaluna had left through.

"No, probably not." She smiled charitably. "And not even you. I thank you for earlier, but you're not going to be able to help me."

"Help you do what?"

She smiled gently. "If you have to ask, you're not ready to know." She rose. "And now I really need to go. The Empire's still looking for Skelly—and if they break Hetto, they could know about my rendez-vous."

Before Kanan could respond, he heard the front door being kicked open. Two stormtroopers appeared there. Turning, he saw two more coming in through the side door.

Hera saw them, too. She sighed. "Speak of the Empire, and it will appear."

Crouching behind a garbage bin, Zaluna struggled to calm down. She'd been right to move when she did. Every Imperial on Gorse was looking for Skelly, and bounty had probably been offered. She didn't know whether he was guilty of what he'd been accused of, but she wasn't going to sit around possibly betraying the Empire while he was anywhere nearby.

Treason! That was what she'd just committed, she realized. Zaluna's breaths came quickly as she looked down at the ground and her open bag. The data cube was there, glinting in the moonlight. By showing the object and its contents to Hera, Zaluna had just thrown away thirty-plus years of faithful service—and for what? To help a woman who might be in league with a mad bomber? Skelly had seemed to recognize Hera. Had his whole tussle with Kanan on the moon been a fraud, to trap her?

Entrapment had been a concern going in, and she'd taken a few steps to prepare for that. They hadn't included an escape route on this side of the building, however. Hearing the clatter of armor as stormtroopers ran past, Zaluna looked furtively for someplace to hide the data cube or something to smash it with. There was nothing. Even the garbage bin was locked.

As the sound of another transport came from the street beyond, Zaluna saw her only possible sanctuary looming large and dark, up the alley. She picked up her bag and ran for it. Either those years in the Transcept exercise room would save her, or they wouldn't.

The clamor inside The Asteroid Belt lessened only a little as the stormtroopers—one male and three female—made their way inside, blasters handy but not raised. Kanan saw Okadiah leave his sabacc game long enough to greet them. "Welcome, Officers, welcome! Happy hour all night!"

Kanan shot a concerned look at Hera. "Only two ways out of here," he said.

"I know. I checked before I came in."

Of course you did, Kanan thought.

Skelly stood up and reached for his hood. "I've had enough of this," he said, beginning to remove his cowl. "I'm trying to see Vidian anyway. I'll just go with them!"

"No!" Kanan and Hera said in unison, each grabbing an arm and jerking Skelly down. Kanan yanked the top of the hood forward so it was almost covering Skelly's nose.

The stormtroopers began working their way through the room, speaking to individual patrons. The drunks weren't cooperating, and the stormtroopers weren't being gentle in return.

"Side door?" Hera asked.

Kanan shook his head. "Hear that sound?"

Hera concentrated for a moment. "Just the bar."

"There's a personnel carrier idling out there. Must be more stormtroopers."

Hera glanced at the exit. "Couldn't it be the hoverbus?"

"Different sound." Only he and Okadiah had the activation code, anyway. Kanan looked around the bar, furtively—until his eyes fixed on the short hallway directly behind their table.

Kanan glanced back to make sure the stormtroopers weren't looking his way. Seeing his moment, he stood, grasping Skelly's arm tightly. "Quick," he said, making for the corridor. "You, too!"

"But that doesn't lead outside," Hera said.

"Just follow—and do exactly what I say."

CHAPTER TWENTY-TWO

"You there!"

"Me there," Kanan said, emerging alone from the short hallway with a white towel in his hand. Less than a minute had passed—and two of the stormtroopers had reached the table he'd vacated.

"We're searching this establishment," the one with the female voice said.

"For what?"

"A spy, here to meet a traitor." The male trooper shoved past Kanan and entered the short hallway.

"You're kidding." Kanan laughed. "Have a look around," he said, picking up his empty mug from the table and rubbing it with the cloth. "If your spy's here tonight, he's blasted off his boosters!"

The female stormtrooper surveyed the cheering crowd. A blitzed Ugnaught, snout-faced and only a meter tall, was riding drunkenly around on the head of a similarly soused Ithorian. The brown-hided, hammer-headed titan had a pitcher in each long-fingered hand and was lumbering around trying to serve both himself and his small passenger at the same time without spilling any ale.

A normal night for The Asteroid Belt, in all respects.

"Maybe that's your traitors there," Kanan said, pointing to them with a smile.

"Never mind," the stormtrooper said. "We're also looking for a pilot from Moonglow. We don't have pictures of him yet, but he's a witness—the bomber stowed away on his ship. We were told he lives here."

"On the floor, maybe," Kanan said, walking to set the empty mug on the bar. "These pilots are in one night, out another." He reached for an empty bottle and pitched it in the trash. "I'm just the bartender. Can I get you something?"

From down the short hallway, the other stormtrooper called out, "There's someone behind this door!"

"Uh-oh," Kanan said, stepping lively to get there first. There was a small door to the left at the end of the corridor, and the stormtrooper that Kanan had seen earlier was about to kick it in. Kanan stepped up and raised his hand. "You really don't want to go in there."

The stormtrooper looked up at Kanan, helmeted head tilted slightly in puzzlement.

And then they all heard it: the loudest, most sickening retching sound, coming from behind the door. Something metallic inside banged loudly against the wall, and then against the door, before the horrible heaving noise began again.

"It's one of the Wookiees," Kanan said, shaking his head. "Always thinks he can handle Trandoshan ale. That stuff can take the finish off a landspeeder."

The female stormtrooper didn't turn away. "But that doesn't sound—"

She was interrupted with a horrific symphony of heaving, louder than before. Kanan looked behind the armored pair. "Bring the heavy stuff, Layda!"

"Excuse me!" Hera, wearing a long apron, appeared in the open doorway on the other side of the hallway. She exited the storage room holding a mop in one hand and a carrying case of industrial-strength cleansers in the other. While the stormtroopers watched, she set the case down outside the door and reached in to find several cloth face masks. She tied one over her face, and then another. "You'll want to get back," she said to the watchers as she placed the third shield over her mouth. "I don't know if those suits will protect you."

"Rrrraaa-arrghh-arrggh-arrrrgh!" came another miserable howl from behind the door. The pounding resumed.

"I think we'll move along," the female stormtrooper said. Her partner's body language showed immediate relief. "If you see any suspicious characters," she said, "call the authorities."

"Gotcha," Kanan said.

Once the front doors closed behind the stormtroopers, Kanan whipped out a key and opened the door. There, inside a small storage closet, squatted a terrified Skelly, holding a metal pail in his hands. "Was that loud enough?" he said, yelling into the pail and producing a noisy echo.

"Get out of there," Kanan said, grabbing at him. "And get out of here!"

Keeping the hood pulled low over Skelly's head, Kanan shoved him back into the main room, along the bar, and out the side door. The stormtroopers and their transport were gone; only Okadiah's hoverbus remained.

Reaching the stoop, Skelly lifted his cowl and called back plaintively. "So, do I get that ID badge or not?"

Kanan answered by slamming the door and locking it.

Hera was leaning against the bar, apron removed, when he turned.

"Nice tactics, there, Kanan." He could tell from her expression that she was impressed. "If you want them to leave, make *them* want to leave. Very smooth."

"I've got a lot of experience avoiding stormtroopers."

"Oh?" she said. "Why's that?"

"I don't like their fashion sense."

She smiled. "Come here."

Kanan did—and was pleasantly surprised when she reached out to touch him. "You've been holding out on me," she said, running her finger along the collar of his shirt.

"I'd never do such a thing." He sidled up closer to her, surprised by this new attitude. If excitement turned her friendly, he wasn't going to object. "You can have anything you want."

"Great," she said. "I want your Moonglow pass."

"I'd—" Kanan said, before her response registered. "You want *what*?"

"Your pass," she said, and jabbed her hand inside his neckline to grab at something. She pulled out a gold-colored card, secured around his neck with a lanyard. "You work at Moonglow. I didn't know that, until Skelly mentioned it. I want your pass to get on the grounds."

"I don't think you can just—"

"I've seen the gate. It's automated." She made a *swish-swish* motion with her hand. "Simple."

"Wait. Why do you want to get into the factory?"

"Denetrius Vidian."

"Ew," Kanan said. He walked back over to the bar, where many of his friends beckoned in comforting glass containers. "Believe me, sweetheart, I'm much better looking."

"I know what he looks like," she said, following him to the counter. "He's the reason I'm here."

"That's even worse," Kanan said. He began pouring them drinks. "Look, I know there's no accounting for taste. But you're way too good for someone like him."

"I'm not in a relationship with him. I'm trying to find out why he's here."

"I'd have thought that was obvious. He's here to get more blood out of stones—or thorilide out of crystals." Handing her a glass, he joined her on her side of the counter. She was really serious about this— *whatever* that she was into. "I never have figured out why the Empire needs so much thorilide."

Hera shook her head. "That's not the mystery here. They're building Star Destroyers at a rate to put one in every home. The mystery is why Gorse," she said, "and why now."

"What do you mean?"

"They were already kicking the stuffing out of you guys to speed you up before Vidian showed up. That's why your pal Skelly—"

"Not *my* pal!"

"—it's why Skelly and a lot of people like him have been so vocal. Gorse and Cynda were not worlds the Empire was honoring with its negligence."

"Careful," Kanan said, taking the excuse to lean closer to her and show her his winning smile. "Treasonous words, there."

"I think I'll trust Zaluna's surveillance sweep. So explain to me this," she asked. "Vidian's administrative domain is centered on Calcoraan, sectors away. But lately, his whole Imperial career seems to have led him toward one goal: getting authority over Gorse and Cynda. And the second he got it, he called up an Imperial escort to take him here." She ticked off the mysteries on her fingers. "Now, does that seem strange?"

"Strange that a smart person has nothing better to obsess over than the life of some Imperial weirdo," Kanan said, shaking his head in disbelief. "Why do you care?"

"Because where Vidian goes, pain follows. Friends of mine have vanished, their worlds have suffered. But everybody wants something. If I can find out what he's after, maybe I can do something about it."

Kanan shook his head. What was she—eighteen, maybe? Taking on an Imperial power broker? "Seriously, how did you come up with all this stuff?"

"I have eyes and ears. I read. I talk to people. I listen."

"You talk to people like Skelly and Zaluna, you really are desperate. Skelly's a mess. And it didn't sound like Zaluna was looking to be a part of any of this. She was fulfilling a last request, not picking up a cause."

A distant look came to her eyes. A little sad, he thought. "No," she said, "they're not really the sort of people who could be—" She stopped herself and started again. "They're not the sort I'm looking for."

"I could have told you that. I did, in fact." He put his hand to his chest. "I'm another story. Very reliable. And I'm about to be available."

"Available for what?"

"For whatever." Kanan stood upright. "I'm leaving this planet—and I recommend the same for you. You've been fun to be around, street fights notwithstanding. Forget this Vidian business, and we can go wandering."

She regarded him with skeptical amusement. "I don't think so," Hera said. "We just met. I don't even know what you are."

"Ask anyone." Kanan waved over the heads of the drunken mob. "Okadiah! Tell her about me!"

Unseen amid the drunken crowd, Okadiah called out, "A fine pilot, an occasional humanitarian, and a somewhat tolerable houseguest. Marry him, my darling!"

"That's an endorsement?" Hera asked, straining to see where the voice had come from. "Can he even see me?"

"Doesn't matter," Kanan said. "Anyone will tell you. I can do anything."

"I don't want you to do anything."

"I know the sector. I know people. I know people who know people." He turned around. "Here, watch this. What was the name from Zaluna's list?"

"The guy the Empire was inquiring about?" She didn't miss a beat. "Lemuel Tharsa."

His eyes scanned the room. "Hang on," he said. *"Okadiah!"*

The old man stepped through the crowd toward them. "You beckoned?" Laying eyes on Hera, the old man bowed admiringly. "Oh, you *definitely* beckon."

Hera lowered her eyes and grinned.

"Did you know a Lemuel Tharsa?" Kanan asked.

"I may have known several Lemuel Tharsas. Is there a shortage?"

"He was around twenty or so years ago," Hera said. "I was wondering if you remembered who he was."

Okadiah shook his head. "It grieves me to disappoint you, my dear. But no. Never on one of my crews."

Hera nodded. "All right. Thank you."

Starting to turn away, Okadiah looked back. "Now, if he worked for the refineries or the Guild administration, I wouldn't have seen him unless he came into the bar. You might ask Boss Lal. She's a lifer at Moonglow—from back in the days when it was Introsphere. She might have personnel records."

"Thanks!"

"But please don't look at mine," Okadiah said. "I don't want you knowing I'm too old for you."

"Get out of here," Kanan said, shoving his friend away. "He's got kidney stones your age," he told Hera.

"Your remark wounds," the older man said, and drifted away.

Hera looked up at Kanan. "Well, now, I *really* want to get in over there. Will you give me the badge or won't you?"

Kanan rubbed his forehead. "I knew you were going to say that. Look, it's been a long day. In a few hours, I've got to run these people back to Moonglow for the morning shift—those that regain consciousness, anyway. I also need to pick up my final pay. You come with us. If you insist, I'll take you to the grounds and get you in." He put up his hands. "But that's it, all right? No crazy stuff."

She studied him for a moment. Finally, she nodded. "Okay. Just this one thing." She raised her glass. "And no crazy stuff. That's my motto."

Hera returned to her ship, resisting Kanan's offer of lodging at The Asteroid Belt. It turned out that "drunks sleeping on the floor" was more than a jocular expression; Okadiah Garson owned the building across the alley, where exhausted revelers, for the princely sum of a credit a head, retired to the luxury of mats on the hard floor. Kanan had offered to give her the more private room upstairs from the cantina—with him either present or absent—but she'd decided to pass. She had a lot to absorb.

Zaluna had never resurfaced, and Hera doubted there was any point in trying to make contact. If Hera had arrived earlier, or if the Sullustan woman hadn't been scared off, she might now have the data cube from Transcept, obviously a treasure trove of information on people and Imperial surveillance methods. But Hera wasn't angry at fate, or herself. Every plan ran the risk of failure due to the unexpected. Recriminations were a waste of valuable time.

But Kanan Jarrus had surprised her, and people seldom did. In Shaketown, she'd seen a brawler, a typical roughneck. But in the bar—beyond his romantic interest, which she had decided to find amusing—she'd seen him act with subtlety and cunning.

It was timely, but likely a onetime thing. She didn't expect to have a chance to find out, in any event.

No, her real quarry remained. Vidian wanted increased production from the world, obviously, but the urgency of his visit had her thinking something else was going on. If Vidian was here on a secret mission—maybe a secret mission for the Emperor—then she wanted to know.

And then there was Lemuel Tharsa. From her ship, she'd checked the public HoloNet and found Tharsa was alive and well and living offworld as a mining consultant, doing freelance work for the Imperial government. Why, then, would anyone aboard *Ultimatum* want to check out his distant past on Gorse? Might he be a potential traitor in Vidian's midst—and an ally for her, were she to warn him?

She would look for answers tomorrow, at Moonglow. She would find the truth—and the truth would tell her what to do. As it always did.

She forced herself to sleep.

Phase Two:

REACTION

"Emperor opens new veterans' medcenter on Coruscant"

"Hunt under way for missing after industrial accident on Cynda"

"Count Vidian arrives on Gorse for inspection tour, traffic delays possible"

—*headlines, Imperial HoloNews* (Gorse Edition)

CHAPTER TWENTY-THREE

For the first time since she entered the Academy, Rae Sloane was late for an appointment. But the Galactic Empire had made the schedule. It could break the schedule.

And it wasn't her fault, anyway. During the descent through Gorse's atmosphere, Count Vidian had emerged from the passenger compartment to reroute the captain's shuttle—*Truncheon*—to a location well south of the factory districts. He'd demanded a flyover of the miners' hospice he had ordered closed.

She hadn't understood the point of making such a trip, if they weren't going to land. There wasn't much to see in the dark. But then she'd seen the reason in a flash—or rather, *with* a flash, as the cube-shaped building abruptly imploded. Vidian had been busy while Sloane had slept, ordering the movement of the personnel, usable equipment, and all patients—so far as she knew, anyway—from the medcenter. With many of the just-evacuated still on the ground looking back from their transports, the Empire's demolition teams had made quick work of the building. Debris removal vehicles were already on the scene; Vidian had plans to turn the site into a more convenient fuel depot. True to his reputation, the man worked incredibly fast. Sloane could only imagine what the bewildered patients watching must have thought, watching their home coming down.

She didn't bother to imagine what Vidian had thought. The man had simply watched the collapse, emotionlessly, before returning to the rear of the vehicle. It was fine with her. Her job was making sure nothing else happened to interfere with his visit. What had happened on Cynda would not happen here.

The count had stops planned all over the muddy megalopolis, so Sloane had decided against using ground vehicles to get to them all. There would be too many routes to secure. Instead, *Truncheon* would fly from stop to stop, bringing its own complement of stormtroopers and protected by electronic countermeasures against ground-to-air attacks while in flight. Such an attack was unlikely in the extreme, but Sloane tried to think of everything.

It meant clearing landing zones everywhere and securing them. That hadn't been a problem. The captain of a Star Destroyer was a naval officer, of course, but she was also the personification of Imperial authority in the system. And while she did not have formal power over the Empire's local authorities on Gorse—except under certain circumstances—captains of capital ships were nonetheless treated like miniature governors. Few petty bureaucrats wanted to argue with someone who could put a dozen AT-ATs on the ground with a comlink call. And so Gorse's local police force had joined with the stormtroopers from the planetary garrison to make ready for Vidian's arrival.

She could get used to having this kind of authority. She certainly wanted to.

"Shaketown," she announced as the ship approached an industrial neighborhood. "Such as it is."

The place was aptly named, she decided: Sloane felt a slight quake as the ship's landing gear settled in the mud. The advance team had decided against having *Truncheon* land on Moonglow's tarmac, where it would have been parked amid explosives haulers; the fugitive had flown back on one and was still at large. Instead, the street in front of Moonglow's front gate had been cordoned off—reportedly over the heated objections of a Besalisk diner owner—to create a reception area.

Such as it is. The ramp down, Sloane surveyed the scene. Vidian's official visit—even *her* visit—on another world would have merited pomp and preparation, short notice or not. Here, there were a few temporary light stands supplementing the waxing moon—and someone had laid some planks over the muddy street. About two dozen citizens stood off to the side, flanked by stormtroopers, watching as a sad little processional approached *Truncheon*. Not the greeting she had ordered or would have liked—but she knew Vidian wouldn't care.

He appeared in the doorway behind her. She'd only known Vidian to march straight into places, not wasting any time—but here, he stood, looking up, down, and all around. And mostly at the factory across the way, where his macabre eyes lingered for long moments. She decided he was just doing whatever it was he did when he prepared to inspect a place. The man could be standing there staring at tomorrow's menu in the *Ultimatum* mess halls, for all she knew.

A tan-skinned human woman waved to them, flanked by two Besalisks. Sloane knew her from their holographic conversation as Shaketown's mayor. "Welcome, Count Vidian. Welcome, Captain. May I present Lal Grallik, chief operating officer of Moonglow Polychemical?"

Vidian broke from his trance and walked down the ramp. No hand was offered. Sloane joined him on the planking.

Lal, wearing a dark business suit, bowed and gestured to the other Besalisk. "This is my husband, Gord—head of ground security."

"I hardly think we'll need him," Sloane said, following Vidian. "And I'm surprised he would be employed here after letting the demolitions man escape." She paused to glare at Lal. "Family or not!"

The male Besalisk growled. "If you think you can do any better—"

His wife shushed him. "I'm sure there won't be any problems now, Captain. Gord's team has triple-checked every square meter of the site."

"Uh-huh." Hearing a high whine coming from the south, Sloane turned to see a weathered hoverbus setting down outside the security line. "What's that there?"

"Part of the next shift for Cynda," Lal said, smiling too broadly. "We're always working here!"

. . .

The stormtroopers waved the battered hoverbus through the checkpoint. The Mark Six Smoothride had already been past its life span when Okadiah bought it; where it had once flown through the skies, not even Kanan ever dared to take it more than a meter off the ground. Okadiah had been so terrified it would skyrocket off uncontrollably that he kept a parachute under the seat. Kanan thought that an unlikely scenario. It was much more likely to die in the street, as it had for him several times. It was good for one purpose: bringing hungover miners back to Moonglow so they could earn enough credits to drink again.

The Imperial Lambda was parked up ahead, its mass completely blocking the entrance to Drakka's Diner. Kanan was certain the chef loved that. In front of the Sienar Fleet Systems shuttle, Kanan saw his boss's husband ambling along, following several steps behind a larger party. Spotting him drive past, Lal waved. "Hello, Kanan! Good to see you didn't quit!"

Kanan replied with a half wave—and then, seeing Vidian out there, quickly pulled his head back inside the window. He gritted his teeth. Yesterday, he had been ready to leave Gorse entirely. Today, he was willingly coming back to an armed camp. But it was just one more day, and there was an excellent reason why. Looking back down the aisle, he saw her chatting amiably with the miners. They were spellbound by Hera. He couldn't blame them.

The stormtroopers waved the hoverbus around to the service gate. The Smoothride groaned as it turned sharply, and for a moment, Kanan thought he heard a thump coming from one of the rearward compartments. It could be anything, he thought. The hoverbus was apt to die on any given trip. Even the door to the restroom was broken.

"I've been having the most lovely conversation with your young friend," Okadiah said, arriving from the back. "We have decided to vacation on Naboo. You may drive us."

"Be careful. She's a woman with a mission," Kanan said as the metal beast settled harshly in the mud. The doors opened, and his passengers filed past him. Kanan remained.

"You're not flying bombs today?" Okadiah said.

"No," Kanan said, nodding toward the back. "I'd like to show some-one the sights."

Okadiah patted his shoulder. "The only job that matters. Good luck."

Kanan smiled, slowly, as the man stepped out. Okadiah hadn't seen the duffel on the floor near the driver's seat—Kanan's belongings, packed while the old man wasn't looking. He'd miss Okadiah, and that was probably good-bye. But the next chapter, he could feel, had already begun.

Even if it was starting strangely. "You really want to do this?" he asked Hera. She was at the window behind the driver's seat, looking all around.

"Yes," Hera said. "I really do."

She slipped off her cloak to reveal an all-black outfit. Good for sneak-ing around in a sunless place, Kanan thought—and better to look at. She checked her holster to see that her blaster pistol was secure. "I really think you ought to hang this and do something else with your time," he said.

Hera replied with a firm look. "I'm sure you have suggestions." She put out her hand.

"Fine." Kanan reluctantly handed her his Moonglow ID badge. "Wave it in front of the sensor at the inner door. I'll be parked out in the street, pretending to have engine trouble." It wouldn't be require much of a lie, he knew. "When you get back, I'll get my pay from Lal and take you to the spaceport—and we'll go to any planet you want."

"We will, will we?" Hera rolled her eyes.

"That's right."

"I have my own ship." She stepped out of the bus.

Huh. That was interesting news, he thought as she disappeared through the door.

Kanan guided the hoverbus back out the gate and parked it within sight of the shuttle. Stepping out, he saw that stormtroopers and local security types were still stationed all around. It was time to start the pantomime.

And there was one small blessing: Skelly hadn't made an appearance after all. *Nobody's that foolish!*

"That's Kanan, all right." Skelly surveyed the new arrivals from his perch hidden among the chimneys atop Drakka's Diner. Only one eyepiece of his secondhand macrobinoculars displayed anything, but that was enough to show him what he needed to see.

He'd realized that he couldn't simply reveal himself. The mining company people wouldn't want him to speak to Vidian, and he didn't trust stormtroopers to deliver him after the episode on the moon. He needed to reach the man when he was alone—and that meant getting into the factory. Thorilide refineries were complicated places: a lot of huge equipment often crammed into tight spaces, offering lots of hiding places.

And Moonglow had something else: an ancient connection to Shaketown's long-abandoned sewer system. Gorse wasn't a particularly rainy place, but the underground water table rose and fell dramatically with the tides. Cynda's movements squeezed the planet like a sponge, causing puddles to spring randomly from the soil. But quake damage had rendered the sewers useless, and only people interested in such places, like Skelly, knew the sewer system existed.

And how to get into it. Prying the macrobinoculars from his hand, he stuffed them into his enormous backpack. Donning it, he found the ladder leading down into the diner's back alley. There, in the middle of a low pool of brackish water, sat the rounded cover he was looking for.

Struggling under the burden of his pack, Skelly fished for handholds around the circumference of the metal disk. He curled his fingers beneath and strained for a long minute. It wouldn't budge. He tried to stand up—only to realize his malfunctioning right hand was locked in position, with his fingers underneath the cover.

Great, Skelly thought. *What else can go wrong?*

Then he found out.

"*Who's back here?*" Drakka, the enormous Besalisk chef, appeared behind him, armed—as if he needed to be—with a huge iron skillet. He grabbed at Skelly with his three free hands, trying to turn him around. Skelly felt pain in his arm as his hand, still attached to the sewer cover, didn't budge.

"Whoa, there!" Skelly said. He was trespassing, he knew—but the Besalisk ought to recognize him. "It's me, Drakka! Skelly! You know me!"

"You say that like it's a good thing!" The Besalisk continued pulling. "You're breaking into my place!"

"Whoa, no!" Skelly winced with pain. "I'm going over to Moonglow to see the Imperials!"

Drakka stopped tugging. He frowned. "I'm closed today because of those idiots." Skelly watched him nervously, for a moment, as the behemoth decided what to do.

Then he reached past Skelly and ripped the sewer cover off the hole, freeing the human's hand in the process. "Besalisks have a saying," he said. "When your neighbors trouble you, send your rodents to their nest." Before Skelly could feel relief, Drakka yanked him from the ground and threw him down the hole.

"Thanks, pal!" Skelly called up from the drenched bottom. He was lucky to have good friends who wanted to lend a hand.

CHAPTER TWENTY-FOUR

Having power to wield on the ground might not be so good after all, Sloane thought. Not if authority meant going on mindless tours of local factories. Hailing from the industrial world Ganthel, she had seen quite enough of shipyards and loading docks. She had gone to the Academy to escape a life working at such places.

But Lal Grallik had insisted on extolling the virtues of every little thing at her company. She was leading them now into the new section, built under her watch; when Gorse ran out of thorilide deposits and mining of the moon started, a new intake center had been required. *Next she'll be showing us the janitorial closets,* Sloane thought.

The one surprising thing was that Count Vidian had said little during the tour. Strange, since he was here to issue directives, and if anyone could stop the Besalisk woman in her time-wasting palaver, he could.

A beeping comlink from the rear of the entourage stopped her instead. "Lal!" her security chief husband called out. "There's a report of someone sneaking around the plant. Personnel department."

"That Skelly person?" Vidian asked.

"They didn't see who it was," Gord Grallik said. He pocketed the comlink and turned around. "I'll check it out."

Sloane gestured to her stormtrooper escort. "Go see."

"No, no," the guard said, heading off. "This is my turf."

"It's all our turf," Sloane said. She pointed after the Besalisk. "Follow him!"

. . .

Skelly watched from his hiding place behind a moving conveyer belt. He had been lucky. An old storm drain opened up right next to one of the newer buildings; he'd had to leave his pack at the bottom to climb up, but he'd been able to dash quickly into the building.

Since then, he'd crept around the high-ceilinged facility, waiting for his chance to get to Vidian. Something had happened to cause Gord to leave, and the Imperial captain had sent her stormtroopers along. Skelly continued to creep closer. He could finally hear their conversations, even over the din of the active belts.

"—and you may find this of particular interest, Captain Sloane." It was Lal, speaking from the foot of the ten-meter-tall mass of titanium at the far end of the room. "This is our heavy-duty bulk-loader vehicle, the newest in use on Gorse. You'll find the cab interior similar to what's in some of your own armored walkers: It's the same manufacturer. If you'll step inside, I can show you,"

Skelly saw the women climbing up the metal staircase and into the passenger compartment of the big vehicle. Creeping ahead, he saw Vidian unaccompanied at the bottom, pacing down the long aisle between the conveyer belts out of the women's sight. Skelly's heart pounded. Whether Vidian was alone a moment or a minute, this was his chance!

"You can come out now." The loud voice was the one Skelly had heard on a dozen management recordings. "I can hear you very well, even in a place like this." Count Vidian turned to face him. "The saboteur, I presume."

"That's not what I am," Skelly said, rising from his knees. He dusted himself off. "I'm a whistleblower, Count Vidian. I'm like you—I think the old ways of doing things have to change. I see what people are doing wrong!"

"I see someone doing something wrong."

Skelly was glad Vidian was talking. He'd heard about the man's cybernetic capabilities: Talking to Skelly meant he wasn't calling for help on his internal comlink.

"If you know me," the count continued, "you know I take problems into my own hands to solve."

"Then you want this," Skelly said, pulling the holodisk from his vest. "My research. You've got to stop the blasting on Cynda. You could tear the whole moon apart by mistake!"

"Madness." Vidian kept walking purposefully toward him. "And if it were possible, and the Empire chose to do it, we would certainly not ask your permission."

Skelly's eyes locked on Vidian's macabre visage, and he stumbled backward. *"I'm trying to help you!"*

"Help by dying." With a mighty swat, Vidian smacked the disk away. It clattered to the floor beneath a conveyor belt. The second swing found Skelly's face.

It had not been a good couple of days for snooping around, Hera thought. There was no getting near Vidian during his tour of the landing field, so she'd started in the personnel department, looking to see if Lemuel Tharsa—the person of Imperial interest, according to Zaluna's files—was anyone important. He'd never been an employee, but the man had been to Moonglow: Visitor badges had been supplied to him on several occasions more than twenty years earlier. Before she could learn more, someone had found her. That was the problem with infiltrating a working factory on a day when the Empire came to inspect. No one had called in sick.

Normally, she liked a challenge. But with the Moonglow security team going one direction and the stormtroopers going another, she'd been forced early into the skulker's last resort: the ventilation shafts. Fortunately, the new building's system was less vile than what she'd found in other factories.

Peering down through another grate, she saw the Besalisk security chief again—Gord, Kanan had called him, the administrator's husband. Gord was telling his aides they had to redeem themselves for losing Skelly the day before. Hera felt a momentary pang of guilt for getting the guy in trouble with his wife and the Empire. But it passed as Gord looked up and pointed, evidently noticing the indentation in the vent housing. That's when the blasterfire started.

Enough of this, she thought, scrambling through another tube. It was time to find Vidian.

Sloane emerged from the cab of the bulk-loader to see Vidian a few dozen meters away down on the factory floor, mercilessly pummeling Skelly. She activated the comlink attached to her wrist and pulled her blaster. "Troopers, to me!"

Vidian lifted the intruder and hurled him through the air. Limbs flailed as Skelly hurtled end over end. His flight ended violently against a control console for one of the conveyor belts.

"This is under control," Vidian said, walking casually toward the spot.

Sloane ran down the stairs anyway. She could see that Vidian's opponent was bleeding and clutching his chest. Skelly stood, facing the approaching cyborg in a daze, before desperately scrambling up the side of the control station. Leaping, he reached for the overhang above and tried to pull himself up.

"Stop!" Sloane raised her weapon.

With a burst of energy that startled her, Skelly pulled himself up and onto the moving conveyor belt. Sloane fired—but the belt carried him around a turn, and her blaster bolt only singed his shin.

Sloane looked back to see Lal, horrified and keeping her distance, up on the metal staircase. "Stop all the belts!" the captain yelled. Lal bustled down the steps to the controls.

"Too late," Vidian said, watching. The conveyor belt led back outside, to the loading area. Seeing Sloane's troopers arriving through a side hallway, Vidian pointed. "After him!"

Sloane stepped up to Vidian. "That was him? Skelly?"

Vidian nodded—and started walking back up the aisle.

"He won't get off the grounds. I'll alert everyone," she said.

"I've just done so," Vidian said, his gaze cast low. He was looking for something, she realized, at the foot of one of the conveyor belts. "But you should go supervise. Someone in authority should be out there."

The whole episode puzzled Sloane. "What was Skelly trying to accomplish? What did he want?"

Vidian knelt. He picked up a small object from the floor. "He wanted to give me this," he said. It was a holodisk, Sloane saw. "It's of no consequence. When you find him, tell him I destroyed it. He should die knowing the futility of defying the Empire."

Kanan removed a bolt from the Smoothride's engine for the fourteenth time. Then he proceeded to put it right back.

He didn't stick his neck out for many—hardly any, really!—but there was something about Hera that had kept him from leaving. He was still working out what it was. She was beautiful, of course—but she knew how to play it cool, something he liked a lot. She also seemed reasonably competent—she'd caught on to his ruse back at the cantina right away. All good traits, suited for whatever it was she was playing at. Kanan still didn't quite know what that was, but that was all right. He could play along, as he had many times before when something or someone caught his interest for a while. He had nothing else to do.

Outside, a siren blared. Looking out from beneath the engine bonnet of the hoverbus, Kanan saw several stormtroopers on speeder bikes racing into the security zone and rushing toward the factory gates. Some were headed toward Moonglow's airfield, where *Expedient* sat parked amid a few other vehicles; others were headed for the main facility.

So much for competence, he thought. Looked like Hera was in trouble.

He slammed the engine lid shut and started to turn toward the factory. He didn't have his badge, but he knew a place around the corner where he could scale the fence ringing the aerodrome.

Reaching the spot, Kanan leapt and swung himself over the railing. Hitting the soft ground, he rolled—

—and was met by stormtrooper blasters pointed in his direction.

Harsh lights flooded the corner of the airfield, nearly blinding him. He could just make out a brown-skinned woman in an Imperial captain's uniform stepping toward him.

"And where," she asked sharply, "do you think *you're* going?"

Skelly had closed the sewer grating over his head just in time. He heard the boots of stormtroopers running past, above, even as he struggled to make his way down the iron rungs of the ladder.

Reaching the bottom, he collapsed in the ankle-deep brackish water, battered and broken. His head was bleeding, and his cheekbones felt as if they were moving beneath his skin. He fumbled with his left hand to count his teeth—and felt anguish when he realized how many were gone. He struggled to roll over, certain his ribs had been cracked.

Skelly coughed, bewildered. Vidian was supposed to be different. The rule breaker. The paradigm destroyer. He had reached the heights of both the public and private sectors by ignoring the bureaucracies and their conventions, by listening to everyone and everything, and deciding based on facts.

Yet he had turned out to be just another sadist, as deaf and blind as he had been before the prosthetics.

Seeing his pack nearby, Skelly fought through the pain and dragged his body close to it. There was a medpac in there—and more. Much more.

If words couldn't save the moon, it was time for something else!

CHAPTER TWENTY-FIVE

Besalisks looked miserable in a way that few species could, Vidian thought. With enormous wide mouths and droopy skin sacs hanging beneath, when they frowned, you could read the expression from orbit.

Count Vidian wasn't interested in Lal Grallik's embarrassment over Skelly breaking in, any more than he was interested in her apologies. The encounter with the saboteur had deterred him from his intended schedule. She had taken him without delay to the refinery building: the oldest part of Moonglow, she'd said, dating back to when the firm was part of Introsphere.

She eagerly showed him her updates—and he ignored her obvious disappointment as he just as quickly undid them, stripping away one safety practice after another. Toxic exposure was a small price to pay to meet the Emperor's quota.

Vidian hated being dependent on surface refineries for thorilide: His comet-chaser harvesters required few workers and were closer to the source. But cometary deposits were already microscopic, while the shards coming from Cynda had to be reduced to a refinable size without damaging the material within. Worse, thorilide-bearing comets were exceedingly rare, and the Empire's insatiable demand for materials had nearly swept the galaxy clean of them. It had idled many of the giant harvester vessels Vidian operated—and had given the slackers in this system job security. It would take forever to replicate Gorse's refining infrastructure on Cynda: He would be reliant on fools like Lal Grallik forever.

Thorilide was Vidian's franchise within the Empire—it, and several other strategic materials. Meeting the need for it had brought him power and position. Now he was failing at meeting his Emperor's demands. And Vidian's rivals knew it.

He'd been preoccupied since Baron Danthe's second message, the night before on *Ultimatum*. Danthe wasn't calling to tell him the Emperor was re-raising production quotas, at least, but what he'd said was almost as bad. Another comet-chaser fleet was returning to Calcoraan Depot, having exhausted what was once a rich supply of thorilide-bearing comets.

And worse, Vidian had learned next from his aides that Danthe had been whispering to the Emperor, casting aspersions on Vidian's whole production scheme. The count knew what Danthe wanted: to turn Gorse into another market for his family's manufacturing droids. Vidian had no quarrel with droids, which could in many cases be much more efficient than organics. But he wasn't about to let Danthe colonize an industry that belonged to him. Vidian had taken out his temper on his stateroom, then—but he'd longed to have Danthe's windpipe in his robotic hands.

Grallik led him to the far wall, and a narrow door. Beyond it was another large room with colossal pipes in the ceiling and the long pools cut into the floor. Long and narrow, like harvesting troughs in a farm for sea life. The droids were here, too, some shoving cartloads of crystals into the roiling green liquid, others trolling the pools with long implements.

"We're very proud of this, my lord. This is a prize project of mine—the only automated xenoboric acid bath on Gorse. The crystals from Cynda start here, and the droids do the rest."

Vidian looked down into a pool. Deep and long, a roiling cauldron with an endless appetite for matter. "And how many days do you lose from droids falling in during groundquakes? Organics would keep their balance better."

"Yes, sir. But the fumes and splashing would be dangerous—and of course, if someone went in, that would be much worse than a droid."

"Worse, how? The baths cannot be used for purification until the offending matter is consumed. Droids take much longer to digest."

Lal was struck speechless by that one. Vidian didn't care. He had a call coming in. He switched his ears to comlink mode.

"Commander Chamas aboard *Ultimatum,* my lord. Message from Coruscant."

"Patch it through."

Lero Danthe appeared before his electronic eyes. "My compliments to Count Vidian."

What was left of Vidian's vocal cords stirred in a growl, a vocalization that for him had no electronic counterpart. The young man appeared life-sized, superimposed over Vidian's surroundings: There was no holoprojector here, but it worked basically the same way. "What is it?" he finally said.

The blond baron smiled. "I've just emerged from another series of meetings with top authorities, working at the highest levels on projects of the greatest . . ."

Vidian stopped listening. He was too busy moving his head around, digitally dumping the chattering baron in one pool of acid after another.

" . . . and to make it all possible, the Emperor will require an immediate doubling of thorilide deliveries. Effective immediately."

Vidian gawked. "What? *Doubling?*"

"Correct."

"A doubling of the original quotas."

"No," Danthe said, explaining as if he were talking to a child. "Your quota was increased by half yesterday, remember? So—"

"So it's really a tripling." Vidian felt his ire bubbling over, angrier than any acid bath in the room. "And you didn't argue against this? This target is impossible. The failure will be yours, too."

The baron shrugged. "I'm attached to your administration, my lord, but I serve the Emperor in all things." He paused, before continuing gingerly. "I *did* suggest a number of things I could do to help—but of course those would require putting some of your territories in my hands."

"I'll just bet you did," Vidian snarled. "This isn't finished, Danthe!"

"So what should I tell the Emperor?"

"That I'll succeed! Vidian out!"

Vidian seethed. This was deception on a grand scale. Vidian had never played games of court well; it was his biggest weakness. The other aristocrats knew it, and one had finally pounced. He was undermined, completely and totally, in a way that he hadn't experienced since years earlier, when he was a different person—

Lal stood near one of the acid baths and looked back in puzzlement. "Are you all right, my lord? You—er, haven't moved for a while."

Vidian wore no emotion, as always. The words came from his neck. "I need triple the output from this factory, immediately."

Lal laughed out loud. Immediately embarrassed, she covered her wide mouth with two of her hands. "I'm sorry. You can't be serious?"

Vidian turned and began stalking toward her. "I am always serious."

She stepped back, nervously. "We can't do that. We were struggling to meet the original Imperial targets."

"Which you never met, either." Vidian stepped up to her. Lal shook, eyeing him fearfully. "Can you meet these targets?"

"N-n-no."

"Then what good are you?" Vidian's arms lanced out, shoving Lal with his open palms. She tumbled backward into one of the boiling troughs.

She screamed, the acid bubbling all around her. "Help! P-p-please!"

Vidian turned and found one of the tending poles, constructed of material designed to withstand the chemical abuse. But instead of fishing her out, he jabbed at her, pushing Lal farther in.

"I am helping," Vidian said, electronic eyes shining. "I need this vat returned to operation. Now hurry up and dissolve."

Hera heard the scream.

She had been staying a step ahead of the Besalisk security chief by entering the refinery and running among the rafters. There were plenty of pipes and catwalks providing routes for one as nimble as she. She'd been hoping to double back, to finish looking for what she'd entered for—when she'd heard the cry. Horrible, unlike anything she'd ever known.

She couldn't help but run toward it.

When she arrived, it was too late. The body was visible from her high vantage point—barely—in the depths of the turbulent pool, but there was no way to get down there without falling in herself. Count Vidian stood at the edge with a tending pole. It had to be him; no one else looked like that. He watched the pool for a moment before dropping the pole, turning, and heading off.

Hera saw a place where she could safely leap down, up ahead. She started working her way toward it.

But Gord Grallik arrived first—and broke her heart.

CHAPTER TWENTY-SIX

On the refinery floor, Gord Grallik wailed.

The security chief had rushed into the room, still looking for Hera. She was heading down the stairs herself when he stopped between the frothing acid pools and looked down. Hera had already seen from above that the four-armed figure in the acid was unmistakably Besalisk.

"Lal!" Gord scrambled around, looking for one of the acid-proof prods. By the time Hera reached the floor, he had given up. He turned to the pool, ready to dive into the acid bath and save his wife.

"Don't!" Hera called out. Skidding to a stop so as not to knock them both in, she grabbed at the security chief's left arms. "It's too late!"

Gord struggled. "I've got to!"

Hera clung to him desperately. She didn't even know if he was aware of her as he struggled to step toward the pool. He greatly outweighed her—and yet she was using every bit of her strength to keep him from jumping. *"You . . . can't . . . do this!"*

At last, Gord stopped. She didn't know if he'd finally registered her presence, realizing she would fall in, too—or if he'd simply seen again what was left of Lal. So little. *"No,"* he said in a low voice. He fell to his knees. "No."

The Twi'lek hung on to his arms. "I'm sorry," she said. She was trying to pull him back from the edge, without much success.

Gord looked at her—and anger blazed in his eyes. "Did you do this?"

"No! I swear I didn't. It was Vidian!" Hera fell away from him but did not run. "Check the security monitors. You'll see!"

Besalisk hands grabbed her. With Hera in tow and murder in his eyes, Gord moved quickly with her to the security control station at the far wall. "I'll see," he said.

Vidian stood outside the refinery and looked up at the moon. He'd killed another tour guide, yes, but there really wasn't any sense in continuing with this tour, or any other. Moonglow was the best-case operator on Gorse. Even if the Empire seized direct control of the factories—a tool in his kit that he found to be of mixed effectiveness—there was no way to make the Emperor's new quotas.

And the first deliveries were due in a week.

Vidian turned and punched the wall. His hand smashed into the permacrete, leaving an indentation. Baron Danthe was at fault for this—a supposed underling, turning him into just another worker scrambling to meet an ultimatum from above. He already knew there was no way to find enough ready thorilide in his territory, or anyone else's. Not without tearing the moon completely apart . . .

Vidian stopped. He played back what his eyes and ears had recorded from earlier, the rantings of the madman Skelly.

"You've got to stop the blasting on Cynda. You could tear the whole moon apart by mistake!"

Remembering, he reached into his pocket. The holodisk was there, the one he had planned to destroy.

Vidian strode purposefully toward a nearby office building. Yes, looking at it would almost certainly be a waste of time for a man that did not waste time. The fact he considered it at all was a true measure of the desperate situation he faced.

Sloane wasn't the first Imperial captain Kanan had met. But she was certainly the best-looking—even if she did insist on pulling that wonderful black hair back beneath the little hat. One of her aides was shining a light into his face, entirely unnecessary under the light from the moon.

"They say you got into the security zone because you were ferrying miners to work," the woman said. "If you're a bus driver, why were you trying to enter the factory?"

"Heading to pick up my pay." Hands manacled behind his back, Kanan flashed a smile at her. "If you want, once I get it I can show you the town."

Sloane's brown eyes narrowed. "Wait a second. I know you! You're that pilot from the explosives hauler. *The mouth*."

"You've got a name for me," Kanan said, grinning. "That's great. I knew you couldn't just fly off. You came all the way down here to see me?"

Sloane stepped forward, reached around to grab his ponytail, and yanked. "Let's not be giving me jobs to do, pilot," she said, forcing him to the ground. "This little act of yours might work with some. Me, I might press you into service and set you to maintaining trash compactors. Or shove you into one!"

"Okay, okay." Kanan shrugged against the stormtrooper's hold. "But if you know I'm a pilot, you know I work here."

"With no pass for the grounds?"

"Lal Grallik knows me. Ask her."

"Making friends?" Kanan heard a now-familiar voice from behind Sloane. The captain spun without releasing him, wrenching his neck in the process. Hera stepped forward from the factory, dangling his pass in her hands. "You left your ID in the plant, buddy."

The Imperials shone their light on Hera. Sloane studied her before looking back to him. Kanan nodded, to the extent he could with the captain holding on to his hair. "Told you."

Sloane released Kanan with a shove, knocking him backward and down into the mud. She turned on Hera. "And where's your badge?"

Hera grinned. "Well, I've got to have it. How could I be in here, otherwise?"

Sloane looked to the sky and growled with frustration. "I've had enough of you people. I think we'll take you all in for—"

"*Sloane!*"

The captain checked her comlink. "Count Vidian," she said. "We're still running down Skelly—and any accomplices."

"Forget them," Vidian replied.

"My lord?"

"The inspection. Everything. Forget it all. I've seen enough here. I have a new strategy that will serve the Emperor. We need to return to *Ultimatum* right away. Gather your team and meet me at the shuttle."

Sloane acknowledged the order and deactivated her comlink. She gestured to a stormtrooper to remove Kanan's handcuffs. Another returned his blaster and holster. "Your lucky day," Sloane said.

"It sure is," Kanan said, nodding to Hera. "I've got the two of you here."

Hera rushed forward and grabbed his arm. "Thank you, Captain. We'll be going." She began pushing Kanan toward the open gate, under Sloane's icy glare. "Sorry to have disturbed you."

"Yeah, good luck with your inspection," Kanan said, before Hera forcibly shoved him out the employee gate.

Hera hustled Kanan around the corner and back to the hoverbus. She seemed perturbed. "You really don't know when to quit, do you?"

Kanan shrugged. "Hey, it worked, didn't it?" He wiped the mud off his trousers. "Being hostile or closemouthed just sets them off. The way to get rid of Imperials is to be so happy to see them that they're thrilled when you're gone. Some Imperials, anyway."

Hera put up her hands. "We don't have time for this. Something horrible happened in there, and—" She paused and looked down, choking up a little. He realized he hadn't seen her looking anything but fully in control before. Now she looked spent.

"Hey," he said, touching her wrist. "You're not kidding. Something bad?"

"Vidian killed the administrator."

"What, Lal?" Kanan was shocked. "He killed her? Why?"

"Because he could," she said, looking up and staring into his eyes. "Her husband saw it and ran off searching for Vidian. And it sounds from that comlink call like Vidian's up to something else!"

"Right about over there," Kanan said, pointing to the Imperial shuttle. Across the muddy boulevard from it, Moonglow's main gate opened. Vidian appeared there, talking with the vessel's flight crew. Sloane and her stormtroopers joined him.

"We've got to follow them," Hera said.

"I can't follow a shuttle in a hoverbus!"

"It's a Mark Six Smoothride," she said. "It'll fly!"

"About a zillion years ago," Kanan said. He looked back to see Vidian marching purposefully along the planking toward the shuttle. Sloane lingered at the gate with the others, evidently giving orders related to her departure.

And then, his eye tracing the path back to the Lambda, he saw something wedged beneath the plank nearest the ship. It looked like a small pouch, several meters away from what appeared to a sewer grating.

An *open* sewer grating.

Kanan didn't need the Force to tell him to grab Hera. *"Get down!"*

The night lit up in Shaketown. The Imperial shuttle exploded, sending blazing debris in all directions. In the street, the shock wave caught Vidian, hurling him bodily into the factory's outer fence even as a fireball blazed overhead.

Kanan caught only a glimpse of the cyborg's fate as, Hera's shoulders in his gloved hands, he dived with her behind the Smoothride. Metallic debris rocketed in all directions, some of it slamming thunderously into the hoverbus. Speeder bikes parked earlier by the reinforcements went spinning wildly; Kanan saw one impale itself in the fencing behind him.

The din subsided. Once certain Hera was all right, Kanan drew his blaster and looked cautiously around the vehicle. Up the way, Vidian was on his knees but alive, his reinforced frame evidently giving him some protection. But the street before the factory was a blazing crater—

and the block of buildings behind it, including poor Drakka's Diner, was now afire. Kanan's instinct was to run toward it, to see if the Besalisk cook was all right.

But something else caught his eye first. A dark figure, scrambling out from the sewer grating he'd seen. The spot was amid the flames but untouched at the moment—and the figure was limping quickly along with a large pack on his back. *Skelly!*

Finding a functioning Imperial speeder bike, Skelly took one look back. Then he mounted it and was gone.

CHAPTER TWENTY-SEVEN

Hera caught her breath as she reached the third-story rooftop. The buildings across the boulevard from Moonglow's headquarters weren't tall, but they all had ladders or some other kind of fire escapes. Everyone knew to expect groundquakes on Gorse. This was another story.

From a concealed spot, she looked down into the street with amazement. The Imperial vessel was still burning below, destroyed by someone they'd hurt. It was something Hera had expected to see one day, something she'd always believed was coming. Just not this soon, and not this way. She wasn't sure what had driven Skelly to do it, but he certainly had been the one responsible, based on what Kanan had seen.

Hera hadn't wanted to linger at ground level after the blast. The street looked like a war zone, and the assassination attempt was sure to send the Imperials over the edge. But she'd helped with the search-and-rescue for as long as she dared, and had to scout the best way out of the security-cordoned neighborhood. Only Kanan had any kind of permission to be on the ground anyway, and he'd hung around down there, trying to free people. She thought well of him that he'd do that. It went very much against the freewheeler mold he seemed to want to fit into.

In truth, she was still reeling from the moment in the factory when Gord Grallik had viewed the recording of Vidian killing his wife. A typical tough security guy, yet he had watched the murder as if his world were crumbling around him. It still wrenched at her heart to remember it.

But that wasn't the worst part, she now realized as she looked down at the street. Vidian, singed but apparently intact, was being hustled from the scene by his escort when Gord appeared at the gate. The Besalisk rushed forward amid the flaming embers only to be stopped by the stormtroopers. She couldn't hear him from this distance, but he was appealing to them, begging them. To arrest Vidian, she supposed. A Moonglow aide handed Gord a datapad: Hera assumed it was the images from the security cam. The frantic Besalisk showed it to one trooper after another, but they would not let him pass.

Hera didn't want to watch—there was nothing at all she could do. Not here, not now. But she made herself. Gord tried to follow Vidian anyway, only to be grabbed by the troopers. It took four of them to restrain the heavy-shouldered security chief: one for each arm.

Then they beat him. This was justice in the Empire.

When the stormtroopers parted, Hera saw Gord crawling back toward Moonglow's gate. She blinked away a tear of anger. Yes, she needed to see these things, to remind her what she was fighting for.

Hera squinted to see through the smoky darkness where Vidian had gone. She spotted him and Sloane in intense discussion, heading between a line of flanking stormtroopers on the way toward—

No, Kanan's not going to like that.

"Are you kidding me?" Having finished his search and joined Hera on the roof, Kanan stared down at the empty spot on the street. "I can't believe this. They stole the hoverbus!"

"I think they call it *commandeering on official business*," Hera said, crouching at the roof edge and pointing east. Kanan saw the outline of the hoverbus bobbing far up the lane. "I'm sure they're headed to the Imperial spaceport to get another shuttle."

Kanan frowned. "Yeah, well, wait until they find the bathroom door's stuck." He flicked wet ashes from his tunic. He'd found Drakka pinned behind his freezer unit; it had taken long minutes to extricate him. Then the cook had stormed out, intent on giving the Imperials a piece of his mind about his destroyed business. Kanan could see from his position that the conversation wasn't going very well, but he had his own problems. "The spaceport's in Highground. How am I supposed to get over there?" It was ten kilometers away.

"I'm more interested in getting out of *here*," Hera said, rising. "An attempt's been made on an envoy of the Emperor—everyone's a suspect. We've got to get out of this neighborhood before half the Empire shows up!" She turned away from the street side of the roof. "Maybe back down those alleys to the south?"

"It's Okadiah's bus," Kanan said. "I can't just forget about it." This was the whole problem with making friends, he did not say: They made it impossible to be truly free.

He looked back across Broken Boulevard—now a more descriptive term than usual—and saw a lumbering gray hovertruck departing Moonglow's loading dock. "Hey, wait," he said, grabbing Hera's wrist before she could leave. "I think we can solve both problems at once."

He pointed to the vehicle. "That's full of refined thorilide." Even trespass, murder, and sabotage couldn't stop thorilide production, it seemed: Every six minutes another one of the transports departed the plant. "It's headed—"

"—straight to the Imperial spaceport," Hera said. "I caught that on my reconnoiter yesterday."

Their eyes met—and a heartbeat later they were running along the rooftops. Hera was fast as she was lithe, hurdling obstacles and leaping one gap after another. Every so often, she looked back to see if Kanan was keeping up.

"I'm fine," he said, keeping a few steps back. "Just trying not to run into you."

She smiled and leapt the next opening. He followed suit.

Reaching the end of the row of flats, they found a door and scrambled down a staircase. Catching their breaths in the doorway, they stopped in time to see the hovertruck move up the street toward them. A stormtrooper waved the vehicle and its golden chauffeur droid past.

As soon as the stormtrooper turned his head, Kanan and Hera bolted toward the approaching truck. Kanan leapt to the running board of the passenger side.

"I am sorry," the droid said. "Riders are not allowed on the—"

Hera, now hanging outside the other door, flicked a switch on the droid's neck, shutting him off. Kanan scrambled inside the cab, grabbed for the control yoke, and ducked. The vehicle executed a wide left turn past the last stormtrooper checkpoint; the sentry never saw the woman hanging outside. Adroitly, Hera opened the door and bumped the robot out of the way.

"I prefer driving," she said, reaching for the controls. "Nothing against you."

Kanan closed the passenger door and stretched his legs. "Sweetheart, you can drive me anywhere." He glanced back at the mess Shaketown had become. "As long as it's away from here!"

Hera had been scarcely more talkative than the deactivated droid, Kanan thought. She'd said nothing about what had gone on in the plant before she'd found Lal.

He didn't know Lal's husband well, other than that he had a short fuse and a big blaster collection. And something else. "That guy lived for Lal," he said.

"I could tell. It was rough."

Watching her, Kanan thought that must be an understatement. "Well, you found out one thing about Vidian. He's evil in a can."

"Being evil doesn't stop you with the Empire. It helps." She sighed. "I didn't even get near him this time—but I guess I found out what I came to Gorse to learn. The secret to Denetrius Vidian's efficiency is murder."

"And where does that get you?"

"Nowhere I wasn't before." She shook her head. "And all I was able to find about Tharsa was that he'd visited there a few times a long time ago. I couldn't find out anything else. First, Gord showed up, then they all started running around looking for Skelly." Guiding the hovertruck around a corner, she sighed. "I don't know what Skelly thinks he can accomplish this way. This loose-cannon stuff—it doesn't get you anywhere."

"And where are *you* trying to get?" He looked at her keenly. "I thought you were going to ditch me after you did your little break-in. And you just said your big mission is done. But here you are."

She rolled her eyes. "I'm helping you get your hoverbus back."

"Uh-huh." Kanan chuckled.

"No, no, it's the least I can do," Hera said. "You were willing to come back inside, looking for me. Unnecessary—and nearly trouble for you. But appreciated."

"Well, you're the only person on this planet I'd take that chance for." That should tell her something, he thought.

"I'm not sure I believe that. You went back to help that Besalisk cook—and Okadiah told me back in the bus about you saving him from Vidian." She smiled. "You even saved Skelly at the cantina."

He put up his hands. "Hey, everyone makes mistakes!"

"Well, we'll see," she said, and left it at that. Kanan liked the look he saw from her. It said she'd come to think he was worth keeping an eye on.

Looking out at the buildings whizzing by, Kanan laughed. "Everything that goes into thorilide—all the security—and here we've just driven off with a truckload."

"We're taking it right where it's supposed to go," she said. "And it's not like we'd find anyone to sell it to."

Kanan shook his head. "You know, I don't even know what the junk is used for."

"Thorilide?" Hera asked. "It's used in granular solid-state shock absorption. They use it on Star Destroyers to keep turbolaser turrets in place after firing."

"Loose cannons again!" Kanan chortled. "They're going to this much trouble for it?"

"They've got a lot of cannons!" Hera's eyes widened as she considered it. "A Star Destroyer requires the use of sixteen million individual components, twenty-seven thousand of which are only produced in a single system, like Gorse." She looked at him, her face animated with passion. "That's why the Emperor needs an Empire, Kanan. It's like a space slug, whose only function is to stay alive. It's got to consume, and consume, and consume."

"You're starting to sound like Skelly."

"He's not all wrong," she said, guiding the hovertruck into Highground. "But he's definitely not all right."

Skelly had taken the speeder bike over rooftops to reach Highground, flying low over their surfaces to avoid any tracking of air traffic. With most of the Imperial attention on getting police vehicles to Shaketown, Skelly had guessed that relatively little attention was being paid to the landing fields. Even so, he knew he couldn't simply fly the bike over the retaining wall. And he was reluctant to dismount, because every step he took off the bike caused him pain.

But now, in the dark at the far eastern end of the compound, his war experience subverting barricades served him again. He'd seen during flights to Cynda that the terrain at Highground had deep drainage ditches leading off to the low side of the compound. It was there, outside the wall in the darkness, that he found a culvert large enough to accommodate both him and the speeder bike. The bars guarding the pipe were no match for the variety of explosives he carried in his pack. It amused him that the same techniques he'd used to mine Cynda for the Empire were now getting him onto its base.

A few muffled blasts later, he was hunched painfully low against the spine of the speeder bike, letting it carry him and his bag of revenge through the tunnel. Inside the compound, he continued to fly the vehicle low through the drainage canals separating the landing areas. The lights here all pointed upward; if anyone had bothered to look down, the sight of his head poking out of the ground and gently sailing along might have given someone pause.

But no one saw. Now, in the shadow of the spaceport's control tower, he waited, padding at his swollen face with swabs from the medpac. He watched the ground transport arrival area, where every few minutes another droid-driven hovercraft appeared bearing thorilide for the waiting Imperial freighters.

This spaceport was it, he thought. The last step before the beauty of Cynda, crushed down and refined, left for Calcoraan Depot and distribution to all the Empire's insane shipbuilding projects. It made Skelly sick to see it.

Time passed. For a minute, he worried that he'd gambled wrong. He'd assumed that Vidian, having lost one ride offworld, would come here next. But shortly the gate opened to allow in—*Okadiah's hoverbus?*

Skelly blinked when he saw it. What was it doing here? Then he saw a group of stormtroopers exit it, followed by Vidian and the Imperial captain. No wonder he had beaten them here, he thought. It would take a genius of a pilot to get the Smoothride to beat a determined person on a speeder bike.

He felt his ribs shifting painfully as he huddled back against the outer wall of the control tower. Skelly was running on adrenaline, now—his own, and stimulus shots from the medpac. But he was undaunted.

He'd missed Vidian before. He wouldn't do it again.

CHAPTER TWENTY-EIGHT

Count Vidian looked up past the control tower. *Cudgel* was descending from space, dispatched from the Star Destroyer to return him to orbit. He didn't want to waste another moment on Gorse. Staying on the planet was unnecessary to his plans.

And now his plans had changed. He didn't have time for the people of Gorse to shuttle back and forth, mining their moon. Even his most extreme notions, erecting dormitories on Cynda and forcing laborers to move there, would take too long. But he now was looking at another alternative—provided by the strangest source imaginable.

Skelly was deranged, just another shell-shocked Clone Wars veteran. But a quick look at the material suggested that he might have stumbled onto something useful. Vidian would need to consult with his staff and *Ultimatum*'s experts to be sure.

The commandeered hoverbus was the least efficient means of reaching the spaceport he could imagine; even Sloane's surviving shuttle flight crew hadn't been able to get it more than a meter off the ground. But he'd used the time well, explaining to Sloane his intentions. She'd reacted to his plans with caution, characteristic of the navy. He hadn't been able to find an iota of imagination in the entire service. Still, Sloane was young and ambitious—and even now, she was suggesting solutions.

"The stores on *Ultimatum* should have what you need, my lord. There's no need to involve anyone on Gorse."

"Excellent."

. . .

The gates swung wide to admit the thorilide hovertruck. The droid—reactivated but muted to prevent its nattering on about its dislike of hitchhikers—guided the vehicle inside as it was programmed to do. No sentry saw Hera and Kanan, ducked down as they were. Within moments, the big vehicle was in the parking area, queued to have its cargo placed on the freighters beyond. Poking his head up, Kanan saw that the line would shortly bring them alongside the parked hoverbus.

That was a relief. He figured he was due to catch a break.

As he dropped back down next to Hera, he chuckled. "It's always an adventure with you, huh?"

Hera smiled. "Yeah, and we're just going to pick up your ride."

"I'm carrying Okadiah's chauffeur license—I should be able to just drive back out," Kanan said. "I don't think I could've just walked up and asked them for it without them wasting my time again. And I've got places to—"

Seeing her expressionless face, he stopped. "Wait," Kanan said. "You didn't come here with me because you wanted to chat, or save me from impound hassles. You're going to go sneaking around checking on Vidian some more!"

Hera responded with a gentle smile.

"This is ridiculous!" He pointed back through the windshield at the Imperial shuttle, settling in for a landing. "Vidian's leaving. What more do you need to know?"

"Something brought him here," she said. "And something's making him leave early."

"Try Skelly and his bomb!"

Hera shook her head. "That's not it, Kanan. I saw him through the electrobinoculars as he was leaving. He's—different. Something's changed. He's got a new mission."

"How do you read the expression of a human droid?" Kanan looked to the floor in aggravation as the vehicle shuddered to a stop. Hera's was the old Jedi way of doing things, he remembered. Master Billaba or

Obi-Wan or someone would get an idea in their heads and chase it all over creation, hiding in closets and creeping around ventilation shafts, spying.

Even when there was plainly nothing to see, as here. Kanan sat up cautiously, took a peek outside, and opened the door on the left side of the hoverbus. He slipped out onto the gravel surface, shielded from the Imperials' sight by the Smoothride. A moment later, Hera lightly touched the ground behind him.

"Look," he said, turning around to face her in the shadows. The space between the vehicles was narrow, and it brought them close together. "I travel alone. But I think you're fun, when you're not running off doing something outlandish." He pointed with his thumb to the hoverbus. "I'm going to take this back to Okadiah's and then I'm heading for the public spaceport. You can come along, or let me hitch a ride on whatever this ship is you say you've got. But I'm done sneaking around here—and I think you should be, too."

There wasn't anything else to say. Obi-Wan's warning and the Emperor's wrath had made him hide part of who he was. But he wouldn't live his daily life skulking about just to have a woman's company—or to support her cause, any cause. That wasn't who he was. Kanan began working his way along the left side of the hoverbus, feeling glad it had open doorways on both sides. He'd wait for Vidian to leave, and then get back to his regularly scheduled life. Either Hera would see sense, or she wouldn't.

He paused to look back. Hera was at the tail end of the hoverbus, trying to peek around at the Imperials. He shook his head. *Guess not,* he thought. *It's a shame. She was something.* Kanan put his foot on the doorstep—

—and heard shouts from the other side of the vehicle. Alarmed, he looked back Hera, but she had already turned and was running in his direction. "What is it?"

"Move!" Without a further word, she shoved him into the hoverbus. He fell onto the floor, and she on top of him. Pinned, he instantly began to formulate a response about how she couldn't live without him—when he caught a sideways glance of what was outside the door on the right-hand side of the vehicle opposite him, in the direction of the Imperials.

Vidian, Sloane, and several stormtroopers were fifty meters away, running away from the *Lambda*-class shuttle that had just landed. In the moonlight, he could just make out the sight of something being hurled toward it, from the shadows of the nearby control tower.

Krakka-boom! For the second time in a little over an hour, the populated side of Gorse saw what seemed to be the light of day as an Imperial shuttle blew apart. Kanan shielded his eyes from the flash—and then held on as the shockwave rocked the Smoothride. When he looked again, he saw debris raining all across the landing field—and then he heard it, as parts of the Lambda slammed against the right fuselage and roof of the hoverbus.

As the din subsided, Hera relaxed her hold on Kanan. "I think that's it," she said. She rose, and he followed. Carefully, they crept out of the right-hand side of the vehicle for a better look.

Fiery smoke blotted out the moon. But they could see that Vidian and all his companions, including Sloane, had been flattened by the blast, some hurled several meters. Vidian was still moving, Kanan saw, but he was definitely reeling.

"Come on," Kanan said, grabbing Hera's arm.

"Yeah, I think so!"

They'd already been bystanders to one attack. They wouldn't be able to walk out of another. But before they could reach the doorway, Kanan heard a high, whizzing whine coming at him from behind—the direction of the explosion. *More debris, now?* It didn't matter. This time, *he* threw *her* down—

—right as a mass of metal screamed just over their heads. Something slammed headlong into the hoverbus, shattering more of its windows. Kanan shielded his and Hera's heads with his arms.

When Kanan finally looked up, he saw something that rendered him speechless. It was a speeder bike, the kind Imperial stormtroopers rode.

Or part of it: Its long nose had shot through one of the hoverbus windows, halting its flight and effectively impaling the larger vehicle.

Outside the hoverbus, hanging upside down from the deeply lodged bike, was Skelly, his right hand holding one of the handlebars in a death grip. He looked as if he'd been through one of Okadiah's blenders. His battered body dangled limply from the frame, and a big backpack hung precariously around his midsection, about to fall.

A subsidiary explosion went off in the field behind them—but Kanan could only look at Skelly, dazzled. The bomber opened his eyes and looked back, wearily recognizing him.

"K-k-k . . . ," Skelly said, his face swollen, his mouth bloodied. "Kanan."

"What?"

"The pack. Grab it."

Not thinking, Kanan took it and then looked inside. "It's full of bombs!"

"Not good," Hera said, grabbing his arm. Across the field, emergency crews were racing from the control tower to put out the blaze, even as Vidian stood up. Vidian hadn't spotted Kanan and the others yet; there was too much flaming debris between them. But Kanan could see the cyborg's creepy glowing eyes as he scanned the area. Fresh stormtroopers ran to the blast scene from the control tower, and several of Vidian's companions rose, looking for their weapons. Overhead, a siren blared—and the ground was suddenly awash with searchlights cutting through the smoke.

"There! At the hoverbus!" Vidian yelled, his voice artificially amplified to its loudest level.

Kanan turned toward the door of the long hoverbus, three meters away, only to see a blaster shot strike just outside the door frame. Out of the corner of his eye, he could see at least a dozen stormtroopers taking positions behind pieces of the wreckage. No one had a bead on him yet, but the vehicle was another story. Hera knew it too. Like him, she was facing the hoverbus—but while she had her hand on her blaster, she hadn't drawn it. She shook her head at him. "Wrong place, wrong time."

Story of my life, Kanan thought. In a nearly autonomic reaction, he let the bag with Skelly's explosives slip from his hands and to the ground. Nothing exploded, which he almost thought was a shame.

"Put your hands behind your heads!" came Vidian's amplified call from behind.

Above and to Kanan's left, Skelly slipped off the bike, his hand finally having given out. He landed with a thud on the gravel.

"Skelly, I'm going to die," Kanan said, glaring down at the man on the ground. "But I'm going to kill you first!"

CHAPTER TWENTY-NINE

When the other guy brought an army, it was best not to argue. Kanan kept his face toward the hoverbus. He could hear blasters being prepared, with more stormtroopers starting to move from cover to cover, working their way across the airfield.

Hera hadn't budged, either, but he could see her thinking. With the smoke blotting out the moon, the Imperials hadn't seen either of their faces clearly yet, but that would change when he turned to run—or fight. And the latter option seemed impossible. They hadn't taken a shot at an Imperial in all the day's chaos, and he didn't want to start now. The odds were just too long.

Skelly sat a meter or so away from the bag, eyeing it. Vidian, with his sharp eyes, noticed. *"Don't touch it!"*

Kanan glanced again at Hera. *It was a good run,* he said to himself. He started to put his hands behind his head.

"Put down your weapons!" called out another voice from behind and to Kanan's right.

"We're not holding any!" Kanan yelled.

"I didn't mean you!" For a moment, the voice seemed strangely familiar to Kanan—until he realized it *was* familiar. Kanan and Hera looked to the right to see Gord walking purposefully from the direction of the cargo intake facility. *"I'm here for Vidian!"*

The bulky security chief was bruised, Kanan saw: Hera had told him about Gord's earlier beating. The Besalisk was also armed to the teeth, prepared to deal death with all four hands. He had come the same way they had, Kanan realized, on one of the other thorilide transports. He'd never seen the security chief looking so serious—or threatening.

"Count Vidian! My name is Gord Grallik, security chief for Moonglow. You are under arrest for the murder of our supervisor—and my wife!"

"On whose authority?" That was Sloane; she sounded stunned.

"Mine," Gord said. "Gorse City has a jail. You'll be treated fairly—more fairly than you deserve!"

"Enough of this," Vidian yelled. "Blast him!"

Gord shot first. And second. And third. Moving with startling speed, the Besalisk peppered the stormtroopers with blasterfire. The Imperials' defensive positions protected them against the hoverbus, but not against anyone coming from his angle off to their right. Before anyone fired a shot in return, Gord hurled something with his fourth hand—a sonic grenade. It detonated amid the group of stormtroopers nearest him, emitting a shriek that sent them reeling.

Hera, pulling her hands from behind her head, looked at Kanan. "Are we thinking the same thing?"

Kanan nodded. "Run!"

They began to move toward the hoverbus—only to both hit the ground as attentive stormtroopers fired at the doorway. As crimson shots struck the gravel ahead of them, Kanan scrambled for the only cover they could find: a chunk of the Imperial shuttle's sublight ion engine, which earlier had hit the hoverbus roof and rolled off.

"Time to join the party," Hera said, whipping out her blaster. She leaned over the metallic barrier, took quick aim, and fired. One of the snipers stopped shooting at the hoverbus.

Kanan looked at her and drew his weapon. He'd done his best to avoid such situations—but this jam wouldn't let go of him, no matter what. *Fine, then!* "Let's dance!"

Kanan fired. Off to the north, Gord was still letting it rip, somehow shrugging off a glancing shot to his left leg. Hera and Kanan supplied him with cross fire, driving the Imperials to move Vidian and Sloane back to a more protected position.

Continuing to shoot, Kanan grew concerned about being outflanked on his right or attacked from behind. Things looked all clear to the south, he saw. And behind him, the hoverbus—

—was *moving*!

Kanan's eyes darted to the ground, where Skelly had lain. The bag with the bombs was gone. He nudged Hera. "The bus! It's being stolen again!"

Imperial blaster shots glancing off it ineffectually, the hoverbus rose a meter into the air—and then slammed into the ground again, nearly tipping over. A mechanical groan sounded above the gunfire, and the vessel lifted once more. But only part of it: One back corner steadfastly refused to lift, and the long vehicle dragged it across the ground as it tried to accelerate.

Hera squinted back through the dust. "Is that Skelly driving?"

Kanan yelled back. "I wouldn't call it that!" Skelly was trying—probably with one hand and certainly in a mad panic—to make the Smoothride fly, something Kanan knew it couldn't do anymore. But at least the vehicle was taking the fire that had been meant for them.

All at once the rear corner of the hovercraft yanked free from the ground. In response, the rest of it lurched, starting a wild sideways swing in their direction. Kanan yelled, *"Look out!"*

He and Hera went flat as ten thousand kilograms of metal careened just over their heads, grinding and snapping away the debris that had been their cover.

Kanan raised his head to see Gord making a running charge across the open ground toward the Imperials—wild-eyed and completely heedless of the hoverbus, now dipping low as it swung widely in an arc toward him.

"Gord, look out!" There was no way for the Besalisk to hear him in the chaos. The spinning bus swept through Gord's position, knocking him off balance and causing him to lose two of his blasters. Gord scrambled

for them, only to take a glancing blaster shot to the chest. That provided the opportunity Vidian needed. He leapt from cover toward Gord. The dazed Besalisk raised his meaty arms, ready to put up a struggle. But Vidian charged forward, knocking his attacker to the ground.

Kanan had no shot. He winced as he saw Vidian raise his fists—and lower them, again and again. But before he could think again about the security chief's fate, the wayward hoverbus completed another revolution—and was heading back for him and Hera. She saw it, too, and was already on her feet, holstering her blaster. "Come on!"

Heedless of the blaster bolts coming his way, Kanan bolted from the ground and followed. The Smoothride yawed wildly toward them with more altitude than it had before. Hera made a running leap for its underside. Kanan followed a second later.

Hera was rewarded for acting first. She had hold of one of the support struts that made up the hoverbus's chassis. Kanan, meanwhile, had only managed to hook his right hand around one of the rings attached to the rear turbofan—putting him right in the path of the straining engine's exhaust.

The hovercraft pitched and fell again, nearly scraping the hangers-on away against a horizontal obstacle. Kanan realized only afterward that it was the outer wall of the Imperial spaceport. They were on their way—somewhere!

From behind the chunk of shuttle wing she'd been using for cover, Sloane watched in stupefaction as the lumbering metal machine improbably crested the permacrete barrier. Her comlink was already in her hand. "Everyone after that thing, now!"

Climbing out from behind the twisted wedge of metal, she dashed toward her charge. "Count Vidian! Count Vidian!"

"Yelling is unnecessary." His voice filled her with relief, for a change. But just for a moment. Vidian rose from the corpse of the Besalisk, his regal outfit bloodied and torn. "I live, no thanks to your forces. Another bomb—and now these attackers. You call this security?"

Sloane fought the impulse to argue. It was the Imperial Army garrison's responsibility to secure the landing area, not hers—but now wasn't the time to quibble. The chase was on. Squat gray Imperial troop transports loaded with stormtroopers were already heading out the west gate, and she had more than that in mind.

"Order the local authorities to put up roadblocks at every intersection—keep them penned into Highground!" she called on the comlink. "Contact ground and satellite surveillance—make sure we know where the vehicle is at all times!"

And across the tarmac, far from the blast site, she saw something she *did* have direct control over: two TIE fighters, parked and waiting. "Get those in the sky," she called out to the spaceport chief.

"Right away, Captain!"

"There were others with the saboteur," Vidian said, looking back at officers heading for the TIEs. "That makes this a conspiracy. I want Skelly shot on sight, but bring the others to me!"

Sloane hadn't gotten a good look at the two who'd been facing the hoverbus, and she doubted anyone else had. One of the traitors had shot out the one surveillance cam covering the area; that someone had known what he or she was doing. But Skelly should stand out—and they wouldn't get far in that monstrosity they were driving.

"I want those renegades," she called out to the troopers. "Now!"

CHAPTER THIRTY

The way to control your fear of being on a ledge, Master Billaba had said, *is not to think about it until you are off the ledge.* Even at the time, Kanan had thought that advice could go two different ways. *Off the ledge* could mean you were safely inside—or it could mean you were plummeting. A lot of Jedi adages seemed to have that problem: They always assumed everything would work out.

Kanan wasn't assuming that at the moment. The underside of a land-speeder normally wouldn't have offered any clearance for a hanger-on—and the Smoothride, while designed for flight, had been little more than a landspeeder for years. Taking it more than a meter off the ground sent the thing wobbling crazily off axis to the left and right. Okadiah's drivers all knew that.

But Skelly wasn't one of Okadiah's drivers. "Look out!" Kanan called forward to Hera as the machine lost altitude. Hera kicked her legs up before they brushed the mud-covered street below. Kanan, taller, felt the front of his boots smack the surface.

Kanan strained, pulling himself upward so he could get a second handhold. Ahead, he saw Hera nimbly swinging her leg upward to catch a hanging support strut. That wasn't an option for him—not with the whirling blades of the turbofan directly ahead. He had to shift his weight and reverse his handholds, turning himself around.

Doing so, he saw the pursuers. Two—no, *three* Imperial troop transports hurtled up the dark lane in the hoverbus's wake, occasionally slowed by oncoming traffic. Skelly wasn't bothered by the traffic at all, Kanan realized: Every few seconds, the vehicle slammed off something to the left or right—or pitched upward, having simply climbed over its obstacle. Kanan had to heave his body upward each time the machine came back down to keep from being scraped off. But there wasn't any choice except to hang on—not with Imperials behind and Hera in danger up ahead.

When the first blaster shot from the twin-cannon turret on the lead transport struck a few meters shy of the hoverbus, Kanan had had enough. Seeing a slight recess just inside the rear of the underchassis, he pitched his legs upward and caught his boots beneath the lower flange. That allowed him to reach off to a more secure handhold on the left, leaving the turbofan housing behind.

With as much care as was possible in the whipping wind, Kanan felt around in the darkness, then began working his way backward across the Smoothride's bottom, feeling a bit like a mynock who'd lost suction. Groaning against the strain, he heaved his body across the opening of the recess to a place he could cling to just the inside of the rear of the undercarriage.

He waited there, breathing hard, as the hoverbus pitched and rolled. Waiting was excruciating—but he had to, for the right moment. Finally it came. The hoverbus struck something hard on the left, causing it to tip almost onto its right side. Seeing air opening up between him and the ground racing beneath, Kanan rolled his body around and onto the rear bumper.

This time, the Smoothride did slam against the ground when it righted itself—and Kanan began to fall backward, off the bumper.

"I've got you, Kanan!"

Kanan looked up, astonished. Someone *did* have him. Skelly was hanging out the shattered back window, his bionic right hand clasped around Kanan's belt. Skelly screamed in agony as Kanan scrambled over his shoulders and through the open pane.

Kanan hit the back floor of the hoverbus, wheezing. But he couldn't stay. The hoverbus had struck the street—anyone beneath would have been dislodged. "We've got to go back for Hera!" he called out. Then he blinked at Skelly. "Who's driving?"

Before he got an answer, the Smoothride again bounced over something, sending Kanan sliding on his back up the aisle as the vehicle tipped downward.

Upside down next to the driver's seat, he looked up. "Sorry," Hera said, grinning. "Still getting the hang of it. But welcome aboard!"

Kanan rolled over and scrambled to his feet. He saw Skelly had somehow made it forward, clearly in great pain but unable to rest. The shorter man was sitting in the stairwell of the open left doorway, his right arm wrapped around the support rail while his other hand fished around in his bag. A moment later, Skelly slung a small pipe bomb out the door.

The landspeeders parked along the left side of the street went up in an inferno that lit the area, upending them. The shock wave caught the rear section of the Smoothride, tipping the hoverbus halfway onto its right side as it hurtled toward an intersection. Kanan grabbed for the support post as Hera ably got control, using the momentum to take the vehicle down a side street.

Skelly just grinned, showing teeth broken and blackened. He reached into his bag again.

"Can you make him stop that?" Hera called back.

"Happily," Kanan said. He stepped over and yanked Skelly's satchel from him.

"Hey!" Skelly said, reaching for it—and nearly tumbling out the open door.

Kanan grabbed him—and immediately regretted it. "I should—"

Before he could finish, blasterfire shattered the windows on the left side. Kanan ducked, trying to protect his head from the flying shards. Through the open door, he could see where the blasts were coming from: one of the Recon transports, ambushing from a side street. A second later the windows on the right exploded with fire coming from the opposite direction.

"We're in a shooting gallery!" Kanan yelled. They had to get out of here—but that meant finding out where they were. Slinging the bag over his shoulder, he pulled his blaster and scrambled atop one of the seats.

It was almost impossible, watching the world whizzing by in darkness. Okadiah had never gotten the vehicle's navigation system working: Who needed it, for runs back and forth to the bar? But Kanan searched in desperation for any landmark.

"There!" The odd shape of Transcept's World Window Plaza, lit from within and without as always, whisked past. "Go right," Kanan yelled. "The old miners' highway. Let's make for The Pits!"

The Smoothride lurched. Hera barely slowed the vehicle—and yet somehow it easily made the turn onto the entrance ramp. The old elevated thoroughfare had the benefit of limited access: Now, rather than passing side streets with Imperial gunners, they were passing buildings and rooftops on either side. They were hemmed in, true—but there was very little traffic to run into on the highway anymore, and Hera opened up the throttle. Kanan scrambled off the seat and ran toward the back.

The Recon transports were racing along behind, he saw. He removed Skelly's bag from his shoulder. There were still close to a dozen improvised explosive devices inside. Now that they were out of traffic, the odds of doing more than random property damage with them were better. He called back to Skelly, still in the middle of the hoverbus. "How do I activate these?"

"Plug in the leads and let it rip!"

Pulling out a cylinder not much larger than a shot glass, Kanan quickly snapped together the two loose wires attached to it. Looking back, he took aim. He hurled it out the rear window and watched as the jetwash took it, whisking it toward the oncoming Imperials.

Fire blossomed before the lead Recon transport. Beneath it, the highway structure, already stressed from years of quakes, shook violently. The first transport flipped trying to avoid the blast, sending the stormtroopers riding outside it hurtling away—but that was better for them, as one after another the rear vehicles slammed into it.

"Three for one!" Kanan yelled, pumping his fist.

"We've got bigger problems!" Skelly yelled.

Kanan looked forward, startled. He hadn't expected clear driving all the way ahead, but it was kilometers from another on-ramp. "There shouldn't be anyone out in front of us yet!"

But before he could run forward to look, light blazed outside the left and right windows, blinding him. Feeling a sudden rush of heat, he realized it wasn't searchlights flooding the hoverbus, or small-arms fire from the Imperials. A high whine passed overhead. "Is that—"

"TIE!" Hera yelled.

The starfighter rocketed over them, a white bulb sandwiched between black hexagonal wings. Kanan looked back to see the twin lights of its ion engines receding in the distance—only to feel the world move again as a second fighter, its level flight path perpendicular to the highway, began strafing them from above.

Hera banked the Smoothride violently, sending her riders tumbling. There was no protection from the TIE's attack—except for the highway itself. The Smoothride's engines objecting, Hera tilted the hoverbus ninety degrees, riding not on the road surface but rather the left retaining wall of the elevated highway. The TIE, which had been aiming low for its pass, found its cannon fire pummeling duracrete rather than its intended target.

Hera twisted the Smoothride back to level again. The TIE shrieked overhead and began to loop—and now the first attacker was back, rocketing up the highway toward them. This time, Hera slammed on the brakes, sending the hoverbus into a spin—and began racing back in the other direction. The maneuver closed the distance with the TIE that had been tailing them such that its shots went harmlessly overhead.

Kanan scrambled to his feet. Hera was the best driver he had ever seen, coaxing things he'd never imagined possible out of the Smoothride. But this couldn't go on—especially not as they were now racing back toward the Recon transports, piled up and blazing. Something had to be done.

Kanan ran forward to the front of the vehicle. Skidding to a stop, he dived to the floor right at Hera's legs.

"What do you think you're doing?" Hera asked, bewildered.

Kanan reached past her feet for something beneath the driver's seat. "This thing used to fly, remember?" He yanked loose a brown pack with straps on it—Okadiah's ancient parachute.

"You're jumping out on us?"

"Hardly!" Getting to his feet, Kanan looked to the ceiling, amidships. "Cut the throttle. When I give the signal, let loose!" He looked back. "Skelly! I'm going to need your help!"

"Great!" Skelly looked at him tiredly. "I'm going to need medication." But he got to his feet.

In the ceiling at the exact center of the vehicle was the emergency exit to the roof: not a bad thing on a planet prone to quakes and mudslides. When Skelly reached him, Kanan was balanced on one of the seat backrests, trying to force open the rusty hatch. "I need you to get up here and hold me!"

The second TIE fighter was making a run along the highway's length when Kanan emerged on the roof. There was no good chance of simply throwing a bomb at it, he'd realized. The wind took him fully as he stood. Skelly had wedged himself in the opening behind Kanan and was holding on to the back of his belt. Kanan was facing down a TIE, which was racing toward him with its lasers ready to fire while he had no weapon at all.

But he had a plan.

"Hera, now!"

Behind, Skelly yelled the call down to Hera. She hit the accelerator—just as Kanan activated the parachute. Attached to nothing, the drogue caught the wind fully and ballooned backward into the air—opening wide into the TIE fighter's path. The fighter veered right, only to find ropes and canvas snagging across its starboard solar panel. Tangled, tumbling, and blinded, the distracted starfighter pilot missed seeing the microwave tower in his path.

"Whoa!" Kanan said, nearly losing his footing as the ship exploded spectacularly. One down. But there was the other one to go, he saw as he turned to look forward. And between the hoverbus and the TIE fighter Kanan saw the smoking pileup that had been the Recon transports. His earlier dirty work lay before them, now, a barrier—and if Hera tried to do another 180-degree turn, he feared he'd go flying. Worse still, there were stormtroopers on the deck of the highway, having emerged from the wreckage. Small-arms fire was flashing—and they were racing straight toward it!

"Pull me back!"

Skelly wasn't in any shape to move Kanan anywhere. But he did lose his hold on the roof opening, falling down into the hoverbus, causing Kanan to tumble backward toward the hole. Catching himself, he struggled to turn himself around and lower his legs inside the hatch.

He heard something from below. "Hera says to hang on!"

Kanan, halfway in the hatch with both hands on the roof, blinked. "Hera, what are you—"

Before he could finish the sentence, the hoverbus barreled through the stormtroopers on the elevated pavement before them, sending several tumbling over the side. Sure that the hoverbus would collide with the smoking wreckage, Kanan put his arm before his face—

—and felt a tremendous surge beneath him as the hoverbus struck the impediment. Struck it, and overtopped it, its repulsorlift jets using the debris as a makeshift ramp. The Smoothride launched into the air—and came fully to life, its ancient engines remembering what they once had been able to do.

Hera had made the vehicle fly! To the stunned surprise of Kanan—and certainly to the shock of the surviving TIE pilot, who veered to avoid a collision, only to crash catastrophically into a smokestack.

The Smoothride stayed aloft, leaving the elevated highway and buffeting over rooftops. Kanan couldn't believe his eyes. Slipping inside the roof opening, he landed roughly and rushed forward to Hera. "This thing hasn't flown in years!"

"You've got to talk to it right," she said, smiling.

"I thought *I* was a good pilot. But you—you're amazing."

"Thank you. But we should probably go somewhere."

Kanan blinked. "Oh, yeah." He pointed. "Back south. The Pits, out near the cantina."

She glanced at him with concern. "We can't just drive up anywhere. They've got satellites. They'll find this thing. We'll have to find a place to ditch it."

"That," Kanan reassured her, "won't be a problem."

CHAPTER THIRTY-ONE

Words could change things. Kanan had been taught that by the Jedi, and it was certainly true when it came to a short document generated by Minerax Consulting, which had changed the face of Gorse four years before the fall of the Republic.

Thorilide mining in the system, before then, had taken place entirely on the surface of Gorse in the wide, drenched plains south of the megalopolis. Then came Minerax's survey, projecting that no more thorilide deposits of any scale remained on either side of the planet. By the time the mines started seeing proof of it, the smart credits had already moved, with producers establishing operations on Cynda. In the space of a year, the strip mines that came right up to the edge of town went from work zones under the big lights to dumping grounds in the dark. The last mine on Gorse closed the day the Clone Wars ended.

So many of the places existed—Okadiah called them "Gorse's clogged pores"—that Kanan couldn't imagine a better place to hide the hoverbus. The endless junkyard was home to many abandoned craft, large and small, including several Smoothrides; it was where Okadiah had found the thing to begin with. Kanan had realized it was the only place they could go, after this long and difficult day, to have any chance of following one of Obi-Wan's directives.

"Avoid detection," Kanan mumbled.

Sliding out from under the left side of the dashboard, Hera looked up at him. "What?"

He leaned against the driver's seat. "Nothing." He shrugged. "I was just thinking—so much for keeping a low profile."

"Well, I may have killed your bus," Hera said, dousing her light. "Forget flying—I don't think it'll run again."

Kanan watched her close the equipment panel. The hoverbus had so many dents and blaster scores, he was amazed the thing hadn't spontaneously combusted.

Hera walked past the driver's seat, her arms sagging a little. She looked tired. "I don't think I've ever had a day like this."

"Stick around Gorse," Kanan said, following her down the aisle. "Every day's a trip to the zoo."

Hera confronted Skelly, who was two rows back, nursing his wounds. Her tone was chilly. "What could you *possibly* have been thinking?"

Skelly stared off in a medicinal haze. "My escape route was all planned. Your hoverbus was in the way."

"In the way of what?" Kanan asked. "Careening into the wall, instead?"

"That's not it," Hera said. "I mean taking us down a main avenue—and then throwing bombs willy-nilly. You were almost a bigger menace than the Empire."

Skelly looked hurt. "I'm trying to save people here. I tried to minimize casualties."

"You sound like you're in a war," Kanan said.

"I am," Skelly said. "It's never ended." He waved his prosthetic hand around.

Hera shook her head, and then she turned away. "Vidian killed Gord. I saw it."

Kanan nodded. "I guess he couldn't live without Lal."

"He wanted justice," Hera said in a soft voice, staring at the wall. "But expecting the Empire to prosecute one of its own is—"

"Dumb?" Skelly said, looking abruptly at her.

Hera shook her head. "I was going to say, *something we have a right to expect.* Which is why people are having second thoughts about the Empire. It's not here to help you. It only exists to help itself."

"Boy, that's right," Skelly said, rubbing his forehead. "I sure got that Vidian wrong."

Kanan thought that was a whole different subject—and that the time for talking was past. The thing now was to get moving, before the Empire put search vessels into the air. "Come on," he said to her. "We're not far from The Asteroid Belt. We can decide what to do from there."

She didn't respond. Reaching for her arm, he waved to Skelly. "You wanted the hoverbus, Skelly? Keep it. We're gone."

"Wait," Hera said. "You're just going to leave him?"

"Wrong. *We're* just going to leave him, if you're smart. I don't think anyone saw you and me clearly at the spaceport, but everybody saw *him*. And that woman and her surveillance firm—their cams are all over the city. How long do you really want to hang around here?"

Hera frowned. "But he's injured."

"Which he did to himself." Kanan looked her in the eye. "I'm not sure what you're trying to accomplish, but whatever it is, this guy isn't going to help you."

She looked at him for several seconds. For a moment, Kanan thought she was going to make a decision.

And then he heard the thumping.

It was amidships, coming from the closet-sized restroom compartment. The door frame had bent slightly as a result of the day's damage to the hoverbus, and a sliver of an opening had appeared. As he approached, the pounding grew louder.

"I know we're in a dump," Skelly said, "but that's the biggest rodent I've ever heard."

Puzzled, Kanan walked to the rear and located a pry bar. Hera and Skelly gathered near the door as he returned. "This door always jams," Kanan said. "And locks itself, and worse. Okadiah spent his summer vacation in there once." He shoved the bar edge into the aperture and pushed. Something snapped.

The door popped open—and a very tired Sullustan fell out.

"Zaluna?"

Zaluna Myder rolled on the floor, gasping and clutching her bag. "Air! Air!" She looked frazzled. She was wearing the same dark clothing from the night before, Kanan saw.

Skelly looked at her in wonder. "Were you in there all this time?"

"Through the bashing and the blasting," she said, her throat dry. "The silly door's too thick—you couldn't hear me!" Zaluna looked up at Hera and Kanan with relieved recognition. Then her eyes fixed on Skelly. *"You!"*

Skelly looked confused as the woman recoiled, sliding backward on the aisle floor. "What's the deal? I don't know you. How do you know me?"

"You're the bomber," Zaluna said, big eyes growing improbably wider. "I ran the surveillance cam that got you arrested."

Skelly blinked. "You what?" Realizing what she'd said, he rocked forward on his seat toward her. "You *what?*"

Zaluna fished in her bag and pulled out her blaster. "Keep him away from me."

Kanan slapped his hands on Skelly's shoulder and pushed him back. "He's not going to hurt you. He has Beatings One through Seven coming from me, first."

"*Three* through seven," Skelly said. "Vidian got me first. And you gave me Beating Number One back on the moon yesterday." He glared at Zaluna. "Did you see *that,* too?"

"Yes," Zaluna said, looking down. "I don't think Kanan should have hit you."

"Thanks," Kanan said. He shrugged to Hera. "See what I get for helping?"

Zaluna put her blaster away. Hera stepped over to help her up into a seat. She looked back into the cramped compartment. "You've been in there how long?"

"Since last night, when we saw Skelly come into the cantina," Zaluna said, struggling to get to her feet. "The stormtroopers were outside. I was looking for someplace to hide, and the bus was there. But I got stuck. I couldn't get a signal out—and the door's so thick you couldn't hear me."

Kanan chuckled and shook his head. "All the bombs going off, all the people shooting at us—and you were right there!"

"I wouldn't recommend it." She looked to Hera. "We'll have to discuss Hetto's data cube later. I've got to get home. I've missed work!"

Hera looked at Kanan with concern. "Zaluna, I don't know that you should go home, or back to work." Hera shook her head gently. "The Empire's not just looking for Skelly anymore. They're after this vehicle, and probably us, too—we don't know. And until we know what they think about you, it's not safe for you to go back."

Zaluna looked bereft. "I really stepped in something, didn't I?"

"It's not mud," Kanan said.

The Sullustan closed her eyes and took a few deep breaths. After a moment, she opened them again—seeming almost at peace. "All right. I've been thirty-some years on one side of the cams. It won't hurt me to know what it's like on the other side." Seconds later, she was climbing atop her seat, stretching for the domed light fixture in the ceiling. It was just within her reach. "When people run, they never run smart," Zaluna said, running her fingers inside the dome. "The secret is to make sure the watchers don't know who's running."

Hera was alarmed. "What is it? There isn't a surveillance cam on board here, is there?"

"This was once a city transport. Those were set up for commercial surveillance thirty years ago." Finding nothing, Zaluna stepped down and moved to the next seat. Climbing, she repeated the process with the next light fixture.

Kanan gawked. "Why would they bug a hoverbus?"

"In those days, to see what beverages you preferred to drink on a commute," Zaluna said, fishing around with her fingers. "These days, it's for the same reason the Empire would watch a cantina, or an elevator. To catch threats before they become threats."

Skelly crossed his arms. "Everyone who called me paranoid, the line for apologies begins to the left."

Zaluna's jowls flared upward in a Sullustan smile, and she removed a small widget from inside the fixture. "Ah. Just like I thought. One of our obsolete recorders. No live feed—it does a batch upload to the satellite once a week." She pitched it to Hera as Kanan helped her down.

Hera rolled the impossibly small recording device over in the palm of her hand. "It won't send anything now, will it?"

"No, it's disconnected from the transmitter. But I admit I'd be interested to see what's on it. I've been in the dark all day. I'd like to know what all the noise was about."

"You were better off where you were," Kanan said. "I'd like to be able to forget it!"

Hera stood in the doorway and looked at him. "Can you hide all of us at the bar until we figure out what the situation is? It's safer if we don't split up."

There was no use grumbling, Kanan realized. If there was one thing he'd learned, it was that he wasn't going to change Hera's mind once she'd decided on something. "All right," he said. "But at the first sign of a stormtrooper, Skelly, I never met you!"

"*Bastinade* is here," Sloane said, sipping from a mug and gesturing to the Lambda descending from the sky.

"Can your people keep this one from being blown up?" Vidian asked. "You only have nine more shuttles."

Sloane hid her expression behind her cup. The control tower's caf was no good, but after the last few hours, any respite was welcome. They'd lost several transports, two TIE fighters—and, worst of all, their quarry. *In* a quarry: an agglomeration of pits filled with refuse and runoff like she'd never seen. The satellite trackers had lost the hoverbus after five seconds in the place. The stormtroopers could be combing the area for months.

Until now, Vidian had said nothing about the incident, choosing instead to review the matter he'd first discussed with her back when they'd commandeered the hoverbus. A very strange matter, indeed, and one with potential ramifications for everyone who lived on Gorse. If it panned out, it might well turn more than a few model citizens into stark raving Skellies.

It probably wouldn't—but Sloane was anxious to get off the planet before something else happened. *Any more time on Gorse,* she thought as she headed for the shuttle, *and I might not even get a substitute command again!*

CHAPTER THIRTY-TWO

It was strange, being in The Asteroid Belt alone. No customers had arrived yet, and he didn't expect any for some time. Moonglow was undoubtedly still crawling with Imperials, and with the hoverbus out of action, Okadiah would have to find another way to get his regulars to and from the cantina.

Kanan had thought a million times about ditching the others. But he didn't want to abandon Hera, and she was convinced Skelly's capture would have led the Empire directly to them. Who knew, maybe she was right. And she wouldn't leave without Zaluna, not when the woman still had the data cube Hera wanted.

At least Zaluna had been useful, leading them on routes she knew weren't under surveillance. Once she had confirmed that the cams in the building were still dead, Kanan had sent everyone upstairs into the attic apartment. He'd lingered downstairs in the dark bar, gathering up whatever food he could find.

Kanan had left that morning assuming he'd never see the place again. Now he had no idea where he'd be in twelve hours. He didn't think anyone had gotten a good look at his face back at the Imperial spaceport, but he didn't want to count on that.

And something had to be done about his other guests.

Someone worked the lock at the side door. Kanan quickly pulled his traveling bag off the bar and put it at his feet. Okadiah walked in, looking grayer than usual.

"You're here sooner than I expected," Kanan said.

"Something's going on at Moonglow," Okadiah replied, somberly placing his jacket on a peg. "You heard about Boss Lal?"

Kanan nodded—and then shook his head. "I didn't hear the whole story. What happened?"

"They said a groundquake knocked her into an acid pool at the plant. She got too close," the old man said.

Kanan shook his head. "Terrible."

"Terrible lie, you mean." Okadiah wandered through the darkness, straightening chairs. "I've known Lal Grallik for longer than you've been alive, my boy. She knew where to walk. She stepped in front of a vicious cyborg, is all—just like the guild chief did." Pausing to wipe something from his eye, he turned. "They rerouted all our personnel transports to Calladan's field. I took a hovercab over."

"That explains the crowd," Kanan said, trying to sound normal as he looked around the empty bar. "I guess it'll be quiet tonight."

"That's one reason," Okadiah said. He walked up to the counter and placed his hands together on it. "Some *gentlemen* met me when I landed."

Kanan found a rag and began to wipe the surface. "Were they dressed in white?"

"Pretty foolish, given all the mud on this planet." The old man walked to the far end of the bar and turned. Looking back, he saw the sack stuffed with food at Kanan's feet. Evidently choosing to ignore it, he joined Kanan behind the counter. "They said the Imperials had to commandeer the Smoothride to the spaceport—and that someone stole it from there and took it for a joyride."

"Surprising," Kanan said. "You'd think a big Empire would be more careful with other people's property."

"It's a good habit to get into." Okadiah opened a bottle and set out two glasses. "Apparently whoever went on this joyride shot up a bunch of stormtroopers and did a hundred thousand credits' worth of property damage." Not looking at Kanan, Okadiah poured. "Is there something you want to tell me?"

Kanan stood, stone-faced. "No, not really."

Okadiah picked up both drinks and looked at him. "That girl isn't getting you into something?"

Kanan didn't answer.

Okadiah watched the young man for a moment, before walking up to him with the drinks. "You've always struck me as a fellow with nowhere to go, Kanan—never as a man on the run." He kept his eyes fixed on him. "Nowhere to go is better. Fewer people come around asking where you are."

Kanan nodded. "I understand," he said, taking the offered glass. He gestured to a spot beneath the counter. "By the way, if you'll check the safe, you'll find some credits. I think someone dropped them behind a table."

"Is that so?"

"Enough to put a down payment on another hoverbus," Kanan said, shuffling a little on his feet. It was half the money he'd saved. "Er—probably not as new as the one you had."

"Then at least fortune smiled on someone today," Okadiah said. He raised his glass in a toast. "May the spirit of death make a clerical error and forget you exist."

"Right," Kanan said. Then he added: "To Boss Lal."

"To Lal."

Kanan downed his beverage and placed his glass in the sink. He picked up the sack of food and made for the staircase.

The raised voices behind the door silenced immediately when Kanan knocked. The latch opened. Seeing him, Hera lowered her blaster and let him inside.

The room was a living space only in the Gorsian sense of the term. A chimney ran up through a low, slanted ceiling; from the street, there was no indication there was an upper level at all. Pipes ran along the floor, bisecting the moldy chamber. Portable lamps provided the only light. A mattress had been thrown onto some crates to create a make-shift bed.

Zaluna sat at the foot of the bed, rubbing her ankles. The compartment had been a cramped place, and she'd slept wrong—when she'd been able to sleep at all. Skelly was seated in front of a little washbasin, doing his best to clean his wounds. And Hera was holding the door, looking as frustrated as he'd seen her.

"Problem?"

"We've just been discussing the day's events," Hera said, speaking evenly. She shot a look at Skelly. "Particularly some things that could have been done . . . *differently.*"

"That's what this crowd needs—a life coach." Kanan walked past and began doling out food. Zaluna and Skelly reached for it eagerly. Kanan walked to the bed and sat down, offering Hera a seat and what remained in the bag. "Your table, madam."

After a moment, she sat with him.

All ate in silence.

"I'm serious," Hera finally said as she finished her meal. "You've been doing this all wrong, Skelly. You need to forget the old way."

"That sounds familiar," Skelly grumbled.

Kanan chuckled. "What's Skelly doing wrong now?"

"It's what I was trying to tell him earlier," Hera said, crumpling the sack. "Gord confronting Vidian. Skelly blowing up everything in sight—it's suicide. It's not the way to do this."

"To do what?"

"To run a—" Hera stopped. She took a deep breath and lowered her voice. "This is no way to make a difference against the Empire."

"They're not trying to make a difference," Kanan said, doling out the food. "They're just trying to strike back."

"And I understand that. But if the people who have a beef with the Empire act solely in their own interests, it won't do anybody else any good. In fact, it might make it harder for any kind of real rebellion to flower—"

"Rebellion?" Skelly snapped. "Who's talking about rebellion?"

Nearby, Zaluna let out a *tsk-tsk*. She spoke to the air in a lilting voice: "This is how you get in trouble."

"Nobody's talking about rebellion, that's for sure," Kanan announced. Zaluna had swept the room for listening devices, but she clearly wasn't comfortable with the words she'd heard.

Hera rolled her eyes. "No, not us. We would never. But in *theory* . . ." She said the word loudly and looked reassuringly at Zaluna.

"They *really* don't like you talking theory," the Sullustan said with a chuckle.

Hera went on. "In theory, say you did have thousands of people—no, thousands of *systems*—enraged at a hypothetical Galactic Empire in a faraway galaxy. But they're all upset over local matters, over particular grievances, and they never get together on anything. So they get no strength in numbers, no strategic advantages from cooperation. They're easy to divide and conquer. And worst of all, no common spirit ever develops."

Skelly looked back in disbelief. "You're saying we don't fight back?" His voice reverberated in the small room. "What they're doing to the moon. What they did to Lal. What they did to *me*—"

"—was horrible, Skelly." Rising, Hera walked over and put a hand on his shoulder. "But you weren't hurt by one person."

"You're right. It felt like an army."

"You were hurt by a regime. You might get vengeance against the hand that hurt you—or that killed Lal. But you wouldn't get justice. Not until everyone gets it."

Skelly's eyes narrowed, and he looked back down in silence.

On the floor, Zaluna drew yet another small device from her bag and started fiddling with it. "Checking my messages," she said to those around her. "It's safe."

Hera nodded.

Skelly stared idly at the leafy stalk of the only vegetable Kanan had been able to find in the cantina's larder. "You know, there were a lot of us that lost limbs in the war. All we wanted from the docs was to be able to do what we used to again. We didn't volunteer to be turned into murder machines." He leaned forward in a daze. "What's wrong with that guy?"

Kanan assumed it was a rhetorical question. He also realized that Skelly had taken a worse beating than he'd imagined.

Zaluna gasped and dropped the gadget she was holding.

The Twi'lek looked to her with concern. "What is it?"

Hands on her knees, Zaluna stared in disbelief at the small device at her feet. "I-I just checked in. My entire team was suspended. And when I didn't show up for my shift, so was I." Her words caught in her throat. "Thirty years with a perfect work record—gone."

Hera covered her mouth with her hand. "Oh, Zaluna, I'm sorry."

"It's more than that. The Empire knows I was friends with Hetto. They're going to find out where I was today. I'm going to lose my job—or *worse*!"

"Some job, spying on everyone," Skelly said, snapping out of his funk.

"It's important!" Zaluna retorted. "At least—it was, once. We did things. Important things."

"I don't see it," Kanan said, standing and walking over to the door. He leaned against it with his arms crossed. The Empire's snooping didn't surprise him, of course. It just seemed like a waste of time. "What's the good in watching a bunch of miserable people going about their boring lives?"

"In the old days—under the Republic—we did more than that," Zaluna said, perking up. "We found missing persons. We stopped crimes. We prevented—"

"Prevented people from questioning anything!" Skelly threw the green stalk he was holding on the floor. "You helped the Empire monitor production. Helped them bust anyone who got out of line!"

"That's *now*," Zaluna said, her voice pitched high. Her words coming fast, she faced Skelly. "Has anything bad ever happened in *your* life?

Anything bad that could have been stopped, if only someone had been paying better attention?"

Skelly took a breath and nodded. "More than once."

"And you, Kanan? Is there something bad that could have been prevented if someone'd been watching over you?"

Kanan shifted. Hera had been listening silently from the corner, but now he could feel her attention focused on him. "I don't know," he finally said, hands in his pockets.

"*Everybody's* got something like that," Zaluna said. "What we do—what we did—was good." She dipped her head fretfully. "And now I'm done for."

Kanan struggled to find something to say. He couldn't think of anything. But removing his hand from his pocket, he found the recording device Zaluna had located in the hoverbus. "Unless someone wants to relive today's disaster," he said, "I'll be crushing this thing."

"No, wait," Hera said, approaching him. She reached for it. "The Imperials were driving the bus for a while earlier. Vidian, and the Imperial captain."

"I didn't hear anybody," Zaluna said, offering Hera her holoplayer. "But then, no one heard me." Hera connected the devices and cued the recording back several hours.

They sat in silence, watching the material from the hoverbus surveillance cam. By the time it was over, Kanan looked up, bewildered. "Skelly was right. *They're going to blow up the moon.*"

CHAPTER THIRTY-THREE

" . . . so we don't have to mine Cynda at all. If what the bomber says is true, the moon could be pulverized, and its thorilide directly harvested and processed in space. No need for slow miners, or the costly processors on Gorse . . ."

Hera shut off the recorder. She looked mystified.

Skelly was apoplectic. *"He stole my idea!"*

"Stole your—" Kanan smirked. "You *gave* him your idea. You nearly got killed giving him your idea!"

"Hey, when I told you the Empire was going to destroy the world by accident, you thought I was crazy," Skelly said. "Now we know they're going to destroy it on purpose. Looks to me I wasn't crazy *enough*!"

"So this is why Vidian left Moonglow so abruptly." Hera shook her head.

"Delusional," Kanan said. Sloane, he'd noticed, had barely said a word during the recording. He wondered if she thought Vidian was insane. "You can't just *dissolve* a whole moon!"

"You want me to show you?" Skelly snapped. "I've got loads of studies I can show you!"

"All on the wall of a bomb shelter across town," Hera said. She frowned. "I didn't believe it, either. Skelly, are you sure?"

"I'm sure! Of course I'm sure," Skelly said. He gestured to his battered face. "Do you think I would've risked all this if I weren't?"

It sounded too incredible to Kanan. Was Vidian really taking any of this seriously?

And yet, hadn't Skelly brought down several levels of Cynda's substrate just by one well-placed bomb?

"It could happen," Zaluna said. "None of the rest of you was born here. I remember when I was young, my mother used to tell me the moon was all brittle, because Gorse loves it and keeps trying to hug it too hard. And the moon keeps trying to get away."

A good metaphor for some of my relationships, Kanan thought.

"She said Cynda would one day break up and come tumbling down. We all heard that story, as schoolchildren." She chuckled darkly. "Maybe that's part of why people on Gorse live as they do—because doomsday's coming. But we were told it wouldn't happen for thousands of years, so not to worry."

Hera nodded. "But what if it happened *tomorrow?*"

The grinning young lieutenant appeared in the doorway of the captain's office on *Ultimatum.* "The projections are run, Count Vidian."

"And?"

Ultimatum's planetary science specialist saluted Sloane belatedly and read from her report. "The bomber was right," Lieutenant Deltic said, "partially. The moon Cynda might be shattered by blasts at the stress points he names, but it would require far more explosives, and of a higher grade, than Gorse has in its stores."

"I have baradium-357 in quantity at Calcoraan Depot," Vidian said, looking meaningfully at Sloane. "As well as a thorilide collection vessel, of the sort that harvests the material from broken-up comets. Would the debris field remain in orbit for sifting?"

"The highly elliptical orbit makes it unlikely that the material would form a ring around the planet," the lieutenant said. "At least some debris would be ejected from the system; some would be captured, falling on the planet. Presuming the thorilide survives, your collector would have more than enough to keep it busy." She chuckled darkly. "The planet's another story, though."

"I don't need to hear about Gorse," Vidian said.

"I do," Sloane interjected. The lieutenant worked for *her*, after all.

"Well, first there's the direct impact—that depends on how energetic the initial dispersal was, and where it took place. You'd have more meteor action if the blast occurred at the upcoming perigee; less if it happened weeks from now, when the moon is farther out. The chunks won't be that large, but their composition will make them harder for the atmosphere to burn up."

"And seismic reactions on Gorse?" Sloane asked.

"Hoo boy," the lieutenant said, her expression suggesting they were well off into the realm of speculation. "Little would change at first, but the system would evolve. As the tidal balance shifted, Gorse would respond. Things could get pretty rocky."

"Groundquakes and meteor storms!" Sloane looked at Vidian. "Sounds cataclysmic."

"That's not even all," the lieutenant put in. "The planet could start spinning again."

"What?"

"The moon is a junior partner in the dance between Gorse and its sun, but an unusually important one. The dynamics of Gorse's atmosphere are extremely sensitive to change—it's already a miracle the dark side's livable at all!"

"The bottom line?" Vidian asked drily.

The lieutenant checked her notes. "Nothing could happen. Or you *could* see the destruction of the whole biome in ten years."

Sloane was amazed. "Ten years!"

"Or not," the lieutenant said hastily. "It's almost worth doing just to see what would happen."

"Enough," Sloane said, rolling her eyes. Glancing out at the moon, hanging large and bright outside her office viewport, she remembered something else the lieutenant had said, something earlier. "You said *if* the thorilide survives the moon's destruction. Why wouldn't it?"

"I'm not a chemist," the young woman replied. "But I know the thorilide molecule is fragile, easily prone to dissolving into its component elements. It's why Cynda's such a great source for it. The crystals that the thorilide's suspended in protect it. But there's a difference between carefully controlled blasts and what we're talking about. You wouldn't know whether the crystals would survive unless you did a test first." She paused. "Be a waste of a good moon otherwise."

Sloane glanced at Vidian, and then back at the lieutenant. "Dismissed."

The lieutenant saluted and departed. The captain looked back at Vidian. "The Emperor will expect such a test," she said.

Vidian idly studied the back of his hand. "I've already considered it. One of the specialists I brought in my entourage has assured me he can make the observations using *Ultimatum*'s sensors."

Convenient, Sloane thought.

"So we can run an experiment posthaste. We will, of course, report everything we find to the Emperor," Vidian said.

Of course. Things were moving very fast—especially considering the seriousness of what they were contemplating. "It's still so hard to imagine. Wiping out Gorse within *ten years?*"

"That's acceptable," Vidian said, walking toward the doorway.

"We would be destroying a habitable world," Sloane said, at once repulsed and amazed.

"We wouldn't be refining the thorilide on Gorse anymore, but in space, using the harvester vessels I have at my disposal," Vidian said, pausing in the doorway to look back out on Cynda. "Those with appropriate skills could apply to join their crews."

"And the rest?"

"The rest are of little use and do not concern me. They can find their own way offworld—and live to be of service somewhere else. But as of this discovery, there can be no doubt: To the Empire, their world is better off dead."

"Pending the test," Sloane said.

"Of course." He turned and left.

Hera watched as the others slept.

Only Kanan had not remained. The discussion had wandered aimlessly after the Cynda revelation, with Skelly concocting new wild theories by the minute. Zaluna, who had been remarkably resilient until now, had let her weariness feed her worry. Hera had tried to give shape to the discussions, urging practicality—and that effort, somehow, had seemed to aggravate Kanan all the more.

"Don't you care about anything?" she'd asked before he left to go downstairs.

"It's never good to care about too much," he'd said, flippant as always. "You're bound for disappointment."

Now she had to decide what she was going to do. Enough hours had passed quietly that she doubted Kanan had been identified at the Imperial spaceport; that meant there weren't stormtroopers waiting outside The Asteroid Belt. She might be able to slip back to her own ship. Zaluna had at last given her the data cube Hetto had prepared for her. That, she knew, would help other dissidents elsewhere.

And she'd learned all she expected to about Vidian—that the famous odds-beating business pundit was a murderous thug evidently willing to entertain outrageous schemes. Like Kanan, she doubted the destruction of the moon was possible; it was too big an idea, too fantastic to imagine. Engineering on that scale just wasn't done—or at least she'd never heard of it. Vidian would surely figure that out. At least while he was doing that, he wouldn't be carrying out any more sadistic "inspections." So there wasn't much reason for her to linger on Gorse.

First, however, she owed it to Zaluna to get the woman to safety somewhere, before the Empire arrested her. It certainly would: Hera had no illusions about that. And for some reason she couldn't put her finger on, she wanted to have one more talk with Kanan. He was self-centered and hedonistic, to be sure—but there had been flashes of something different, moments that made her wonder who he was and where he had come from. He was good at staying a step ahead of the Empire, and she'd seen him perform remarkable physical feats.

But none of that mattered, if the man lacked a conscience. It took more than talents to bring about a revolution. It required spirit.

And not everyone had it.

CHAPTER THIRTY-FOUR

One of the perks of living in a place without daylight, Kanan felt, was the large number of options it offered for those who didn't want to be seen.

A group of tourists had lost their shirts—or rather, their fine and expensive cloaks—to Kanan weeks earlier in a sabacc game. The wraps had sat useless in the cantina's storeroom ever since, unable to be pawned. It turned out that in the dark, the cloaks looked just like the robes a group of weird blood cultists wore as they wandered the streets every full moon, chanting their mantras and looking for escaped house pets to practice their religion on. Not only did the Empire tolerate the cultists, it had shut down Gorse City's animal control department to reap the savings.

Kanan had cursed his fellow players, who certainly must have known that "creepy maniac" was a fashion statement nobody wanted to make. But now he and the others put the cloaks to work. "Keep walking," he said from under his hood as he led the others up the long avenue in the industrial district. "If you see anyone, keep your head down and growl like you're hungry."

No one had bothered them. The full moon was approaching soon enough that other blood cultists were about and making for the cemeteries where they liked to hold their rites. It was a good time to be out and gruesome. Kanan had lashed his traveling bag to his back beneath his cloak; mad monks carried no luggage, and he thought the hunchbacked look it gave him was a nice touch.

"Seems to be working," he said. "We won't get away with it more than once, but it'll get us across town."

"You keep surprising me," Hera said. She was walking directly behind Kanan, keeping a careful watch all around.

"Yep, it's the whole lunatic family out for a crawl," Kanan said. "Mom, dad, grandma, and the weird uncle we keep in the basement."

"*You're* the grandma," Zaluna said.

Kanan grinned. The Sullustan woman had run out of steam the night before, but sleep had seemed to return her spirits. He still thought she was a little strange, but she amazed him nonetheless. He'd had the routine of a lifetime disrupted, years earlier—but he hadn't lived remotely as long as she had. And yet Zaluna seemed to have bounced back. He wondered what her secret was.

Skelly was in worse shape. He was moving slower, now, he saw: The latest round of meds hadn't lasted the whole walk. He was looking up at the moon as he trudged along. "You know," he said, "I think I really always wanted to be a rock guy."

Kanan looked at him. "A what?"

"A mineralogist. They used to study Cynda before they started ripping it up. I'd have had to go to school for it—everything I know I learned on my own. But coming here was nice. It showed me that the underground's more than just a place to plant mines."

"Or people," Kanan said, gesturing ahead. "Beggar's Hill, ladies and gentleman."

Beggar's Hill was no hill at all. A square clearing defined by little-traveled streets, the cemetery was populated by the aboveground sepulchers that Gorse's moist soil necessitated. Nightferns and crawling yettice had overtaken most of the ancient crypts, wearing all the names away. Catching a little light now as it did at this time of Cynda's orbit, it had the look of a peaceful grotto.

Kanan watched Hera as she stepped down the little path between the graves, moonlight in her eyes. *She really is something.*

Skelly staggered up and looked around. "I guess there won't be any place like this for Lal—or Gord. I didn't get along with them, but still . . ."

"Yeah," Kanan said, but he didn't think on it long. Wakes weren't for him. The Jedi were big on funerals, but no one had memorialized any of them. A death meant it was time for the living to get moving.

And it was. "All right, I've done what I can," Kanan said. "This is the western edge of Shaketown—Moonglow's just a few blocks away. We're in the middle of everything here. Hera, you said your ship was parked two kilometers to the west. Zaluna's apartment is two blocks to the southeast. And the nearest commercial spaceport," he said, turning and pointing north, "is ten blocks that way. So wherever you want to go, you're almost there." He took his hood down. "We're done."

Hera looked over at Zaluna, who was wandering around looking at the monuments. "Have you decided?"

"I want to go with you," she said, "in your ship." The woman gestured to the graves. "Almost everyone I've known on this planet is just a name on a screen—or a name on a stone. I don't want to work at Transcept anymore, even if they let me back. And it would be nice to see an actual sunrise someplace."

"Should we go to your place and pick up your things?"

Zaluna shook her head. "They're watching it by now. And my life wasn't at that apartment anyway." She looked up at the moon. "Let's get started."

Hera turned to Skelly. "And what are you going to do?"

Skelly opened his cloak and patted his satchel with his left hand. "I'm going to cut off this problem at the source—by blowing up the explosives plant that's near the spaceport. If they can't bring baradium from Gorse, they can't destroy the moon!"

Hera looked reproachfully at him. "You do know there are other sources of explosives besides Gorse, right?"

"If I cost them a day, it's worth it." Skelly jutted out his chin. "Besides," he said, "what else is there for me to do?"

Kanan nodded in agreement, despite himself. Skelly had just summed it up. Futile efforts—that was all anyone on Gorse had left. Kanan, of course, knew all about being cut adrift with no guidance as to what to do next. He'd figured out the secret: never again identifying with anything or anyone so much that losing it left him with no other option. But not everyone was as smart as he was.

He walked up to Hera. "So, where do you want to go after we drop her off? Wor Tandell's nice. Or there are some casino worlds I think you'd love."

Hera shook her head. "I hate to sound like that droid from yesterday, Kanan, but I don't take riders."

Her serious tone startled him. "What's that again?"

"I'm not traveling the stars looking for companions or places to see," Hera said. "I have goals. I don't need anyone who isn't interested in them slowing me down."

"But Zaluna—"

"—has performed a service to the galaxy in providing data about the Empire's methods, and needs to start a new life where she can be safe. You, as near as I can tell, roll with whatever happens—and with whoever's in charge."

"That's harsh."

"It's what I see," she said. She offered her hand. "I do thank you for what you've done. Good luck to you."

Tongue-tied, Kanan simply accepted the handshake. "Okay," he finally said. "You're sure?"

Hera nodded pleasantly, took her hand back, and turned away. "Oh," she said, reaching into her cloak. Facing him again, she withdrew a small pouch and began counting out Imperial credits. "For your help."

Kanan was startled. "What am I, a mercenary?"

"No. But I saw you putting money back into Okadiah's safe, to pay for the hoverbus." She offered the cash. "Take it. You'll go farther."

So I'm a hired hand now, Kanan thought. *Oh, well.* He took the money.

He looked at Skelly and Zaluna. "So long," he said—and walked back toward the street. It would be a long trek to the spaceport, and sweaty in the robe. He doffed the cloak and threw it into the nightferns. He'd take his chances, as he always did.

Where the path met the street, he turned to get one last glimpse of Hera. They were all still there, getting ready to go their separate ways. He shook his head, wondering what was keeping him. Kanan Jarrus never looked back. He always looked upward, outward, following the pull of the beyond. Cynda, hanging big and bulbous, was the glowing light pointing the way to his future. Up to the sky, where . . .

The moon exploded!

The Gorse skyline lit up, awash in the light of a dawn for the first time in a geologic age. No explosion of Skelly's had lit the cityscape so, and Kanan staggered, expecting some kind of thunderous sound. But there was none. And as the flash waned and his eyes adjusted, Kanan saw that, no, the moon hadn't exploded.

But it wasn't intact, either. Near the darkened lower limb of the near-full disk, a colossal plume of white ejecta was spreading downward and outward. It almost looked as if Cynda was shedding a teardrop—a teardrop a hundred kilometers across and widening as it moved.

Kanan had seen comets and meteors striking moons before. Those didn't look like this. This was an eruption. *An eruption,* on a world volcanically dead.

And he knew that spot on Cynda. He landed there every day.

He looked back at the street. All traffic had stopped. People were outside their vehicles, next to their speeder bikes, looking up in fascination and horror. Kanan looked past them to the big glowing clock on the waterworks building behind. It said what the sickness in his stomach had already told him: Okadiah was on shift on the moon.

Everywhere, people began talking all at once, like the buzz at a sporting event. Kanan could hear Hera's voice, too, the voice he loved hearing, calling out to him from behind. But he didn't listen. He was running to a speeder bike paused in the middle of the street, grabbing it from the hands of its stunned rider. She and the speeder bike's owner were still yelling as Kanan tore away down the thoroughfare, racing into Shake-town.

The world shook beneath Skelly. To one side, Zaluna's voice was filled with horror. *"It's happening."*

"No," Skelly said, looking up in wonder as the ground rumbled. "The groundquake's just a coincidence. Call it a sympathy pang."

He had removed his hood: No one was going to be looking at him. Not now. And a graveyard seemed to him the perfectly appropriate place to be witnessing the beginning of the end of the world. He looked back at Hera as the tremor subsided. "That was nothing compared with the quakes we'll feel if they keep it up."

"The Empire's doing it," Hera said, looking up in amazement. "They really are doing it."

"You didn't think they would?" Skelly asked.

"If they can do something, they will do something." She shook her head. "I just didn't think it was possible—or that it'd happen this fast."

Zaluna tugged at the Twi'lek's sleeve. "Do people need to leave, Hera? Is something going to happen to the planet?"

"Skelly says we're okay. But we should get back to my ship, just in case." She looked back to the street. "That's what I was trying to tell Kanan." Hera had something in her hands, Skelly saw—some device she'd been struggling with since not long after Kanan fled the scene. "I've been trying to get any information I can, but there's too much interference on the airwaves."

"Everyone's talking," Skelly said.

A Recon transport drove past as if nothing were happening, aiming a searchlight in the opposite direction from them. Skelly could hear an-other approaching down an intersecting street.

"They're still after us," he said glumly. "Even with what's going on up there."

"Then we can't wait around," Hera said, pocketing the gadget.

"Looks like your plan's been overtaken by events, Skelly. Let's head for my ship."

"To go where?" Zaluna asked.

"I can drop you both someplace safe," Hera said, removing her cloak. "But first, I may need to stop Kanan before he does something rash." She glanced up at the sky with worry. "I think I know where he's going. There's only one pilot in a million that could navigate that debris up there. I'm afraid of—" She stopped herself. "Let's go." She headed down the path out of the cemetery.

Skelly tried to follow. But before he could limp to the street, the roar of engines came from above. And light. Not as bright as before, but closer, and more directed. Skelly yelled out. "The Empire's found us!"

"I don't think so," Hera said as the dark mass of a starship descended toward the street.

"Your ship?" Zaluna asked, quivering.

"It's Kanan!" Skelly exclaimed, recognizing the shape. "It's *Expedient*!"

The rear ramp descended as the mining ship settled half a meter over the street. Kanan appeared in it. "Hurry," he called to Hera. "I need you to get me to that blast site. Next to you, I'm an amateur!"

Hera gestured toward her companions. "They come with us!"

"I don't care. I've got Okadiah's team on the comm," Kanan said. "They're dying!"

CHAPTER THIRTY-FIVE

Expedient rocketed through the exosphere into space. Kanan had guessed right. He'd missed two work shifts, but with Lal dead and Vidian's appointed caretaker not yet in place, his ship hadn't been reassigned to anyone. His identification had gotten him onto the tarmac—but nobody was looking at the ground anyway. He found that the passenger seat had been replaced, but the ship hadn't yet been reloaded with explosives. The latter fact was helping *Expedient*'s handling enormously.

Only he wasn't the one handling it.

"Busy," Hera said, guiding the control yoke. From the passenger seat, Kanan could see that all the traffic normally headed toward Cynda at this hour had joined the ships fleeing it. A colossal cone of silvery debris rose into space from Cynda's southern hemisphere, blooming outward like an upside-down snowfall. Contact with the fast-moving ejecta could be catastrophic, and the other freighter pilots knew it.

Kanan knew it, too, which was why he'd surrendered the controls to Hera. After their experience on the hoverbus, he'd been left with little doubt that Hera wasn't just a good pilot; she was great. At the moment, he was upset, not the master of his emotions—and he knew how that could compromise the focus and reflexes necessary to do the kind of piloting that was about to be required: They had to go exactly to the one place everyone else was fleeing.

"No more info on the comm," he said. There'd been nothing but static for long minutes, ever since he'd heard Okadiah's team send their distress call. The other companies' channels had similarly gone dead. Looking at the long-range scope, he could see why. The fragments emanated from a point less than a kilometer away from the main entrance to the mining complex. He couldn't make out a single landmark. What hadn't blown outward had caved in.

Hera weaved *Expedient* through the rush of oncoming freighters. Half of them didn't seem to know where they were going, Kanan thought: All were seeking refuge, either on Gorse or around it. "They're afraid it's going to happen again."

"Good bet," Hera said. "But not today."

Maybe it's just a natural disaster, he thought. That, or an industrial accident. He wanted more than anything for his worst fears to be wrong. Would the Empire—would *anyone*—really test a far-fetched theory while everyone was still at work? It made no sense. But then he looked out onto *Ultimatum,* the only ship not in motion. It simply sat, the indifferent observer at a safe distance. No rescue vehicles had been released: only probe droids, headed toward the debris field.

Hera swung the ship out of traffic and onto a wide approach vector to the moon. Kanan looked back into the windowless rear of the cockpit. Light reflecting from Cynda intensified, casting his and Hera's shadows darkly upon their passengers. Skelly sat, unusually mute and reserved, on the acceleration couch to the left, his head bowed. Zaluna was on the little chair behind Kanan's, facing in the opposite direction. Initially excited by the takeoff, she'd refrained from looking out the forward viewport as they closed in on the disaster site.

"All those people," she said in a low voice. "I watched them every day." In an odd way, Kanan thought, the woman had been going with them to work on the moon for years.

Kanan looked forward as Hera expertly brought *Expedient* into a roll. He saw the length and shape of the debris field now. "No, that doesn't look suspicious at all," she said. "It's like a funnel."

"Yeah. Channeling outward." He blinked. "None of it's falling back down!"

"It won't," Skelly said morosely. "A normal blast would emanate outward spherically. You'd have a lot of fragments raining down again. This was the result of a shaped charge—a bunch of simultaneous blasts placed to direct most of the debris up and out at escape velocity."

Kanan stared at the unnatural-looking formation. "How do you know?"

"It was my idea." Skelly groaned. "It was on the holodisk."

Kanan grew sick as he studied the sensors. "Outgassing at the main landing bay. The complex has been ruptured." He unsnapped his restraint and headed for the rear of the compartment. "I've got to get down there."

Hera punched several buttons. "I can needle us in beneath the cloud. Where do you want to go?"

Skelly unhooked himself and came forward. Studying the scene, he pointed. "The auxiliary bay!"

Half in the space suit he'd retrieved, Kanan came forward to look. "Yeah, I think you're right."

Skelly directed Hera toward a small dark indentation clear of the blast zone. The auxiliary bay had been the shipping-and-receiving area for a smaller network of caverns, long since abandoned for the richer veins of the main expanse. An airlock separated the sections, installed due to fears that the old complex might vent to space.

Now that the opposite had happened, Kanan thought, it could provide the only way in.

Hera directed the ship into a deep crater. The surface beneath was coated with ashen residue from the blast, but the rectangular opening cut into the southern wall was intact.

"Magnetic field's still holding," she said. "But it's dark."

"Lights are on a different power grid," Kanan said, putting on his boots. "Can you handle it?"

"Of course." Effortlessly, Hera guided *Expedient* toward the maw.

As the ship entered the blackness, Hera activated the exterior floodlamps. At once, the occupants of *Expedient* were bathed again in light—

their own, mirroring off and coruscating through the thousand stalag-mites on the cavern's ceiling.

"We saved a lot on lighting this way," Skelly said.

Zaluna leaned around Kanan's chair for a look as *Expedient* touched down. She gasped at the beauty—and then retreated into her seat as Cynda rumbled. The moon hadn't quaked before to Kanan's memory, but he didn't care. He was already donning the helmet of the environ-ment suit. The air in the bay was fine, but what lay ahead might not be. "I'm patching my suit comm into Moonglow's audio channel. Hold station here."

"I'm going," Hera said, rising. "You've got two suits."

Stuffing a bag full of oxygen masks, Kanan shook his head. "I need you here. Someone's got to fly these guys out of this place."

She was already suiting up. "Is this a rescue or a suicide mission? Now get the ramp open, because I'm going!"

Kanan felt like an insect making its way into a pile of brambles—in the dark. That was what had become of the region beyond the reinforced airlock. Passageways that had been horizontal and shafts that had been vertical had both gone diagonal as gravity sought to fill in the gap left by the explosion.

The thorilide-rich crystals that were the Empire's goal were, in fact, the only reason there was room to move at all: Even damaged by the blast, their tensile strength was amazing, giving the place a continued semblance of structure. Kanan didn't have time to think on the irony. He kept going downward, inward, ever farther into the darkness, lit only by his and Hera's helmet lights.

Hera had somehow kept up with him, even as he'd scrambled over and under and around barriers. She was unspooling a microfilament cable they'd found in the landing bay; there was no expectation of get-ting back to the ship otherwise.

Kanan couldn't rely on positioning technology to guide him down here in the underworld. All he had was the distress signal in his helmet, still being weakly broadcast from somewhere in the chaos. Every so often, they had seen a sign of past occupation: a cart, smashed and sideways, or the arm or leg of a droid. But there had been no indication of life.

He found a dark triangular opening up ahead. Shining his light into it, he saw what amounted to a floor several meters down. He pulled the loop of cable he'd been carrying from around his arm and lashed it to a seemingly solid crystal support. "Wait here," he said into his helmet mike.

"No."

There was no time to stop and argue. He slipped over the side and dangled, trying to find the surface somewhere beneath him. Letting go, he hit the ground—and slid downward into the darkness.

"Kanan!" Hera called.

"I'm all right," he said, shining his light around where he'd come to rest. "We're getting close."

She rappelled down the cable and slid down behind him. "Close? How can you tell? It's hard to see anything!"

"I can tell," Kanan said. He pointed his light to illuminate a battered head, sticking out from the ceiling.

"Oh," she said.

"Yeah." It was Yelkin. His body was crushed, embedded in the new strata of the moon.

Kanan could tell the sight chilled Hera. It didn't do him much good, either. But as the opening started to go more horizontal, they saw more corpses, dropped like sticks this way and that amid the broken crystal columns. It was like tunneling into a graveyard. Kanan recognized a uniform next—and then a hovercart, like the one he used daily. He was in the right place.

"Kanan!" Hera called.

Crawling over a mound of debris, he found her kneeling beside a half-buried equipment console. "That's your distress beacon," she said, looking around. "But I don't see—"

"Okadiah!"

Kanan leapt over jutting obstacles in the dark, hurrying to a spot up ahead. It was an elevator car, diagonal but still held in shape by the frame of its onetime shaft.

Okadiah was under it. Kanan shone his light on the old man's face. Okadiah's skin was blue; his eyes and lips were covered with frost. The volume of air in the underground network was vast relative to the new vents to space, and further collapses had closed those portals off. But pressure had dropped considerably, and the air that remained was frigid. Kanan whipped his pouch open and removed an oxygen mask. Carefully wrapping it around the miner's head, he was relieved to hear the old man cough.

"Kanan—"

"Don't move," Kanan said.

"That . . . a joke? Not funny."

Kanan pulled the thermo-wrap from his bag and covered Okadiah's chest and shoulders. Then he looked to the old man's legs. They had been crushed beneath the elevator car, but not fully pinned. "Hang on!"

Kanan turned and looked for something to use for leverage. Hera was right there, gripping a tough-looking stalactite. Kanan took it from her and inserted it beneath the side of the car. "You pull him out," he said to Hera—and heaved. The mass, already lopsided, gave way in the opposite direction, tilting backward enough for Hera to slide the old man free.

Kanan collapsed, panting, on the ground next to Okadiah.

Okadiah struggled to say something. "S-s-stormtroopers . . ."

"What?"

"Stormtroopers. Came in . . . ordered us out of Zone Sixty-Six. Had their own charges . . ."

Kanan exhaled. "I knew it." Feeling strength returning to his muscles, he got to his knees. "We're going to get you out of here."

"Too . . . late," Okadiah said.

Kanan looked back at Hera. She was looking away, off into the darkness, respectfully.

"C-c-come here," Okadiah mumbled. "Where . . . I can see you."

Kanan cradled the old man's battered frame in his arms. "What is it, Okadiah?"

"Not . . . you," Okadiah said, before coughing. "The . . . *pretty one.*"

Hera stepped to the other side of Kanan and knelt. "I'm here."

"Ah," he said, smiling as if laying eyes on her were medicine enough. "You . . . listen. This boy . . . is good to have around." Okadiah coughed again, this time much more violently. "You ought to . . . stick by him. Think . . . he needs . . ."

Okadiah stopped talking and closed his eyes. The inside of the transparent oxygen mask, once fogged, went clear.

No. Kanan reached for the man's chest, certain he needed to do something, but unsure of what. He knew conventional first aid, but Okadiah's injuries seemed past that. He felt useless, as useless as he had when Master Billaba had died—and the turmoil of that moment mixed with this one, clouding his concentration. He struggled to focus—

—only to feel the gentle touch of Hera's hand on his arm. She shook her head. "He's gone, Kanan."

"I tried."

"You did," she said, her touch turning into a firm grip. "We need to leave now."

Kanan looked back at her and shook his head. "No. Not without him."

CHAPTER THIRTY-SIX

"It's a triumph," Count Vidian declared. "A triumph, pure and simple!"

He strode onto the bridge, holding a datapad high. He didn't need it, but not everyone had his eyes. "It's the report from my lead researcher," he said, approaching Captain Sloane. "Ninety-seven percent of thorilide molecules in the effluent remained intact. Only a small portion broke down!"

"I don't recognize the name," Sloane said, pointing to the lead researcher. "*Lemuel Tharsa*. He's aboard?"

"Part of my team. He boarded with me." Vidian glared impatiently, bothered to have had his good news interrupted. "You'll find him checked in on your ship's manifest. What difference does it make? The important thing is what he *says*."

Sloane read from the report. " 'The moon Cynda may be effectively pulverized using deep-bore charges, yielding an amount of ready thorilide equating to what could be mined in two thousand years, using conventional methods—' " She looked up in disbelief. *"Two thousand years?"*

"Imagine the Emperor's response!"

"We'll have increased efficiency, all right."

Vidian looked past her to the sky outside *Ultimatum*. "What's the status of the mining cargo fleets?"

"We've ordered every empty vessel to hold position, awaiting your next command," she said, handing off the datapad to an aide. "Two hundred seventy ships, counting thorilide carriers and explosives haulers."

"We'll need them all," Vidian said. "And all the ones on Gorse. We'll be bringing back thousands of metric tons of baradium-357 from Calcoraan Depot. We can retrofit the thorilide carriers for use there."

Sloane stepped over to examine a monitor. "There also appears to be at least one intact explosives freighter remaining on Cynda."

"Hardy."

"Or foolhardy. Our sensors showed it going *to* the moon, even after the explosion. Someone was determined to deliver his payload." Sloane studied the screen in more detail, before looking up with concern. "We count thirty-six vessels destroyed in Cynda's main hangar, both personnel carriers and cargo ships. All attendant personnel presumably lost."

"Acceptable," Vidian said. "If we'd alerted the miners to our plans, you'd have seen true unrest. There'd be dozens like that bomber."

"One was plenty," Sloane said, straightening. "But won't people on Gorse wonder what happened?"

Vidian began walking back to the elevator, accompanied by Sloane. "I've prepared an alert for broadcast," he said, "calling the event a comet strike. That explanation alone accounts both for why the workers were caught unawares—and for Cynda's ultimate fate."

"Efficient."

"We won't need miners anyway, when our plan works."

The captain's dark eyebrows shot up. "*Our* plan?"

"This could be big for you, Sloane," Vidian said, standing in the lift doorway. "I'll send up final instructions shortly."

"We're ready, my lord."

Vidian nodded, stepped back, and watched as the door closed in front of him. He could no longer smile, but he felt it. It *was* a triumph.

But not pure and simple. He hadn't told Sloane everything. Certainly, destroying the moon would help him meet the Emperor's goal now—but later was another story. That little inconvenient distinction had been revealed to him in the past hour, and he had shared it with no one.

He'd expected such an eventuality, however, and he had a means of dealing with it. It would get him past this crisis—and then he would lay a trap that Baron Danthe could never escape. Vidian knew something Danthe didn't, a secret that would solve all his problems.

In one stroke he would keep the Emperor's favor—and eliminate his main rival once and for all. Efficient, as always.

Together with Hera, Kanan had managed to move Okadiah's body back up the long and twisted route to the still-pressurized auxiliary bay. There, after removing their environment suits, they'd found Skelly and Zaluna outside the ship. Skelly was lying on his back, looking up at the lights, as Zaluna wandered as if in a daze, marveling at the kaleidoscopic effects.

"I watched the place on the cams for years," she'd said. "But I never imagined anything could be so beautiful."

Kanan had considered taking Okadiah's body back to Gorse for burial. But on reflection, Cynda seemed a much more fitting resting place for his friend. He and Hera had found a side grotto, where they laid the body down and covered it with rocks.

With the damage to the complex, Kanan couldn't imagine anyone mining the moon again, not in the normal way. That meant the Empire had gone all in on the moon-shattering scheme.

"You're blinking," Skelly said, looking up at Kanan.

Kanan noticed the flashing light on the device on his belt. "Call coming in." It was strange to see, now, of all times. "It's my Moonglow pager."

He activated it, and Vidian's voice echoed through the massive chamber. "Attention, all traffic associated with the Mining Guild. All empty mining cargo ships on Gorse or in orbit are instructed to follow *Ultimatum* to the Calcoraan system. All off-shift pilots on Gorse are ordered to report and fly whatever vessels are available."

Skelly sat up. He gawked, trying to calculate. "That's got to be a thousand ships!"

The transmission continued—only now, it was Sloane speaking.

"This alert is for Gorse Space Traffic Control. No other traffic of any kind is allowed to depart Gorse until further notice. The space lanes must be kept clear until our return. We're leaving a TIE patrol to enforce the restriction." The message ended.

"No one can leave Gorse?" Zaluna asked, fretful.

"And if we go back, we're stuck," Skelly said. "So much for warning people."

"What is this about?" Kanan asked. "What's Calcoraan?"

Kneeling near the exit to the landing bay, Hera looked through the magnetic shield and out to space. "It's Vidian's base of operations. A nerve center, a supply hub for the Empire in this sector."

Skelly snapped his fingers. "Three fifty-seven!"

Kanan blinked. "What, *baradium-357*?"

"It's in my research," the bomber said. "I ran the numbers on the worst case, what it would take to blow the moon apart. Plain old baradium bisulfate can't do it, not even a thousand ships full. But the isotope could. That's the evil stuff, weapons-grade."

You're the expert, Kanan thought. "And they've got it there."

"They invented it there," Hera said, walking over to join them.

Zaluna spoke in a worried voice. "So what do we do?"

No one said anything.

Kanan finally shrugged and gestured to *Expedient.* "We *could* do what they want us to do."

Hera turned to face him. "Yeah?"

"That's an explosives hauler. I'm a pilot for one of the mining firms. You just heard my orders. We can't go anywhere else, more than likely—not without a fight." He put his hands before him, palms upward. "So we go."

"We follow Vidian?" Skelly's eyes narrowed. "What would we do?"

Kanan glowered at him. "We're not blowing the place up, I'll tell you that!"

"But *maybe*," Hera said, "maybe we won't have to."

Kanan looked at the ship, considering the possibilities.

"We can't decide to go without everyone's consent," Hera said. "That's the Empire's way."

Kanan looked back at her in disbelief. "What, you want a vote? We can't exactly sit around in a circle debating all year."

Hera walked into the middle of the group, addressing each of the three as she turned. "Listen, I think we all understand the stakes—at least, I hope we do. You know the Empire needs to be stopped here, and you've also got individual reasons to care. But for us to have any chance of working together, we've got to be united. We've all got to see the same big picture."

Zaluna watched her. "Tell us."

"I've been around to see it. All across the galaxy. This is an Empire motivated by greed—that delivers injustice. That rules through fear—and that prospers through deceit." Hera started counting on her fingers. "Greed, injustice, fear, deceit. You can see them here, can't you?"

"They've certainly got the greed part down," Skelly said, looking up at the ceiling. "I can't believe what they've done—what they're going to do to this place. And for what?" He waved his good hand. "Whatever. I'm in. And I think if Gord Grallik had lived, he'd go with you on the injustice part."

Hera nodded. She turned to Zaluna next. "Do you want to go home, Zaluna? Because if you do, we all will. No one will judge you."

Zaluna didn't say anything for long moments.

Finally, summoning the words, she spoke. "You know, I always liked to tell myself I was a brave person. But the fact is, I've been a coward," she said, looking down. "The place I felt safest was in a place where I could watch over others. But it's changed. Hetto, Skelly—they're far from the only ones. I've seen *hundreds* of people arrested. Based on things I heard them say and do." She shook her head. "And I never saw any of those people on the screens again. Nobody comes back!"

"The Empire doesn't keep watch in order to protect, Zaluna. It keeps watch to scare."

"I know. *I've* been the terror." Eyes full of defiance, she looked over at Hera. "I don't want to make innocent people afraid anymore. And I won't let *them* do it, either."

Hera smiled gently. Kanan knew Hera didn't want to show it, but he could tell she was immensely proud of Zaluna.

"We . . . we won't have to hurt anyone, will we?" the woman asked.

"Not if we can avoid it," Hera said.

Now she turned her eyes on Kanan. "And what about you?"

"I lost track," Kanan said. "What did you leave me with, injustice?"

"Deceit," Skelly offered.

"Well, I think I've got that covered," Kanan said, gesturing. "All those bodies down there. Nobody had to be here."

He was scratching his beard, deciding whether to offer anything else, when the next words came out anyway. "And they're not the only friends of mine that the Empire's deceived."

Hera studied him, perhaps deciding whether to ask him to elaborate. Instead, she smiled a little. "So what do you suggest doing about it?"

"Something." Kanan paused. "I don't know what. But somebody sucker punched a friend. I won't let that pass."

"Good enough." Hera stood up straight and gestured to the ramp. "It's your ship, Captain."

"You're the pilot."

"And you're the tactician." She grinned. "Let's see what you can do."

It was more than a risk, Hera thought: Going to an Imperial depot at this stage of her project bordered on madness. The Empire, as yet, hadn't identified her. Getting tagged now would be just as bad as getting caught.

But what was happening to Gorse and Cynda was beyond serious. It was the sort of thing she'd vowed to stop someday. The day had just come early—too early, before she'd assembled a capable team. Not exactly the new dawn she'd had in mind.

Skelly would have been arrested if she'd left them behind on Gorse, she still believed; that could have put the Empire on her trail. But he wasn't revolutionary material. And Zaluna had resolve now, but she would be out of her depth soon.

No, it was Kanan she wanted to see in action. She watched him from the pilot's seat, as he punched hyperspace coordinates into the nav computer. He seemed different to her now. Not obsessed, as Skelly seemed— but focused, directed. She'd seen him act that way in short bursts when heroism was required; now it was a sustained effort. It was clear that what had happened on Cynda had affected him deeply.

She hadn't lied earlier. She did want to see what he could do. But she was more interested in seeing what he *would* do.

Phase Three:
DETONATION

"Count Vidian leading Mining Guild in heroic effort to stabilize moon"

"Blast investigators turn eyes to mining firms"

"Tourism industry watchers suggest busy season for travel ahead"

—headlines, *Imperial HoloNews* (Gorse Edition)

CHAPTER THIRTY-SEVEN

A child's snow globe, filled with blood. That was how one of the first visitors to behold Calcoraan had described the world. It was a wonder anyone had ever returned, given that description—and Rae Sloane agreed.

Looking out from *Ultimatum*'s bridge, she saw a planet that heaved and churned crimson, the result of a planetwide ocean thick with chromyl chloride. There wasn't anything living down there—not on a sea where a drop of water could unleash not one, but two potent acids. But both the liquid and the ocean floor beneath it held uses for starship manufacturing, and so Calcoraan Depot had been constructed in orbit to service the many robotic factories already in space.

It was just another bizarre stop on what had, for Sloane, become a tour of the galaxy's strangest planets. The Empire tended to like these punishing environments, she thought, like an extremophile bacterium in a volcanic rift. It made sense to her, philosophically: True power could only be claimed by those brave enough to go and get it.

And Gorse could soon become another hellish place, losing what little livability it had.

Calcoraan Depot was Vidian's design and domain, and the thing seemed an architectural expression of his philosophies. The vast polyhedral hub of the depot sat like the biggest atom in an extensive molecule, connected to all the orbital factories by a triangular lattice grid of passageways. New supplies kept moving through those tubes to the hub and its main warehouse or directly to departing vessels for snap delivery.

The hub's central position also gave its occupants a view of everything around, including the approaching flotilla of cargo ships from Gorse. *Keep moving! Destroy barriers! See everything!* was fully at work in Vidian's station.

Sloane could see Vidian's minions fully at work, too, on a curious giant of a spacecraft at the far end of the sprawling complex. Vidian was over there now, overseeing final preparations and calling every thirty seconds to inquire as to when the rest of the cargo fleet would arrive from Gorse. It was a ship like none Sloane had ever seen. Seven bulging black spheres connected on a long axis, it looked like a segmented insect. But where a bug might have had legs, the vessel instead had long antenna-like structures running from the frontmost pod backward the entire length of the vessel.

"Forager," the science officer said excitedly. "That's a real beauty."

The captain nodded. Lieutenant Deltic got on her nerves, but Sloane had ordered her here anyway. She felt she needed to understand the process she was being asked to protect. "What are those long things along the spine?"

"Electrostatic towers—sixteen of them." The lieutenant fidgeted with the pins on a hat gone lopsided. "They'll fan outward when it's in operation to become the spokes for the collection wheel. I saw a ship like that in action once. It just plows through the debris field, snapping up all the goodies."

"The goodies?" Sloane shook her head. "I don't think I can handle all this technical jargon."

"The thorilide molecules. They're drawn to the spokes and shunted inside the vessel. There are automated processing centers in each of those big pods—taking the place of much of what the refineries on Gorse would've done. Just above the thrusters, that tail-end pod has the landing bays for shipping the stuff out. They'll churn out more pure thorilide in an hour than the miners did in a month."

Sloane nodded. The vessel was heavily shielded, as anything that barged into asteroid fields and comet tails needed to be; the turbolaser cannons on the outside of each pod and on the forward command hub probably also cut down on damage from errant debris. Once *Forager* was in place, Gorse would have its own Calcoraan Depot—for as long as the thorilide lasted.

Which seemed to be forever. The lieutenant was dizzy with her math again. "Even if ninety percent of the debris were to strike the planet, that machine could supply a *hundred* Empires the size of ours for a century!"

"There is only one Empire," Sloane said sternly. Then she looked at the lieutenant. "Ninety percent of the debris falling? Is that possible?"

The younger woman shrugged. "I told you. Might be a drop, might be a deluge." She grinned. "We have a betting pool going on down in Planetary Sciences. If something takes out the World Watch Plaza building in Gorse City in this calendar year, I'm taking my shore leave on Alderaan!"

"Dismissed," Sloane said. *Out the airlock,* she wanted to add.

Still, she'd found out what she wanted to know. It was amazing, seeing up close the work involved to source and service just one component of the Imperial arsenal. And this was just one of countless facilities. How many other projects were out there, similar to what Vidian had in mind? How many had he run, and how many was he running personally?

Playing bodyguard to an efficiency expert hadn't interested Sloane in the beginning. But now she saw clearly that her mission was, in large part, about the basic business of the Empire: to keep going. To keep growing. It all suggested to her that Vidian, in his eccentric way, was as vital to the Emperor as Lord Vader—and that escorting Vidian was easily more important than chasing down pirates on the Outer Rim. Things had to be built.

All interstellar empires rose and fell, ultimately, on their ability to deliver on this one simple, unexciting thing: logistics. Her military history studies had told her of the war forges of the ancient past—she didn't doubt that Vidian had studied them, too. He could well be the great armorer of future legend—and she, his preferred deputy.

It was just still a little surprising to her that an entire planetary population might wind up between hammer and anvil. Even as motley a group of specimens as lived on Gorse. The workers on her homeworld, so much closer to the galactic center, were much better behaved.

Commander Chamas approached from the door to her ready room. "I see Lieutenant Strangechild has left you in peace."

Sloane rolled her eyes. "You want something?"

"You have a call," her first officer said. "I think you'll want to take it. A very important person."

"Vidian again?"

Chamas smirked. "A different important person."

She had seen him once at the commencement ceremonies at the Academy. He'd stood on the stage and shaken some hands. Not hers, but she could hardly forget him. Baron Lero Danthe spent more on a suit than her family spent on its house on Ganthel.

"My lord," she said. "To what do I owe the honor?"

"You and your crew do the honor, by your service," the young man said, bowing. "I heard about the attempts on Count Vidian's life. I was calling to thank you for protecting him."

"Most generous." Extremely so, considering the bad blood she'd heard to exist between Vidian and his subordinate in the administration. "They haven't made the saboteur who can foil the Empire."

The golden-haired man smiled. "Very glad you're on our team."

She liked hearing it. They were separated by title and fortune, but she and Danthe represented the New Imperials—the media's catchphrase for the first generation of people to ascend to adulthood under the Empire. With few exceptions, her naval superiors were part of a class that had struggled to reach the top, only to see all the rules change; now they were spending every waking moment trying to keep pace. Perhaps not Vidian, she thought. But it was tiring dealing with them all. The Empire would be a better place once people her and Danthe's age were in charge.

But in the military as in government, the time of apprenticeship had to be respected. She knew Danthe was already fabulously wealthy, having inherited control of a firm manufacturing heavy-duty droids for use on fiery worlds like Mustafar. But Vidian's holdings were wider, his name already established. And given the cyborg's health, she couldn't imagine him handing off power for decades to come.

Not that the young man wasn't eager. "The count hasn't had time to fill me in on this special project of his involving Cynda. How would you say it's faring?"

"I couldn't judge, my lord. I'm simply the escort."

"Hmm." Danthe frowned ever so slightly, before brightening. "Well, I am sure you will do well in that. I want you to know, Captain, if you ever have the smallest need, please contact me immediately. My people will put you through directly."

"I . . . thank you, my lord." The transmission ended.

Vidian, now Danthe? Were all interim captains this popular with the elite?

CHAPTER THIRTY-EIGHT

Through his own reflection on the passenger-seat window, Kanan beheld the whole of Calcoraan Depot. He'd seen other such sights in his travels: enormous examples of Imperial ingenuity and excess. They seemed to get bigger every year.

But his focus was on his reflection—and the question he now asked himself. *Caleb, what are you doing?*

He hadn't gone by that name in years, and he didn't consider it relevant to the person he was now. Yet whenever Kanan stuck his neck out further than was comfortable, Caleb Dume was usually the culprit. Caleb, the little Jedi cut off before his date with destiny, his career as a galaxy-saving superhero stunted. He couldn't believe now that he'd ever been that person. That kid didn't know what real life—or real fun—was like. That boy was a nobody, a never-was. An unwelcome squatter in the back of his gray matter. Whenever Kanan had an idea that Caleb Dume would have agreed with, it was usually better to stay inside and order a double.

As much as the Emperor, Caleb was responsible for making Kanan's early adolescence miserable with his constant regrets. Caleb was all counterfactuals and what-ifs, all mental replays of the deaths of Depa Billaba and the other Jedi, always looking for some way disaster could have been averted. It was just as well that he was avoiding other people then, because it had made the young fugitive unbearably morose. While the other teenagers in the hangouts he'd tried to blend into were thinking about podracing, he was off in the corner trying to figure out how Jedi Master Ki-Adi-Mundi could have better protected himself on Mygeeto, or Master Plo Koon on Cato Neimoidia. Every name he'd found out about in those days had just set the whole thing off again, making it impossible for him to forget.

A waste of time. Except for one thing: All that thinking and hiding in those early days had trained him to analyze situations quickly and thoroughly. The tactical smarts Hera seemed to like had sprung from there. In that case, he thought, there was one good thing that had come of it. Because looking at her in the pilot's chair now, he determined that he'd follow her anywhere.

If he didn't get her killed first. Or if she didn't do the same to him.

Hera was chipper as she braked *Expedient.* "Told you we'd catch up," she said as the ship neared the tail of the freighter convoy. It had been open to question whether they would arrive at all. *Expedient* had left Cynda just as the straggler freighters were following *Ultimatum* into hyperspace. Kanan, who had never used the ship's hyperdrive before, had worried that it might not work at all. Ships on the lunar run were there for the very reason that their long-haul days were past. But the fact that none of the other ships was better off made them catchable for the right pilot, and Hera had talked nicely to *Expedient,* getting her way. She did that a lot.

It had worked that way with him, too. He liked that Hera had direction and drive. All women were magical creatures to Kanan, but there were happy forest nymphs, and then there were wizards. There was so much more to Hera, and it might take days or weeks or years to find out what was motivating her.

Time, he had—but he wouldn't stick around long if it meant constantly letting Caleb Dume call the shots. Hera had seemed to sense that old dutiful instinct in him, and had gotten him to come this far by appealing to it. The problem was, that person was someone he'd never really been, and could never be again. Okadiah's death deserved an answer, yes, and Gorse needed to be protected if possible. But both were responsibilities of a kind he had avoided for years. He intended to keep avoiding them.

Hera was clever, and pretty, and he loved her voice. If the only way to keep hearing it, though, was to play at her cloak-and-dagger games, he might have to be on his way, with thanks for the memories.

"Okay, you're up," Hera said.

"Hmm?"

"I'm not the pilot of record," she said, sliding out of her seat. They were approaching the outer security perimeter, an invisible energy shield surrounding Calcoraan Depot. TIE fighters circled the station, demarcating the location.

"Right." Kanan squeezed past her—a not unpleasant experience—to take his usual seat. Grabbing the control yoke, he slowed *Expedient* to a stop just short of the barrier indicated on his viewscreen.

A gruff female voice came across the comm system. "What's your identifier?"

"Moonglow-Seventy-Two," Kanan replied.

"Not anymore."

The response startled Kanan for a moment. "What do you mean?" He pushed a button. "Here, I've switched on the ID transponder. You can see who I am. I'm from Moonglow—"

"And I said not anymore," the woman answered. "You're now Imperial Provisional Seventy-Two. Name, license, and personnel."

"Kanan Jarrus. Guild license five-four-nine-eight-one." He paused to look back. "Passengers, three laborers."

"That's two more than you're supposed to carry."

"We'll get loaded up faster," Kanan said. "What do you care?"

"Not at all. Continue on your heading to landing station seven-seven. Follow the lights, and go slow."

Kanan did so. *Expedient* cruised into one of the largest assortments of starships he'd ever come across. Every Baby Carrier he'd ever seen in the skies between Gorse and Cynda was here, and more from elsewhere. And yet, unlike on the lunar run, all the ships were moving in an orderly and precise fashion. He soon realized why, as *Expedient* shuddered and he felt the control yoke go dead in his hands.

"Tractor beam parking attendants," Kanan said. "Nice. I hope we won't owe anyone a tip." He sat back, a passenger again like all the others.

Hera watched as *Expedient* circled the facility. "Are we going to have a problem getting back out?"

He shook his head. "Doubt it. These beams are for traffic manipulation. This place is so well protected, they wouldn't need tractor beams rated to yank fleeing ships from the sky."

"That's a relief."

Kanan stood up to stretch his legs—and thought back. There was one thing the controller had said that had disturbed him. "Weird. They changed our call sign."

"I know why," Zaluna called. Kanan turned to see her on the chair across from Skelly. As soon as they'd left hyperspace, she'd gotten her datapad out and started looking for news on the public channels. "They changed your name because there is no more Moonglow."

"What?"

"Moonglow has been blamed for the big blast on Cynda."

Across the aisle, Skelly gawked. "That's not true!"

Zaluna shook her head. "It was a Moonglow team that found your first bomb, remember?"

Kanan rolled his eyes. "I was there. Don't remind me."

"I was in the Transcept monitoring room when the word went out on that," Zaluna said. "They called it a natural occurrence, so nobody would get spooked about the mining company's practices—"

"Or would see that a dissident existed," Hera put in.

"Right. Now they've totally changed that story, saying that the collapse earlier this week and the giant explosion were both Moonglow's doing. The company has been dissolved, with its assets placed under Imperial control."

"Nothing like stomping all over someone's good name after you've killed them," Kanan said. Lal Grallik had been nice to him. Count Vidian was starting to roll up some big numbers in the debt column.

Expedient traced a long arc toward a massive disk-shaped landing station connected by huge spars to the rest of the facility. Several open ports revealed a sprawling loading area.

The comm system came to life again as the vessel cruised into the landing bay. "On landing, debark and begin loading product as it arrives on the conveyers. Take standard precautions—you're on our turf now."

"Great," Kanan said when the transmission ended. "Now I guess I work for the Empire." He looked to Hera. "What's the plan?"

"The plan is, you do what they tell you," she said, standing up and checking her comlink. "Load the ship. And wait for my call."

Kanan's eyes widened. "Wait. You're leaving?"

"That's right," she said, adjusting the blaster in her holster. "I'm going to destroy the station."

CHAPTER THIRTY-NINE

Kanan nearly fell over Hera's feet trying to get between her and the door. "Destroy the station?" He couldn't believe his ears. "I thought you were all about being careful and undercover. Now who's the loose cannon?"

"I know what I'm doing." Hera looked directly up at him and explained, a little less patient than she had been until now. "Cynda isn't just some little rock in the sky above Gorse, Kanan. I read up in the ship's gazetteer while you were sleeping. Zaluna was right. It's a rogue planet that entered the system and got captured—massive enough they might start revolving around each other in a million years, if Cynda doesn't break up first."

She pointed her thumb toward the aft of the ship. "But you saw how many starships are here. They're going back to break up the moon for sure, and not in a million years. They're doing it *now*. The people down below on Gorse are in danger *now*. So something has to be done *now*."

Kanan refused to budge. "Here I thought *I* was the suicide flier."

"I call it logic." She crossed her arms and tapped her foot on the deck. "Now, are you going to get out of my way or not?"

Shaking his head, Kanan stepped away from the airlock door.

She looked back at the others. "I'm sorry things worked out this way. If I don't make it back, you should try to warn people somehow. Then Kanan can take you someplace safe." She paused. "Somewhere besides Gorse."

Kanan looked at Zaluna, who was clutching her bag tightly to her and shaking her head over the thought of losing her homeworld. "The Jedi used to take care of these things."

The remark startled Kanan. Jedi were a topic people weren't supposed to speak of. "What do you know about the Jedi, Zaluna?"

"More than that silly story the Empire put out about them." She looked up wistfully. "I saw Jedi in action, you know, long before you were born. If innocent lives were threatened, they would figure out what to do. Even in a no-win situation."

Hera nodded. "We could use one, now."

"Or maybe it's time for people to be their own Jedi." Emboldened by the subject she was speaking on, Zaluna looked confidently from Hera to Kanan. "They weren't gods—just people like us, who saw a need. If they could find a way, I'm sure we can."

Maybe, Kanan thought.

And then it came to him.

"Wait," he said, as she started to work the door handle. "Let's say you somehow blow this whole monstrosity up. Are there other depots like this?"

Hera looked back at him, nodded. "Not exactly like this, but there are stockpiles in every sector."

"So if the Emperor thinks having a bunch of easy thorilide is worth ruining the Gorse system already, wouldn't he just try it again?"

"I imagine so."

"Then I don't get what you're trying to accomplish," Kanan said. "You're the one that thinks futile gestures are stupid."

"I'm buying time."

"For what? Is it worth sacrificing yourself to delay the inevitable?"

Hera shrugged. "I don't want to sacrifice myself, no. But you're describing a situation where we just sit back and let the Empire do whatever it wants."

"No, no. There's another answer. It's not enough to prevent it now. *We've got to make them never want to try it again.*"

Kanan's mind raced. Hera watched him, curious. "Go on."

He began talking, not yet sure where he was going. "Okay, look. The Empire didn't even have this fool idea until they got it from Skelly—"

"Fool that I am," Skelly interjected bitterly.

"—and then they tested it, back there with that big blast. But how did they know the test worked—that it didn't destroy the thorilide it freed?"

"I saw probes searching the debris," Hera offered.

"So did I," Kanan said. He began pacing. "Vidian wouldn't just demolish a moon without the Emperor's say-so. He'd have to send a report." He paused and snapped his fingers. "So we send another report—or 'fix' the one he's about to send."

"Yeah, just let me at it," Skelly said, interested. "I can throw cold water on the whole thing. I'll say crushing the moon will ruin what they're going after!"

"So we say the test didn't work." Hera nodded. "It would cause confusion—maybe slow them down until we can warn people. But can we make it look legitimate?"

"No problem," Zaluna volunteered. "Where would something like that be kept?"

"With Vidian," Kanan said. He scratched the side of his head and looked at Zaluna. "Would you be able to find him using the station's surveillance?"

"Maybe," she said. Then, "Yes. Just get me to a terminal I can slice."

Hera seemed pleased. "I like it better than blowing the place up. But this will be harder than just me sneaking around. Skelly's known, and we may be, too, for all we know."

Kanan nodded. Then something told him to turn around. Outside, a flash of color caught his eye. "Wait," he said, recognizing what it was. "Look!"

Hera and Skelly joined Kanan far forward and looked out onto the landing deck of the shipping node. A dozen other freighters—Baby Carriers and former thorilide haulers alike—were parked with their ramps down. Under the watchful eyes of ranks of stormtroopers, individuals short and tall descended from the vessels, all wearing head-to-toe coverings in fluorescent orange.

"Hazmat suits," Hera observed.

"We're here to load baradium-357, all right," Kanan said. "That's *Naughty Baby.*"

Supporting himself against the back of the passenger seat, Skelly nodded. "It's like we guessed. They need the big stuff to destroy the moon. I ran the numbers on it in my report—wishing I hadn't."

Hera stared. "What are the suits for? Does it blow up if you *breathe* on it?"

"That's not the reason for them," Skelly said, hobbling back to his seat. "The canisters have an outer shell full of toxic coolant. Nasty stuff, if it leaks."

"Will it kill you?"

"Maybe. But *you'll* kill a bunch of people first. It's psychoactive—produces irrational violent impulses."

Kanan laughed. "Check around your house for some, Skelly. It'd explain a lot." Then something dawned on him. Kanan snapped his fingers and turned. *Expedient*'s supply cabinet was between the forward compartment and the cargo area. Opening the door, he beheld his own supply of bright orange outfits, hanging neatly from a rack. Masks sat on an upper shelf. "I've seen these in here but never used them."

Hera stood before the door and stared. "You've got your own wardrobe?"

Kanan removed a suit. "That's Lal's thinking. We never knew what we'd be carrying from day to day, and she didn't want anyone getting hurt. The suits are meant to be thrown away, so they're cheap enough. And one-size-fits-all. Or most, anyway."

Efficient, Kanan thought, though he decided against mentioning that Vidian would probably approve. He looked back to Skelly and Zaluna. "We'd need you both with us. It could be dangerous—"

"Tosh," Zaluna said, rising. "We know what's at stake."

Skelly rolled his eyes. "Let's go before my meds wear off, and I start thinking clearly."

"Okay," Hera said, pulling down the masks. "We try this your way. But if this doesn't work out, we go back to my plan."

"Dying is never a plan. But you've got a deal."

CHAPTER FORTY

It was the rare space station that a Star Destroyer could dock with. Among Calcoraan Depot's many arms was a long astrobridge that mated to an airlock on *Ultimatum*'s hull. Sloane figured Vidian had calculated some minuscule time savings in it.

He had met her at the connecting port. *Greeted* was too strong a word, since as usual he seemed to be engaged in silent comlink communication with someone else. Given how many sights they passed, their ride in the tramcar from node to node felt like a tour—only a tour in which the guide had almost nothing to say.

They passed an arrival area in which heavily plated robots were being disassembled. She had never seen anything like them. "What are those?"

"Droids."

"Of what sort?"

"Heat-tolerant. The depot supplies projects across the sector, not just Gorse."

She was anxious to show what she knew. "Heat-proof. Baron Danthe's firm made them, then? He holds the monopoly."

Vidian visibly bristled at the baron's name. "Yes. Many firms supply the Empire, including his."

"But those are employees of one of your firms taking them apart." She recognized the logos on the uniforms.

"Standard maintenance." Vidian accelerated the tramcar, indicating the subject was closed.

They rode on past several more junctions, offering opportunities for more glimpses of the depot's shipments and more terse exchanges with Vidian. Sloane wondered if Vidian even remembered that he had asked her here.

"It's an amazing place," she finally said. "I appreciate the opportunity to see it."

"You don't find the logistical world too tedious?" he asked as their car began to slow.

"It's what makes the Empire go."

"Agreed," Vidian said. He pointed to a small cabinet in the car. "You'll want what's in there."

Sloane opened the compartment and withdrew a transparent face mask. Donning it, she saw a sign for landing station 77 up ahead. There were hazmat-suited workers all around the floor, taking meter-high cylindrical drums from pneumatic tubes and delivering them to freighters. "The explosives," he said, gesturing. "Being loaded here and at several other nodes, for return to Cynda. Testing has shown that organics will move explosives more quickly than droids will. Fear is a useful motivator."

"Of course." She looked at Vidian, maskless. "Don't you need—?"

"My lungs have been augmented to reject poisons."

The car stopped, and Vidian stepped out onto the shipping floor. Sloane followed.

"The explosives must be deposited deep within Cynda using shafts drilled at precise locations." He paused and looked at her. "My prep teams are already en route to the moon, but your military engineers could help speed things along."

Now we're to it, Sloane thought. "Of course. They're at your disposal."

"Fine." A red-clad human stepped forward to Vidian, offering him a datapad. The count passed it to Sloane. "Convey these instructions to your crew."

As a pair of workers passed carrying drums, another tramcar arrived from a different direction. Vidian gestured toward the loading floor. "I must finalize my report for the Emperor. Stay and educate yourself." He walked toward the vehicle. Then he paused and looked back at her. "It's good to have an ally in the military who understands what I'm doing."

It was the closest thing to warmth she'd seen from him. She bowed her head. "Your lordship commands."

"That's our boy," Kanan mumbled as he set a canister on the deck of the loading floor.

Hera nodded, anonymous in her orange getup but for the big bumps on the loose-fitting head covering where it protected her head-tails. "He hasn't sent the report yet," she said, her lovely voice muffled by the mask. "More luck that he'd drop by here!"

"If you can call it that."

"Skelly!" Hera called out.

Kanan pivoted to see the hooded Skelly limping through the crowd of busy workers toward Vidian. Worse, he was carrying his pouch of explosives. His blood running cold, Kanan picked up the baradium canister and started walking quickly in that direction.

Skelly was a dozen meters away from Vidian's back and reaching for his bag when Kanan interposed himself. He shoved the canister into Skelly's hands. "Here you go, buddy. Back to the ship."

Skelly, his expression invisible through the opaque faceplate, seemed poised to keep on going. "Don't you see?"

Vidian? You bet, Kanan wanted to say. Instead, he twirled Skelly around. He nodded to one of the stormtroopers standing guard. "Sorry. Big place. Easy to get turned about."

Skelly resisted as Kanan pulled him away from the tramline. Vidian was in the car already, seemingly none the wiser. "Skelly, have you lost your mind?"

"But he's right there, Kanan!"

"Not now!" Kanan pulled him back across to where *Expedient* was parked. "You want to blow us all up?"

"It's him or us."

"That'd be him *and* us," Hera said. Stepping over, she took the canister from Skelly's hands while Kanan pulled the bag off his shoulder.

"Watch him," Kanan said, turning to *Expedient*'s ramp. "I'm putting this where he can't get it."

Kanan shook his head as he locked the sack of bombs away. Time had only seemed to magnify the injuries Skelly had suffered at Vidian's hands; it was getting harder to get the guy to see reason through his pain. As he disembarked, Kanan saw that Hera had stationed Skelly by the ramp with a datapad, pretending to take inventory. That was the best place for him, right now.

Zaluna approached carrying a canister as gingerly as she might carry an infant. "Will they blow up if you drop them?"

"Just a little," Skelly said.

"He's kidding," Kanan said. "But if you do, make sure that hood is secure." He didn't want to imagine Zaluna on a chemically induced killing spree.

Minutes later, Hera returned from a nonchalant walkabout of the loading floor. "Okay, Vidian's gone to the hub," she said in a low voice. The layout was on Skelly's datapad now, having been downloaded from a nearby terminal by Zaluna—but it had taken too long to get, and *Expedient* was nearly fully loaded. They'd be expected to leave the station after that.

"We need to slow this down," Hera added. "And I don't know how we can get over there."

Kanan suppressed a chuckle. "And you were thinking you were going to have the run of the place."

"I'm not taking this bunch through the ductwork," she said, looking about. "And the stormtroopers are everywhere, making sure we're where we're supposed to be."

Kanan looked back the way Vidian had departed. There were three parallel portals there: a service hallway, with the canister-delivering pneumatic conduit on the left and the tramcar tube opening on the right. Kanan put his finger in the air. "There's the answer," he said. "We change where we're supposed to be."

Before she could ask him anything, Kanan stepped away.

Whistling to himself, he casually strolled over to the conduit where canisters, gingerly moved along on a gentle cushion of air, appeared in the loading area. Glimpsing left and right and seeing no one looking, Kanan disappeared up the service tunnel.

He saw there what he'd seen when walking past earlier: a spindly-looking silver droid, minding the controls on the outside of the tube. Kanan walked past to a maintenance door on the tube's exterior. With a twist, he snapped the hatch open.

"Wait!" the droid chirped. "You can't do that!" It clanked toward Kanan—who then grabbed it, shoving it bodily into the meter-wide tube. With a shove, he jammed its torso backward, fully lodging it inside. Then he slammed the maintenance panel shut.

The blockage light was already flashing outside the opening when he stepped back out onto the loading floor. Kanan looked at the light and swore loudly. "The stupid thing's stuck."

Workers gathered at the opening. Sloane marched over. "What's going on here?"

"I'll tell you what's going on," Kanan said, peering up the dark opening. "Your dumb droid's messed up the whole works!"

Sloane waved her hand dismissively. "Someone send for a repair crew."

"Yeah, you do that," he replied, pleased as he backed out that she could not see through the faceplate of his hazmat suit. He turned away from the group and marched back to *Expedient*.

"Wait," the captain called. "Where do you think you're going?" But Kanan was already heading up the ramp.

When he returned, he saw Sloane waiting with an armed storm-trooper. "Coming through," he said, pushing *Expedient*'s spare hover-cart down the ramp. Smaller than the one he'd ridden to survival on

Cynda, it bounced on the air as he pushed it toward Sloane's feet. "I've got a deadline, lady. Move it."

Sloane stepped back, seemingly surprised by his presumption. "What are you doing now?"

"You're paying us to move this stuff," Kanan said. "If your depot can't bring the junk to me, I'm going to it." He looked back at Hera. "Come on, Layda. Bring your cousins."

Hera saluted and gathered the others. They followed Kanan and his hovercart toward the service hallway, even as other loaders on the floor got the same idea and went for carts of their own.

Sloane shrugged in irritation and stepped back. She looked at the stormtrooper beside her. "This is not what I went to the Academy for."

CHAPTER FORTY-ONE

Skelly leaned back against a pillar, wheezing. "Next time . . . we take the tram."

"Yeah, that wouldn't be suspicious," Kanan said, pushing the cart up another seemingly endless hallway. They hadn't encountered anyone but service droids like the one he'd accosted, but the distance was the real test. They'd gone from one node to another, working their way toward the hub.

He looked down at the hovercart in annoyance. *I thought I gave this up when I quit Moonglow!*

Walking alongside Kanan, Hera paused and looked back. She pulled on his arm, and Kanan turned to see Skelly sitting in the middle of the floor. "I'm fine," the bomber said. "Just . . . come back . . . for my body."

He looked at Hera. He couldn't see her face, but he could imagine the expression of concern. This wasn't going to work. They'd both realized on the trip from Cynda that Vidian had injured Skelly more than he was letting on; he'd gotten this far by doping himself from the medpacs, but he was starting to fade.

Kanan stopped and turned the empty cart. "Here," he said, helping Skelly climb onto the flatbed. "You make one crack about me being your nursemaid, and I'm dumping you on the floor."

"Check." Skelly collapsed flat on his back.

Hera looked up at the fat disk on the ceiling up ahead. "What have you got, Zal?"

"These are Visitractic 830 factory surveillance cams," Zaluna said. Walking in front of the group, she waved one of her devices like a dowser with a divining rod. "Quality stuff—only a few on Gorse. They're not used for facial recognition. More to make sure the product keeps moving."

"Can you kill them?"

"I'm freezing them before we come into view. As long as nobody's walking into the scene around us, it won't look odd."

"You can do that?" Kanan asked. "I thought you said they were quality cams."

"They are," Zaluna said, unsnapping and removing her hood. "But nothing leaves a cam factory without a defeat code. Too many embezzling executives have been caught by their own technology. When I was younger, we used to use the codes to mess with other operators. You'd learn about them on Hetto's data cube."

Hera pulled off her head covering and smiled at Kanan. "And *that* is why I came to Gorse."

Kanan yanked his own cowl off. He was dripping with sweat. "These masks sure aren't for marathons. How far to the hub?"

Hera looked at her datapad. "Five hundred meters to another junction, then eight hundred more. There's a reason they use the chutes and conveyer belts."

"I never want to see another conveyor belt again," Skelly mumbled.

"Wait," Kanan said. "Zaluna, will your cam trick work if we go faster?"

"It's an infrared signal. It works as soon as we get into range."

"Fine. Both of you on the cart with Skelly," he said, cracking his knuckles. He set the hovercart's repulsors to maximum and grasped the pushbar. "I did this once with a ceiling falling on me. Get ready to hang on!"

Standing behind a wall of containers on the enormous warehouse floor of Calcoraan Depot's hub, Kanan decided he was done with riding hovcrcarts for one lifetime. The ride across Cynda's sublunar floor amid an avalanche had been harrowing enough, but by putting his formidable muscles into a running start before leaping aboard the cart's back bumper, Kanan had turned the floating pallet into an unguided missile, caroming off the walls of the hallway. Hera, sitting up front, had nearly ground the heels off her boots bringing the thing to a stop at the end of the second, longer run.

Replacing their masks on entry, they'd found that Calcoraan Depot's hub was every bit as busy and noisy as Kanan had expected. Robotic arms, vacuum hoses, and magnets were employed here, plucking materials from a forest of towering storage units and routing them to outer parts of the station. Zaluna had wryly pointed out a wire bin the size of *Expedient* that looked as if it held replacement latches for restroom doors.

"We take this place out," Skelly said, "and we can make half the Imperial fleet prop the door shut."

At least Skelly seemed to be feeling better. Kanan wasn't. They'd found a quiet spot—*quiet* being a relative term—to park the hovercart near a far wall while Hera did some reconnaissance, looking for a route to Vidian's executive chamber. Zaluna's map showed that it was somewhere through the wall but at least one floor up—but there were no details about how to get there. Gantries and catwalks leading over the main floor hadn't worked. Elevators were secured and guarded. The maintenance hatch in the wall behind him was their last chance.

Kanan stared down at Hera's hazmat suit, rolled up in a bundle on the hovercart. She'd taken off the bulky suit so she'd have more freedom of movement for sneaking around. He wondered where she was, and thought about opening the door to follow her.

Before he could act on the impulse, Hera cracked the door open. She looked frustrated.

"This is no good," she said, opening the hatch wide. The corridor behind was lost in shadows. She raised her portable light to reveal narrow apertures lining both sides of a passage that seemed to go on forever. "The entrance is at the far end, upstairs, but it's a long hallway guarded by stormtroopers. And we have to go past a bunch of Vidian's red-suits at their desks before you get to that."

"I guess we could say we were delivering lunch," Kanan said. He was about to give up when he saw something moving behind her, passing through one of the narrow openings on the right. "Look there!"

It was tall and mechanical, entering the corridor in the faraway darkness. Kanan stepped through the hatchway to get a better look. The droid had a gray tubular body and a flat head that rotated all the way around, casting a single red light about as it did.

"That's not a guard droid," Hera said, watching it disappear through a small opening to the left of the passageway. "That's a Medtech. FX-something."

"You get a lot of medical droids at an office complex?" Kanan asked. He waved to the others outside the hatch to follow him inside. "Be careful—it's pretty dark in here."

"No light, no problem," Zaluna said, big Sullustan eyes widening as she entered.

"I'll go anywhere that's not here," Skelly said, rubbing his ear. "This place is giving me a headache on top of everything else."

The door sealed, Hera led the way, creeping toward the darkened exit the droid had taken. "I didn't go this way before," she whispered.

"Allow me." Kanan drew his blaster and rounded the corner. Nothing leapt out at him. Hera's light on uniformly placed girders cast long, deep shadows across a wide circular expanse. The place was empty but for what appeared to be furnishings in storage, including a bed, several operating tables of different types, a wardrobe, and a chair large enough to be a throne.

The medical droid ignored them as they entered the area. It simply glided next to what appeared to be a console and stopped.

Skelly squinted. "What are we—"

"Wait," Kanan said. Light sliced into the area from a quadrilateral opening in the ceiling above the medical droid. With a mechanical whir, robot and console both started rising into the rafters, lifted by a hydraulic press. The rays from above illuminated the rest of the room in front of them before the door in the ceiling closed back. "We're under Vidian's health clinic!"

"Great," Skelly said, staggering in a daze toward a cabinet. "I could use a medcenter." Opening a drawer, he slumped against the side of the fixture. The others watched as he began pawing blindly at it with his gnarled right hand, completely missing the inside of the drawer.

Zaluna looked fretfully at Hera. "Is he going to be all right?"

"The faster we get in and out, the better for him." Kanan could see the Twi'lek studying the other furnishings: All were on similar platforms. "But now we've got our way in."

"You keep saying *we*," Kanan said.

"This was your idea—and the last meter's always the hardest. Besides, we've been lucky so far," she said, grinning. "Maybe he's asleep."

"Or getting a personality transplant." Kanan sighed as he pulled at the zipper of his suit. "But I doubt it. People never get what they need."

CHAPTER FORTY-TWO

Vidian sat at the center of his web and watched it all.

His home, like everything else in Calcoraan Depot, had been built to his specifications. A hemispherical room at the center of the station's hub, it was a place for him to contemplate his plans while he recuperated from the regular maintenance surgeries conducted by his medical droids. He had no need for grand windows looking outside, or giant stellar cartographic displays in the dome above him. He could make his cybernetic eyes display all the images he wanted.

Others were rarely allowed to enter, but when they did they saw only a neutral gray ceiling, dimly lit by a ring of lights. But when Vidian, chest now covered in a post-operative white robe, looked up, he saw the space station in action, as if he could see through its walls. He inhabited every corner of its durasteel frame, watching the supplies being brought in and sorted for redistribution. He saw the movements of the ships outside the station, and their destinations far beyond. The whole galaxy spread out before him, ready to be transformed by his force of will.

It hadn't always been this way. He had been powerless, once, in ways no one knew about. Vidian's official biography painted him as a heroic whistleblower for a military contractor, but in truth, he had been that most useless of creations: a safety inspector for an interstellar mining guild.

He had lived under another name, then. That was when he'd learned all he knew about the thorilide trade—and that was when he came to understand the hypocrisy practiced by those with money and power. Lives meant nothing to the manufacturers he visited, and so many of his superiors were bribed that the reports he filed were beyond pointless.

It was on an inspection trip to Gorse, of all places, that he'd finally been fed up. He decided to get in on the game, asking for and receiving bribes from several of the firms he'd visited. But before he could spend a credit, he fell ill in a mining company lobby. In the miner's medcenter, he learned his travels had caught up with him. The toxins he'd inhaled, the biological agents he'd touched in countless filthy factories had unleashed a degenerative disease, destroying his flesh. It wasn't a theatrical end, like falling into a vat of acid, but it took the same toll. Soon, all that remained of that once-energetic young man was a parched sack of organs, somehow coaxed into continued function by the efforts of the surgeons.

He'd never been much of a person, by his own admission, but now even that was gone. All that remained was a mind, trapped, with no way to reach out. He lay there lost, at the edge of madness, contemplating his existence—or lack of it. Seething with anger over the powerlessness of the life he'd led, and hatred for those who'd won while he had played by the rules. After two years steeping in the acid of his mind, he found a rudimentary way to communicate with one of the caretaker droids.

And the guild inspector's deathbed became Denetrius Vidian's birthplace.

From there, his life had progressed more closely according to the well-known legend—the only part of his biography that was remotely true. Avenging himself against the industry bigwigs required a new identity, a figure on the same level or higher. Vidian began as a cipher, a name on an electronic bank account. But soon he became the greatest corporate stalker the Republic had ever seen, all while still in the medcenter.

The Republic had protected the thorilide mining industry against corporate raiders during the Clone Wars, so instead he'd taken stakes in firms manufacturing comet-chaser harvesting vessels. He'd bought a secret stake in Minerax Consulting, pushing out reports that wiped out surface mining on Gorse and other worlds; many of the companies that he once inspected failed—including Moonglow's predecessor firm.

Revenge, perhaps, but he didn't really care. With his cybernetic prostheses, he had been mobile by then, having left Gorse and its bad memories for riches and financial fame. He had left it all behind. He'd become someone powerful, someone he had never been in his old identity—and if he did not have Palpatine's ear, he at least had his respect. The Republic was full of ill-functioning industries. Vidian was seen as the man who could fix them all.

He wasn't about to let a snotty upstart like Baron Danthe undermine him. The Emperor encouraged vigorous competition in his administration; it was a sensible strategy, forcing everyone to give his or her best. But Danthe could only tear down those more talented. The baron had desperately been searching for some weapon to use against Vidian; it was one reason the count had sought Imperial authority over Gorse. He'd managed to demolish the medcenter of his long-ago confinement—and any trace of his true past—with no one the wiser.

Still, the fool kept trying. The baron had contacted him again, earlier, fishing for information about his plans. Calcoraan Depot operators had even intercepted Danthe calling Captain Sloane, trying to get the same thing. To her credit, Sloane had told the man nothing.

There was no reason to wait any longer. Vidian stepped from the chair and sent it back down to the basement. He crossed to the secure terminal on the side of the chamber and entered his passkey. With the tap of a control, he sent the document he had prepared to Coruscant. It had been crafted with utmost care; the Emperor would support his action. Vidian was taking a risk with his present course, yes—but he'd also laid a trap, one that would take Danthe out of his nonexistent hair for good. Sloane was a part of his master plan, as were droids he'd shown her earlier.

When all was done, Vidian would remain in the Emperor's favor, and the Empire would grow, uninterrupted, because of it. And who knew? There might even be a bonus. Vidian knew the Emperor was interested in projects to create giant weapons of intimidation. He didn't know all that existed, but it was hard to hide much from someone involved in so many strategic supply networks. The destruction of Cynda, if it could be done, might be of military interest. Moons with its peculiar structure, orbit, and proximity to its parent planet were rare, but it paid to have a variety of tools in so large a galaxy.

Vidian closed out his connection with the Imperial throneworld and paused. The place was still, apart from the whirring and clacking of the FX-4, motoring between the operating table and the tall diagnostic console beside it. "I know you're here," the count said, his back to the rest of the room.

He heard nothing. And then, light footfalls heading to his left, behind the bank of computer equipment to the right of the sealed entryway. Vidian strolled casually away from the communications terminal and gave another silent order. A fresh operating table, this one with restraints, rose into view. "I've heard you since you entered, *both* of you. You rode up behind my chair." He stepped past the medical droid. "There's no surveillance in this room. It's just me. I've heard your motions, your hearts beating. I've seen your breaths coloring the infrared. Don't make me hunt you. It's tiresome."

Vidian whirled and leapt back toward the terminal on the wall to the right of the entrance. Looking over it, he beheld a crouching young green-skinned Twi'lek woman pointing a blaster in his face. "You're new," he said.

He heard someone move behind him. Vidian stood granite-still as the blow came: a metal surgical stand, smashed over the back of his head. The Twi'lek flinched as the stand's attachments broke free, clattering off the top of the console. Vidian whipped around and lunged for his attacker in one blinding motion.

"You're *not* new," he said, clutching the dark-haired man by the neck. The broken shaft of the surgical stand was still in the man's gloved hands. Vidian lifted him from the floor and looked keenly into his blue eyes. "The gunslinger from Cynda. I may have deleted your image, but I never forget a fool. I'm fascinated to learn what brings you here."

CHAPTER FORTY-THREE

Choking, Kanan struggled in vain to strike Vidian with what was left of his makeshift weapon. "Shoot him!" he said between gasps. "Shoot him!"

Hera did exactly that, leaning over the computer console and firing a point-blank shot into Vidian's back. Plasma coruscated over Vidian and fed into Kanan, shocking him. Through the pain, Kanan could see the robe that covered Vidian's chest was tattered, revealing a silver sheen beneath.

"I wouldn't do that again," Vidian said, ripping off the shreds of the garment with his free hand without loosening his hold on Kanan at all. "My skin graft is a cortosis mesh—a holdover from the days when I advised manufacturers in the field late in the Clone Wars. I can assure you, young lady—every bolt you fire against me will carry directly into your friend."

Kanan saw Hera stand erect, keeping her eyes on Vidian. "You want to know why we're here? Put him down!"

"Certainly." Vidian lowered Kanan—but just as the tips of the younger man's toes touched the ground, the count delivered a mighty open-handed slap with his left hand. Kanan felt his jaw nearly go sideways.

And still, Vidian continued to hold him by the throat. Kanan struggled to speak, but only unintelligible sounds came out.

Vidian loosened his hold a little. "What's that? You want mercy?"

Kanan coughed once and glared at him. "I said, 'That was a cheap shot.'"

"Glad you approve." Vidian looked back to Hera, whose eyes darted between him and the door. "You needn't worry. These walls are sound-proofed, and I haven't called for help. I rarely get to entertain—I don't want anyone to interfere."

Hera looked at Vidian—and then moved, vaulting athletically over the console. She fired her blaster just past Vidian's head, purposefully missing him, as she hit the floor. She was there just a moment before bounding forward, charging toward the cyborg. Vidian, startled by the frontal attack, reached out with both arms to grasp for her, releasing Kanan in the process. Hera instantly changed her target, diving low and tackling Kanan around the midsection while Vidian's arms crossed, catching nothing. The force of her jump propelled her and Kanan to the floor, two meters behind the count.

Vidian spun, amused rather than alarmed as the two stood. "Well done."

Kanan, breathing again, pushed Hera away from him just as Vidian charged toward them. The count was a shirtless brawler in a cage, now: the sort of opponent he'd dealt with in many a cantina. Kanan met the advancing cyborg with a roundhouse kick to his lower back. It felt like kicking a sack of titanium hammers—and Kanan felt dumber than one for the attempt when Vidian snatched his leg and shoved. Kanan tumbled backward, smashing through a lab table.

Hera opened up on Vidian again, clearly convinced no one outside would respond to the blasterfire. Vidian shrugged it off and charged her. She leapt high, vaulting over his back as he dived. But this time, his legs kept their balance, and he pivoted in time to catch her by a head-tendril. Vidian yanked, hurling her violently across the room.

"Hera!" Kanan yelled, rising from the debris. Vidian had thrown Hera hard enough to smash her against the far wall—and yet she hadn't landed at all. Blue light from a ceiling-mounted stasis beam captured her in midair.

The count looked up at her in high spirits. "Marvelous! Perfect aim. Don't move, now."

Of course, she couldn't—but before Kanan could wonder what Vidian was doing with a paralyzing suspension beam in his living quarters, the cyborg was moving toward him again. "Now, where were we? I used to spar in physical therapy."

"Oh, yeah? I used to put people there." Kanan stepped gamely toward him.

Vidian lunged with his right. Kanan stepped aside just as quickly, feeling the stroke go past. Balling his gloved fist, he pounded Vidian's left ear. The rest of the man might be sheathed with something tough, but Kanan bet that Vidian needed his ears for balance like anyone else. He was right—at least for an instant, the cyborg recoiled. It gave Kanan enough time to grab Vidian violently by what passed for his ear. Whipping the count's head around, Kanan bowled forward, smashing Vidian face-first into a cabinet with a colossal clang.

Like a spring-loaded weapon, Vidian snapped back around. His face was expressionless, but his mechanical voice betrayed excitement. "Now we're to it!"

Kanan and Vidian punched at each other for long seconds. Kanan used all his speed to prevent Vidian from landing a solid blow—and all his own technique to keep from breaking his hand on the count's metallic hide. He'd battled enough tough-skinned opponents to know to avoid head-butts or anything else more threatening to him than to Vidian. But that didn't leave him a lot of options, except for trying to knock Vidian off balance.

He tried—and the room paid for it, as the two overturned cabinets and more stands in their melee. But the cyborg was just too fast.

"We're done," Vidian said, his right arm lancing out. Catching Kanan's wrist in his viselike grip, Vidian delivered a left jab to his temple. Kanan didn't see anything for a few moments after that. But he felt motion, as Vidian grabbed his tunic and shoved him.

When the lights in his mind stopped blinking, Kanan realized Vidian had him against the main operating table. The count snapped Kanan's right hand into one metal restraint. When Kanan struggled, the cyborg smacked him again. A moment later both Kanan's hands and feet were bound to the surface.

Vidian straightened and stretched, as one refreshed. "That was invigorating." He looked around. "Any other guests? Are we done? No grieving Besalisks to the rescue?"

Seeing no other new arrivals, Vidian turned around. "Fine then," he said, facing Hera and Kanan. "It's time we got to know one another."

Kanan swallowed and looked at Hera, who, still suspended, managed to shake her head. Skelly, down in the basement level, was in no shape to do anything, and Zaluna would never come up into the middle of a fight. Nor would they want her to.

Vidian rummaged in a wardrobe. "You flew for Moonglow, gunslinger. I killed your boss. Is that what this is?" Vidian took out a gold-colored shirt and put it on. "Friendships are costly. They make you do things outside your best interests."

Kanan said nothing.

"I'm sure you'd tell my interrogator droid more," Vidian said as he walked through the mess his room had become. "And I may have another use for you."

Struggling against the stasis beam, Hera glared. "What do you mean?"

"I might let my droids practice on you." He turned to face Kanan and scratched his chin—a move that seemed more an affectation than anything motivated by an actual itch. "Can you imagine what it is to live without senses, without any means of interacting with your environment?"

"After a few drinks."

"The mind is a dynamo in the dark, an engine endlessly running, powering nothing. It thrashes in the night, seeking daylight, inventing its own." He walked around the table, looking for the surgical stand. Finding a bent tray, Vidian knelt beside it and began meticulously replacing the scattered surgical instruments on it. He held up a scalpel before his eyes. "*Controlling nothing.* Consider that! The youngling and the aged experience it—the struggle with ineffectuality. Controlling nothing is the true death."

He rose, holding the tray. "But I have come back from the dead. And through me, the Empire will control everything." He set the tray back on the stand. "You've heard my slogan, perhaps: *Keep moving, destroy barriers, see everything?*"

"You were talking on the holo in a spaceport once," Kanan said. "Nobody was watching."

"I'm not offended. A trite bit of management advice. But for one amputated from everything, it is more. It's a prescription for being." Vidian walked back to Kanan, scalpel in hand. "I was without contact for two years. Let us see what happens if you go without for ten. Who knows? You might even become interesting."

"Wait!" Hera said, still dangling.

Vidian looked over with impatience. "Yes?"

"I thought you were going to interrogate us first."

Kanan rolled his eyes. "Oh, yeah, torture me before you torture me. Wouldn't want to forget that!" What was she thinking?

Vidian set the scalpel aside. "She's quite right." He went silent for a moment. "I've just sent for my assistant. Be patient."

Another slot in the floor opened. A black, bug-eyed globe levitated upward through it. Kanan, struggling to get loose, recognized it as an Imperial interrogator droid. Their reputation was well known—and the large syringe it wielded identified it unmistakably.

"Hold still," Vidian said. "It'll be over in a second."

Kanan's mind raced as the thing approached. Master Billaba would have advised him to use the Force. *Cast the thing against the wall! Unlock your bonds! Hypnotize Vidian into taking a long walk out of a short airlock!* He'd tried never to use the Force openly in the past, yet this was serious. Kanan started to focus—

—but before he could do anything, the interrogator droid rotated just a few degrees and extended its needle right toward the injection port on Vidian's exposed neck.

"What?" Vidian swatted at the hovering droid, sending it tumbling into a far wall. He fell to his hands and knees.

A large door opened within the floor. Vidian's throne rose into the room. Skelly sat on it, with Zaluna standing beside it, holding the remote control for the droid.

"I don't think that's truth serum," Hera said.

"It sure isn't." Skelly patted the small mountain of vials in his lap. "I know my pharmaceuticals." He grinned through broken teeth at Vidian. "Nighty-night, sweetheart."

Lying diagonally on a separate table from Vidian, Skelly enjoyed a bacta rub from one of the count's medical droids. "I don't know about you guys," he said, "but I think we delete him. Enough's enough."

Kanan rubbed his throat. "Show of hands on that one?"

Skelly forced his right hand up with his left.

Hera shook her head. "I want to do the right thing here," she said. "I'm not against killing if it's necessary. But something strange is going on. I want to know that killing him won't cause something worse!"

"Worse than him blowing up the moon and leaving Gorse a graveyard?" Skelly asked.

Hera shook her head. "No, I mean—bad, but different. If we assassinate Vidian here and now, and we're caught, the Empire's going to think it's got a rebellion on Gorse!"

"A rebellion? *There?*" Kanan chuckled. "It's not exactly a hotbed of political thought."

"It'll get hot when the purges start," Hera said. She pointed to Zaluna, working at a console at her side. "Zal knows better than anyone—they've been taking names. It won't be random, like rocks dropped out of the sky. It'll be targeted." Hera blinked. "Or maybe it *will* be random, whole neighborhoods firebombed from orbit just to make an example!"

Zaluna goggled. "Has . . . has that happened before?"

Hera looked away. "You don't see everything," she said softly.

Silence fell across the room. Vidian had been as good as his word on a couple of things, at least: As far as they knew, no one outside had heard anything from within his chamber, and no one had seen the fight. Zaluna had already swept for cams. Kanan had wondered why Vidian wanted protection from the eyes of his own people. But at least his room didn't suffer from lack of restraining devices. They'd move him into the stasis field if he started to stir—but according to the medical droid, Skelly's cocktail would keep him out for a couple of hours.

Which it looked like they would need. "There's no getting into this system," Zaluna said in frustration.

Hera shook her head. "Still the last passkey?"

"It's a code, entered by hand," the woman said. "He couldn't do it by voice. If there was a cam or something around here, maybe it would have seen. There'd be something I could look at. But there isn't."

The room fell silent again.

Kanan stared. "Wait a second. Maybe there is." He stepped over to Vidian and turned the man's head. There, in his left ear, he saw a small dataport. A moment's revulsion struck and passed. "All right," he said. "Who wants to download Vidian's brain?"

CHAPTER FORTY-FOUR

Zaluna sat at the portable terminal next to Vidian's bed and looked back along the clear thin wire. It stretched to a dataport hidden in the count's ear. "This is the strangest thing I've ever done. And after the last couple of days, that's saying something."

Kanan laughed and moved a piece of fallen equipment that was obstructing the holoprojector. "We're clear," he said. "Show us what he's got."

"I've deactivated his eyes and ears so they're not recording, and I've also deleted his entire encounter with us," Zaluna said. "That's pretty easy. But I can only show you what he's seen in the last day—that must be this subsystem's limit." She pushed a button. "There."

The lights in the room dimmed. Across the floor from Vidian's throne, life-sized holographic images appeared, cast by the overhead emitter. The holograms were simply stereoscopic, comprising images from Vidian's left and right eyes—but they had unusual crispness and depth.

Hera shook her head in amazement. "We're seeing through Vidian's eyes!"

"Yeah," Kanan said. "Makes you want to throw up."

Zaluna forwarded and reversed the visions through elapsed time, stopping only for a fraction of a second before setting them moving again. The images came and went so quickly that Kanan was often unsure what he was looking at, but the Sullustan seemed to know. "You can watch that fast?" he asked.

"Every day for thirty years," Zaluna said, manipulating the controls. She seemed more comfortable than he'd ever seen her. "Most people's lives aren't very interesting. You learn to skip around pretty quickly."

She reached a stretch seemingly recorded recently, here in the sanctum. A data terminal came into view—the one across the room. "There," Hera said.

Zaluna was way ahead of her. "He's entering his data key," she said, framing the sequence backward. "Right . . . *here*."

Hera quickly read the code and dashed to the terminal on the far side of the room. A few seconds later, she called back happily, "We're in!"

Skelly, nicely medicated, hobbled over. "What have you got?"

"The list of subspace data messages to Coruscant," Hera said, reading. She frowned. "He's already sent the Cynda test results to the Emperor."

Skelly found a chair and pulled it up beside her. "Find the original. We'll create a revised version, saying the tests failed. We'll say there was a measurement error."

"I don't know if we can send anything. It looks like accessing the Emperor's direct channel requires a different passkey. He must have entered it earlier and logged out."

"It must have been a while earlier," Zaluna said, still searching through the images from his eyes. "There's no other code being entered."

"We can't get lucky twice," Hera said. "But maybe there's another way." Her fingers moved quickly on the controls. "Here's the file with the lunar test results. Let's have a look."

Skelly looked on as Hera began reading. After a few moments, she paused, staring at the screen in bewilderment. "This is confusing."

"I'm sure it's technical," Kanan said. "That's why we brought Skelly, to lie in their language."

"That's not why it's confusing," Hera said, exiting the document to look at another. "I can't do it."

"You can't make the change?"

"No, there's no need," she replied, both surprised and confused. "The original results *already* say that the test blast caused most of the thorilide to disintegrate. *The version Vidian sent the Emperor was a lie.*"

"What?" Kanan had begun to think a year wouldn't be enough for them to make sense of the count's world.

Hera read aloud from it. The original report said there was thorilide in the space debris kicked up by the blast that had killed Okadiah, but that much of it had been destroyed outright. An exponentially progressive decay process had been triggered in the rest; within a year of the moon's destruction, all unharvested thorilide would cease to be. And yet Vidian had told the Emperor there was a two-thousand-year supply. Hera was flabbergasted. "Why would he want to destroy Cynda when it'll ruin the thing he's there to get?"

Kanan had the same question. "Who gets to destroy something the Emperor wants?"

Zaluna looked at Hera. "You don't think . . ."

"That he's a revolutionary, like me?" Hera stifled a laugh. "I doubt it. This seems like a good way to wind up dead."

"Or with a desk job on Kessel," Kanan said.

Skelly rubbed one of his bruises. "Well, we know he's a sadistic crazoid. Maybe that's enough, in his world."

Hera shook her head. "He's not suicidal. There's got to be a reason he wants to do it, and a reason he's not worried."

The room fell silent, except for the quiet clicking of Zaluna's hologram controller as she continued to follow Vidian throughout his day.

Kanan found Vidian's chair and collapsed on it. He cast his tired gaze onto the flood of images. It was the ultimate spy tool, he'd thought— but all it had gotten them so far was the passcode. He looked down to the floor.

And then back up, where an image caught his eye. "Frame that back," he said.

Zaluna complied. "Now, there's a well-dressed man," she said. It was a young blond human, wearing regal business attire: a richly decorated suit of clothes, with gold buttons and a half cape slung over his right shoulder. But the image seemed different from the other pictures they'd seen. "The resolution of this image is different from everything else. Strange."

Hera saw the figure. "That's Baron Danthe, the droid magnate." Hera seemed to know everything, as usual, but now she seemed confused. "He's in Imperial government, too—he's Vidian's attaché, back on Coruscant. I found him in my research. He was here?"

"He *wasn't* here," Kanan said, snapping his fingers. "He looks different because he's a hologram."

"A hologram in a hologram? Shouldn't he be blue and fuzzy?"

Zaluna shook her head as she adjusted the controls. "Not if Vidian has messages piped straight to his eyes. And it's a message, all right. It looks like Vidian saved the audio from the conversation."

The images began to move, and they heard Vidian's disembodied voice. *"Baron Danthe, how can I do my work if you won't leave me alone?"*

"I'm only the messenger. The Emperor wants immediate assurance you can make this year's thorilide quota," the young man said.

"My plans will yield all the Emperor requires—providing you don't talk him into raising the totals again."

"Count, I'm hurt. I would never—"

"Spare me. I'm about to send His Imperial Majesty the report."

"Wonderful. If you would copy me on that—"

"I will not. This is my domain, not yours." A pause. *"If you want the responsibility so much, Baron Danthe, fine. After I successfully meet the Emperor's targets this year I'll ask that he transfer management of Gorse to your office."*

"That's generous, my lord. I don't know what to—"

"Say nothing. Just stay out of my affairs!" The image of the baron disappeared.

"Boy, they don't like each other at all," Kanan said. "Did you catch the smirk on that baron guy's face? I wouldn't trust him to hold the door open for me."

"It makes sense," Hera said. "The Emperor's leaning on Vidian to make a quota, so Vidian's got to crack Cynda like an egg. He gets a year's worth of thorilide, so he makes his quota. And by the time it runs out prematurely, Danthe will be left holding the bag!"

"Evil," Kanan said, regarding the motionless Vidian. "I knew he had it in him."

"Wait a minute," Skelly said. "The Emperor wouldn't take Vidian's word on this report. Vidian's a management guy, not a scientist. What's the name on that report?"

Hera looked at the screen again. "I can't believe I missed this. *Lemuel Tharsa!*"

Kanan blinked. "That name again. Who was he?"

Hera whipped out a datapad from her pocket. "I found that earlier. According to the HoloNet, for fifteen years Lemuel Tharsa has served as chief analyst with Minerax Consulting, producing studies on raw materials for private and, more recently, Imperial government use."

Zaluna perked up. "That's the man someone on the Star Destroyer asked us about. There wasn't much on the data cube about him—just the standard bioscan at customs."

Hera looked at her. "Check Moonglow's refinery, twenty or so years ago. I found he'd been issued entry credentials."

"Ah," Zaluna said. She opened her bag and produced Hetto's data cube. Switching off the link to Vidian's visual memory, she connected the cube to the terminal she was working at. "Moonglow was Introsphere then. We were definitely monitoring the building."

Skelly rolled his eyes. "Why am I not surprised?"

"A lot of this old material hasn't been mined—we probably didn't know where to start, when the inquiry came in." Zaluna's nimble fingers flew across the console. "I'm running a visual search on the name, limited to security badges."

"What *can't* you do?" Kanan rubbed his forehead. Hiding his Force talents even from himself made a lot more sense, now.

"Got him," Zaluna said. "Here he is." The holoprojector activated again, and a human male appeared. Kanan stood and approached the life-sized image.

The biometric data Zaluna had found in the customs files said the man was just shy of thirty at the time of the visit, but he looked far older: like a harried middle manager, prematurely balding, with a few tufts of rust-colored hair hanging on. His suit was dingy, his shoes scuffed. He could have been anyone.

And yet Kanan thought there was something oddly familiar about Lemuel Tharsa. His posture, his gestures as he ranted to an executive who clearly couldn't have cared less what he was saying. "What *is* he saying?" Kanan asked.

"Looks like we only caught a snippet." Zaluna pressed a button.

"*. . . don't have to tell you people again what the guild's safety rules are. It's the same everywhere in the trade. You've been doing it wrong. Forget the old way!*"

Skelly laughed. "There's old Vidian's motto, before Vidian said it."

Kanan and Hera looked at each other, at the prone count, and then back at the image. The voice was different, for sure, but the intonation was similar. Hera rose and approached Zaluna. "You said there were biometrics on Tharsa?"

"Right here." Zaluna punched them up on the console. "We do a little work with them at Transcept. The main spaceport requires them of all arriving visitors." Kanan bristled, glad he'd arrived on a tramp freighter that avoided that routine.

"I can't believe I'm going to ask this." Hera glanced over at Vidian. "Is Vidian's biodata in that medical console?"

"It should be." Catching Hera's drift, Zaluna ran a comparison. The results appeared on her screen. "Genetic markers are identical with Tharsa's sample on entry. No way to compare eyes, voice, or prints—but somewhere in there, that's the same guy."

"Whoa," Skelly said, looking between Vidian and the image of Tharsa. He scratched his head. "No, no. That's wrong. I saw the biography piece on the HoloNet. Vidian was a defense contractor, nearly died of Shilmer's syndrome. He wasn't some safety inspector." He chuckled. "How ironic would that be?"

"Very," Hera said, studying the results. "But that's him."

Skelly was stunned. "Then Vidian's war bio was a hoax? He was supposed to have been a whistleblower, helping the troops!"

Hera gave Skelly a sympathetic look. "Come on, are you really surprised?"

Skelly threw up his hands. "It's more fun when *I* think of the conspiracies."

"So Tharsa got sick and became Vidian." Kanan crossed his arms. "Was that on Gorse, too? Are there medcenter records?"

"The Republic had privacy laws, then," Zaluna said. "It was the one place we didn't have access. The only records would be on the site."

"Or not." Hera's brow furrowed. "Vidian had a medcenter demolished on his visit. But I don't know why he'd care about covering his tracks now—or why someone on the *Ultimatum* would be asking about Tharsa."

Kanan looked at her, puzzled. "That's not the only thing I don't get. Why wouldn't he keep his original name?"

Hera thought for a moment—and brightened. "Because he wanted to keep Tharsa alive. He's still on the Imperial rolls as an adviser, remember?" She rushed back to the terminal on the far side of the room. She pointed at the screen. "And look what he's been responsible for!"

Kanan stepped behind her and read. It was a long list of things, some dated recently. "I . . . don't get it. What are these?"

Hera ran her finger down the entries on the screen. "Technical reports from Minerax Consulting. Tharsa's name is on many of them as the preparer." Her eyes scanned the titles. "There are dozens of worlds, dozens of projects. Some are things Vidian worked on for the Empire—and some are before, from back in the Republic days."

"He's his own independent auditor?" Skelly hooted. "There's an efficient way to bilk your customers. Do your own fraudulent research!" He leered at Vidian's motionless body. "I'm impressed. You're the master. Really."

Kanan nodded. Things were falling into place. If some Imperial was asking around about Tharsa, maybe Vidian had covered his tracks on Gorse to keep anyone from making the connection. Tharsa's name would still be good with the Emperor, providing he didn't suspect anything; Vidian's plan to destroy the moon would sail through.

Hera squinted. "There's another file here tagged with Tharsa's name—older, but accessed today. But I can't get it open."

"No problem," Kanan said, turning. "Zal?"

"Reporting," Zaluna said, skipping over the cable attached to Vidian's head.

Hera stood up and stepped over to Kanan. He smiled at her. "This is something, right?"

"It's something," she said, looking around at the outer doors. "I'm just not sure what."

"We send the correct version to the Emperor, that's what," Kanan said.

"Not on that system," Hera said. "And I don't exactly think the Emperor checks his own messages—particularly not ones from random dissidents."

She turned her eyes to the ceiling. She had that look again, the one that said she was five moves ahead of him in whatever game it was she was playing. He liked the look, even if it made him a little uncomfortable. He looked back. "Any luck, Zal?"

"I can't decrypt it," Zaluna said. "I'm not a slicer. Kidnap one of those next time."

Kanan looked over at Vidian. Time was running out. They could dose the count again—but someone would be around for him eventually.

Kanan looked at Hera. "You really think there's something important in that file?"

She nodded. "It's the only one protected like that. And," she added, cautiously, "I've got a feeling."

"Good enough for me," Kanan said. He walked back to Vidian's table. "Get that medical droid back over here. I've got a plan."

CHAPTER FORTY-FIVE

"Step lively, there! If you were loading torpedoes on my ship, I'd be launching *you,* next!"

The orange-clad workers began moving marginally faster, but now they were walking so as to avoid Sloane, negating any increase in speed. It wasn't going well. Three of the miners from Gorse had dropped canisters, causing coolant leaks that cleared the floor for ten minutes each time. And while the repair workers had removed the fool droid that had somehow gotten itself crammed into the pneumatic tube, they had put a long gash on the inner cushioned wall in the process. Now *that* was being repaired. *Civilians!*

At least this experience gave the lie to a little of Vidian's legend, she thought. If Calcoraan Depot was supposed to be the domain of the man who saw everything and kept everything moving, he was sleeping on the job.

There'd been no sign of trouble otherwise. Aware that the bomber from Gorse might be among the workers drafted to load explosives, she'd accepted a pistol and holster from the stormtroopers. It hadn't been necessary. Neither had any of the workers tripped to what they were really assisting in: the possible destruction of their own homes. That, she thought, could get ugly.

Her comlink beeped. She reached for it. "Sloane."

"Captain," droned a familiar voice.

"Count Vidian," she said briskly. "The loading is almost complete. We'll be ready to return to Gorse shortly."

"I need you. Report to my executive chambers—alone."

Sloane's brow wrinkled. "Is it something about the report to the Emperor?"

"You could say that," came the reply. "Come at once."

"Yes, my lord." She snapped off the comlink. She was growing tired of being at Vidian's beck and call—but *Ultimatum*'s regular captain could show up to reclaim his command at any moment, sending her back to the waiting list with everyone else. She had to do as told.

She passed a lieutenant as she marched toward a waiting tramcar. "Tell Commander Chamas to monitor the loading," she said. "I'll be back shortly."

Vidian's antechamber was lavishly appointed, but the workplace's occupants seemed oblivious to their surroundings. Two dozen men and women of various species, all "enhanced" with cybernetic computer implants, wandered the opulent room like monastics, nodding as if listening to music. Not one noticed Sloane's arrival. Each was tuned in to events many systems away, all managing the flow of goods and services vital to the functioning of the Empire in Vidian's managerial domain. Sloane wondered if anybody had ever walked into an open elevator shaft while his or her mind was on moving widgets from Wor Tandell.

Identifying herself to the stormtroopers standing guard, she entered a long hallway. The double doors at the end opened as she reached them. The room beyond lay in darkness.

Sloane rolled her eyes. *More weirdness.* Taking a deep breath, she took a step inside. "Count Vidian?"

Another step—and the doors behind her clanged loudly shut. Sloane heard movement in the dark. She reached for her sidearm—only to feel pain in her wrist as someone kicked the blaster from her hands. The weapon clattered off in the dark. A lithe, shadowy figure whisked by to her right: her assailant. The captain reached again, this time for her comlink—when someone grabbed her arms tightly from behind, spun her around, and shoved.

Sloane didn't hit the floor, or anything else. She heard the hum in the air above, felt the strong pull of an invisible force holding her body in place. It was a stasis field, like the ones in her brig. The person who had pushed her walked ahead in the dark before turning and shining a bright portable light in her face.

"Captain Sloane?" It was Vidian's voice, coming from the direction of the light.

"Count Vidian? What's going on?"

The light shifted—and Sloane saw that while Vidian's voice had indeed spoken to her, the man himself was strapped to a table, motionless. The light traced slowly across the count's form. There was a dark recess in his neck ring where his electronic speaker belonged.

"Glad you got my message." This time, Sloane realized the voice was coming from the person with the portable light—and squinting, she could just make out the figure pressing something against his own neck. "Nifty little doodad. Triggered by the throat muscles."

"You impersonated him!"

"And well," the speaker said, still using the device. His light shifted back toward Vidian, and the speaker turned his back to her. "Get this hooked back up," she heard him say to someone in a different, softer voice. Someone else in the room shuffled toward the table.

Sloane strained to see, to move, to do anything.

"Release us now," she said in her most commanding tone. "You won't get away with this!"

No answer.

"The count had better be alive and unharmed, or you'll have a death mark in every system in the galaxy!"

Still no answer.

Sloane grew concerned. Fanatics like the bomber on Gorse might not care about getting away. After a short silence, she decided on another tactic.

"Look," she said more calmly, "I can get your grievances a hearing. But that'll only happen if you let me and the count walk out of here right now."

The figure with the light directed it at her again. "Oh, don't go so soon. This is our first date!"

She recognized that voice. Gawking, she said, "You're the mouthy pilot!"

He moved the light underneath his chin and flashed a devilish smile. "Nice to be remembered."

Sloane was flabbergasted. "We checked your badge back on Gorse. Kanan something."

"Kanan Something will do." He shone the light on her again.

She put the pieces together. "A pilot at Moonglow. That's how you got here." She glared into the light. "You've wandered off the tour, mister."

"I had to see *you*," he said, voice sugary. "You missed me, right?"

"Kanan!" came a loud whisper from the shadows.

Sloane's eyes darted to the speaker. "Ah. The co-worker." She was the person who'd kicked at her, she realized. And there were other shadowy figures in the darkness, including a slender person at the table fiddling with Vidian's vocoder. "Did you *all* come with him? You're accomplices. What did he ask you to do?"

"Forget about them," Kanan said. "Haven't you figured it out? I *am* an infiltrator—but on a mission you'll approve of. I serve the Emperor." He paused, before adding: *"Directly."*

Sloane stared down at Kanan for several seconds. Then she burst into laughter. "*You*, an agent of the Emperor?"

"What?" Kanan scowled. "It's possible."

Sloane struggled to stop laughing. "I think he can do better than *you*! What do you suicide fliers do, drink your way from port to port? Did you wander off from your keeper?"

Kanan thumped his chest. "I'm a man with a mission."

"You're an oaf with a delusion. Do you know what the penalty for impersonating a personal agent of the Emperor is?"

"No."

"A personal agent of the Emperor would!"

"You're wrong. There is no penalty—because nobody would ever do such a thing." Kanan sat the lamp on the floor, angled to point up at Sloane. He walked to a control panel near where she was suspended and touched a dial. "Now listen to what's going to happen. I'm going to give you my message, and be on my way. The stasis field's timer will release you with enough time to do what you need to do, before Vidian wakes up. Is that understood?"

"Let *me* tell *you* what will happen instead," Sloane said. "You'll let me down, turn on these lights, release Vidian—and then we'll march you down to the detention block. You can do your talking to an interrogator droid."

"That would be a mistake." Kanan began pacing around the darkened room. "I have information that's vital to you—and to the Emperor."

"If you're the Emperor's agent, you're already reporting to him directly. What do you want from me?"

"Vidian controls all communications from this depot. I can't afford to have this intercepted. I need an Imperial captain, with her own resources." He looked at her cannily. "You *are* resourceful, aren't you?"

"I can tell when I'm being played." She strained against the stasis beam. "Enough of this. Someone is going to come looking for me."

"Then I'd better talk fast," Kanan said. "And you'd better listen. *Like your life depends on it.*"

CHAPTER FORTY-SIX

Back in his hazmat suit, Kanan heaved another baradium-357 canister off the hovercart and onto a shelving unit in *Expedient*. "The seed's planted."

Through her mask, Zaluna looked at him. "That was both the most exciting thing I've ever done in my life—and the most exhausting. What do we do now?"

He locked the cylinder into a magnetic support. "Ditch these forever," Kanan said, peeling off his hazmat mask and throwing it to the deck. Once the canisters were secured, the bulky protective wear could be dispensed with.

As Zaluna pulled off her mask, Kanan saw that the Sullustan woman looked winded. "I meant, what if what you did doesn't work?" she asked. "With the captain, back there?"

"Don't worry, it'll work," Kanan said, climbing out of his suit. "Sloane was sold. I could tell."

"You could, could you?" Once the airlock door sealed behind her, Hera removed her mask and frowned. "Sloane thought you were cracked."

Kanan waved dismissively. "*Skelly* is cracked. *I* sounded like a responsible adult."

"Who wanted to buy her a drink. That charm thing of yours is not for every situation, Kanan." Hera hustled past him and slid into the pilot's seat. "See to Skelly."

Skelly, facedown where he'd collapsed on the acceleration couch, feebly tried to peel off his hood with his one working hand. He finally succeeded when Kanan gave the mask a yank. The man looked rough. They'd had to load the explosives and make their way back to the ship quickly, and there hadn't been room left on the hovercart for Skelly to ride. The walk had been hard on him, and Hera and Zaluna had supported him part of the way. They'd been the last crew to make it back, just barely avoiding notice.

Skelly looked up, his face twisted in pain. "I still think . . . we should have killed him."

Kanan shook his head. He wasn't going to explain it again. He pushed Skelly upright in his seat and strapped on an oxygen mask. "Trust me, everybody. This'll work."

"If . . . it doesn't," Skelly said between breaths, "we need . . . to warn Gorse."

"What's the point?" Kanan asked, shuttling forward. "The Empire's declared full groundstop on Gorse. Nobody can take off."

"There are tunnels," Skelly said. "And bomb shelters."

"Hera tells me they make fine homes," Kanan said, settling into the passenger seat beside her. "Let's hope it doesn't come to that."

Zaluna looked forward as the engines revved. "You need to talk to everyone on the planet at once . . ."

Kanan looked back at her. "You got something?"

She shook her head. "It—it's nothing." She slumped back in her seat, weary. "We've done too much already."

Hera turned to face Zaluna. "Come on, Zal. You have a way to help, don't you?"

Zaluna let out a deep breath. "I think there's a way," she finally said. "But I can't do it with this ship's transmitter. I need something built in the last thousand years."

"Hey, I'm sure there was a refit a century ago," Kanan said, looking up at the bulkhead. He wasn't about to get defensive about *Expedient,* no matter how much he and the ship had been through. He looked at Hera. "How about your lovely ride?"

"It's got everything," she said, pulling back on the control yoke. *Expedient* heaved off the deck. "My ship should be up to date for whatever you need. If we can land on Gorse and get to it."

"We'll be shot at on the way down and up again."

"*Up* I'm not worried about." She smiled.

I have got to see this ship, Kanan thought again as *Expedient* turned in midair. "What have you got in mind, Zaluna?"

"I still have Vidian's passcode from earlier. If we can send a signal mimicking an Imperial override request, we can push out an emergency message onto every electronic system on Gorse that Transcept is spying on." She looked at Kanan with trepidation. "We'd only be able to do it once, ever. They'd close the door immediately."

"One message, then. It'll have to be enough," Hera said, guiding the ship through the magnetic field into space. "We'd have to get there and do it before he changes the passcode."

"If he doesn't realize we did anything," Kanan said. "And he won't." He gestured forward. Traffic was moving along outside the station, and he could see the TIE fighters routinely flying past. "See? Nobody's shooting us out of the sky."

"That's just because your *new friend* hasn't called out the heavy artillery yet," Hera said—

—and as she did, *Expedient* shuddered violently. Zaluna yelped. Kanan and Hera glanced warily at each other.

"Just the parking tractor beam guiding us out," Kanan finally said, nodding forward. The ship was turning, making progress toward the perimeter.

Hera took a deep breath and let out a whistle. "We'd better hope this thing lets go of us before the stasis beam lets go of Sloane."

"I'm telling you not to worry," Kanan said, leaning back and stretching his legs. "None of this is necessary. Vidian is done for. Sloane is sold."

.   .   .

"My lord! My lord!"

Count Vidian roused. Awareness always returned quickly to him after sleep, medically induced or otherwise. His eyes activated a second after his ears did, and he saw the fraught face of the Star Destroyer captain leaning over him.

"Sloane? What's going on?"

She yanked at the straps binding him to the operating table. "You were unconscious," she said, straining to remove one of the durasteel cuffs binding his wrists. "Are you all right?"

"I believe so." Whispering a command, he cycled back through everything his eyes had recorded in the last several hours. There was nothing there from the time he was under—not even any of the feedback his nightmares had been producing lately. And neither had his senses recorded anything from the hour before, during the battle with the pilot and his companions. A glitch, caused by damage in the fight?

The servos in his hips activated, and he sat up on the table. He looked around at the mess of his living space. "Someone drugged me."

"There were intruders here," Sloane said, moving to work on the cuffs holding his ankles. "They attacked me, too, when I entered. They trapped me in your stasis beam. Then they left."

Vidian looked around. "Through the floor?"

Sloane nodded. "It was dark—I couldn't see much. What did they want?"

"Me." Vidian leaned down and ripped at the ankle cuffs with his metal hands. The manacles were designed to withstand his thrashings, and yet they couldn't survive against his rising anger. "I want a full search. Lock the station down!" He opened a channel on his internal comlink and prepared to give the command.

Sloane spoke before he could. "My lord—one of them *talked* to me." Her dark eyes were full of concern. "He claimed to be an agent of the Emperor."

"What?" Vidian closed the audio channel and stared at her. "Who?"

"One of the people who waylaid me," she said.

"An agent of the Emperor?" Vidian rose from the table and stood, turning his back to the captain. "What . . . did he say?"

"A lot of nonsense. He claimed you were acting against the Emperor's interests in the Gorse project. That your plan was to destroy the moon and its thorilide, regardless of the yield."

Vidian froze. Cautiously, he turned to face her. "Most amusing. Pray tell, what reason did this mystic give for my doing such a thing?"

"It was senseless ranting, Count Vidian. I didn't listen."

"Perhaps he thinks I'm some kind of traitor? Some kind of plant in the hierarchy?"

Sloane laughed. "I think he was insane." She looked at him. "Have you called for security already, or should I?"

"I'm doing so now," Vidian said. But directing his eyes to check the station's surveillance reports, he found precious little for his staff to go on. Nothing unusual had been seen aboard Calcoraan Depot in the last few hours. He'd recognized the gunslinger from Cynda, and he'd remembered Skelly. But all the workers aboard were in hazmat masks, and the ships had already departed. Even a check of the data feeds from his medical droids in the room confirmed that their memories had been wiped.

The infiltrators were good, whoever they were.

Reports from the TIE sentries on the system perimeter confirmed that all the ships had gone to hyperspace on the same heading: toward Cynda, as ordered. If his assailants weren't still aboard the depot, there was only one other place for them.

Vidian thought quickly about his next move. He wasn't sure who his attackers were, but neither was he sure what they would say if found. All that mattered was making sure nothing interfered with the destruction of Cynda.

And he had a way to do that. "*Ultimatum* will arrive in the Gorse system before the last of the baradium haulers?"

A little startled by the change of topic, Sloane nodded. "They haven't built the freighter that can outrun a Star Destroyer."

"Good. I want your whole complement of fighters deployed, managing the final delivery. Bring in additional TIEs from here, using the Gozanti freighter carriers. If any hauler moves a centimeter out of line, I want that ship destroyed, cargo and all. Regardless of any danger to the pilot doing the shooting. Is that understood?"

"They'll do their duty—for me." Sloane looked at him searchingly. "You think the intruders are headed for Gorse?"

"It pays to be ready." Vidian walked across the room to a fallen cabinet. Righting it, he thought about his other problem. He highly doubted the gunslinger was an agent of the Emperor; while Palpatine was fond of testing his underlings' devotion, he was never as clumsy as this. But neither could he see a bunch of amateurs successfully boarding his station, simply looking for revenge for Lal Grallik's death.

What Vidian could easily see, however, was the pilot and his friends being part of some plot by one of his many rivals. And that meant he had to be cautious. He had no idea what the pilot had said to Sloane—but he had to be certain of her loyalty, and his eventual success. "I appreciate your freeing me, Sloane. This could have been . . . *embarrassing*."

She shrugged. "My duty is to you, sir."

"Then I will do mine to you." He paused for several seconds before speaking aloud again. "I have just sent a verbal instruction to the staff at my offices at Corellia. In a few days Captain Karlsen will be receiving a very lucrative offer to join the private sector."

Surprised, Sloane put up her hand in protest. "Sir, I wasn't expecting—"

"At that time, *Ultimatum* is yours to keep."

The news appeared to take her breath away. *Good,* Vidian thought. "Return with *Ultimatum* as planned while I finish the preparations aboard the collection ship. Once the moon is destroyed and *Forager* begins to do its job, the Emperor will see the return, and our work together will be vindicated."

"Together, my lord?"

"You'll have the credit you deserve for helping to make this happen so quickly. I might even request you and *Ultimatum* be permanently detached to me." He eyed her. "Who *is* the youngest admiral, I wonder?"

CHAPTER FORTY-SEVEN

There wasn't always much to do when a ship was in hyperspace, the interdimensional realm between stars. There was even less when flying *Expedient,* a ship with no galley or living quarters. Worse, the cockpit area offered no privacy at all; Skelly was snoring away on his seats, and Zaluna, unshakable for so long, had taken to nervously fidgeting around with the contents of her magic bag. Well, even the strongest had their limits—especially when death was coming for their homeworld.

The only getaway existed in the far rear of the ship, down one of the branching aisles of the cargo hold. And there, at the far end, standing amid the shelves of secured baradium-357 canisters, waited the person he wanted to see.

"Cozy back here," Kanan said. "We could send out for flatcakes."

"Very funny." Hera held the smile for only a moment. She looked tired. "We need to talk."

"My pleasure." Kanan found a spot at the end of the aisle with no canisters on either side, creating two makeshift seats on opposing lower shelves. "I fixed the ID transponder like you asked. It'll say we're a different ship than landed on Calcoraan Depot—in case they've finally figured out we were the ones that messed with Vidian."

Hera still wore the same worried expression, he saw. "I'm guessing you had a different problem?" Kanan asked.

"It's Skelly," she said in a low voice, nodding in the direction of the cockpit. "I think he's in trouble."

"He's always in trouble."

"I think he's *dying*," she said. "The joking around is a cover. He's in bad shape."

Kanan inhaled deeply and nodded. He'd seen the same thing. "Vidian did a number on him. Broken bones, internal bleeding." He shook his head. "I caught a look at the readings that medical droid took of him. It wanted to open him up, right then and there."

"We need to get him to a medcenter," Hera said. "He's navigating on force of will alone."

"He's got plenty of that. But where can we take him? We're about to tell everyone on Gorse to run for their lives."

Hera sighed. "You're right. They come first. He's just going to have to hang on."

She looked toward the small viewport to her left, at the end of the aisle. Stars streaked by. Kanan thought she looked striking even now, facing likely defeat. "This isn't what you came to Gorse for, was it?"

She chuckled darkly. "Not even close. I've been talking to people who have grievances against the Empire—but only to find out the scope of what's out there, what's possible. I wasn't expecting to *do* anything against it. Not yet, anyway. Not for a long time."

"That's the problem with people," Kanan said. "They never need help on your schedule—only theirs."

She nodded. Then she looked back at him. After studying him for a moment, she spoke. "Where are you from, Kanan?"

"Around," he said. "You?"

"Same."

"Fair enough."

She smiled gently. "That's not what I really wanted to ask, anyway."

Kanan smirked. "Fire away, then."

"Why are you doing this?"

"Sitting with you? Wouldn't miss it."

"No, I mean *this*. Flying around fugitives and trying to take down Vidian. I know why Skelly and I are doing this," she said. "Even Zaluna. But not you."

He shrugged. "I love a party."

"Seriously."

He scratched his beard. "You were there. You saw what happened to Okadiah, and all the others—"

"And that's awful. But by your own admission, you move around. You were about to leave Gorse forever when I found you. So while I appreciate your being here, I wonder if there's something else going on." She eyed him. "I mean, you're not here for the politics."

He laughed. "Definitely not."

She smiled. "Yeah, you don't strike me as a victim of oppression."

Kanan's grin melted a little on hearing her words, and he looked away. "You never know," he muttered. "Appearances can be deceiving."

"What?"

Feeling her eyes on him, he faced her again and smiled. "Nothing. Hey, it's like I said at the start. I'm just going where you're going."

Hera's nose wrinkled. "Hmm," she said, after a moment.

"Hmm what?"

"I think I liked your first answer better."

Zaluna stood before the onrushing stars. It was an amazing spectacle, something she had never expected to see. Her salary wasn't enough to take her far, and besides, she had nowhere to go. Her office was her universe.

And now that Skelly was snoozing and Kanan and Hera were gone, somewhere in the back, this was her last chance to get it back.

Her last chance to change her mind.

She'd completely ruined her life in the last few days. She'd only wanted to fulfill Hetto's parting wish, not go running around the galaxy like some kind of secret agent. Infiltrating an Imperial depot? Tampering not just with the computers of an important official, but with his very body? Who *was* that person? It certainly wasn't the woman she'd imagined she was.

But here, she had an opportunity to undo everything. She'd seen the big red light on the forward control panel, earlier: It had signaled when the vessel was about to exit hyperspace. Dark now, it sat adjacent to the comm system—and that was something Zaluna knew how to use.

And she *could* use it, right as they reentered realspace, to contact the Empire and get off this ride.

They might still believe her. She could say she was kidnapped, forced to help the would-be radicals. Skelly and Kanan were violent characters who'd attacked Imperial agents. Hera was the mastermind, trying to lure her into betraying the Empire. Zaluna was innocent, a pawn, a foolish woman with nothing but good intentions. She could say she was trying to entrap the agitators when she got trapped herself. They'd taken her into danger. She didn't owe them anything.

And the moon might still be saved. If Vidian was doing something he shouldn't, the Empire would stop him, wouldn't it? And how was any of it her business anyway? Maybe the deadly predictions of what might happen were wrong. Who was she to second-guess decisions made from so far on high? It would be an irrational Empire indeed that would ignore its people's best interests.

Only . . . the Empire *had* done exactly that many times that she had seen. And its minions had *never* listened to anyone's defense before. They only listened to what people said about the Empire. Zaluna knew firsthand, having been the state's ears and eyes on Gorse and Cynda for years. She'd heard—but never comprehended. She watched, but never saw.

And now that was changing. The others had started her thinking.

Hera had listened patiently to Zaluna's concerns several times during their journey, and each time had spoken frankly and firmly. Fear was understandable and forgivable—and no one expected Zaluna to do more than she was capable of. "But seeing and doing nothing isn't the worst thing," Hera had said. *"The worst thing is to see and not to care."*

Zaluna had seen Imperial minions do many things. Bad things, that Transcept's watchers were ordered to look the other way on. She'd done as commanded—but it had never made sense. Wasn't being a watchperson her job? What good was being a witness if the laws could be changed at whim by the lawgivers?

Then there was Skelly. He was troubled, for sure, but she'd come to understand that he truly was interested in protecting Cynda and Gorse. The Empire cared little for those damaged by the Clone Wars, and even less for people who had qualms about its industrial activities. She could tell that for Skelly, the impending destruction of the moon was like watching death approaching for someone close to him.

And finally, there was Kanan, who seemed to go from disaster to disaster as if he were wandering from one cantina to another. Nothing seemed to touch him—yet she knew that wasn't true. Yes, he played the roustabout, working a dangerous job and pushing back against those who pushed him. But that day with Okadiah was not the first time she'd seen him come to someone's defense. They were always small acts; often, the person helped hadn't known he'd done anything. He seemed to want it that way, for some reason.

She could also tell he was tired of living the way he had been: tired of going from one pointless job to another, looking for a place where he could live his life his own way. She'd seen the look a hundred times on the faces of other migrant workers—and the Empire had made it into a perpetual state for many. Kanan was young—but his secret soul was much older. And Zaluna knew the Empire was somehow responsible.

But Zaluna had the right to a life of her choosing, too—and time was running out.

The red light on the nav computer flashed. A buzzer, half broken and barely audible, sounded. Her eyes went to the comm system controls. It would be so easy . . .

"Your only value to the Empire is what you can do for it," said a voice from behind.

Unsurprised at hearing Hera, Zaluna turned over her words in her mind. "You know," she said calmly, "Hetto used to say that exact thing."

"He was right."

Zaluna saw Hera's reflection in the viewport, against the streaming stars. She was motionless behind her, not approaching. "Aren't you afraid?" Zaluna asked.

"Anyone would be. But the Jedi had a saying about fear. It leads, ultimately, to suffering." Hera paused. "Someone has to break the chain."

"People can't talk about the Jedi anymore."

"Maybe they should."

Zaluna nodded and looked back at the control panel. "It *was* better then." She felt her strength reviving. She was more than an extra set of eyes and ears to a sadistic cyborg—and to a faraway Emperor. She was no revolutionary, but she could at least try to stop them now.

Zaluna moved her hand to the nav computer and shut off the buzzer. "I was just coming to get you," she said. Turning to Hera, she smiled. "We're here."

CHAPTER FORTY-EIGHT

Kanan thought it sounded foolish to say aloud, but leaving hyperspace was just like entering it, except in reverse. The stars through the forward viewport went from blurred lines back to twinkling dots. Only this time, few could be seen from *Expedient*'s cockpit. Cynda hung above, a brilliant crescent from their angle, while massive Gorse sat up ahead, its cities in their eternal night.

And there was something else: more TIE fighters than he had ever seen. Swarms lay ahead, peeling off in quartets as *Expedient* entered the area.

"Vector right seven-five degrees, down-axis twenty," snapped a voice over the comm system. "Follow the formation if you want to live."

Kanan flinched. This was normally when he'd give the Imperials some lip—but he wasn't flying, and it wasn't smart. Not now. Hera complied, banking the vessel and bringing it into line with a queue of ships far ahead. Each freighter had a pair of TIEs either above and below it or on either side, defining a corridor: Kanan could tell from the sensors that two flanked *Expedient*, on the port and starboard sides. Ahead, the sky went black for a moment, as the hexagonal wing of another TIE zipped past their field of view.

"They're crisscrossing," Kanan said. "Keeping us all separated."

Hera frowned. "They're limiting the damage a saboteur can do. They're afraid there's another Skelly out here."

"They'd be right," called Skelly from behind. Holding his midsection, Skelly hobbled toward the front of the cockpit. He reached for the side of Kanan's seat and missed. Zaluna hopped from her seat and grabbed onto him. Skelly seemed almost unaware of the woman steadying him. His eyes were locked on the outside. "Somebody means business."

Expedient followed the convoy across the terminator dividing Cyndan night from day. There they saw it, sitting off in space: the gang boss to their work crew. Zaluna gasped at the sight. "Another Star Destroyer!"

"No, the same one," Hera said.

Kanan nodded. It was one of the more unnerving consequences when ships of differing speeds used hyperspace. *Ultimatum* had been in their rearview cam, parked at Calcoraan Depot, when they'd gone to lightspeed; now it was sitting in front of them over Gorse, disgorging even more TIE fighters.

Hera looked in unsettled wonder. "These TIEs can't all be from the Star Destroyer. *Imperial*-class has sixty, maybe seventy."

Kanan pointed out other vessels orbiting off Cynda's horizon. Long and bulky like the thorilide cargo craft, the ships had docking ports for four TIE fighters each. "Looks like the Empire's refitting Gozanti freighters these days."

"And they beat us here, too!" Hera was as aggravated as he'd seen her. She was clearly used to flying a faster ship. "We're lucky they didn't have time for shore leave." She looked at the scanner and raised her hands in frustration. "I don't know that we can get to Gorse at all through this blockade."

"I thought you were good," Kanan said.

"Not that good. Not in this thing."

The TIEs led the convoy on a long descent path, several hundred kilometers off the surface of Cynda. Hera rolled *Expedient* 180 degrees so the ground could be seen from the cockpit. "Construction work ahead," Kanan said. He flipped a switch, triggering the viewport's magnifying overlay.

Skelly staggered forward and half collapsed against the forward panel between Hera and Kanan. Arms splayed forward across it for support, he gawked at what he saw. "We're too late," Skelly said, staring at a large metal tower on the surface over their heads.

"What? What are those?" Kanan asked. He could see at least six others, spaced seemingly randomly across the moon's surface.

"Injection sites. They're pumping in xenoboric acid, punching holes deep into the mantle. They'll run the baradium charges down on suprafilament next." Skelly looked from tower to tower. "Down below, Cynda's got flaws, just like a diamond. They'll set off the charges in a precise order, seconds apart. The primaries will cleave it. The secondaries will crush it. The tertiaries will disperse it."

Kanan stared at him. "How do you know all this?"

"It's my idea. I did it as a thought experiment—just to prove my point. It was on the holodisk." He sighed and sagged to the floor. "Why do I always have to be right?"

Hera studied the workers on the surface. "They're in a real hurry," Hera said.

"Vidian's in the hurry," Kanan said. "He's got to destroy the moon before the Emperor gets wise to what he's doing here." He smirked. "And that's who's missing. Him and his big collector ship. I told you, you just had to trust—"

"Attention, newly arriving freighters," said a familiar voice over the comm system. "This is Captain Sloane of *Ultimatum*. I have important information about a change in plans."

Kanan smiled at the others and gave a thumbs-up signal. "This is it!"

"The accident earlier this week left the moon's mines dangerously unstable," Sloane said over the comm system. "Imperial scientists have determined the only way to prevent future disasters is to release all the stresses that have built up—now, with no one in the mines. By doing so, we assure safe mining can continue, in the name of the Empire."

"Yeah, that Empire's really looking out for them," Skelly said. "They're talking our own people into committing suicide!"

"You will be guided to sites on the Cyndan surface where you will off-load and leave immediately," the captain continued.

Kanan frowned. "Wait a minute. That wasn't what she was supposed to say. She was supposed to say Vidian's a goner—and send us all home!"

"That doesn't sound like a woman who just squealed to the Emperor," Hera said.

Kanan stared at the comm system. "No, it doesn't." He shook his head.

The hyperspace anomaly alarm flashed blue and squawked loudly. Ahead, Vidian's gigantic thorilide harvester vessel appeared in the only free patch of space available.

"Welcome, *Forager*," Sloane said over the comm system. "The final freighters are here and the last charges will be injected in forty minutes. You should receive a data hookup with Detonation Control down there in one hour."

"Excellent work, Captain Sloane," they heard Vidian say. "You'll make a fine admiral one day."

Kanan looked at Hera. "This is making me sick. They're on a date."

"Jealous?"

"Blast it, I thought she'd listen!" He pounded his fist on the dashboard. "That's the Imperial way, all right. They're always stabbing their friends in the back!"

Sloane spoke again over the device, sounding more concerned. "Count Vidian, time will be of the essence. Lieutenant Deltic's staff says you will have one hour from the Detonation Control linkup to trigger the process."

"I won't need that much time," Vidian responded, drily. "I've been ready—and *Forager* will be ready."

"To collect the thorilide after he's blown most of it up—along with the moon," Skelly muttered as the transmission ended. "Senseless." He turned around on the floor and slumped with his back against the cockpit control panels. He dabbed his nose with his hand. There was blood there. "Just drop me off anywhere. Maybe I can die on Cynda before they blow it up."

Hera looked at Skelly for a moment—and then back outside. Her eyes focused on something ahead. "Skelly, why did she say there was a time limit to detonating the explosives they're planting in the moon?"

Skelly rubbed the side of his head, his eyes closed. "It's the xenoboric acid they're injecting. Wait too long and any of the junk that's left down there will eat its way through the baradium drop cables and containers. No boom then."

Hera looked at Kanan. He caught the drift. "You said there was a chain reaction here—that some of those towers were primaries?"

Skelly sniffed, eyes opening. "Yeah. Four of them."

"Which four?" Kanan asked.

"I'm trying to remember. I'd have to look." Skelly tried to get to his feet, but only fell back down on his rump. Zaluna sprang again from her seat and helped him stand, bracing herself between the two forward chairs. Skelly looked ahead and squinted at Cynda's bright surface.

"Will killing the towers stop the reaction?" Kanan asked him.

"Yeah. But those are our people down there working those sites— and flying cargo to them."

"I know." Kanan reached down for his headset and put it on.

"That's only patched into local comm traffic," Hera said. "We can't send Zaluna's warning on it."

Kanan ignored her and worked the latch on the panel in front of his knees. A door swung open, and he pulled at what was inside. Reluctant hinges cracked and groaned. With effort, Kanan craned a targeting system with handles up toward his chest.

"Do I want to know what he's doing?" Zaluna asked.

Hera stared at him in puzzlement. "I'm not sure I know, myself."

"The meteor chaser," Kanan said, waving to the ceiling. The single cannon perched above the crew compartment had a field of fire that covered a wide arc on either side and ahead of *Expedient*. "Every Baby Carrier has one. Baby doesn't like being bumped."

"Neither do I," Skelly said, looking nervously at him. "You can't expect to fight off the Imperials with that?"

"Not more than a few," Kanan said, testing his microphone. "But if I do it right, a few's enough!"

CHAPTER FORTY-NINE

The command center of the collection ship looked like a cathedral for some ancient religion. Vidian's comm station, in the middle of the room, resembled an altar. Idle comparisons, both. But the reality was not lost on Vidian. From here, he would sacrifice the moon to his Emperor, winning his favor for another year. And the ashes of the world would smother his rival once and for all.

Intentionally or not, the collection ship's designers had built a supernatural feel into *Forager*'s bridge. Situated frontward on the foremost sphere on the ship's linked series of pods, the huge round room looked ahead through tall windows that rose and curved to a ceiling twenty meters above. More consoles like Vidian's circled him like miniature megaliths in a place for idol-worshipper rites. A catwalk two stories up ran around the front arc of the room, providing additional workstations between the windows for Vidian's droids and cybernetically enhanced assistants. He could see the metallic figures moving back and forth on the decking, digital priests backlit by the shining moon.

"Spokes deployed, my lord," one of them said. "We are ready for the collection process to begin."

Vidian nodded. It was up to Sloane and her people now. Switching his visual feed from cam to remote cam, he looked approvingly on the Cynda work sites. Sloane had done a remarkable job, throwing *Ultimatum*'s thousands of staffers at a project that, days before, had been a fantasy on a holodisk from a deranged assassin. Now they were thirty minutes away from doing something that still existed only at the outer edges of Imperial capability: the destruction of a moon, and perhaps the world below.

It had been critical to get Sloane's cooperation early on. Any extra time, any deliberation would have brought the Emperor's corps of engineers into the picture, and they would have questioned the yield from the test blast. Vidian could use Tharsa's name to falsify a report and defraud an ambitious captain, but more would be difficult. And this couldn't wait. As Vidian cycled his messages before his eyes, he saw not just more from the nuisance Danthe, but several from the Emperor's inner circle. All were almost comically urgent, suggesting that if Vidian didn't deliver thorilide in record amounts instantly, the entire Imperial fleet would have to be mothballed. The baron had really gone to work on the Emperor's people.

Well, he would finish it soon enough. He would deliver thorilide beyond anyone's fantasies—and then stick the grinning Danthe with a ticking bomb.

One of Vidian's cybernetic aides stepped forward. "Something's coming in, master, on the Mining Guild channel."

"Eh?" Vidian whispered commands until the sound reached him.

"—don't know what's going on. Feeling so . . . weird. These blasted Baby canisters—some of them started leaking these, I don't know, these *fumes* . . ."

"What's this nonsense?" Vidian said aloud.

"—don't know how it happened. Faulty loading, faulty material, faulty something—just like everything in this wretched job. I've hated it all, y'know." The voice went from woozy to bitter. "And I've hated all of *you*."

"It's one coming from one of the freighters," Vidian's aide volunteered. "The coolant lining the baradium-357 canisters has been known to cause psychotic episodes if it gets—"

"Yeah, you know me," the broadcaster interrupted, sounding angrier by the word. "You know my voice. I put up with all of you, for Okadiah's sake. In the mines, on the hoverbus, in the bar. Lot of bums, all of you. Think you're such *tough* guys. You make me sick!"

Vidian seethed as he recognized the voice. *The gunslinger!* "Zero in on that transmission," he ordered. "Find him!"

The speaker was raging now. "Filthy, stinking miners! I can see your ID transponders—I know who you are. Think you're hot stuff, hauling bombs. Let's see how hot *I* can make it!"

Vidian toggled his comlink mode. "Now hear this! This is Count Vidian. Disregard these transmissions and finish your deliveries! You've just heard the ravings of a crazy man, a provocateur—"

The pilot boomed in response. "I'm crazy? *I'm crazy?* Fine! I don't care about your stinking starfighters, Empire-man. I'm telling everyone—if you see me coming, run, because I'm going to blow every ship I see out of the sky! *Starting with the miners!*"

A horrific squawk erupted from *Expedient*'s comm system: Imperial jamming on the guild channel. Hera looked at Kanan, stupefied. "I thought you were going to warn them about the moon!"

"They wouldn't have believed it. *I* barely believe it. Right now, they're only afraid of the TIE fighters. But they're about to become more afraid of me!" Kanan flashed her a wild look. "I need you to fly like a Wookiee whose hair is on fire—and who thinks *everybody* lit the match. Can you do that?"

She seemed to get the idea, if reluctantly. "Got it."

He pointed at the TIE fighter beginning its intersecting run across their convoy corridor. "Dive when I signal."

The Imperial starfighter whisked into their field of view, its wings resolving into a fat hexagonal target. Kanan used it as exactly that, pulling the trigger on his gunnery controls. "Hera, now!"

Orange fire ripped from the weapons turret positioned over and behind their heads, tearing dead-center into the wing of the TIE fighter passing before them. Hera slammed the control yoke forward and hit the throttle, causing *Expedient* to dive. The TIE exploded into a blaze of bright flame above—but now Cynda was all they could see, its icy surface filling the viewport.

Zaluna lost her hold on the side of Kanan's seat and fell forward, mashing Skelly against the forward control panel. He called out in pain.

"Hang on!" Hera brought *Expedient* into a roll, bringing one of the two Imperial fighters that had been flanking them into Kanan's sights. He fired again. Hera didn't wait to see the result, moving once more to bring the ship lower. Cynda's gravity began to take hold.

Zaluna tried to help Skelly up. "I'm so sorry," she said. "I'm not used to this!"

"Who is?" Weakly trying to fend off her attempts to stand him up, he appealed to the air. "Please, just let me go sit down . . ."

"We need you here," Kanan said, struggling to find their other flanker on his scope. The TIE was shooting at them: He could see the flash of energized particles to his right. "Where is this guy?"

"Right here," Hera said, slamming on the braking jets. The glowing ionic thrusters of the third TIE appeared in the space before them. Kanan swung his targeting mechanism and hit the trigger. Hera pumped her fist as the starfighter blew itself apart.

Kanan glanced at Skelly, looking rocky as Zaluna held him up. Skelly outweighed the woman, but she was doing her best to keep him in place. Kanan implored him. "Come on, Skelly. We're there. Focus!"

Skelly squinted at the surface as Hera descended. There was a tower on the far horizon, nothing more than a needle on an ocean of white. A cluster of ships could be seen heading for the area. "That way!"

The alert clarion sounded on the bridge of *Ultimatum*. "Scramble wings fourteen, fifteen, seventeen," Sloane said. "Pursue freighter, hereafter tagged Renegade One. Take them down!"

The captain stood by the holographic tracking display and watched the action with bewilderment. She'd ordered the Star Destroyer to remain on its station, overseeing the convoy route and protecting *Forager*—but what was going on over the surface of Cynda defied belief. And it had all started with that bizarre message from Kanan.

"Renegade One is pursuing the other baradium haulers," said a fresh-faced ensign. Young Cauley had been trying his best to track the zigzagging renegade—but nothing it did made any sense.

"They're trying to destroy the freighters?"

"No, Captain. Just the TIE fighters accompanying them. The freighters should be easier targets, but it's just, well—" The headset-wearing ensign gawked at his monitor. Sloane stepped behind him to watch the chase. The runaway was peeling away the escorts of the fully laden cargo ships—and then seemingly shooting to miss, aiming just in front of the vessels.

"Harassing fire," she said. Kanan—pilot, insurrectionist, would-be Imperial agent? Whatever he was, he was definitely aboard that ship and trying to prevent the others from landing their cargo. His threatening message had set the stage for chaos. "Method to the madness. He's scaring them away."

"And doing a good job of it," Ensign Cauley said. He pointed to the screen. "He gets anywhere near a freighter and they try to peel off."

Sloane looked back at the holographic tracking display. One by one, baradium freighters were switching off their ID transponders, fearful of having Kanan come after them. It was only adding to the confusion. *Has everybody on Gorse tangled with this character?*

Cauley tapped his earpiece. "I've got a TIE pilot chasing after the hauler he's escorting now. It's fleeing, afraid of being targeted by Renegade One. Our pilot's asking if he can shoot his hauler down."

"What? No!" Sloane froze. She'd told Vidian she'd allow nothing to interfere with the explosives delivery, and they'd sent more than his project needed. But how much more? "Tell our pilot to stick with the ship he's convoying as best he can until our reinforcements arrive. Tell him if he can run interference—"

"Never mind," Cauley said, removing his headset. "Renegade One just shot our pilot down."

Sloane clenched her fists. "Pull all escort wings in that area off their duty. Send them all against Kanan!"

"Against who, Captain?"

"Renegade One!" Quaking in anger, she pointed outside. *"The guy shooting at everyone!"*

CHAPTER FIFTY

Kanan checked his sights again as Hera banked *Expedient* into another S-turn. She'd been weaving between the injection tower on the Cyndan surface and the landing area nearby, where tracked Imperial ground vehicles were moving baradium canisters across the ice from the freighters.

He wasn't about to target anything directly: Shooting the tower, Skelly had said, might set off the world-destroying reaction by accident. And killing mining workers in the freighters or on the icecrawlers would make him no better than Vidian. Instead, he continued strafing the areas the workers had to cross, while preventing any more ships from landing. He wouldn't kill civilians, but he had nothing against scaring the daylights out of them for a good cause.

"Not exactly an ideal way to raise a collective consciousness," Hera said as he fired another volley just beneath a freighter attempting a landing.

"Recruit allies on your own time. This is getting attention, the Gorse way!"

Trouble was, he was running out of targets. "Skelly, where's the next primary tower?"

"Forget it," Hera snapped. Yanking on the control yoke, she sent a reluctant *Expedient* into a groaning upward spiral. Kanan saw why as the ship twisted: a sky full of TIE fighters, rocketing toward them.

A loud beeping noise came from his gunnery controls. The indicator said the weapons turret was overheating. He looked at Hera and shook his head. "This thing's rated to move some pebbles around. That's about it!"

"I think our engines could go at any minute." She sighed in exasperation as *Expedient* hurtled back toward orbit.

"Safest thing on board is the baradium!" It was a perversely lucky thing, Kanan thought: The many bumps, slams, and near-misses *Expedient* had suffered would have set his regular cargo off in a heartbeat. The ridiculously more powerful Baby on board at least had the benefit of containers that secured to the shelving.

Gorse appeared in front of them again, with *Forager* hanging before it. Its spokes were open, a gigantic metal bloom at the front of the vessel. Kanan blanched at the size of it. "Can we take out that thing?"

Hera checked her instruments and shook her head. "Big energy shield around it." She pointed *Expedient* outward, away from the ever-approaching wave of TIE fighters. It gave them a better look at *Forager* from the side, but that was about it. It was useless.

Kanan released the gunnery controls. He'd left imprints on them with his hands, he saw. He rubbed his forehead. "Anybody else got a plan?"

No one said anything for a moment.

Then a voice came from behind. "I think we can do Plan Two."

Kanan looked back to see Zaluna trying to squeeze past Skelly. She was looking outward, at *Forager*. "Which one was Plan Two?" Kanan asked.

"I thought Plan Two was slowing down the injection process," Skelly said, hanging on to Hera's chair.

Zaluna shook her head. "No, that's Plan Three. Plan One was informing on Count Vidian. Plan Two was warning people. Plan Three was slowing down the injection—"

"Can we stop this?" Hera pleaded. She nodded to the left and smiled politely at Zaluna. "TIE fighter fleet in two minutes, remember?"

The woman pointed ahead at *Forager*. "Okay. Look up there." Behind the rimless wagon wheel that was the collection array stretched seven globes, connected in a line. The one at the ship's front, nearest the spokes, had a lighted crew area at top—and a big round dish atop that. "That's an Imperial subspace transmitter."

"I didn't see that," Kanan said. "Good eyes."

"That's what they paid me for." Zaluna grinned. "I can tap into the Transcept systems on that thing and send our warning to Gorse. They won't know to jam that."

Kanan stared. "That ship's where Vidian is now. We'd have to get you in there to do your thing."

Zaluna shrank a little at that, but didn't shirk. "I know."

"And maybe we can even keep Vidian from sending the trigger command to Cynda," Hera said.

"Two for one," Kanan said. "Happy hour."

"You're going to want a stiff drink or two after this," Hera said, bringing *Expedient* around in a wide arc. She looked at him. "This is not what you'd consider a safe bet. Are you sure *you* want to do this?"

Kanan took a deep breath. It wasn't even a dare he'd take on his drunkest day. It was insane—but it had all been. And he had to admit he'd felt better these past few days doing something—even a stupid something—than he'd felt in years of running. "I've got nothing else to do. Let's go for it."

"All right." Hera looked at the Sullustan. "Strap yourself in, Zal. Everybody else—hang on!"

Vidian had had quite enough of people telling him what he couldn't do.

As a guild safety inspector, he'd given edicts to police but had no power to enforce them, as his corrupt supervisors constantly undermined him. He'd transformed his image and position such that no one could say no to him—and yet people tried anyway, trying to protect their old ways of doing things.

The gunslinger and his friends, it was obvious, were trying to prevent him from destroying the moon. Were they saboteurs working for Baron Danthe? The baron had set up the near-impossible production threshold for Vidian to meet; he might well fear the acclaim success would give the count. And Vidian knew the baron had spies about, inquiring after Vidian's "independent consultant," Lemuel Tharsa. If so, then Vidian was all the more ready to destroy the moon. No one would say no to him in this.

He retained the upper hand now, through his logic and careful preparations. The berserk antics of the fool pilot had changed nothing. He'd added his own precautions to Skelly's scheme, and those included dispatching more baradium haulers than were necessary. Already, the redundant vessels were moving into the area recently harried by the renegade. It would only mean a little lost time, not enough for the xenoboric acid to destroy the bombs he was implanting in the moon. It was the same kind of acid Lal had fallen into on Gorse, a refining necessity; *Forager* was full of the stuff. But it wouldn't devour his plan.

And the one random variable was about to be canceled out. The run-amok freighter was out of space to roam, hemmed in between the collector ship's weapons and the swarm of TIE fighters now arriving on the scene. He'd thought of everything. It was his strength, his power. One day, the difference between success and failure for the Empire might be a simple thing someone else would overlook. It would not be his fault, and would never happen on his watch. He would see everything, and act.

"We are at a safe distance from the target moon," he said. "Reorient to face it."

The engines thrummed, and Cynda came fully into glistening view. Vidian didn't bother to look at it for more than a second.

"Give me an update on the enemy," he commanded the nearest cybernetic assistant. Vidian never used the bald woman's name; it didn't seem necessary, after her surgery.

"The freighter has not attacked," she droned. "It is circling. Probing *Forager*'s energy shield."

"Is there a weakness?"

"No, my lord. The only gap in the energy shield is rearward, along the horizontal axis of the vessel. The thrusters produce a flux when ignited."

Vidian froze. The engines had just been activated a few moments earlier. And it was at the tail of the ship, above the thrusters, where the shipping bays sat, open to space . . .

"Proximity alarm!" the female cyborg said. "Unauthorized vessel on approach!"

Vidian was already looking at the scene, his optical feed having been switched to the rear external cams. Pursued madly by half a dozen TIE fighters—and those were just the ones in firing range—the errant freighter raced toward *Forager*'s aft. "What are you waiting for?" Vidian said. "All defensive turrets, fire!"

Outside, *Expedient* rocketed through the cross fire toward the rear of *Forager*. Rows of landing bays perched atop and tucked beneath the glowing thrusters, open to space. "An open door's as good as an invitation," Hera said.

But the freighter was going far too fast, Kanan thought. "This'll be close!"

At the last instant, Hera fired *Expedient*'s attitude control jets, spinning the vessel around 180 degrees. The ship entered the bay tail-first, piercing the magnetic screen. Hera fired the main thrusters, burning off speed—not to mention the chrome off any loader droids in their path.

Expedient struck the landing surface, scraping noisily across the deck as it slid inward. It was a long hangar, and the freighter needed all of it to slow down. Kanan clutched the armrests, knowing the back wall had to be there somewhere . . .

A violent jolt shook the vessel, rocking Count Vidian's underlings. Above, a droid slipped between the catwalk and the railing and fell to the main deck with a crash.

Vidian, prepared for the impact, was unshaken. "All troops aboard *Forager*," he transmitted, "stand by to repel boarders. Enough is enough!"

CHAPTER FIFTY-ONE

"We're still alive!"

Skelly had said it, but Kanan was as amazed as anyone. And Hera was simply straightening her gloves as if nothing had happened.

"You're incredible," Kanan said. "I'm permanently moving to the passenger seat."

"Time to get out of it." Hera stood, checked her weapons, and made for the airlock. "Come on, Zal!"

Zaluna took a deep breath and retrieved her pouch of electronic magic from behind the acceleration couch. She met Hera at the door.

Vidian was almost certainly at the head of *Forager*, where the transmitter was. "Do you have anything else aboard we can use?" Hera asked Kanan. "We don't know the layout."

"I think so." Adjusting his holster, Kanan walked down the aisle to a storage compartment. He knelt before the bin and opened it. There, beside Skelly's bag of improvised explosives, which he'd hidden for safekeeping, was part of the Cynda emergency kit: a rappelling gun with an automatic winder. He passed it to Hera.

He was about to close the bin when he glanced at his traveling pack—the one he'd carried with him when leaving Gorse. A thought occurred to him, and he unzipped it and felt around for something inside.

His lightsaber.

It was there, hidden innocuously inside the canvas carrying case for a blaster riflescope. Kanan hesitated for a moment before removing the case and strapping it to his left leg, opposite his holster. He wasn't going to use it, of course, but unlike on Calcoraan Depot, the chances of the ship being searched were pretty good. He didn't want anyone to find it.

He turned back to see Skelly watching him. For a moment, Kanan worried he would ask about the scope case—he had no rifle, after all—but he quickly realized Skelly was eyeing his bag of death.

"I'm not having you blow us all up," Kanan said. He lifted Skelly's bag. "This is coming with me for safekeeping."

"You'll blow yourself up just carrying that." Skelly forced himself to stand. "It's all right. Leave it. I'll go with you."

Kanan frowned. "You can barely walk!"

"So I can keep up the rear. Put that down and let's go."

Forager's interior was one huge automated factory floor, Kanan discovered. The seven spheres that formed the body of the ship intersected in a row, producing a single atrium several stories high that stretched forward out of sight. Vats, centrifuges, conveyor belts, pneumatic tubes—it was a Denetrius Vidian production, if ever there was one.

Standing at a railing overlooking the area, Hera momentarily marveled at the sight. "It's like someone crammed all of Moonglow's refineries into a starship."

"Hurry, so we can save the real one," Kanan said. He could see the stormtroopers down on the main floor now, running toward them from the far end. Metal stairs led down to what would be more than a kilometer of hard fighting, nearly the length of a Star Destroyer.

"Can I . . . go back . . . and get my bombs?" Skelly said, panting at the railing. He'd fallen behind twice—and simply fallen once—on the way here from the landing bays.

Kanan shook his head and looked at Hera. She was staring up at the rafters. "What have you got?"

"Things are looking up," she said, pointing. "There!"

Kanan squinted. Up top, a tramcar track suspended from the ceiling ran the length of the room between two banks of industrial lighting.

Kanan's eye traced back toward his location—and the rungs of a ladder attached to the wall behind them, fifteen meters high or more. The ladder was the only route to the tramcar: There was no way the rappelling gun could carry more than one at a time.

Hera had the idea; Kanan made the plan. It was how things were working out between them. Kanan sent Hera up the ladder first, having her stop at intervals to turn and provide cover fire, if necessary, against any arriving Imperials. Then he sent up Zaluna, who went without complaint. Heights were apparently one more thing Zaluna wasn't afraid of.

Skelly was his problem. He'd figured the guy had to go up ahead of him or he'd never go at all, but it was making their progress impossibly slow. Skelly was in pain—and reluctant to use his right hand for a grip.

"Go on, Skelly!" Kanan yelled, after the third time he tuckered out.

Skelly dangled precariously, his right arm looped around a rung. "Just give me a—"

Skelly never finished his statement. Blasterfire peppered the wall around him, causing him to lose hold. Kanan grasped vainly at the man as he fell past, flailing. "Skelly!"

The man fell outward, his body slamming against the railing of the balcony they'd been standing on earlier. Limply, Skelly fell over the side and out of sight—presumably toward the factory floor. High above, Hera opened fire on Skelly's attackers.

Hanging partway off the ladder, Kanan craned his neck to see any sign of Skelly. He couldn't see anything—and now, more shooters were moving into the area. Hera called down from above. "Kanan, come on!"

Kanan scrambled up the ladder, narrowly escaping being shot several times in the process. Reaching the apex, he stepped out onto the short metal landing next to the parked tramcar. Hera was in it already, hanging over the front and looking down. "No sign of Skelly," she said. She looked back, her face fraught. "I don't think he could have survived that!"

"Nothing to do," Kanan said, piling into the tramcar with the others. "We'll look when we come back—*if* we come back. Let's move!"

Once activated by Hera, the tramcar rattled along across hundreds of meters. It rode on a single rail—probably electrified, Kanan thought—attached to the ceiling by metal framing.

Things went quietly for a minute, until the stormtroopers below tripped to where the intruders were. Then it was open season on the rafters, with blaster shots deflecting off the girders, the ceiling—even a few off the tramcar itself. Passing control of the vehicle to Zaluna, Hera and Kanan fired back, but the targets were too small and numerous. And they hadn't even traveled halfway across the factory floor.

"We've got to do something before they bring out the heavy artillery," Hera said.

Kanan nudged her. "Check that out!" He pointed down and ahead to enormous cylinders on the factory floor, made of some kind of special clear composite. Inside was liquid, a shocking green in color. "Xenoboric acid—like in Lal's factory!" It made sense: This was a thorilide refinery, after all. Kanan and Hera looked at each other, shrugged simultaneously, and then turned their weapons on the nearest vat.

Multiple blaster shots struck the container at the same place. A sick groan later, the protective material gave way, releasing a fountain of acid. A stricken stormtrooper dropped his weapon and howled so loudly they heard it near the ceiling. The vat's structure failed completely then, unloosing a gusher onto the floor. Now all the stormtroopers were on the move, rushing to alcoves to escape the effluent and throw off their boots and affected armor.

Kanan and Hera targeted another vat, and then another, as the tramcar advanced. The trick was clearing their way better than any army. He grinned at Hera, hoping to see her smile in return.

Instead, he saw her grimace as the tramcar ground to a halt. Hera moved to Zaluna's side and punched futilely at the control buttons. "That's it for the free ride," she said. "Someone knows we're here."

"I would think those guys," Kanan said, pointing down. Laser shots were striking the ceiling again, but with less accuracy than before: The shooters were all huddled on top of control consoles and other equipment, avoiding the acid flow. He looked at the tramcar's control panel. "I guess I can rewire this thing."

"I know I can," Hera said, scrambling over the side. "You keep shooting! We're running out of time!"

Kanan turned to do exactly that—when Zaluna poked him. She pointed above, to where the frame of the tramcar track connected with the ceiling. A row of girders ran the length of the line, offering a small, protected crawl space above. But Kanan realized it would be a long hands-and-knees scramble—and it would take someone small and athletic to get up there.

"I don't think I could make it up there," Zaluna said. "But one of you could go."

"We don't know how to access the global communications systems you talked about," Hera said.

"Wait a minute," Kanan said, getting an idea. "Hera, get back in!"

As she did so, he put down his blaster and reached for the rappelling gun. Anchoring his legs behind the dashboard, he leaned out and fired at one of the horizontal supports, far ahead. The hook snapped taut, and the motorized winder groaned into action. The current might have been cut from the track, but the tramcar still moved along it—if slowly.

"We're too heavy," Hera said. She looked up to a debarkation area, far ahead. "All three of us will take forever. I'll take the upstairs route."

Zaluna looked at her, face fraught. "Hera, I don't think you should go alone."

"And you shouldn't, either," Hera said. "Kanan, make sure she gets there. Get that warning message out!" She climbed onto the side of the car and leapt. Nimbly grabbing the side of one of the supports, she twisted her body around and disappeared into the small horizontal space, safe from the stormtroopers' shots.

The cable rewound, Kanan released the hook and prepared to fire again. Zaluna, looking up in vain to catch any sight of the scrambling Hera, shook her head. "We're going to have to send the message while Vidian's in the room, aren't we?"

"You've come this far, Zal. The hard part's over." Kanan grinned and fired the grapple. His Jedi teachers had warned him about lying to his elders, but he figured this time it was for a good cause.

"*Forager* reports being boarded," an ensign called from a terminal. "Incursion force small. Three, maybe four."

"Stand by." Captain Sloane walked to the junior officer's station and looked over her shoulder. *Ultimatum* was receiving some security feeds from the collection ship, but it was difficult to see much. For a moment, she thought she caught a glimpse of a running Twi'lek—and then she definitely spotted the arrogant space jockey.

She shook her head. "Is *Forager* asking for help?"

"No, Captain. Count Vidian is continuing the countdown, waiting for the final injection site to finish its work."

Sloane nodded. Vidian had his own stormtroopers and personal guards over there. It would be unlikely he would need assistance. Still, it was difficult just sitting here, not knowing what to do. It was times like this when she missed being a junior officer herself, having someone around with the answers—

"Captain!"

Sloane turned to see Commander Chamas rushing onto the bridge toward her. "What is it?"

Chamas looked pale. "We have a priority-one message for you."

Sloane stopped. "From the Admiralty?"

"No," the commander said, breathless. *"From the Emperor."*

The captain's eyes bulged. "I'll take it in my ready room." She was already to the door by the time she finished the sentence.

CHAPTER FIFTY-TWO

Commander Chamas appeared in hologram, speaking to the *Forager* command crew. "Your linkup to Detonation Control is live, Count Vidian. We read ten minutes until the last charges are implanted."

"I see it." Vidian was already watching the progress at the last injection site. "The delays that fool freighter caused weren't fatal."

He was still aggravated by the failure of *Ultimatum*'s fighters to stop the renegade, but the ship crash-landing on *Forager* hadn't cost him much. The infiltrators had found a way around his stormtroopers, but he had shut down the tramcar line. They'd damaged the refinery area, truc—but he had many other harvester vessels on the way.

He looked up at the hologram. "Where is Sloane?"

"The captain is . . . *indisposed*." Chamas seemed agitated.

"She'll miss the show."

"Do you require assistance against—"

"No. *Forager* out." Vidian cut the transmission, and Chamas disappeared. The cyborg had never had any use for the man, and didn't want to talk to him any more than necessary. Not now, in his moment of success.

The sounds of blasterfire came from the southern hallway, one of three portals on the ground floor leading into the command center. Vidian switched to the security cam feed from the hallway and saw nothing unusual at all—just his stormtroopers standing guard. But something was wrong with the image. It was frozen, the soldiers halted mid-movement like statues—even as the sentries in the room with Vidian were firing through the southern door. They saw something he couldn't.

"Lower the security doors on the command floor level!"

Heavy barriers slowly descended from the door frames in the three large entryways. Still shooting at whoever was in the hallway, one of the stormtroopers charged the exit, moving to get through it before the door sealed. But a blaster shot caught him in mid-stride, and he fell on his side. The massive door came down on the soldier's collarbone. It stopped there, leaving a half-meter-high space between the bottom of the door and the floor beneath.

Vidian heard the blasterfire cease. The opening was too small for the attacker to easily exploit, whoever he was. He checked the cam feed again. It was still on the guards standing around motionless, and the door was still open in the image. "Someone's been interfering with what I can see."

A pinging noise came from his command console. A critical moment had passed: The very last set of baradium charges were being loaded onto the derrick for descent into Cynda's deep interior. He couldn't afford any more distractions. There weren't blast doors at the entrances on the upper level of his chamber, but he could place his remaining sentries up there. On his command, the stormtroopers dashed up the steps to the catwalks. That left one route into the room, by which he might root out his real enemy once and for all.

He turned to the command console, his back to the main door. This would be a simple matter.

Kanan stood on guard amid the fallen stormtrooper bodies. They'd beaten Hera here, as he expected, but there was no good way to sneak up on stormtroopers on alert. Now there was at least a way into Vidian's chamber—for one of them. "Ready?"

Looking at the fallen troopers, Zaluna shuddered. "I don't know."

"You knew you'd have to do this alone, didn't you? We can't both sneak in."

"I didn't think we'd get this far." Zaluna put the widget back in her pouch. They'd needed to defeat the surveillance cams on their approach, as on Calcoraan Depot, but the trick didn't work as well when anyone was in the frame. There was no way around that now. "Are you sure you don't want a tutorial on slicing Imperial communication systems?"

"I would if I could," Kanan said. He could hear more troops running in the hall, searching for them. "We're out of time."

"It happens."

The stormtroopers were closing in. Kanan knelt, protecting the doorway in front of her. "I'm sorry you have to do this, Zaluna. You never asked for any of this."

"Neither did you," she said, securing her pouch. "You're a decent person, Kanan, no matter what show you put on for the world. You keep being that way."

With a dutiful salute, Zaluna got down on all fours and peeked beneath the blast door propped up by the body of the unfortunate stormtrooper. She looked back and whispered, "All cyborgs, all the time. It'll be just like evading cams." Then she shimmied under the door.

The room was frighteningly large, with lots of computer consoles about. More places to hide. Zaluna crawled behind one. Vidian's cybernetic assistants were here and there, but their minds appeared to be on their work.

Zaluna quietly moved from one workstation to another, hoping the artificial ears in the room couldn't hear her joints cracking or her heart pounding. *It's just like working my way across the floor of that cantina the other day,* she told herself. It wasn't, but thinking it helped.

Finally, she found a console near the eastern wall that looked to have a connection to the comm system—and a nice little nook behind, where she could tap in and send her warning.

Text would have to do. She'd prewritten it on the tramcar ride: *"People of Gorse, beware . . ."* She would send it and hope for the best.

She was about to connect to the port when a voice came from overhead. "And here's our rodent."

Grabbed by the back of her shirt, Zaluna was yanked upward and outward. Spun about, she saw the moon outside the windows. She saw stormtroopers running down the metal steps to the main floor. And now she looked directly into the terrifying eyes of Count Vidian.

He shook the woman violently. Her bag fell open, spilling forth her blaster and all her devices. Vidian surveyed the instruments. "So they brought a slicer. I knew there was someone else." His other hand on Zaluna's collar, he brought her back face-to-face with him. "If you know about surveillance cams, you should have remembered something else: You don't always know where they are."

He turned and hurled her across the room.

In the middle of firing at oncoming stormtroopers outside the doorway, Kanan heard Zaluna's cry.

The gambit had failed. Kanan shot and shot again, putting his last attackers on the deck. Holstering his blaster, he turned to the door. It had descended farther since Zaluna had gone underneath it: The servos were grinding away, trying vainly to push through the armored obstacle.

Kanan placed his hands along the underside of the blast door and heaved upward. His muscles screamed, fighting against both the heavy door and the mechanism holding it in place. Metal groaned, and then something snapped. He forced the door up half a meter from where it had been—where it would go no farther. It was enough. He slid his legs beneath it and rolled, even as the door began to move again.

Righting himself, he saw the count stalking toward Zaluna's motionless body. Kanan stood. *"Vidian!"*

A stormtrooper charged at Kanan from the left side of the door, his blaster raised. Kanan moved like lightning, grabbing the rifle by its barrel and shoving. The soldier stumbled backward, allowing him to wrest the weapon free. Another trooper came toward him, from behind. Kanan spun, smacking his attacker in the side of the helmet with the weapon.

Vidian charged. Kanan turned the stormtrooper's rifle around. Three blaster shots slammed point-blank into Vidian's body, searing his tunic. Kanan knew that wouldn't stop him—but he had to get the man away from Zaluna. Vidian charged, grabbing for the barrel of the blaster rifle. He ripped it away and shattered it in his bare metal hands.

"Hurry up," the count said, unruffled. "I have a schedule to keep."

Kanan moved his hand to his holster before changing his mind. He'd learned something from their first fight. Instead, he dived to the side as Vidian lunged, hitting the ground long enough to leap again—onto Vidian's back.

Enraged, Vidian clawed at him, raking at Kanan's clothing. His heels digging into the cyborg's metal hips, Kanan wrapped his arms around the back of Vidian's neck and hung on for dear life.

Hera darted from hall to hall, careful to avoid stormtrooper details. They were numerous in this end of *Forager*—and apparently much exercised by her friends' earlier infiltration.

Kanan's been here, all right, she thought, peering around the corner at the bodies of stunned troopers. Other stormtroopers were tending to their companions and helping to defend their station. She wouldn't be able to follow the path Kanan had taken.

Opening a portal leading off the main hall, she stepped into a storage area full of equipment—and loading vehicles, all unattended. There were even several hovercarts like the one Kanan used on Cynda.

A power forklift caught her eye. A heavy-duty repulsorcraft, narrow enough to navigate hallways—with a cab that offered some degree of protection from attackers ahead.

Hera grinned. Driving loading equipment was Kanan's trade, but she'd show him what she could do.

Zaluna awoke to a nightmare. The sound had reached her first—Vidian stumbling about, driving his back into consoles and walls as he tried to dislodge Kanan. Horrific squawks came from Vidian's speakers as electronic circuits tried to express his animal rage.

And yet Kanan kept moving, shifting his hold every time Vidian came close to dislodging him. From headlock to arms around the cyborg's shoulders to a headlock again, the younger man squirmed in response to the count's every move.

Zaluna forced herself to sit up. Her leg hurt horribly where she'd landed—but the only stormtroopers here were on the floor. Vidian's cybernetic assistants milled about near the walls, looking on as the pair wreaked havoc on their work space. Vidian staggered past again with Kanan, nearly stepping on her. She rolled—

—and saw her pistol, on the floor where she'd dropped it. Vidian had a handhold on Kanan's left ankle now, she saw. She had to help her friend. Zaluna dived for the blaster and rose to face the count.

"Zal, no!" Kanan yelled.

Vidian swept forward, releasing his hold on Kanan and reaching for her blaster. She tried to fire—but he had hold of the barrel now. He squeezed. Zaluna saw a flash brighter than lightning as the blaster's energy pack discharged in their faces. She fell backward—and saw no more.

The flash subsided. Kanan, who had remembered what happened when blaster shots struck Vidian, had leapt clear an instant before the flash occurred. His eyes adjusting to the light, Kanan saw Zaluna collapse. "No!"

Vidian staggered, holding his face in his hands. Kanan quickly surmised the man had overestimated his ability to shake off energy attacks. Blaster bolts were one thing; power packs exploding point-blank were something else. Kanan scrambled past him to Zaluna's side. The woman was still breathing, he saw, but her face was burned.

So, he now saw, was Vidian's. Recovered, the cyborg had pulled his hands away from his face. His synthskin facial coating was charred and melted, revealing the metal man beneath. He straightened and stared down the pair.

"This ends now, gunslinger. Draw your weapon."

Kanan was about to—when he heard something else: blasterfire echoing through the huge chamber. He couldn't tell where it was coming from. Looking around, Vidian acted as if he couldn't figure that out, either—nor could he identify the gruesome, grinding sound that accompanied it.

Then everyone saw it: a massive hover-forklift powering its way through one of the upper doorways onto the catwalk above. Two hapless stormtroopers had already been collected by its massive arms—and a third, caught by surprise, tumbled backward over the railing to the command center floor.

The vehicle kept on going, smashing through the catwalk barrier. Vidian, astonished at the new arrival from above, dived to the side— even as Kanan moved to protect Zaluna. With a deafening crash, the forklift and its pinned troopers slammed onto the floor between the infiltrators and Vidian. The lifting arms snapped violently off, one nearly taking out the count's shins.

Hera clambered out of the cab. Vidian looked at her in amazement. "You!"

"That's the trick with surveillance cams, Count. You can't watch all of them at once." She drew her blasters.

Vidian started to claw his way up the pile of wreckage toward her. "You should have tried to run me down. You know your blasters won't hurt me."

"No, but this might." Hera turned and aimed each one at a different tall viewport. "These viewports aren't magnetically shielded—and these blasters are set on full power. I can decompress this whole compartment. If you make a move on my friends—or try to give the detonation command—you'll have a whole new address!"

Vidian responded with a digital snort. "And which of us do you think would fare better in such an event?" He stepped over to a console and clamped his left hand on it. "I won't be going anywhere. And my respiration is augmented already." He shook his head and let out an electronic cluck. "But I find what you've said much more interesting. We've come to it, at last. You want to save the moon, Cynda." He looked around at his workers—and at the few mobile stormtroopers, recovering and raising their weapons. "Tell me who you're working for, now!"

"I'm working for everyone. The people of Gorse. The people of the galaxy!"

Vidian seemed surprised. Then he laughed. "I think we have an agitator here!"

"If you destroy the moon, you'll destroy the thorilide," Hera shouted. "The Emperor won't stand for that!"

"Don't be so sure," Vidian said. "I'm smarter than you think." He turned to face the console. "I am going to do this. And then I am going to find out who each of you really is. And the Empire will destroy everyone important to you."

Kanan glared. "You're a little late on that one."

"And your time is running out. Four minutes until optimal detonation window." He smiled back at Kanan. "Shall we all wait together?"

CHAPTER FIFTY-THREE

Sloane knew back on Calcoraan Depot that she had walked into a trap. She just didn't know whose trap it was.

The mouthy pilot had told her about Vidian's double identity, his fraudulent test results, and his desire to make the Emperor's deadline by destroying Cynda—and Gorse along with it. She'd thought it all nonsense, and very likely some bizarre test of loyalty from Vidian. After the speaker and his shadowy companions sank into the floor on the hydraulic lift, Sloane had been ready to dismiss the entire thing.

But Vidian had laid it on too thick. He'd tried too hard to ensure her cooperation, insisted too much on speeding the project to a conclusion. Her elevation to permanent Star Destroyer captain—ahead of all the others with more seniority—was more than a bribe. It was a bludgeon, something no one could refuse.

And the suggestion that he might have some way of elevating her to admiral—her, a green captain without a permanent posting yet—was simply insulting to her intelligence and to the service to which she'd devoted her life.

Vidian, the mystery man had said, lived by terrorizing people into meeting quotas. Yet fear of loss of standing was driving him to destroy a resource that the Emperor could have expected would produce for years to come.

And Sloane believed him.

But there was no reporting the pilot's information up the chain—not the usual way. It was too explosive. Instead, she'd returned from Calcoraan Depot to *Ultimatum* where Chamas had arranged a secure connection with Baron Danthe, using the contact information the latter had provided. It was highly irregular to involve a civilian, but Danthe was the only person she knew who had a hope of directly reaching the Emperor or one of his minions.

Silence had followed, during which she'd done her job as ordered. Then, finally, she'd heard back from them in her ready room. The Emperor's people had confirmed that everything the young man said was true. And there was more.

Vidian had already launched one scheme to defraud the people of Gorse, starting before the days of the Empire. By secretly purchasing and controlling Minerax Consulting, he had issued the critical report accelerating the end of thorilide mining on Gorse. That single act damaged the guild he once worked for while lifting the interests of the comet-chaser industry, which he mostly controlled. On Gorse, mining work had literally gone to the moon then, defacing what had been a famous natural preserve.

That had been enough for Vidian, until the past week, when he returned to the system for the first time in years—and Sloane's part in it began. On his return to the system, Vidian had cut the last connection between him and Lemuel Tharsa by using her and *Ultimatum*'s power to eliminate the miners' medcenter where he had convalesced. But that matter was minor compared with the problem he faced meeting the Emperor's new production targets. The newly discovered prospect of destroying the moon for thorilide had been a sudden blessing, and his metal fingers grasped at the reed with full force. There, again, he had used Minerax to lie, asserting that the project would be a successful producer, long-term. Minerax, and its chief researcher: Lemuel Tharsa.

As Vidian had expected, Tharsa's name and reputation had been enough to gain Imperial approval for destruction of the moon. The man and his résumé were real. Hadn't Tharsa been a veteran of the Interstellar Thorilide Guild, before dropping out to change his line to consulting? And hadn't he given the okay to dozens of projects over the past several years, some of which redounded to Vidian's personal profit?

Yes, and no. Because the renegade pilot had spoken truly. Vidian *was* Tharsa. But Vidian had also kept Tharsa's name alive, using it in order to advance his goals and to enrich himself. Moreover, Tharsa's supposed existence helped hide the count's past from others, who might have found his true origin—as a functionary for a guild where everyone was on the take—less compelling than his self-scripted myth of a military ship designer who had taken on his superiors in the name of the troops.

There had been one other consequence: The Emperor hadn't known the truth, either.

Emperor Palpatine's reach and resources were immense. Little went on in the Galactic Empire that he didn't know about—usually, before it even happened. It was a good thing, and it worked to the advantage of all his subjects. But Vidian had spent well to cover his tracks. And perhaps Vidian's past image as a fame-seeking business guru had caused the Emperor to accept his identity as it was described. As long as Vidian was as effective as his reputation advertised, what difference did it make that he lined his pockets playing the show-off?

A whole lot, Sloane now understood. Because "Kanan"—the Emperor's agent, she now accepted—had, through her, supplied his master with the truth. Vidian *had* lied about the lunar test results. Before passing the report along, Sloane had *Ultimatum*'s technical staff confirm the man's claim: Within a year, the vast majority of unharvested thorilide from the moon's remains would decompose in space, destroying the Emperor's precious prize.

Vidian's aides aboard her ship—the ones that existed, anyway—had helped to rig the test, ensuring that false data would be reported. While still docked at Calcoraan Depot, her crack technicians had reexamined every probe droid in *Ultimatum*'s stores. Vidian's people had done a good job of hiding their tampering, but not good enough. In order to fast-track the destruction of Cynda, Vidian had been forced to prepare his deception too quickly.

Of course, the truth would have come out a year after the moon's destruction: Vidian had to know the result would enrage His Highness. And yet, here the count was, going ahead with the project. Sloane wondered whether the quest for revenge had driven the man mad.

But Vidian wasn't insane. He had a plan, outlined in a supplemental document given her by the stranger: an encrypted file from Vidian's computers. The Emperor's experts had cracked it just minutes before, prompting his call. Her anger rose now as she read the file.

Cynda would be destroyed, and within a year would be worthless rubble—but by that time, it would be the responsibility of someone else: likely his underling and greatest nemesis, Baron Lero Danthe. The baron would naturally point at Vidian, who would in turn blame Sloane and her demolition crews' incompetence. He would call her appointment to interim captain premature. And then he would rush to the rescue with another revelation: something so startling that she could barely believe Vidian had concealed it all this time. It was a fact Minerax Consulting had discovered fifteen years earlier, and that Vidian had bought the firm in order to bury.

The moon Cynda did have more thorilide than the nightside of Gorse. But Gorse's dayside held *incalculably* more, all buried under the blazing heat of a sun that never left the sky.

It would otherwise have been a useless bit of knowledge: Organics couldn't toil in that heat. And at the time, the suppliers of heat-resistant droids belonged on the side of the Separatists in the Clone Wars. The stuff was unreachable. And when the war ended, it left Danthe as the monopoly supplier. Such a prize would make Danthe incalculably rich and powerful, she realized. No wonder Vidian had hidden the fact.

And it further explained what she had seen on Calcoraan Depot: workers of Vidian's, trying to reverse-engineer Danthe's droids. Vidian's file described a one-year timetable for having his own droids ready to rush to Gorse's dayside, able to fill the need when Cynda's remains ran out of thorilide. In a sequence of events typical of his preference for neat solutions, Vidian would eliminate a competitor and save the day for the Empire—all while turning a huge profit.

But he would destroy Gorse's population in the process. And worse, he would ruin Sloane's career.

She wouldn't allow that. And neither would the Emperor. The Emperor had no quarrel with destroying places for short-term gains or with dealing harm to rivals. But the galaxy and all its assets belonged to him— and he alone would decide where and when such actions were taken.

That made her next command easy. Walking from her ready room onto the bridge, she knew the next moments would startle her crew as much as her would-be patron.

"Channel to Count Vidian," she said.

Chamas, looking at her with a mixture of curiosity and concern, snapped his fingers. Count Vidian's holographic image appeared.

"Ah, Sloane," he said. "You're back just in time. I'm just about to detonate the charges and pulverize the moon."

"Then I *am* just in time," she said, taking a deep breath before continuing. "*Ultimatum* technical crews—rescind the Detonation Control link to *Forager*."

"What?" The shimmering Count Vidian looked at her in surprise—as did the very real form of Commander Chamas, standing nearby.

Sloane clenched her fist. "And all stormtroopers aboard *Forager*, in the name of the Emperor: *Arrest Count Vidian!*"

CHAPTER FIFTY-FOUR

It had happened this way to the Jedi, Kanan remembered. Responding to some command from the Emperor, clone troopers had eliminated the Republic's cherished fighting force. It had been a dark day—by far, the darkest in Caleb Dume's young life. Kanan Jarrus usually avoided thinking about it.

But seeing the stormtroopers turning on their master: That was both amazing and delicious. Even if the Imperials were also pointing their weapons at Kanan and his friends. More troops hoisted open the main door, bringing the total number of white-armored guards to a dozen.

Up atop the bulk-loader, Kanan saw that Hera didn't know what to think. But there was no mistaking Vidian's reaction to the holographic captain.

"This is a rash act, Sloane. Have you lost your mind?"

"You're under arrest for multiple violations of the Imperial legal code. Falsification of testimony to the Emperor. Profiteering without permission of the Emperor. Breach of faith with the Emperor. Attempting to damage or destroy strategic assets deemed vital to—"

"The Emperor," Vidian finished, anger rising. "You dare invoke his name?" He pointed at Kanan. "These—*anarchists* have poisoned your mind against me. They're Gorse partisans, seeking to hinder our project." He looked back outside the viewports at the moon. "A project that must go on!"

"Forget it, Vidian," Sloane said. "You won't be destroying anything today."

Kanan could hardly restrain his response. His gambit had worked, after all.

Vidian stared as the pair of stormtroopers approached him, as if deciding what to do. "I don't think so," he said. He looked over to a pair of his cybernetic assistants. "Restore the Detonation Control uplink."

Sloane snapped at him. "We already disconnected—"

"You disconnected nothing. The injection towers, the logistical systems—you only installed them. My workers manufactured them—and my workers can take back control for me at any time."

"If that's the way you want it," Sloane said. "Death warrant extended to all workers on *Forager*'s bridge. Stormtroopers, fire!"

The stormtroopers executed their order—and several of Vidian's aides—immediately, at point-blank range. Vidian yelled something, but Kanan didn't hear it. Blasterfire blazing all around, he hit the deck. Scrambling behind the smashed remains of the forklift cab, he saw Zaluna. She looked rough, her face a scorched mess.

We've got to get out of here. He looked back to see Hera scrambling down the bulk-loader to the floor, dodging shots as she did. All around, Vidian's droids and aides fell.

Blaster in hand, Kanan considered joining in before having second thoughts. For an older man—if any man was still in that body—Vidian had worked into a superhuman rage. Whatever source powered the man's limbs, it had yet to run out of juice. Shaking off a blaster shot from a stormtrooper, Vidian launched himself at his attacker, crushing the man's helmet in his hands. A horrific scream later, and Vidian was on to another stormtrooper.

Kanan spotted a newly opened portal to the side. Hera provided cover fire as Kanan lifted Zaluna's body. He rushed to the exit and set her down outside the door.

"Wait here," he said.

"That . . . a joke?" she muttered.

"Sorry." Kanan turned back to face the room.

Hera, even amid chaos, remembered what they most needed to do. "The comm console," she called out, pointing past the latest melee. She leapt out from behind the forklift, even as Kanan bounded from the other side.

Vidian was already there.

The last stormtrooper had already fallen, Kanan realized too late. To a person, Vidian's workers were all down, too—just more workplace casualties in the count's machine. Only he, Hera, and Vidian remained here alive. And Vidian had just completed punching in a series of keys. "Detonation Control linkup restored," Vidian said. "Just over a minute to spare."

It was the same smug, self-satisfied voice they'd always heard from Vidian—but the man himself was much changed. His tunic was in tatters; his artificial skin and nose had been scorched off his face, leaving just a charred silver mask. Sparks flew from his mechanical joints. Yet he was unbowed. He turned back to Kanan and Hera. "I don't know what you told Sloane. But once the Emperor sees my results, it won't matter."

"Your results?" Hera yelled. "Destruction and genocide!"

Vidian snorted. "You're going about this wrong, you know. You'll never get anywhere against the Empire. You're too undisciplined, too disorganized."

"We'll learn," Hera said, brandishing her weapon. "The people will stop you. We'll stop you."

"We've had this fight before, the three of us. You don't have anything that can hurt me."

"Maybe *I* do." Kanan felt for the holder on his left leg where his lightsaber was hidden.

"Nonsense," Vidian said, waving his hand dismissively. "If you had anything, you'd have used it already. Right?"

Hera looked searchingly at Kanan as Vidian turned back to the console. Kanan began to reach for his secret weapon—but then he paused. Something, somewhere told him: *No, not that. Not now.*

Not yet.

"Forget him, Twi'lek," the cyborg said, reaching for the console. "He doesn't have what it takes to stop me."

"But I do," said Captain Sloane, hologram flickering back into view. Her expression was icy, her eyes narrow. "*Ultimatum* gunnery control, target the transmission tower and fire."

Now Kanan moved. Moved the way his instincts told him to go. He dived not at Vidian, but at Hera, bowling her over even as one of the viewports behind the count lit up like a hundred suns.

If there was a sound, Kanan didn't hear it. There was only light, and motion, and heat as *Forager* wrenched violently under the impact of the Star Destroyer's turbolaser barrage. Rolling away from Hera, it took what seemed like an eternity for his eyes to adjust. The lights were out in the command center, and Vidian was staggering around like one caught in a hurricane. Kanan realized why, looking out the windows. It wasn't just *Ultimatum*, now, but the TIE fighters pummeling *Forager's* energy shield. The vessel was in one piece—for the moment—but every strike on the shield shook everything inside madly.

Somehow, Vidian reached the console again. Kanan was ready to go after him, even shaken—but this time it was Hera who grabbed him, keeping him down close to the floor. He saw the reason. *Forager's* superstructure was holding, but the transmission tower, visible through the room's viewports, shook itself to pieces under a direct hit on the shield from *Ultimatum*.

Sloane had called her shot, Kanan realized. And her gunners had done their jobs.

His chance to destroy Cynda gone, Vidian howled and turned. He ran back through the main entrance, paying Kanan and Hera no mind. Finding his blaster on the floor nearby, Kanan rose to follow Vidian.

Behind him, Hera called out. "Kanan, no!" He looked back. She was still getting to her knees near the door he had dragged Zaluna through, beneath the catwalk that had been damaged earlier. "We have to get to a—"

Time stopped for Kanan. And then it started again, slowly.

He saw everything. He saw the TIE bomber outside, unloosing its torpedo at *Forager*'s energy shield. He saw the bridge shake violently, in response. He saw the heavy durasteel catwalk, already weakened from Hera's forklift entrance, snap from its moorings. He saw it fall toward Hera. Hera—not oblivious, but in no position to get out of the way.

He recognized the obstacles between them—the debris and the bodies, lying across the fastest route. Without thinking, he swept them away with his mind, clearing a path. No barrier blocked him from Hera.

And he moved. He moved faster than when he'd saved Yelkin, faster than he'd remembered moving in years. All in the hope of grabbing her and diving beneath the doorway.

Except time moved faster, too—faster than his hopes. He reached her too late, just as he'd been too late to save Master Billaba. The Force had been too late for many that day. But it was with him now, as he slid to the floor by Hera's side. Hera, knowing the danger she was in, put her hand up as if to shoo him away, to safety. Kanan looked instead upward, waving with his hand—

—and suspending the giant catwalk in midair, centimeters from his and Hera's heads.

She stared at it, dumbfounded—and then at him. Self-conscious, Kanan shoved at the air, pushing the levitated mass off to the side. It landed with a colossal crash.

Forager shuddered again under the Imperial attack. The view outside was a thing of perversely wondrous beauty, he thought: flashes of light before the moon as the starfighters made their runs. But it all paled before the look he saw here in the darkness, in Hera's eyes.

"But—" she started to say. "But you're—"

With a wry smile, Kanan put his finger to her mouth. "Shh. Don't tell anyone."

She looked at him for a long moment in wonderment before understanding came to her—and a gentle smile came to her face. She nodded. "Let's go."

CHAPTER FIFTY-FIVE

The life pod soared from *Forager*. Kanan hunched over the small circular viewport and looked back at the collector ship. Several other small pods were jettisoning away, he saw—and the Empire was watching every one.

"TIE fighter on our tail," he said.

"We don't have a tail. We barely have an engine." Hera guided the small stick directing the vehicle. It was about the only control she had. "I think the TIE's just following."

"I know." There wasn't anything to do. Kanan turned from the viewport and returned to dabbing gingerly at Zaluna's burnt face with a bacta-infused pad from the medpac.

Ultimatum was still pounding away at *Forager;* as soon as it finished, Kanan knew it would likely begin sweeping up all the life pods. Sloane would be looking for Vidian, but she'd find Kanan and company instead.

"You still can't see?" Kanan asked Zaluna.

"There's nothing good to see anyway," she replied.

Vidian waded through a river of acid. It was everywhere on the factory portion of *Forager:* ankle-deep in some places, waist-high in others. It was destroying the flooring, and had already eaten into the bulkheads below; he anticipated explosive decompression at any minute.

The crossing had started as a panicked mechanical run—and then slowed to a hideous slog as his legs wasted away to skeletal struts. His arms had been further damaged, too, in the trip. There had been no other choice, no other way to his destination.

He'd remembered something. The intruders had come in a baradium hauler. It was intact, he saw through the few still-functioning surveillance cams: ready to go. He would use it, eschewing the one-trip life pods. The freighter might be lost in the confusion, he hoped; he might be able to make it to one of the drill sites on Cynda, where there was still time to detonate the explosives and meet the Emperor's quota. He would find a way.

This was Baron Danthe's doing, somehow. It had to be. It was impossible to imagine a few would-be rebels and a substitute captain could've reduced his reputation and career to shambles. Detonating the moon, he was sure, would restore him—between the moon and the sunward side of Gorse, the Emperor would have thorilide for a thousand fleets.

And if it didn't, the freighter still had hyperdrive and a full cargo of baradium-357. That was an important resource, and something to build upon someplace else if necessary. He had come back from nothingness, before. Perhaps it wouldn't take twenty years this time.

But he wouldn't have to do that. He would finish the project.

Vidian staggered on failing limbs into the landing bay. The place was a mess of fallen beams and bulkheads—but the troublesome freighter was right where it was supposed to be, ramp open. He thought it ironic that it, of all things, would be his deliverance.

Reaching the ramp, Vidian looked out through the landing bay's magnetic field. *Forager,* tumbling out of control, now, was turning to face Cynda. Convenient for a quick trip, Vidian thought. *Efficient.*

Vidian staggered up the freighter's ramp—and then could go no farther. He looked down. There, on the landing deck slumped against the side of the ramp, was Skelly. The man was a battered, bloodied mess—and yet he had summoned the energy to reach for Vidian's leg strut as he'd walked up the ramp. Skelly clutched Vidian's onetime ankle now in his right hand.

The count tried to shake him off, but couldn't. "Release me!"

"That one . . . doesn't let go," Skelly said. He coughed. "Don't . . . mind me. I've just been . . . out here looking . . . at the moon."

"Don't get used to it," Vidian said, straining to keep climbing. But his acid-damaged legs couldn't give him any leverage.

"Sorry, Vidian. Blowing things up . . . is *my* job. Guild rules, y'know." Skelly shifted around—and now Vidian saw the device in his other hand, connected to a long microfilament line. Vidian's eyes followed the line up and into the doorway of the ship. "I told Kanan . . . we wouldn't need my bag of tricks," Skelly said. "But I didn't say . . . I wouldn't come back for it."

Realization came quickly. *"No! No, don't!"*

"I don't take orders from you." Then Skelly looked out the landing bay entrance at Cynda. He winked. "I saved you, sweetheart!"

He pushed the button.

The flash blinded Kanan at first. The explosion began at the rear of *Forager*, quickly consuming the landing decks and ripping forward. His eyes adjusting, Kanan recognized the familiar characteristic color of a baradium explosion. But this was bigger and more energetic than he'd ever seen.

"Hera, go!"

There was little she could do, except put the life pod's reentry heat shield between them and the blast. The TIE fighter pursuing them was slower to react. Superheated particles from the explosion ripped through the vessel's hexagonal wings, causing the starfighter to tear violently apart. A shock wave comprising not air but plasma and matter expanding outward from the blast zone slammed into their life pod.

Shaken by the impact, Hera fought with the controls, angling the life pod to catch the wave. All around, Kanan saw more effects of the blast. Less fortunate life pods were disintegrating, as were their TIE pursuers. And the electrostatic towers that had been *Forager*'s spokes were flung off in all directions—including toward *Ultimatum*. A long, ragged beam slammed off the surface of the Star Destroyer's hull, opening a fiery gash.

It was enough distraction for Hera, who took the chance to make for Gorse's atmosphere. She powered down the interior cabin lights, and the life pod went dark as it soared, just another piece of debris.

In the darkness, Hera reoriented the vessel so the passengers could look back at *Forager*'s remains. There wasn't much to see. Kanan had no doubt that *Expedient* with its shipload of baradium-357 was the reason. "*Very* naughty baby," Kanan said.

Zaluna shuddered. She hadn't seen the explosion, but she'd felt it. "I—I was hoping Skelly might have survived earlier. That he might have made it."

Hera held her. "It's okay. We got out. Maybe he did, too."

"No," Kanan said, thinking aloud. "He didn't."

Somberly, Hera looked out at the firestorm in space. "The landing bay must have taken a hit from the Star Destroyer."

Kanan shook his head. "No. Skelly did that."

"If you didn't see it," Zaluna asked, "how do you know?"

Hera studied Kanan for a moment. He had gone silent. "He just knows," she finally said. "He just knows."

She turned back to the controls. The life pod sank into the clouds of Gorse's endless night.

Final Phase:

DAMAGE ASSESSMENT

"Emperor's robotic mining plan for dayside brings new era to Gorse"

"Baron Danthe granted oversight of industrial region"

"Vidian's HoloNet site goes dark as disease relapse claims him"

—headlines, Imperial HoloNews (Gorse Edition)

CHAPTER FIFTY-SIX

Apart from her promotion ceremonies, Sloane seldom had use for her dress uniform. But this night was different, and it was always night on Gorse.

The regional governor was here in the mayor's regal residence—easily the nicest place on the planet. She recognized several other Imperial captains and an admiral; he had brought with him a Moff, one of the highest authorities in the government. They were all here to drink and gab and celebrate the most important event in the history of industrial production of thorilide: the opening of the sunward side of Gorse to Baron Danthe's heat-resistant mining drones.

It was a huge moment for the world, liable to transform its economy in amazing ways. Gorse's refineries would be necessary; not even the Emperor would destroy the moon and devastate the planet for a one-time benefit when the long-term reward was much richer. And it was all being directly attributed to a discovery by Sloane and *Ultimatum*'s science team. It wasn't, of course; she had simply passed along Vidian's secret report to that effect. But she was being given the credit, and would take it—alongside her crew.

Her crew. Unrelated to Vidian's machinations, Captain Karlsen's posting had just been permanently awarded to her. She was glad Commander Chamas had sent Deltic and her co-workers home to the ship immediately after the commendation presentation, before they embarrassed her in front of anyone else. But they were her embarrassment now. *Ultimatum* was hers.

And the proceedings were only beginning. Later, they would all ride the luxurious shuttle to Cynda, restored once again to its status as a tourist destination. The zone damaged by the test blast was only one of many former natural preserves on the moon; the Empire had wasted no time in reopening another. It would be made available for visits from the rich and powerful: those who had served the Emperor well and those whose influence he sought to court. *That includes pretty much everyone in this room,* she thought.

Taking a drink from the tray of a GG-class serving droid, Sloane thought back on the events of the days since Vidian's death. An intermediary from the Emperor had met with her to follow up on the whole situation. Sloane had spoken completely and truthfully, of course, and he had seen no problem with her testimony. But he had expressed puzzlement over her tale of the young pilot, speaking to her in the dark. This "Kanan" was no agent of the Emperor's, she was told. It didn't make sense, and neither of them had pressed the issue. Did Vidian have another rival, loose, somewhere in the Imperial system? Or was it someone else entirely?

Sloane hadn't shaken the feeling that there was another player out there. Someone allied with the young pilot, pulling the strings. She wondered if she would ever find out.

There was something she *had* found out. She had learned that someone on *Ultimatum*'s senior staff had queried Transcept about Lemuel Tharsa on their arrival. She hadn't authorized it, and it made no sense that Vidian would have done it. She realized what had happened—and outside, on the balcony, she spotted the men responsible.

Nibiru Chamas drank there with Baron Danthe. Danthe saw her and smiled. He was even more radiant and robust in person, she saw. "My good captain," the baron said, raising his glass. "Please join us."

"I am yours to command," she said.

And so was Chamas. *He'd* sent the inquiry about Tharsa, she'd realized, using his authority as an *Ultimatum* officer to help Danthe investigate Vidian's phantom consultant. She wondered how long Chamas had been on the baron's payroll as informant.

Smiling darkly, Chamas raised his glass of wine to her. It didn't look like his first. No wonder, for she had supplanted his position with his patron. Danthe had been grateful, and she saw his hand in the *Ultimatum* staffing move. Perhaps Chamas had sought her chair. If so, then no matter: This was the way things worked in the Empire.

She stepped to the railing with the baron. Chamas, realizing his glass was empty, excused himself. It was humid as always on Gorse, and none of the visitors were out here—but she had gotten used to it. She looked up at Cynda, well past full now. It would continue to shine, and to set Gorse to rocking every so often. And one day, it would probably tear itself apart and rain down, as Vidian intended. But it wouldn't be in her lifetime, and tonight she planned to enjoy it.

Baron Danthe watched her as she stared up at it. "I do thank you for alerting me."

"I was alerting the Emperor."

"Of course." Danthe chuckled. "Such a life we lead. Did you ever think that stabbing people in the back would be a way to get ahead?"

"It's the way the game is played," Sloane said, a little surprised at his openness. "I prefer flying my starship."

"And defending the Empire against—*whatever*." He grinned. "Have you learned any more about the others that were involved?"

"Nothing."

He gave a derisive sniff. "I don't think we need worry too much. A single rebellious act isn't the start of anything. This was a blip. A glitch in the system. Nothing more."

"Maybe." *Or maybe they'd awakened a sleeping gundark.*

Sloane decided there would be opportunities for advancement in a galaxy like that, too.

"To interesting missions ahead." She clinked her glass against his.

·   ·   ·

The sun rose, and nobody died. Zaluna had lived her entire life where that was impossible.

This was a different world with a different sun, and while she couldn't see it, she could feel its rays warming her body. She could feel the cool air of night gently giving way, hear the dew on the grass crunching as she walked. And all around, she could smell the flowers of the garden waking up.

Kanan had left them after their return to Gorse, thinking it best to meet again here on this sparsely populated agricultural planet sectors away. Zaluna didn't know the name of the planet Hera had brought her to, but then she'd never asked.

She was taking her first step into a new world: a world disconnected from the grid.

It still wasn't clear that the Empire was looking for her for her part in the *Forager* affair. Before bringing her from Gorse to the agrarian world on her fancy ship, Hera had stopped by Zaluna's apartment for her things. It showed signs of having been entered by the landlord, but it hadn't been ransacked. And certainly no video surveillance imagery from aboard *Forager* identifying Zaluna had survived.

The news had made Zaluna wonder. Maybe she hadn't been the focus of any planetary dragnet, along with the others. Maybe it had been all in her mind. Maybe she could've come back from her suspension and gone back to work at Transcept, as if nothing had happened.

But she couldn't. Because something *had* happened. A lot of somethings. And it meant she could never return to that life, if she even wanted to. And she didn't.

Still, she was glad that life on Gorse wouldn't be quite so bad anymore for those she'd left. The miraculous news of thorilide in quantity on Gorse's dayside meant that work was already going ahead, using legions of heat-resistant droids Baron Danthe had ready and waiting. No further damage would be done to Cynda or the places where people lived on Gorse. The miners, by far the roughest customers on the world, would migrate elsewhere. And while the refinery work would stay, the

Empire now controlled its own firm in Moonglow: a place where a far-sighted Lal Grallik had, in life, made safety improvements that would now become the model for all the other factories there. The Empire had gotten the efficiency it had wanted out of Count Vidian's trip after all—and yet people would be safer all around. Hera had particularly liked that thought. *"Victory through unintended consequences,"* she'd said.

The house they had found for Zaluna was abandoned and half in ruin, but it was cheap and quiet. The person Hera bought it from had said the garden out back had been planted by another older woman, long since dead; it was direly in need of care no one would give. Most of the planet's settlers had moved to places like Gorse to find work.

Brushing her fingers against the blooms, Zaluna couldn't imagine a sillier prospect.

She felt for the steps beneath her feet. There was a tree at the end of the path; walking up to it reminded her of the cemetery at Beggar's Hill, with its large monuments.

"Keep walking, Zal, and you'll bump into it."

Zaluna smiled. "You're still here, Kanan!"

"Enjoying the weather. Gorse was a steam bath." Zaluna felt his hand on her shoulder. "You doing all right?"

"Better than ever," she said. She began to walk past the tree, with Kanan's hand still on her shoulder. "What do you think of my garden?"

"It's good," Kanan replied. "You know you can get those eyes treated, right? To get your sight back."

"Like Vidian?" Zaluna chuckled and shook her head. "No, I think I've seen enough. I have a place to live, and there's a little girl who visits daily to help me with things. But I'll be helping myself soon." She gestured backward. "And look! I have a tree!"

Kanan laughed.

"I'm thinking it's Skelly's tree," she said. "A nice monument, don't you think?"

"Well, there are some twisted clinging vines over there I would have thought of instead."

Zaluna lifted her head to face the sky and sighed. "No, Skelly's ashes are probably still back there, raining down on Cynda. I think he'd like that."

Kanan didn't respond for a moment. And then: "That works, too."

She heard someone coming up the walk from the house. "I'm ready to go," Hera said.

"Always on the move," Zaluna said.

She felt Hera's hands on hers. "Are you sure this is what you want, Zal? You have skills. There are others you could help."

Zaluna shook her head. "I can't save Hetto—not now. I know what you're up against, and it's beyond me. Wherever he is, Hetto would never want me to risk my life trying to save him. And if he's in a bad place, he'd probably rather imagine me living somewhere nice like this. It's certainly better than where we were!"

Kanan laughed. "She's got you there."

Hera hugged her. "Take care—and thank you."

Zaluna walked to the edge of the gravel road with them. "And now," Kanan said, "I get the pleasure of walking this gentle lady back to this mysterious starship of hers." Kanan had been dropped off by a tramp freighter, and had yet to get a look at what she and Hera and had arrived in.

"I see," Zaluna asked. "Are you traveling together?"

"We haven't discussed it," Hera was quick to say.

Zaluna smiled. "You'd better take him with you," the woman said, "or I'll put him to work." She turned and walked back toward the garden.

CHAPTER FIFTY-SEVEN

Kanan and Hera walked the long sylvan road from Zaluna's house.

"I think she'll be fine," Hera said for the third time. "The medic I took her to said she's healing nicely."

"Oh, sure," he replied again. They had done an excellent job of talking about nothing on the walk—indeed, since the life pod landed on Gorse. They'd parted quickly then, allowing Kanan time to leave a trail placing him on Gorse during all the previous action. Sloane might know his name, but as far as Imperial surveillance was concerned, he was just one more suicide flier who'd left Gorse when the work dried up.

They approached the small hangar she had rented outside the little town. Not turning toward him, she asked, "So what's next for you?"

"Well, you know me. A force always in motion."

"I do know you." She kept walking. "So what do you think about what Zaluna said?"

"What, going with you?" Kanan shrugged. "Well, you know what I've said. You're great company." He eyed her. "But I don't think you're looking for a traveling companion, are you?"

"Not like that." She stopped outside the door to the closed hangar, and he did the same. She looked up at him. "What's happening to the galaxy is serious, and I mean to do something about it. If you mean only to mind your own business," she said, offering her hand, "then I wish you luck in your travels."

He looked down at her hand, and then at her. "I still haven't seen this ship."

"And you won't. The fewer people see it, the better."

He scratched his beard. "It sounds pretty large. Must be a lot on it to keep up."

She stared at him for a moment—and nodded. "Yes, there is."

"You might need a crew for something like that." He looked at her pointedly. "Not a traveling companion. Not a revolutionary. Crew." He thrust his hand into hers.

She flashed a shrewd smile—and shook his hand. "I can live with that."

Kanan turned and clapped his hands together. "Great! I just hope it's not as big a mess as the ship I just left."

"Well, you're going to love this," she said, opening the door to the hangar.

So. Kanan Jarrus was a Jedi. Or rather, he had been in training to become one when the Emperor betrayed them all.

It was just a guess. He hadn't said anything more to Hera about that moment aboard *Forager*. It was possible that he was just some random person who happened to have the ability to use the Force. Someone who, in a rush of adrenaline, had reached out to the universe for a great feat—and who had seen his prayer answered.

But Hera didn't think so. When she was a girl, the Jedi had helped her people in the Clone Wars. Although she had been too young then to remember specific events from those days, her father had told her, time and again, of the Jedi in action. Later, she'd watched many historical holos—all of them now banned—of Jedi in action. She understood that Jedi abilities weren't some suit of superpowered armor that someone could leave at home, or abandon in a garbage can. The Force influenced and enhanced every action of a person touched with it, whether they were conscious of it or not.

And no one but a Jedi could do the things she had seen Kanan do. The brawl in Shaketown, the escape on the hoverbus, the battle with Vidian—in each, she'd seen a man acting at the outer edge of human performance. And in all cases, she'd somehow thought him capable of doing even more. It seemed as if he'd identified a line that he would not cross, and had stuck to it.

Kanan had gravitated toward a dangerous calling on Gorse, because to him it wasn't dangerous. And it was a solitary trade, so he secretly could call on his prodigious talents if danger struck. She suspected that described all the odd jobs he'd taken on in his life. It was the strategy of someone trained in a certain discipline, and yet forbidden from practicing it. That, his nomadic nature, and his lack of family ties all added up.

Kanan probably wasn't yet a Jedi when the massacre came. She doubted he even had a lightsaber—all he had in the galaxy was one bag of clothing, and if he'd hidden it in there, she would never go looking for it. Hera wondered how young Jedi became apprenticed. She didn't know, and such information was harder to come by now than just about anything else.

Where had he been, when the great betrayal had happened? Who had he been with? Had someone warned him?

And did that someone yet exist?

Kanan might tell her, someday. Or he might not. She was all right with that. The Emperor had disenfranchised souls across the galaxy, people from all walks of life. A reluctant near-Jedi was just one more of their countless number. Many people would be required for a rebellion to work, all contributing their unique talents. All would be equally important, in their own ways.

He obviously liked her starship, she could see as he walked around it. That was good. He was also smitten with her, she could tell—and she was all right with that, too. She didn't want to tell him that her war had already begun, and that in war, there was no time for anything else. He would probably understand that eventually.

No, she thought, things would be fine the way they were. Kanan would be a great asset to her in the days to come even if he never returned to the Jedi ways.

But she couldn't help but wonder: *What would happen if he did?*

Kanan Jarrus was in love.

The *Ghost,* Hera had called it. It was the ship he'd admired as it passed him on the way to Cynda days earlier—and it was a marvel. Roughly hexagonal in shape, it was a light freighter with lots of modifications—all of them, as near as he could tell, improvements. The two main engines jutting out the back were top-notch pieces of equipment, better than anything he'd seen on Gorse or anywhere else. A cockpit sat front-and-center above another bubble housing a turret for a forward gunner. It had symmetry many Corellian cargo ships lacked—and even a small excursion module mounted aft.

After piloting dingy freighters and explosives haulers, after riding in nasty commercial liners and the holds of mining ships, Kanan found *Ghost* a breath of pure oxygen. He would kill to fly it—and as Hera had joked, he might have to. It was hers, all hers. That was fine. He'd welcome the ride.

A nightmare had begun for everyone, years earlier, and it continued in almost every way that mattered. The galaxy hadn't awoken from it yet, and maybe it never would. But Kanan had always been about going to perdition in style, and *Ghost* was a great way to get there.

Particularly with the company.

She was watching him as he admired the starship. Hera had hidden it well, constantly looking away or fiddling with some part—but Kanan was well trained in knowing when female eyes were on him. Things had changed there, too. Hera had been mildly curious about him before, but the events on *Forager* had definitely influenced her attitude toward him. That, or he had somehow gotten a lot more attractive.

Either reason was fine. Any excuse to be in her company was a good one, as long as she didn't push the matter. Hera knew one little thing about his past now, which was one more than he knew about hers. He hoped she'd figure out it had no bearing on who he was. If delivering pinpricks to the Empire was what gave her a thrill, he could certainly help her without getting into all that.

Perhaps the answer will come to you in another form, Master Billaba had said years earlier when he'd asked what a Masterless Jedi should do with his time. He'd sought answers in dangerous jobs and travel, in cantinas and carousing. Hera was a new and very different answer: as good a way to spend his time as any.

The people who had taught Kanan as a child had left him with a handful of skills and some parting advice. Nothing more. That had been their total legacy. Heeding their instructions was all he owed them. He would continue to avoid Coruscant, to avoid detection. He didn't understand what he needed to "stay strong" for, but he'd continue to defend himself against anyone who challenged him.

And the Force? Well, it might be with him, or it might not. Kanan would get by, either way. He always had.

He slapped the underside of the *Ghost* and winked as he made for the ramp. "Let's go somewhere."

About the Author

John Jackson Miller is the *New York Times* bestselling author of *Star Wars: Kenobi, Star Wars: Knight Errant, Star Wars: Lost Tribe of the Sith—The Collected Stories,* and fifteen *Star Wars* graphic novels. A comics industry analyst and historian, he has written comics and prose for several franchises, including *Conan, Iron Man, Indiana Jones, Mass Effect, The Simpsons,* and *Star Trek.* He lives in Wisconsin with his wife, two children, and far too many comic books.

Read on for an excerpt from

Star Wars: Tarkin

by James Luceno
Published by Del Rey Books

BLOWS AGAINST THE EMPIRE

The door to Tarkin's quarters whooshed open, disappearing into the partition, and out he marched, dressed in worn trousers and ill-fitting boots, and with a lightweight gray-green duster draped over his shoulders. As the adjutant hurried to keep pace with the taller man's determined steps, the strident voice of the protocol droid slithered through the opening before the door resealed itself.

"But, sir, the *fitting*!"

Originally a cramped garrison base deployed from a *Victory*-class Star Destroyer, Sentinel now sprawled in all directions as a result of prefabricated modules that had since been delivered or assembled on-site. The heart of the facility was a warren of corridors linking one module to the next, their ceilings lost behind banks of harsh illuminators, forced-air ducts, fire-suppression pipes, and bundled strands of snaking wires. Everything had an improvised look, but as this was Moff Wilhuff Tarkin's domain, the radiantly-heated walkways and walls were spotless, and the pipes and feeds were meticulously organized and labeled with alphanumerics. Overworked scrubbers purged staleness and the smell of ozone from the recycled air. The corridors were crowded not only with specialists and junior officers, but also with droids of all sizes and shapes, twittering, beeping, and chirping to one another as their optical sensors assessed the speed and momentum of Tarkin's forward march and propelling themselves out of harm's way at the last possible instant, on treads, casters, repulsors, and ungainly metal legs. Between the blare of distant alarms and the warble of announcements ordering personnel to muster stations, it was difficult enough to hear oneself think, and yet Tarkin was receiving updates through an ear bead as well as communicating continually with Sentinel's command center through a speck of microphone adhered to his voice box.

He wedged the audio bead deeper into his ear as he strode through a domed module whose skylight wells revealed that the storm had struck with full force and was shaking Sentinel for all it was worth. Exiting the dome and moving against a tide of staff and droids, he right-angled through two short stretches of corridor, doors flying open at his approach and additional personnel joining him at each juncture—senior officers, Navy troopers, communications technicians, some of them young and shorn, most of them in uniform, and all of them human — so that by the time he reached the command center, the duster billowing behind him like a cape, it was as if he were leading a parade.

At Tarkin's request, the rectangular space was modeled after the sunken data pits found aboard *Imperial*-class Star Destroyers. Filing in behind him, the staffers he had gathered along the way rushed to their duty stations, even while others already present were leaping to their feet to deliver salutes. Tarkin waved them back into their swivel chairs and positioned himself on a landing at the center of the room with a clear view of the holoimagers, sensor displays, and authenticators. Off to one side of him, base commander Cassel, dark-haired and sturdy, was leaning across the primary holoprojector table, above which twitched a grainy image of antique starfighters executing strafing runs across Rampart's gleaming surface, while the marshaling station's batteries responded with green pulses of laser energy. In a separate holovid even more corrupted than the first, insect-winged Geonosian laborers could be seen scrambling for cover in one of the station's starfighter hangars. A distorted voice was crackling through the command center's wall-mounted speaker array.

"Our shields are already down to forty percent, Sentinel . . . jamming our transmiss . . . lost communication with the *Brentaal*. Request immediate . . . Sentinel. Again: request immediate reinforcement."

A skeptical frown formed on Tarkin's face. "A sneak attack? Impossible."

"Rampart reports that the attack ship transmitted a valid HoloNet code upon entering the system," Cassel said. "Rampart, can you eavesdrop on the comm chatter of those starfighters?"

"Negative, Sentinel," the reply came a long moment later. "They're jamming our signals net."

Peering over his shoulder at Tarkin, Cassel made as if to cede his position, but Tarkin motioned for him to stay where he was. "Can the image be stabilized?" he asked the specialist at the holoprojector controls.

"Sorry, sir," the specialist said. "Increasing the gain only makes matters worse. The transmission appears to be corrupted at the far end. I haven't been able to establish if Rampart initiated countermeasures."

Tarkin glanced around the room. "And on our end?"

"The HoloNet relay station is best possible," the specialist at the comm board said.

"It is raining, sir," a different spec added, eliciting a chorus of good-natured laughter from others seated nearby. Even Tarkin grinned, though fleetingly.

"Who are we speaking with?" he asked Cassel.

"A Lieutenant Thon," the commander said. "He's been on-station for only three months, but he's following protocol and transmitting on priority encryption."

Tarkin clasped his hands behind his back beneath the duster and glanced at the specialist seated at the authenticator. "Does the effectives roster contain an image of our Lieutenant Thon?"

"On-screen, sir," the staffer said, flicking a joystick and indicating one of the displays.

Tarkin shifted his gaze. A sandy-haired human with protruding ears,

Thon was as untried as he sounded. Fresh from one of the academies, Tarkin thought. He stepped down from the platform and moved to the holoprojector table to study the strafing starfighters more closely. Bars of corruption elevatored through the stuttering holovid. Rampart's shields were nullifying most of the aggressors' energy beams, but all too frequently a disabling run would succeed and white-hot explosions would erupt in one of the depot's deep-space docks.

"Those are Tikiars and Headhunters," Tarkin said in surprise.

"Modified," Cassel said. "Basic hyperdrives and upgraded weaponry."

Tarkin squinted at the holo. "The fuselages bear markings." He turned in the direction of the spec closest to the authenticator station. "Run the markings through the database. Let's see if we can't determine whom we're dealing with."

Tarkin turned back to Cassel. "Did they arrive on their own, or launch from the attack ship?"

"Delivered," the commander said.

Without turning around Tarkin said: "Has this Thon provided holovid or coordinates for the vessel that brought the starfighters?"

"Holovid, sir," someone said, "but we only got a quick look at it."

"Replay the transmission," Tarkin said.

A separate holotable projected a blurry, blue-tinted image of a fan-tailed capital ship with a spherical control module located amidships. The downsloping curved bow and smooth hull gave it the look of a deep-sea behemoth. Tarkin circled the table, appraising the hologram.

"What is this thing?"

"Begged and borrowed, sir," someone reported. "Separatist-era engineering more than anything else. The central sphere resembles one of the old Trade Federation droid control computers, and the entire forward portion might've come from a Commerce Guild destroyer. Front-facing sensor array tower. IFF's highlighting modules consistent with CIS *Providence-*, *Recusant-*, and *Munificent*-class warships."

"Pirates?" Cassel ventured. "Privateers?"

"Have they issued any demands?" Tarkin asked.

"Nothing yet." Cassel waited a beat. "Insurgents?"

"No data on the starfighter fuselage markings, sir," someone said.

Tarkin touched his jaw but said nothing. As he continued to circle the hologram, a flare of wavy corruption in the lower left portion of the hologram captured his attention. "What was that?" he said, standing tall. "At the lower—there it is again." He counted quietly to himself; at the count of ten he fixed his gaze on the same area of the hologram. "And again!" He swung to the specialist. "Replay the recording at half speed."

Tarkin kept his eyes on the lower left quadrant as the holovid restarted and began a new count. "Now!" he said, in advance of every instance of corruption. "Now!"

Chairs throughout the room swiveled. "Encryption noise?" someone suggested.

"Ionization effect," another said.

Tarkin held up a hand to silence the speculations. "This isn't a guessing game, ladies and gentlemen."

"Interval corruption of some sort," Cassel said.

"Of some sort indeed." Tarkin watched silently as the prerecorded holovid recycled for a third time, then he moved to the communications station. "Instruct Lieutenant Thon to show himself," he said to the seated spec.

"Sir?"

"Tell him to train a camera on himself."

The spec relayed the command, and Thon's voice issued from the speakers. "Sentinel, I've never been asked to do that, but if that's what it's going to take to effect a rescue, then I'm happy to comply."

Everyone in the room turned to the holofeed, and moments later a 3-D image of Thon took shape above the table.

"Recognition is well within acceptable margins, sir," a spec said.

Tarkin nodded and leaned toward one of the microphones. "Stand by, Rampart. Reinforcements are forthcoming." He continued to study the live holovid, and had begun yet another count when the transmission abruptly de-resolved, just short of the moment it might have displayed further evidence of corruption.

"What happened?" Cassel asked.

"Working on it, sir," a spec said.

Repressing a knowing smile, Tarkin glanced over his right shoulder. "Have we tried to open a clear channel to Rampart?"

"We've been trying, sir," the comm specialist said, "but we haven't been able to penetrate the jamming."

Tarkin moved to the communication station. "What resources do we have upside?"

"Parking lot is nearly empty, sir." The comm specialist riveted her eyes on the board. "We have the *Salliche,* the *Fremond,* and the *Electrum.*"

Tarkin considered his options. Sentinel's *Imperial*-class Star Destroyer, the *Core Envoy,* along with most of the flotilla's other capital ships were escorting supply convoys to Geonosis. That left him with a frigate and a tug—both vacant just then, literally parked in stationary orbits—and the obvious choice, the *Electrum,* a *Venator*-class Star Destroyer on loan from a deep-dock at Ryloth.

"Contact Captain Burque," he said at last.

"Already on the comm, sir," the specialist said.

A quarter-scale image of the captain rose from the comm station's holoprojector. Burque was tall and gangly, with a clipped brown beard lining his strong jaw. "Governor Tarkin," he said, saluting.

"Are you up to speed on what is occurring at Rampart Station, Captain Burque?"

"We are, sir. The *Electrum* is prepared to jump to Rampart on your command."

Tarkin nodded. "Keep those hyperspace coordinates at the ready, Captain. But right now I want you to execute a microjump to the Rimward edge of this system. Do you understand?"

Burque frowned in confusion, but he said: "Understood, Governor."

"You're to hold there and await further orders."

"In plain sight, sir, or obscure?"

"I suspect that won't matter one way or another, Captain, but all the better if you can find something to hide behind."

"Excuse me for asking, sir, but are we expecting trouble?"

"Always, Captain," Tarkin said, without levity.

The hologram disappeared and the command center fell eerily silent, save for the sounds of the sensors and scanners and the tech's update that the *Electrum* was away. The silence deepened, until a pressing and prolonged warning tone from the threat-assessment station made everyone start. The specialist at the station thrust his head forward.

"Sir, sensors are registering anomalous readings and Cronau radiation in the red zone—"

"Wake rotation!" another spec cut it. "We've got a mark in from hyperspace, sir—and it's a big one. Nine-hundred-twenty-meters long. Gunnage of twelve turbolaser cannons, ten point-defense ion cannons, six proton torpedo launchers. Reverting on the *near-side* of the planet. Range is two hundred thousand klicks and closing." He blew out his breath. "Good thing you dispatched the *Electrum*, sir, or it'd be in pieces by now!"

A specialist seated at an adjacent duty station weighed in. "Firing solution programs are being sent to downside defenses."

"IFF is profiling it as the same carrier that attacked Rampart." The spec glanced at Tarkin. "Could it have jumped, sir?"

"If the ship was even there," Tarkin said, mostly to himself.

"Sir?"

Tarkin shrugged out of the duster, letting it fall to the floor, and stepped down to the holoprojector. "Let's have a look at it."

If the ship in the orbital-feed holovid was not the same one that had ostensibly attacked Rampart, it had to be her twin.

"Sir, we've got multiple marks launching from the carrier—" The spec interrupted himself to make certain he was interpreting the read-ings correctly. "Sir, they're *droid* fighters! Tri-fighters, vultures, the whole Sep menagerie."

"Interesting," Tarkin said in a calm voice. One hand to his chin, he continued to assess the hologram. "Commander Cassel, sound general quarters and boost power to the base shields. Signals: initiate counter-measures."

"Sir, is this an unannounced readiness test?" someone asked.

"More like a bunch of Separatists who didn't get the message they lost the war," another said.

Perhaps that was the explanation, Tarkin thought. Imperial forces had destroyed or appropriated most of the capital ships produced for and by the Confederacy of Independent Systems. Droid fighters hadn't been seen in years. But it was even longer since Tarkin had witnessed HoloNet subterfuge of the caliber someone had aimed at Sentinel Base.

He swung away from the table. "Scan the carrier for life-forms on the off chance we're dealing with a sentient adversary rather than a droid control computer." He eyed the comm specialist. "Any separate channel response from Rampart?"

She shook her head. "Still no word, sir."

"Carrier shows thirty life-forms, sir," someone at the far end of the room said. "It's astrogating by command, not on full-auto."

From the threat station came another voice: "Sir, droid fighters are nearing the edge of the envelope."

And a thin envelope it was, Tarkin thought.

"Alert our artillery crews to ignore the firing solution programs and to fire at will." He pivoted to the holotable. A glance revealed Sentinel Base to be in the same situation Rampart appeared to have been in only moments earlier, except that the enemy ships and the holofeed were *genuine*.

"Contact Captain Burque and tell him to come home."

"Tri-fighters are breaking formation and commencing attack runs."

The sounds of distant explosions and the thundering replies of ground-based artillery infiltrated the command center. The room shook. Motes of dust drifted down from the overhead pipes and cables and the illumination flickered. Tarkin monitored the ground-feed holovids. The droid fighters were highly maneuverable but no match for Sentinel's powerful guns. The moon's storm-racked sky grew backlit with strobing flashes and globular detonations, as one after another of the ridge-backed tri-fighters and reconfigurable vultures were vaporized. A few managed to make it to the outer edge of the base's hemispherical defensive shield, only to be annihilated there and hit the coarse ground in flames.

"They're beginning to turn tail," a tech said. "Laser cannons are chasing them back up the well."

"And the capital ship?" Tarkin said.

"The carrier is steering clear and accelerating. Range is now three hundred thousand klicks and expanding. All weapons are mute."

"Sir, the *Electrum* has reverted to realspace."

Tarkin grinned faintly. "Inform Captain Burque that his TIE pilots are going to enjoy a target-rich environment."

"Captain Burque on the comm."

Tarkin moved to the comm station, where Burque's holopresence hovered above the projector.

"I trust that this is the trouble you were expecting, Governor."

"Actually, Captain, most of this is quite unexpected. Therefore, I hope you'll do your best to incapacitate the carrier rather than destroy it. No doubt we can glean something by interrogating the crew."

"I'll be as gentle with it as I can, Governor."

Tarkin glanced at the holotable in time to see squadrons of newly-minted ball-cockpit TIE fighters launch from the dorsal bay of the arrowhead-shaped Star Destroyer.

"Sir, I have Rampart Station Commander Jae on the comm, voice-only."

Tarkin gestured for Jae to be put through.

"Governor Tarkin, to what do I owe the honor?" Jae said.

Tarkin positioned himself close to one of the command center's audio pickups. "How is everything at your depot, Lin?"

"Better now," Jae said. "Our HoloNet relay was down for a short period, but it's back online. I've sent a tech team to determine what went wrong. You have my word, Governor: the glitch won't affect the supply shipment schedule—"

"I doubt that your technicians will discover any evidence of malfunction," Tarkin said.

Instead of speaking to it, Jae said: "And on your moon, Governor?"

"As a matter of fact, we find ourselves under attack."

"What?" Jae asked in patent surprise

"I'll explain in due course, Lin. Just now we have our hands full."

His back turned to the holoprojector table, Tarkin missed the event that drew loud groans from many of the staffers. When he turned, the warship was gone.

"Jumped to lightspeed before the *Electrum* could get off a disabling shot," Cassel said.

Disappointment pulled down the corners of Tarkin's mouth. With the capital ship gone, the remaining droid fighters could be seen spinning out of control—even easier prey for the vertical-winged TIE fighters. A scattering of spherical explosions flared at the edge of space.

"Gather debris of any value," Tarkin said to Burque, "and have it transported down the well for analysis. Snare a few of the intact droids, as well. But take care. While they appear to be lifeless, they may be rigged to self-destruct."

Burque acknowledged the command, and the holo vanished.

Tarkin looked at Cassel. "Secure from battle stations and sound the all clear. I want a forensic team assembled to examine the droids. I doubt we'll learn much, but we may be able to ascertain the carrier's point of origin." He grew pensive for a moment, then added: "Prepare an after-action report for Coruscant and transmit it to my quarters so I can append my notes."

"Will do," Cassel said.

A specialist handed Tarkin his duster, and he had started for the door when a voice rang out behind him.

"Sir, a question if you will?"

Tarkin stopped and turned around. "Ask it."

"How did you know, sir?"

"How did I know what, Corporal?"

The young, brown-haired specialist gnawed at her lower lip before continuing. "That the holotransmission from Rampart Station was counterfeit, sir."

Tarkin looked her up and down. "Perhaps you'd care to proffer an explanation of your own."

"In the replay—the bar of interval noise you noticed. Somehow that told you that someone had managed to introduce a false real-time feed into the local HoloNet relay."

Tarkin smiled faintly. "Train yourself to recognize it—all of you. Deception may be the least of what our unknown adversaries have in store."

About the Type

This book was set in Galliard, a typeface designed in 1978 by Matthew Carter (b. 1937) for the Mergenthaler Linotype Company. Galliard is based on the sixteenth-century typefaces of Robert Granjon (1513–89).